ROOTS RUN DEEP

ONCE AND ALWAYS
BOOK 2

MELODY CLAIRE

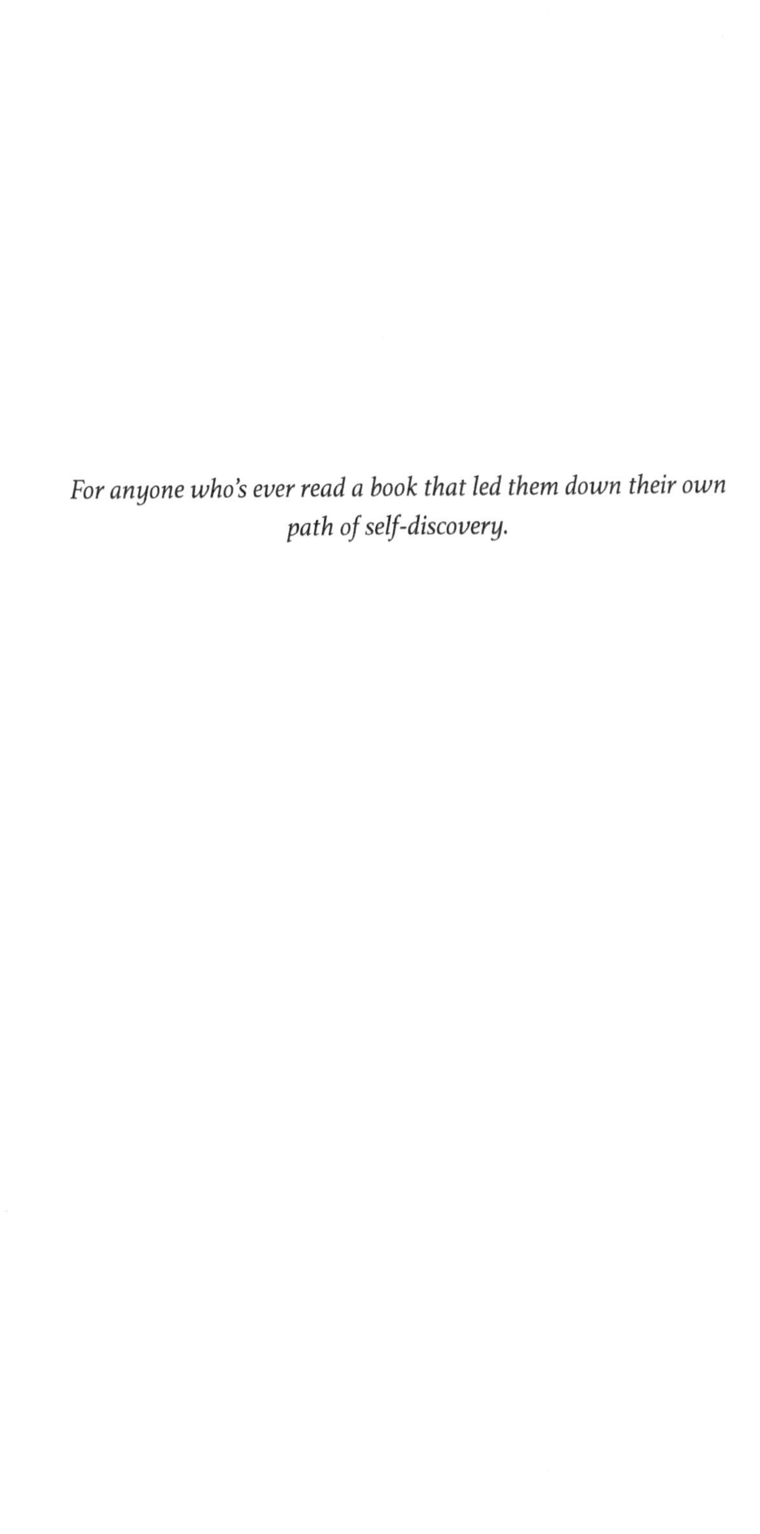

For anyone who's ever read a book that led them down their own path of self-discovery.

TRIGGER WARNINGS

Your mental health should be your first priority! Take care of yourself!

This book contains subjects which may be triggering for some readers. A list of trigger warnings can be found on the following page.

For those who would prefer to skip the trigger warnings and go in blind, please skip the following page.

Questions may be directed to mel@melodyclaireauthor.com.

TRIGGER WARNINGS

grief/death of a parent (off page and in the past, but heavily discussed)
panic attacks (on page)
PTSD
light alcohol use
nightmares
discussions of foster care/adoption

PART I

ONCE

1

ZACH

JUNE

THE SOUND of bows aggressively attacking violin strings assaulted my ears as I climbed into my father's black BMW late in the afternoon on a Friday in mid-June. The display read *Paganini: 24 Caprices, Op1: No. 5 in A Minor*, which didn't make a damn bit of sense to me, but neither did my father's fascination with Classical music. I wasn't sure if he genuinely enjoyed the musical genre or if he thought it made him appear more cultured, which was ridiculous since we lived in fucking Nebraska. Not that people here didn't have any cultural knowledge, they just didn't care who else did or didn't keep up with such things.

"How was camp?" Dad asked as he pulled away from the curb, navigating the airport traffic with practiced skill while I buckled my seat belt and settled my duffel bag on the floor below me.

"It was fine."

"Just fine?" There was a bite to his tone, indicating his displeasure with my response.

I stared out the window as we headed north toward the highway. The truth was, the answer to his question was complicated. I'd flown to California earlier in the week to attend a mini-camp with the UCLA soccer team I would be joining as a freshman in the fall. I'd been nervous to meet the guys, hoping I'd fit in, hoping the coaches wouldn't take one look at me and decide they'd been wrong to offer me a full-ride scholarship.

It didn't matter that I'd always made friends easily or that I'd been scouted by soccer teams nationwide since I was in the eighth grade. There was always a part of me that thought *this time* they'd see right through me and discover the guy they thought they saw, the popular star athlete, was really just average at soccer and nothing but an uptight nerd.

As it turned out, the camp had been pretty great. I'd clicked with most of the other guys, and the coaches had seemed pleased with my abilities. Practicing with older, more experienced players had been challenging in a way the sport hadn't been for me in a long time. It made me want to work harder, to show them I deserved a spot on the team.

I loved soccer, had always loved soccer, but the problem was that my dad sucked the fun right out of it. For a long time now, conversations about soccer revolved around being the best on the team, getting noticed by the right coaches, and getting a scholarship to the right school. It was never about what I wanted or whether I was having fun or achieving my dreams. It made me want to lie, to tell him it was a shitty camp and I'd hated it there, just to piss him off.

"Yeah, it was fine." I didn't have to look at him to know he was irritated. Annoyance radiated off him.

"You could be a little more grateful. I'm sure plenty of others would love to take your spot on the team."

"I know."

"Zach, you really—"

"Did you get to see any celebrities?" my sister, ever the peacekeeper, chimed in from the back seat.

I turned and looked at her, flashing a smile. Drea was three years younger than me and a pain in my ass. I adored her and would miss her when I went to school this fall. "I didn't leave campus."

She threw herself back against the leather seats and crossed her arms. "You could have seen someone at the airport."

"Sorry to disappoint. I guess you'll just have to come out and visit."

"Really? That would be amazing." Her thumbs began flying over the face of her phone. "I have to tell Mandy. She's gonna die."

The sound of her chatter washed over me, and my eyes drifted closed as we turned onto the highway toward Astaire. As I floated on the edge of sleep, I could almost believe it was my mom talking. The inflection and tone of Drea's voice were so similar.

It still hurt to think of my mom. I felt a squeeze somewhere behind my heart at the thought of the woman who'd been my biggest cheerleader. She'd been the light of our household, her humor and warmth contagious, and when it was stolen from us by a car accident almost two years ago, we were plunged into a darkness so deep, I wasn't sure we'd ever completely recover.

The car slowed and I opened my eyes just as we passed the city limit sign for Astaire. I'd gotten used to this little town when we'd moved here last fall, and I supposed it was an okay place to live, though I couldn't imagine spending the rest of my life here. I needed someplace with a little more action. Where you could go to concerts and professional sporting events and take a date to a restaurant a little more upscale than Sherry's Soft-Serv or Fred's Diner.

Our house backed up to the lake just outside of Astaire, and it was one of the few things I'd actually liked about moving here. All of the bedrooms in the house faced the water, and though I'd never really given it any prior thought, I'd come to realize that living here had brought me a sense of peace unlike anything else since Mom passed. I'd spent many a sleepless night staring across the lake, sometimes watching long enough to catch the sun rising over still waters. I'd watched it transform with the seasons, reflecting the golden hues of fall foliage, freezing over during the Nebraska winter, and bursting into life again this spring.

"How was camp, really?" Drea approached, standing beside me at my bedroom window while we watched a canoe cut its way through the water on the far side of the lake.

"It was really good, actually."

"Why didn't you tell Dad that when he asked?"

"You know why."

She sighed, leaning her head against my shoulder. "He doesn't mean to be such a dick."

"I know. But that doesn't mean he gets a pass for it. How was your week?"

I felt her shrug, but her head remained on my shoulder. It was a comfort. "It was fine."

"Was it really?"

"It was. I hung out with Mandy mostly. Went to dance class. Went shopping with Aunt Amy. It was chill."

I waited, debating whether to press, but I had to know. "Did you eat?"

Another sigh, though it felt more like resignation rather than frustration. "Yes. Three meals a day." She pulled away and looked at me. "I'm okay, Zach. I'm eating. I have an appetite. You don't have to worry."

"I'll never not worry."

"Well, *try* not to. I'm much healthier than I was a year ago. I take my meds. I talk to my therapist. I miss Mom. I'm still sad. But I'm not depressed. It's not the same."

I looked at her big brown eyes, so bright and lively, and I believed her. I still saw some sadness there, but it wasn't the same as that haunted quality she'd had when we'd lost Mom and she'd fallen into depression and stopped eating.

"You promise you'll tell me if you start struggling again?"

"What are you going to do about it from California?" she sassed, and damn if it wasn't my biggest worry.

What would happen when I was fifteen hundred miles away? Would Dad go back to working late, leaving Drea to fend for herself? What if she fell into a depressive episode and Dad was so absorbed in his own shit that he didn't notice until it was too late?

"I'm serious, Drea. I can't leave Nebraska if there's a chance you're not going to be okay. It'll kill me."

"You can't ever know that, Zach. I can't promise I won't have an episode again. And you can't live your life sitting around waiting for it to happen. You have to trust me when I say I'm taking my meds and talking to my therapist. Aunt Amy helps too."

She'd grown up so much in the last two years. I swore she was fifteen going on thirty. "I can't help it. Worrying about you is kind of my thing."

"I love you too, big brother."

I tugged her ponytail but pulled her in for a hug. Dammit, I was going to miss her in the fall.

2

JASON

"What time is Will picking you up?"

I scooped up some potato salad, piling it on my plate next to my burger, and then passed the container to my dad. "He'll be here in twenty," I said, answering my mom's question.

"Picking you up for what?" My sister, Mandy, turned her big blue eyes on me, her expression excited and curious, and I knew she was angling for an invitation.

"A bonfire at the lake. One that you are definitely *not* going to."

"That's not fair," she said, turning those blue eyes on my father. "How come he gets to go and I'm stuck here with you guys?"

Dad snorted. "Thanks, kid. Why don't you go over to that one girl's house? What was her name? Her brother's the soccer player."

"Drea? Why can't you remember any of my friends' names?"

"Because it feels like you've got a stream of 'em parading through here every other day, and I can't keep up."

"I do not. And besides, Drea's pretty much been my best friend all year. You should totally know her name by now." She sat back in her chair and folded her arms. "She went into Omaha with her dad to pick her brother up from the airport and wasn't sure what time she was getting back."

I let the conversation flow around me, enjoying the fact that my sister turning the attention on herself meant it was taken off me. I loved my family, even my bratty younger sister, but I hated being the center of attention. I'd already told my parents I was heading to the bonfire tonight. I'd graduated a couple of weeks ago, and they'd lifted my curfew as long as I promised to be safe, not drive under the influence, and not knock anyone up. I was ninety-nine percent sure I was asexual, so knocking someone up was pretty damn unlikely, but they didn't know that. And out of all my friends, I'd always been the most responsible one, taking care to not only make sure I was safe, but that my friends were safe as well.

My phone buzzed with a text from Will, letting me know he was in the driveway. I stuffed the rest of my burger in my mouth, then grabbed my ball cap off the counter and shoved it on my head backward. "I'll text if I'm going to be late," I said, tugging on Mandy's braid as I passed. I was pretty sure I heard her mutter "dick" under her breath, but it was quiet enough that I couldn't be sure.

I pushed through the storm door, waving to Will as I made my way to the passenger side of his Jeep. Normally, I would have driven my truck, but Dad's car was in the shop, so he'd commandeered mine.

"Thanks for the ride," I said as I buckled myself in.

"No problem." He backed out of the driveway and turned us toward the lake.

We rode in comfortable silence with the windows down,

allowing the warm summer breeze to whip through Will's Jeep and ruffle his dark-brown hair. Will was a pretty cool guy. We'd played sports together until he moved away when we were eleven. He'd moved back a couple of weeks ago, and we'd rekindled our friendship. In fact, as odd as it sounded, he was quickly becoming one of my closest friends despite the fact we hadn't really talked in years.

It wasn't that I was a loner or anything. I hung out with a ton of guys from our graduating class and pretty much got along with everyone. I just had a hard time getting close to people. But there was something about Will that made him easy to talk to. I was comfortable with him in a way I wasn't with many people.

By the time we arrived at the lake, the sun was about thirty minutes away from fully setting and the sky was awash in purples, oranges, and reds. Someone had built the bonfire up until flames were shooting into the sky, and I eyed it, assessing its safety. It looked sturdy enough at the moment, but I had a feeling I'd be keeping an eye on it most of the night. I wouldn't be able to relax otherwise.

Music and laughter filled the night air as we crossed the sand to where several pickups were lined up with their tailgates down. One of them held a keg, and in unspoken agreement, Will and I made a beeline for that one. I typically wasn't a huge drinker, but I didn't mind a beer or two, and since Will was driving, I figured I could enjoy a few.

With our cups full, we chatted with some of our other friends, mostly lifeguards from the pool where we worked, mixed in with some other kids from our class and the class below ours. There was a lot of talk about college plans for the fall and upcoming visits for freshman registration, none of which I was going to be participating in, at least not at the university level. I was enrolled in an EMT course at the community college in Brinkley. It was a semester-long program that would have me ready to get to work starting in January.

I'd thought a lot about college over the last couple of years—it was pretty impossible not to since it was shoved down our throats in high school—but I just couldn't imagine myself in any of the careers that came with a four-year degree. I was smart enough, I supposed, but going into debt over college loans for a job I wasn't even sure I would like just didn't make sense. I wanted to help people and I wanted to stay active, so going the EMT route made sense. I was mostly content with my choice, but there were times like now, when everyone was talking about college and all the things they were looking forward to, that I wondered if I would be missing out.

"You alright, man?" Rafi, one of our lifeguard friends, asked as he passed me a freshly filled cup. He tried to pass one to Will, but he'd been distracted since he'd spotted Sammy, another kid from our graduating class, walking across the sand on the other side of the fire. I wasn't sure what Will's orientation was, but I suspected something was going on between the two of them. I didn't like it. Not because I cared if Will was into guys but because Sammy had a bit of a reputation for being a troublemaker, and I didn't want Will to get hurt.

I nudged Will to get his attention, though my eyes were on Rafi as I answered his question. "I'm fine. Why?"

Will took the second cup from my hand as Rafi responded. "You just seem, I don't know, sad or something."

"Nah, man. I'm good." I played it off. The three of us turned as cheers went up next to us. Hannah Sinclair and Sonny Gordon, a couple who'd graduated with me, were chugging beers from a funnel while the crowd around them chanted their names. The chant got louder and louder as Hannah showed signs of winning. When she finished first, she let out a whoop and held the funnel up in the air, shouting, "Hell yeah, bitches!"

Sonny finished a moment later, shaking his head at his loss, but he smiled and laughed with Hannah as they kissed, then hopped down from the tailgate where they'd been standing.

"Those two are crazy." I shook my head, laughing. It was hard to imagine intentionally putting myself in a situation like that, with people cheering me on while I made a spectacle of myself. I was far more comfortable casually hanging with my friends, sipping my beer, and watching while others made asses of themselves.

And so it went. People continued drinking, laughing, and bullshitting with friends while the fire licked away at the logs in the sand. Every so often, someone added a couple more logs to keep it going before moving on to another group of friends.

I was talking to a very drunk Hannah and Sonny when Will bumped into me. I reached out to steady him, and he brushed me off, insisting he was fine. He set his empty cup down, then turned and began making his way across the sand toward the trees. I'd taken his keys about a half-hour ago and knew he was pretty wasted, but I figured he probably just needed to piss. If he wasn't back in five minutes, I'd go find him.

"Who's the drunk?"

I turned my attention to the voice over my shoulder. Zach Jacobs stood behind me, eyes tracking Will as he pingponged through the crowd. I didn't know Zach well. His family had moved here last summer and we'd only had one class together this year. Despite being new—or maybe because of it—he'd quickly become popular, getting voted homecoming king and captain of the soccer team.

Objectively, he was attractive, with deep brown eyes and thick dark hair that hung over his forehead. His status as soccer team captain had come with good reason. I'd heard he played for a club team and drove into Omaha several days a week to practice with them. Apparently, he was going to UCLA in the fall on a full-ride scholarship. I didn't know much about soccer—I'd been more of a football and baseball guy—but he'd led the team to State, so I figured he must be pretty good. At the very least, he was in shape. The polo he wore fit him like a glove.

Even as I took in his appearance, my dick was flatly uninterested. You could make an argument it was because I wasn't gay, but my dick had never taken an interest in a girl either. Add it to the list of evidence that I was ace.

"That's Will Hartley," I said, realizing I hadn't answered his question. "He just moved back for the summer."

"Moved back?" Zach stepped up next to me, sipping his beer as we watched Will disappear into the trees.

"He lived here when we were kids. His stepdad is Mr. Johnson."

"As in our principal Mr. Johnson?"

"Yeah. He moved here last summer to take the principal job, but Will and his mom stayed in Grand Island so he could finish his senior year there."

"Must be nice," he muttered into his cup as he took another sip, but before I could process what he'd said, he turned toward me with a wide smile and changed the subject. "How's your summer been?"

"Decent. I'm lifeguarding at the pool with Will, Rafi, and a bunch of other guys." I turned toward him so we were facing each other. "What about you?"

"I've barely been home. I worked a soccer camp in the city the first week of June, then flew to Cali for their summer mini-camp. Just got back today."

"Oh yeah, my sister said something about you getting picked up from the airport today." I laughed when his face screwed up in confusion. "My sister, Mandy, is friends with your sister. They're in the same grade."

He squinted at me, his look of confusion turning to disbelief. "I'm pretty sure Mandy's spent the night at our house several times. You guys look nothing alike."

Mandy was a dancer and built like one, with a slender frame and long legs. She had blue eyes and blond hair, just like my mom, while I got my linebacker build from my dad. "We get that a lot. I—"

"I'm taking your boy home. Give me his keys." Sammy shoved between Zach and me, holding out his hand for the keys I was definitely not going to give him.

"What?"

"Will. He's shitfaced. I need his keys so I can take him home. You'll have to find your own ride."

I dragged him away from the crowd to the other side of the row of trucks, shooting Zach an apologetic look as I went. Despite the cooler air on this side of the trucks, my blood was boiling.

"You and Will haven't spoken since we were kids, and tonight, you've decided you're friends?" I looked him up and down, trying to determine what he was playing at. Will and I'd talked about Sammy the other day after Will had helped Sammy's brother, Jimmy, through a panic attack. Sammy and Will had been friends when we were all kids, but as far as I knew, they'd lost touch when Will moved.

"We're not."

"Then why are you trying to take him home? I was the

one who rode here with him. I have the keys, and I'll take him." I crossed my arms and glared at him. I was a big guy, and though I wasn't a fighter, most people were intimidated by my size. Not Sammy though. He just glared at me right back.

"Man, just give me the damn keys."

I raised an eyebrow but didn't move.

"Look," he huffed. "I'm not going to violate him or anything. Just give me the keys and go back to your friends."

"I don't fucking trust you."

He shrugged. "I don't really care."

We were locked in a stare-down. I didn't think Sammy was a terrible guy, but he'd always been a loner, so I didn't know him all that well. I was really having a hard time understanding just what his motives were here.

"Give me your number."

"What?" I asked.

"Give me the keys and your number. I'll send you proof of life as soon as I get him home."

"That can be faked."

"For fuck's sake. Just do it."

I searched his face, looking for a clue that he really had Will's best interests at heart. He didn't flinch. Just continued to stare me down with his chocolate-brown eyes, and something in my gut said it would be okay. God, I hoped I was making the right choice.

"Fine," I spit out. We exchanged numbers, then I gave him the keys and said, "I don't like this."

"Noted," he said and walked away.

3

ZACH

"What was that all about?" I asked as Jason approached with a scowl on his face.

"Sammy's taking Will home."

"And that pisses you off?"

He blew out a breath, took off his hat, ran his hand through his short crop of hair, then put the hat back on, his movements jerky and agitated. "I just don't know if I did the right thing giving up Will's keys like that. And now I don't have a ride."

"I can give you a ride."

"Yeah?" His blue eyes lifted to mine. There was a quiet intensity about him that I didn't see in most guys our age. I found it...intriguing. "That'd be great. Thanks."

He shifted from one foot to the other, almost like he couldn't decide what to do with himself. "Do you want me to take you now?"

"Nah, I don't want to keep you from the party."

"It's cool. I don't mind. I barely know most of these people." I looked around, and while I recognized many faces, I hadn't developed a close relationship with anyone in particular. I'd gotten along with my classmates and the guys on the soccer team, but it had all been superficial. Flash a smile, make a joke, and get along with everyone. It was the formula for convincing people you were okay. That you weren't the sad kid without a mom. The player with an over-bearing soccer dad. The lonely kid without any true friends.

Jason's forehead creased in a frown, so I doubled down on my smile. "Come on. My car's up the hill." I nodded in the direction of the parking lot and the road beyond.

Bodies jostled into us as we maneuvered through the crowd and across the sand. I nodded and smiled at people as I passed, my popular pretty-boy facade locked in place like a coat of armor. Eventually, the mob of people thinned out and the sounds of laughter and music trailed off as we trudged up the path to the lot. Up here, away from the press of bodies, the air was the tiniest bit cooler. "My car's down the road a little way," I said, leading Jason through the lot and toward the road beyond.

We walked side-by-side, the June air thick with humidity and heavy with the weight of Jason's worry. I searched for some other topic of conversation to distract him.

"What are your plans for the fall?"

"I'm taking an EMT course at the community college in Brinkley."

"That's cool. What made you want to do that?" I gestured for him to go ahead of me as we filed onto the road. There wasn't a sidewalk out here away from town, so we hugged the shoulder as we walked past the other cars parked half in the street, half on the grassy shoulder. It amazed me that everyone in Astaire turned a blind eye to the clear evidence there was a party full of underage drinkers happening at the lake. I supposed there were some perks to living in a small town.

"I don't know, really. My grades in school were pretty decent, but I just can't imagine paying for an education I wasn't even sure I wanted. I liked the idea of helping people. And not being tied to a desk. Plus, the program's only like four months." He stopped in front of me, causing me to pull up short before I ran into him. "I just realized I don't know what car I'm looking for," he said, glancing over his shoulder.

I grinned. "It's the blue Lexus two cars up." He blinked at me owlishly but didn't say anything. Just turned and continued on until he arrived at the electric-blue car.

We both climbed in, and I bit back a laugh as the big guy squeezed himself into the passenger seat, immediately trying to locate the button that would slide the seat back. "Sorry. The only one who rides with me regularly is my sister, and she doesn't require nearly as much legroom."

"I'm used to it. It's one of the reasons I drive a truck."

I punched the button to start the engine. "You definitely strike me as a truck kind of guy. Where are we headed?"

"I live over on Woodson. You know where that is? Just past the high school."

"Yeah, I think so."

I pulled the car onto the road, heading in the direction he indicated. We rode in silence for a bit, but it wasn't uncomfortable. Though I didn't know him well, Jason had never struck me as the type of guy who needed to fill a space with idle chatter. He did appear restless, though, shifting in his seat several times and fiddling with the hem of his shorts.

"You okay?" I asked, giving him my attention while I was stopped at one of the three traffic lights in town.

"Sorry. I'm just worried about Will. I shouldn't have given up his keys so easily."

I couldn't figure out if he was just a worrier or if Will meant more to him than it appeared on the surface. I'd never seen Jason date anyone, though I supposed it was possible he had a thing for Will.

"Is Sammy really such a bad guy? I had a couple of classes with him this year. He mostly kept to himself, but I didn't catch a vibe or anything."

"He's... I honestly don't know him very well. We've both lived here our whole lives, but he's just, like, really hard to know." He nodded toward the light, which had turned green while we were talking.

I started to ease through the intersection, but after a quick check of my mirrors to see if traffic was clear, I turned right instead, pointing us in a new direction. "Where are you going?"

I flicked a quick glance his way, catching the confused look on his face. He didn't look pissed, though, so that was a good sign. Returning my eyes to the road, I said, "I can turn back if you want, but I thought maybe you could use a distraction. If I take you home now, you'll just stew all night."

He blew out a breath, but there was a touch of humor in his tone when he responded. "You're probably right. Did you have someplace in mind?"

"Not really. I just thought I'd drive for a bit without any particular destination in mind."

"My grandparents have some land outside of town. There's a spot on the back edge of the property that over-looks the creek. We can head out there if you want..."

"Sure. Just tell me which way to go."

Ten minutes later, we pulled onto a gravel road that I would have missed if Jason hadn't pointed it out. Trees crowded in on both sides of the drive, making it feel like I was in a scene from *Jurassic Park*. It was only about a quarter-mile before the trees opened into a small clearing where I parked my car and we got out. Stars blanketed the night sky like someone had scattered salt over a black tablecloth. Out here, away from Astaire, the vastness of the space made me feel infinitely smaller. Insignificant.

Alone.

So much so that I almost forgot Jason was with me.

"Grandpa used to bring me out here when I was a kid." His voice was soft and low, gentle as the breeze. "He had this old rusted-out Ford pickup that he kept just for driving around the farm. The seats were cracked and lumpy, and I used to giggle at the way they bounced up and down when he drove over ruts in the dirt."

The look he gave me was sheepish, like he was embarrassed about telling his story, but I smiled, hoping he'd continue. I liked the gentle sound of his voice, the smooth way it floated across my skin.

That was a weird fucking thought.

"Sometimes he'd bring my sister with us, but most of the time, it was just us two. He called it 'guy time.'" His chuckle was soft, almost like he'd forgotten I was there. "I wasn't allowed pop until I was in middle school, but he'd pack a couple of cans of Coke in a cooler, winking at me as he popped the top, telling me it was just between us men."

There was a fallen tree near the edge of the overlook. We made our way over and sat on it, looking out over the creek and fields beyond. I thought about my grandparents, what little I could remember of them. My dad had been estranged from his parents, so they'd only visited a handful of times, flying in from Arizona for quick visits that always left us feeling relieved once they were gone. I was pretty sure I'd been in middle school the last time I'd seen them. They hadn't even bothered to come out for Mom's funeral.

By contrast, my mom's parents had been the quintessential grandparents, warm, loving, and kind. Grandma had spoiled us with cookies and sweets, while Grandpa had loved a pun and always given us a two-dollar bill on our birthdays. We still saw them occasionally when they came into town to visit my Aunt Amy and her family, but since Mom had passed, their relationship with my father had become strained. We still spoke over the phone and by email, but I missed seeing them in person.

"None of my grandparents live here. One set is in Arizona and the other in Florida." I didn't elaborate, not wanting to open myself up to this guy I barely knew. I didn't open myself up to anyone, really.

"Do you see them?"

"Sometimes."

I felt the weight of the questions he hadn't asked. He wanted to know more, but he was too polite to push. And I was too private to say more.

So neither one of us said anything, letting the silence hang between us.

It was odd, that silence. How comfortable it was, despite my refusal to part with the personal information I knew Jason was curious about. I hadn't spent a lot of time in the quiet, typically seeking out other people and their noise. And on the rare occasion I did find myself alone, my AirPods and playlist were never far away. I didn't like the silence. I didn't like being alone with my thoughts. My memories. My grief. It was why I'd gone to the bonfire tonight, despite my exhaustion from camp and travel.

On cue, I yawned, long and hard, my eyes watering.

Jason pulled out his phone and looked at the time. "Do you want to go? You're probably exhausted."

"Nah, I'm good," I said, waving him off. "It's been a long day, but I don't know if I want to go home yet."

His eyebrows pinched in concern. He did that a lot, I noticed. He was a worrier. "Why?"

"Why don't I want to go home?" He nodded, and I shrugged. "Just family stuff. It's not a big deal."

With a brief nod, he turned to look out over the fields, letting the quiet fall around us once again. This time the silence felt itchy, like a tag in the back of a shirt poking at the skin of my neck. I searched for something to say, something to drown out the buzzing beneath my skin, an inane topic we could discuss to deflect from the personal.

But what came out of my mouth was, "My father's kind of a dick. Like, I know he loves me and my sister, but there's always this insane amount of pressure to be the best at everything we do. For me, it's soccer. For Drea, it's dance. And grades for both of us. Our rooms have to be kept immaculate, our beds made every day. Clothes unwrinkled and not a hair out of place. There's no room for error, for being human."

I dragged my hand through my hair, annoyed that I'd opened my big mouth but unable to stop the stream of words. Jason watched me carefully, his eyes full of concern, but he didn't interrupt.

"I got a full-ride scholarship to UCLA, but that wasn't good enough. He wanted me to go to Clemson because they're ranked higher in the preseason polls. Astaire played the State Championship this year for the first time in school history, and Dad was pissed because I didn't score the game-winning goal. It's never enough for him. So when he picked me up from the airport today and asked how camp went, I told him it was fine."

I stood, restless and unable to sit still as the words bubbled out of me. "I knew that word—*fine*—would piss him off, but I said it anyway because it wouldn't really matter what I said. Everything pisses him off. He gave me shit about how I should be more grateful for the opportunity, so I faked sleep the rest of the way home."

"Do you want to play soccer?"

I stopped pacing, hands on my hips as I looked out over the creek and fields beyond. Once upon a time, the answer would have been unequivocally *yes*. But now? Now, the joy and freedom of running down the field, dribbling the ball, moving in tandem with my teammates, the challenge of reading and anticipating my opponent's move, and the exhilaration of scoring that perfect goal was buried under a layer of expectation. It was like a poison had infiltrated everything I'd once loved. Infused it with something insidious until I no longer recognized the sport I'd given my heart to.

But this week, I'd found a sliver of that passion again. Without my father breathing down my neck, without his constant scrutiny, I'd felt a glimmer of the joy I'd once known. On the second day, I'd even had my phone out of my pocket, ready to call Mom and tell her all about it, as if I was a young boy recounting my first day of school. Then, I'd remembered there was no *Mom* to call. It had taken all my self-control not to throw my phone across my dorm room as I blinked back the tears.

So when my father had asked me how it went, I'd responded with "fine" because I wasn't willing to give him anything more. I didn't want him to twist it into something ugly when I'd only just gotten started.

I dropped my chin to my chest, letting out a breath. "It's complicated," I said, copping out on my answer to Jason's question. The flood of words that had burst out of me moments ago suddenly dried up, leaving me with nothing more to say.

"I shouldn't have dumped all of that on you. I don't usually..." I let out a frustrated breath, chancing a look at him. I didn't know what I'd expected to see, maybe discomfort, maybe pity, but all I saw was quiet concern. "I think maybe I do want to go home." I scrubbed my hand over my face. "It's been a long day, and I think I just need to get some sleep."

He was quiet for a moment, those dark eyes penetrating, likely seeing more than they should. I struggled not to squirm under his gaze. But then he stood and simply said, "Alright," and started walking to the car.

It took fifteen minutes to get back to town. Fifteen minutes to wonder why the fuck I'd spilled my guts to a guy I barely knew. Why I'd bared my soul to him when I'd never bared it to anyone other than Drea.

I pulled into his neighborhood, following his directions as he told me when to turn left and right. His house was dark, though the porch light was on, like a beacon of welcome as I pulled into the driveway.

"Thanks for the ride," he said softly, making no move to get out of the car.

"It's no problem. Sorry if I made it weird back there." I tried to make a joke out of it, make it out to be no big deal.

One corner of his mouth turned up, though his eyes remained serious. "I don't mind. We all need someone to talk to sometimes."

I didn't know what to say to that. I didn't really have any intention of letting it happen again. It had left me feeling exposed, like someone had scraped out my insides in order to examine them closer. No thank you.

Not wanting to be rude, I nodded but didn't offer anything more.

"Goodnight," he said, then climbed out of the car and made his way inside. I told myself I was watching him go because I wanted to make sure he got inside, but the truth was there was something about Jason, some pull, that I couldn't turn away from.

When he got to the door, he turned back and gave a small wave before disappearing inside, and I was left with the oddest sense of loss.

What a weird fucking night.

4

JASON

JULY

A BEAD of sweat ran down my temple as I entered my second mile of the morning. It wasn't even seven o'clock and temperatures were already in the upper seventies, with a predicted high near one hundred. Anything above sixty was hotter than I liked for running, but it was the humidity that really made it unbearable this morning. June had been unseasonably hot and humid for Nebraska, and it looked like July was only going to get worse, but if I wanted to be in shape for my EMT training in the fall, I would have to push past the discomfort.

In truth, I was surprised by how much I actually enjoyed running. After adjusting to the early morning wakeup—the time necessary to avoid the blazing hot temperatures—I'd discovered something gratifying in the solitude of watching the world come alive. Sometimes, I ran through my neighborhood, but more often than not, I found myself driving down to the lake to run on the paved trail that snaked its way around the perimeter. There was just something about it that fed my soul and made me feel alive.

I concentrated on my breathing, knowing I needed to pace myself if I was going to make it to my five-mile goal in this heat. I didn't see Zach until he was practically on top of me. He came around a bend in the path, his expression focused on the pavement in front of him as he breathed in and out in a steady rhythm. I hadn't seen him since the night of the bonfire. But I'd caught myself thinking about him at the oddest moments, wondering how he was doing, how he was handling the pressure of his soccer career with his dad breathing down his neck.

When he caught sight of me, his face lit with a smile as he tapped his earbud. We slowed to a stop, and I bent at the knees, trying to catch my breath, while Zach took a drink from his water bottle. He offered it to me, and I took it gratefully, having forgotten mine at home. I handed the bottle back to him, and he eyed me up and down, his Adam's apple bobbing as he tipped his head back and drank.

"I wouldn't have taken you for a runner." He swiped his hand across his mouth.

I quirked a brow. "Why not? I was a two-sport athlete."

"Yeah, but you're built like a tank."

"Big guys can run. It's not just for skinny guys like you." I knew I was a big guy, just like I knew he was flipping me shit. But that didn't mean I couldn't flip him some right back.

"Skinny? That's some bullshit right there."

He wasn't wrong. He did have a slender frame, but it was packed with the kind of muscle that came from training at an elite level. I had no doubt he could kick my ass if it came down to a footrace.

Laughing, I shook my head at his mock outrage. "How many more miles you got?"

He looked at his watch. "Three-ish. You wanna run together?"

"Sure. If you think you can keep up." I flashed a shit-eating grin.

"We'll see about that," he said, turning to run back in the direction he'd come from.

We set out at a relatively easy pace, feeling each other out as we fell into a comfortable rhythm. His posture was loose and relaxed despite the heat, showing just how in shape he was, while I did my best to concentrate on my breathing and not make an ass of myself.

I'd played football and baseball for as long as I could remember, and I sometimes swam laps before my life-guarding shift, so I wasn't exactly out of shape. But running long distances took a different type of endurance, and I was still working up to it.

"I haven't seen you around much lately," I said when I'd found a comfortable enough rhythm that I could talk.

"I've been in the city coaching a soccer camp."

I didn't know what I'd expected, but that wasn't it. "Do you like it? Coaching?"

"It kind of depends on the age I'm working with. The first week I was working with seven- and eight year-olds. They're kind of cute, but they drive me a little nuts. This last week, I worked with middle school kids, and surprisingly, they were pretty fun."

Zach swiped his forearm across his brow before he continued, "They're dumbasses for the most part, but they make me laugh. And while they act like they don't care, they're actually pretty eager to learn and get better. At least, when they're not trying to one-up each other."

I wasn't looking directly at him as he spoke, my eyes focused on the path in front of me, but there was a thread of pleasure in his tone. Excitement that I hadn't heard the last time we spoke.

He'd seemed out of sorts that night at the overlook, contrary to the persona he'd carried our senior year. He'd always seemed so laidback, like nothing ever phased him. Friendly. Always wore a smile. The teachers and our classmates liked him. I suspected the side I'd seen last month was one he rarely let anyone else see.

"Have you ever thought about coaching? Like as a profession?"

I felt rather than saw him shrug beside me. "I don't know. Maybe? I haven't really thought about it."

Something in his voice made me think he wasn't giving me the full picture, but I didn't push. I was sure he had his reasons.

"What about you? You lifeguard, right? You ever give swim lessons? Or coach Little League?"

"I've never taught swim lessons or coached, but I've reffed baseball and hated it. The kids were fine, but some of the parents were jackasses. The last straw was when I had to eject a dad because he got up in my face over a call. His kid was in the 8U league. Most of those kids barely know which way to run to first base and are more excited about what kind of snack they'll get afterward, but this dad took everything way too seriously. He'd been hollerin' at me the whole game, but when I called a strike on his kid, he lost his shit. Came over, got in my face, and started yelling. It took both coaches to get him off the field. It was ridiculous."

Zach was quiet for a moment but then said, "My dad can be like that sometimes. He's gotten ejected a couple of times. It's embarrassing as fuck."

"That sucks, man. I'm sorry."

"It's one of the reasons I wanted to go to school on the coast. Makes it harder for Dad to come to my games. He's loaded, so I'm sure he'll fly out for some of them, but at least it puts some space between us. I just need room to breathe."

It was the second time he'd opened up to me about his issues with his dad. Either he wasn't as private as I'd thought, or he'd decided that it was too hard to stuff every thing back in since he'd opened up already.

We came around a bend in the path and had to go single file to avoid a large puddle. I thought to change the subject to something lighter, but he continued before I could, "I'm worried about my sister. She's had...a tough couple of years, and Dad's not quite as hard on her with her dancing as he is with me and the soccer, mostly because I don't think he understands the dance world, but he still pushes. At least with me here, his focus is divided, but with me gone..."

He'd mentioned his grandparents lived in other parts of the country, and I'd never heard him talk about his mom. I figured there was a reason, so I didn't bring it up. "Do you think she'd call or text you if shit got bad? Or maybe she'd talk to my sister? They're pretty tight, I think."

"I don't know. I mean, yeah, I think they're pretty good friends from what Drea's told me, but I'm not sure how much she'd open up if she's having a hard time. She's really good at putting on a happy face for the world while underneath it all, she's drowning."

I gave him the side-eye. "Must run in the family," I said before I thought better of it.

Thankfully, he snorted a laugh. "Yeah, maybe. At least with everyone else. You seem to be able to get me talking."

"Me? I didn't do anything."

"I don't know. There's just something about you. You're easy to talk to."

We came around another bend and the path took a sharp turn to the left. Stairs cut up the hill leading into the neighborhood that backed up to this section of the lake. Most of the lake was for public use, but this quarter-mile section of shoreline was private. The neighborhood wasn't gated, so it was perfectly fine to cut up the stairs and run on the sidewalks through the community until it sent you back down to the lake on the other side. I typically turned around at this point and headed back in the direction I'd come from instead.

I started to do just that, but Zach stopped me.

"You don't want to go this way?"

I shrugged, taking a moment to catch my breath. "I usually turn around and head back at this point."

"Come on. We can stop by my house, and I'll get you a bottle of water."

"You live in this neighborhood?"

"That's my house down there." He pointed a little way down the shoreline. "The white one, three houses down."

The backside of the house he pointed at was almost entirely glass, with windows stretching up two stories. It sat on a bit of land that jutted into the water with a dock stretching out into the lake. A boat sat in a covered slip on one side of the dock and a pair of Adirondack chairs sat at the end. I thought it would be a pretty spectacular place to catch the fireworks this evening.

Realizing I'd been staring and hadn't responded to Zach's question, I turned to face him. "Sure, we can head up that way."

He smiled, then led the way up the stairs to the sidewalk along the road. We didn't bother to jog since his house was just a little way down, and I appreciated the opportunity to catch my breath. Five miles in this heat had been an ambitious goal, but I'd wanted to keep up with him.

I tried not to gape as I took in the front side of the house. There weren't nearly as many windows on this side, but it was no less impressive. This side of the house was mostly stone in shades of gray mixed in with large beams stained a dark espresso color. My eye was immediately drawn to the entrance, which featured a vaulted covered entry in what I thought I'd heard called Craftsman style on one of my mom's HGTV shows. It was tall enough to drive a car under and had one of those driveways that curved from one side of the yard across to the other.

"You coming?" Zach asked with a small smile. Despite my efforts not to gawk, my steps had slowed as I'd taken it all in.

I ducked my head, feeling awkward at getting caught staring. "Sorry. Your house is...nice," I finished lamely, the word completely underrepresenting the impressiveness of it.

He chuckled. "My dad's a lawyer. I have no idea what kind, but he makes a shit-ton of money and spends more time at work than at home, which is fine with me because it's easier on all of us that way."

He said all this with a smile as we stepped into the house, but my heart sank. It made me sad to know that his relationship with his father was so bad he'd rather not see him. I may not live in a house quite this impressive, but we were comfortable, and more importantly, I knew the people in that house cared about me. We cared about each other.

I kicked off my shoes by the door and followed him through the living room into the kitchen. The whole area was completely open, with ceilings that rose to a peak running from the front of the house to the back, where windows made up an entire wall of glass overlooking a good-sized deck, lower patio, and the lake beyond. I stepped up to admire the view, watching as a lone paddle boarder pushed through the water into the center of the lake.

I jolted and let out a hiss as Zach tapped my shoulder with a cold water bottle. "Jesus," I exclaimed, turning toward him. He laughed and held the water out to me. I shook my head but smiled as I took it from him. It was nice to see this playful side of him again. It was more in line with the persona he'd put forth all school year, and while I suspected it was a front to hide some deeper side of himself, his smile was nice to see.

"You going to the bonfire at the mayor's tonight?" he asked between gulps of water. "I've heard the fireworks are amazing over the lake."

"You didn't see them last year?"

"We moved in about a week after the Fourth."

"They're pretty awesome. Though I've never seen them from the mayor's house. We usually go out to the farm and set some off ourselves, or we watch from the other side of the lake."

"You should come with me. It'll be fun."

A weird little thrum of energy ran through me. He was smiling at me, but there was an intensity in his eyes that had me locked in his gaze. "Yeah, I could come. I don't think my parents have decided what their plans are just yet."

"Ugh, it's too early." Zach's sister walked into the kitchen, pulling her long, auburn hair into a messy bun. I usually ignored my sister's friends when they were over at the house, so I didn't think I'd spoken more than a few words to Drea before, but I definitely recognized her as one of the girls who frequently hung out with my sister. She squinted at the light streaming in the window behind us and scrunched her nose. "You guys stink. And you're dripping sweat all over the floor. Boys are so gross."

She reached into one of the cabinets, pulled out a bowl, and then disappeared inside the pantry. We could hear her muttering as she rummaged around then finally came out with a box of Lucky Charms. "You're still here? Shouldn't you be showering or something?"

"Drea is not a morning person," Zach said, stating the obvious. If a glare could do bodily harm, he'd be in the ICU, though he seemed impervious. "You want to finish our run?"

"Actually, if you don't mind, can you give me a ride back to my car? I'm gonna run home, shower, and check in with my parents. What time does the thing at the mayor's start?"

"I think it starts at three, but we can head over whenever."

"Let me talk to my folks and get back—"

"Are you coming tonight? To the mayor's?"

I looked over at Drea, whose face had transformed into hopeful anticipation.

"Yeah, probably..." My eyes darted between Zach and Drea in confusion. I wasn't sure why she'd taken a sudden interest in my plans with her brother.

"You're Mandy's brother, right? Can you bring her with you? Otherwise, I'm going to die of boredom making small talk with a bunch of rich assholes. Please! Please! Please!"

Zach rolled his eyes, though there was a hint of a smile on his lips. "God, you're so dramatic sometimes."

I chuckled. "Yeah, I can bring Mandy."

"Yes!" she exclaimed, then tore down the hallway, leaving her half-eaten bowl of cereal sitting on the counter.

"Sisters, right?"

I chuckled and followed him out to his car.

5

ZACH

"No. Go change."

"What?" I looked down at the clothes I was wearing, trying to figure out what was wrong with a navy-blue T-shirt paired with red swim trunks and flip-flops. Everything was clean. There were no wrinkles. And it was red and blue. Patriotic as fuck.

"You look like a fucking hippy who lives out of a van. Go put on a pair of chinos and a polo."

"You're serious?" My voice was incredulous. I had no idea where he'd gotten the hippy thing. I looked like a fucking Gap ad.

"I don't have time for your antics. Just go change."

"It's ninety-five degrees out, and you want me to wear pants to a lake party? We're in Astaire, Dad. Guaranteed if I wear chinos, I'll be in the minority."

Drea walked out in a strappy cotton sundress and flip-flops. I could see the strings of her bikini peaking out from underneath her dress. Her eyes darted between us in concern before she pasted a bright smile on her face and popped on her sunglasses.

"Ready to go?" she asked in an overly cheerful tone.

"I'm ready."

"No, you're not. Go. Change," he bit out.

"Nope. Either I go like this, or I don't go at all." I crossed my arms defiantly.

"Daddy, he looks fine. Let's just go." She grabbed the oversized bag full of towels and sunscreen off the counter and started walking toward the door. "Zach, grab the cookies out of the pantry."

Dad clenched his jaw but didn't say anything when I brushed past him on my way to the pantry. I grabbed the cookies she'd made yesterday and followed them outside.

The mayor's house was just a few houses down from ours, situated in a cove on a property with the longest stretch of shoreline in the private part of the lake. We had been there one other time around the holidays, when the lake was partially frozen and the trees barren of leaves. Now, in the peak of summer, the oversized cottage was beautifully landscaped with a small patch of lawn in front and surrounded by trees, making it look like a forest retreat.

We followed a stone path that led us toward the back of the house, where we could hear music and voices coming from partygoers down by the water. People were talking in clusters, some standing, some sitting in folding chairs, decked out in swimsuits, sundresses, and a whole lot of red, white, and blue.

There was a large brick patio with a sunken firepit on one side, though it was unlikely it would see any use in this heat. The patio ran across the entire back of the house and included an outdoor living space, a massive grill, and, on the other end, a putting green. Near the grill area was a long table covered in a festive tablecloth and laden with food.

I headed in that direction to add Drea's cookies to the

dessert end of the table. I set them between a plate of Rice Krispies treats covered in red and blue sprinkles and a plate of chocolate-dipped strawberries melting in the heat.

"What was that?" Drea asked as we scanned the crowd, looking for people we knew. Dad had immediately separated from us, looking for the drinks and, thankfully, leaving us to our own devices.

"What was what?"

"Back at the house. What was Dad's deal with your outfit?"

I snorted. "No fucking clue. I've given up on trying to figure out what his problem is."

"You must have done *something* to piss him off."

"Breathed, probably." I turned to look at her. "There isn't always a reason. You know that. He finds fault with everything I do. I've given up trying to please him." Which was bullshit, but maybe if I said it enough, I'd actually believe it. "Let's get some food and then head down to the water. It's hot as balls out here."

We piled our plates with burgers, watermelon, and pasta salad. Most of the seats were occupied, so we sat on the edge of the patio with our feet on the sandy beach and balanced our plates in our lap while we ate. I itched to get out there and play sand volleyball, but I suspected that if my father saw me, he'd give me shit for risking injury and ruining my soccer career.

As I finished my burger, a shadow fell over me, and I looked up to see Jason and Mandy standing just over my shoulder. I scrambled to my feet to greet them. "Hey. You made it!"

"Took us forever to find a spot to park my truck, but here we are."

"No worries. We've only been here about half an hour. Did you want to get some food?"

"Nah. We ate at my grandparents before we came. Mom made us go over there first."

"Cool."

And then we stood there awkwardly. I was tongue-tied, I realized, which was really fucking weird for me. I didn't think I'd ever struggled for words in my life.

"Why are y'all acting weird?" Drea asked. She and Mandy exchanged a look before dissolving into giggles.

"J!" a voice called from behind me. "I didn't know you were coming today."

I turned to see the guy from the bonfire—the one Jason had been worried about—walking toward us from the lake. Will, I thought his name was.

"Hey, man. Last-minute invite. What's up?"

"I'm so glad you're here. I barely know anyone." He looked at me curiously. "Hey, I'm Will."

"Zach," I said with a smile.

"Can we get in the water now?" Mandy asked no one in particular. "I'm dying of heat stroke."

Jason rolled his eyes. "We literally just got here."

I laughed. "Let's do it."

WE SPENT the afternoon splashing each other in the water, eating more food than we should, and playing cornhole. It was a really great day, despite my father's nagging this morning and the girls kicking our asses at cornhole. We'd retaliated with an epic water-gun fight I was pretty sure I'd pay for later.

As Jason and I sat in the sand watching the sunset, I

marveled at how easy it was with him. Easy in a way it hadn't been with anyone except Drea. And that was different anyway. I loved her, but she was my sister, and she was three years younger.

I'd never lacked friends over the years. I'd guess you could say I'd been popular in school. Even here in Astaire, when I was the new kid as a senior, I'd still been voted homecoming king. Teachers liked me. I hadn't had any trouble getting dates when I wanted them. There'd been a few teammates over the years who'd been jealous of the attention I got from coaches, but for the most part, I'd gotten along with the rest of them. But getting along with people and being friends was not the same thing. I wasn't sure why I'd always struggled to let people in, but somehow, Jason had snuck past my defenses.

He was easy to talk to. Easy to be around. He was a good listener. More thoughtful in his responses than most. And though he wasn't the type of guy who cracked jokes right and left, when he did snapback on someone, it was sharp and funny as hell.

"In about a month, it's going to be real weird around here."

"Yeah?"

"Most of my friends are heading to college, at least the ones I'm close to. I've known some of them my whole life. It'll be weird to not see them every day."

I could hear what he wasn't saying. He'd said it would be weird, but he meant it'd be lonely. As much as I was looking forward to going away, from getting out from under my father's thumb, Jason was staying behind. He was staying by choice, but that didn't make it any less difficult to watch his friends go.

"We can keep in touch. Text or whatever."

"I don't think I have your number."

We pulled our phones out and exchanged numbers. I was just pocketing mine when my dad approached. "Zach, I need you to come over and meet someone."

I started to argue, to insist I was already in the middle of a conversation with a friend, but I caught the look in his eye and decided against it. As much as he pissed me off, sometimes it was easier to go along. We'd already argued this morning, and I didn't want to fight again.

"I'll be back," I said to Jason as I followed my father over to where a couple was standing with a girl who looked to be around my age.

"Zach, this is Shannon and Joseph Palmer and their daughter, Leslie. Joseph is a state senator in the Nebraska legislature." I smiled politely, nodding my acknowledgment. "Leslie is a year younger than you. She's heading into her senior year."

Leslie's smile was polite, but I recognized the same look in her eye I was sure I had when my father was forcing introductions on me. She was pretty, with blue eyes and long blonde hair. She wore a sundress that accentuated her curves but wasn't overly revealing. With her father in the unicameral, I figured her outfits were probably pre-approved for events like this.

"You look familiar. Did we have any classes together?" I didn't think I'd had any classes with anyone outside of my grade this year, but there was something familiar about her.

"We were on the homecoming court together. I was the junior class princess."

"That's it! I was still new at the time, trying to learn everyone's names."

"Zach," my father interrupted, "why don't you show

Leslie where the drinks are? Fireworks should be starting soon."

Ignoring the fact that Leslie's family had probably been to this party more times than we had and likely had a good handle on where the drinks were located, I gestured for her to follow me toward the beverage station. I grabbed a can of Coke from the bin full of ice, but she bypassed it, pulling out a can of seltzer instead. She pulled a red cup off the table and poured the seltzer into it, discarding the can with efficiency.

"I've been dying for a drink all day," she said, tipping back the cup and taking a healthy swallow.

I debated putting the can of pop back and grabbing something alcoholic, but I wasn't really feeling it, so I popped the tab and took a drink.

"Rough day?" I asked.

My question was directed at her, but my eyes scanned the crowd, looking for Jason. I felt bad that I'd left him by himself. At last, I spotted him sitting a little distance away, talking to Will. The sight had me feeling oddly conflicted. I was glad he'd found his friend, but I kind of wanted it to be me sitting with him instead.

"Eh. Not rough, exactly. Just long." I dragged my attention away from Jason and back to Leslie, not wanting to be rude. "This is the fourth party we've been to today. Dad insisted on stopping by three others and making the rounds before finishing with this one. I've been introduced to more people than I can count."

"That does *not* sound like a good time."

"I'm a people person, so it's not like a huge hardship, but I'd rather hang out with my own friends on a day like today, you know?"

"I feel that."

The breeze ruffled her hair a little, the blonde strands shimmering in the low light of dusk. "It's not a big deal, really. Don't mind me. I shouldn't complain."

"It's okay. I'm sure it can be a drag sometimes."

"It's—"

A boom echoed across the lake a second before the sky lit up with the first round of fireworks. I caught the look of wonder on Leslie's face moments before I turned to watch the display. The spot where Jason and I had been sitting earlier was still open so I led Leslie over to have a seat, my eyes again scanning the crowd to see if Jason was still with Will.

When I finally found him, Will was nowhere in sight, but Jason was sitting in the sand next to our sisters. They sat near the water's edge with their backs to us, heads tilted toward the sky. Another large boom sounded, followed by a bunch of smaller crackles, and Drea tapped Jason's shoulder, pointing at the sky with glee. It was good to see my sister laughing, though I wasn't surprised Jason had brought that side out of her. He had a way of making people feel comfortable enough to let their guard down.

Leslie laid her head on my shoulder, which surprised me, considering we'd just met, but I didn't push her away. It felt nice to have someone lean on me like that.

The night wrapped up fairly quickly once the fireworks finished their grand finale, setting the sky ablaze with bursts of light coming rapid-fire, one after the next. Everyone clapped, then began looking around them, gathering discarded towels and chairs and encouraging overtired kids to help. I lost Jason in the crowd, disappointed that I didn't get a chance to say goodbye, but I shot him a text asking if he wanted to run again later in the week.

And though Leslie kissed my cheek before fighting

through the crowd to find her parents, it was still Jason I thought about when lying in my bed that night. I thought about how he listened when I spoke, like he was truly interested in what I had to say. The way he'd teased his sister mercilessly while playing cornhole, yet had made sure she'd been drinking water and reapplying sunscreen throughout the day. And the sadness in his eyes when he thought about his friends leaving in a little over a month.

I thought about that most of all.

6

———

JASON

After that first time on the Fourth of July, Zach and I started running together several times a week. It was nice to have a running partner who kept me accountable. Sometimes, we ran in companionable silence, and others, we chatted about whatever was on our minds. It was comfortable and easy.

At least it was easy most of the time. Every so often, Zach rolled in like a thundercloud. Those were the days he ran with an almost inhuman determination. He'd set out at a punishing pace, and I'd spend the next thirty minutes trying to keep up with him. He never spoke about what set him off, but based on what he'd told me earlier in the summer, I assumed it was something to do with his dad.

It was a cloudy morning in late July when I met Zach on the path at the lake just a few minutes late. I hadn't been able to find one of my shoes and it had taken me longer than usual to get out the door. I'd sent Zach a text letting him know the situation, but he hadn't responded, so I'd just headed over and hoped for the best.

The expression on his face was thunderous, unlike

anything I'd seen from him before. "Hey, man. Sorry, I'm late. I—"

"It's whatever. Let's just go." He turned and started running without waiting for a response.

My heart clutched. He might have been irritated by my tardiness, but I was sure this was something else. Something was bothering him and I hated seeing him so upset. Hoping the run might burn off his foul mood, I followed him.

Temperatures were cooler this morning, dipping below seventy for the first time in weeks, but the humidity was still high, and with the clouds dark and heavy above us, I figured we were due for a storm. Sweat trickled down my back as we pounded the pavement, the pace he set relentless.

I focused on my breathing, trying to maintain a steady rhythm, but after the first two miles, I fell behind. I didn't ask him to stop, figuring he needed to continue chasing his demons, but I did slow to a more reasonable pace, keeping him in my sights.

Eventually, he stopped and stood in the middle of the path with his arms resting on top of his head, staring me down until I reached him. I bent over, resting my hands on my knees, taking in big gulps of air as I willed my heart rate to come down. My stamina had significantly improved over the last several weeks of running, but not for the pace he had set this morning.

Three fat raindrops landed on the pavement in front of me, and for a moment, I thought they were drops of sweat, but when I felt a couple more land on my neck and arms, I knew we were about to be caught. Before I could react, the skies opened up. We ran for the closest cluster of trees, but it was too late. We were soaked to the bone in seconds, though standing under the trees did offer some protection, softening the sting of the raindrops that had been pelting us out in the open.

"This fucking sucks," Zach said through gritted teeth, and I thought he wasn't just talking about getting caught in the rain. He turned and leaned against the rough bark of the oak tree next to him, tilting his head back with his eyes closed and letting the rain wash down his face.

I stood awkwardly facing him, unsure what to do. Pain and anger radiated off him. It was in his tone of voice, his posture, the way he'd carried himself since I'd met him on the trail this morning. I wanted to help him, to take some of it away, but I didn't know the cause. Didn't know if he'd let me in. He'd given me a few glimpses of his personal life, but we mostly kept it to the superficial stuff. He seemed more comfortable that way.

I was about to ask if he wanted to talk about whatever was bothering him when his face crumpled and a small sob escaped. I took a step closer, unsure what to do, but without warning, he launched himself at me, burying his head in my chest as his body shook with sobs. My arms came around him automatically, and I held him while he clutched my wet T-shirt in his fists.

I don't know how long we stood like that, my hands rubbing his back while he cried, but by the time he was finished, the rain was too. Or at least it had faded to nothing more than a steady sprinkle.

He pulled away, hastily swiping at his eyes and nose, looking at the ground and refusing to meet my eyes.

"I'm sorry. That was… I don't know what that was."

I put my hand on his shoulder, and he finally looked at me. "It's okay to have feelings. You don't have to apologize."

"I should probably tell you today is the anniversary of my mom's passing."

Damn. The pain in his words sliced through me, making my heart ache for him. I'd wondered about his mom but figured he'd tell me about her when he was ready.

"Man, I'm so sorry. That's...that's gotta be so hard."

He shrugged and nodded at the same time in an awkward gesture, like he couldn't decide how he felt about it all.

"Can we walk? I think it would be easier to talk about it if we're walking."

"Sure, though you don't have to tell me anything if you don't want to. You don't owe me an explanation."

"I don't talk about it with anyone, really, at least not here in Astaire. Everyone knew at my old school, and I got tired of people treating me differently, so I didn't really tell anyone after we moved." His eyes were piercing as they met mine. "But I want to tell you."

Speechless that he'd trust me with something he was usually so private with, I nodded, and we made our way back to the path, turning toward the parking lot.

"Two years ago, my mom was killed in a car accident. It wasn't even late at night. It was the middle of the afternoon on a Tuesday as she was coming home from the grocery store.

"My family—we were already somewhat dysfunctional, but my mom was the glue that held us together. She ran interference between my dad and us when he was riding our asses about school or sports or whatever. One look from her, and he'd lay off. He always had a soft spot for her. No matter my father's faults, I never doubted how much he loved her."

He kicked a pebble as we walked, then shifted his gaze to some spot in the distance, lost in memory. I didn't say anything, just kept walking by his side, giving him the space to continue whenever he was ready.

"Things got really bad after that. Dad was unbearable. Barely spoke to us, and when he did, it was usually to pick at us for something. Drea fell into a depression and stopped eating. Lost a ton of weight. And I was so buried in my own shit that I didn't even notice.

"Thankfully, that Thanksgiving, my Aunt Amy insisted on hosting us for dinner and pulled my father aside and told him to pull his head out of his ass and pay attention to what was going on. Drea started seeing a therapist and started eating again. She still struggles from time to time, but she's learned to recognize when she's slipping and needs to talk to her therapist.

"Oh God." He stopped in his tracks, putting his hand on my elbow to stop me. "You can't say anything to your sister. And don't tell Drea you know either. She'd kill me if she knew I'd said anything."

"It's fine. I won't say anything. I wouldn't do that to you. Or her."

He relaxed, his shoulders slumping in relief, though he still radiated sadness.

"I miss her. I miss my mom so much I can't breathe sometimes. But when everything fell apart, I was the one who picked up the slack. I made sure Drea had what she needed for school. I helped her with her homework and drove her to dance classes. Eventually, Dad started stepping up—probably because Aunt Amy threatened to kick his ass if he didn't—but he's been such an asshole, I sometimes wish he would stay away."

"I'm sorry. I can't imagine how hard it's been for you."

"I just want her back. I want to be able to call her from college and tell her how it's going. I want to fight with her about what color sheets I want for my dorm room. I want to know that when I leave next week, Drea will be taken care of."

"I can look out for Drea if you want. I won't make it weird or anything. I'll just keep an eye on her. She's always hanging with my sister anyway."

"Thanks. That'd be…nice."

"I know it's not the same as you being here, but it's something. And I'm here for you too. Whenever you want to talk."

We stopped at the edge of the parking lot and faced each other. "I feel kind of weird about what happened back there. I don't think I've ever lost it like that."

"Maybe it was time you did."

"Yeah, maybe." He pushed his soggy hair off his face. "Anyway, thanks."

"Anytime."

"Same time tomorrow?"

"Yeah, though, maybe I'll check the weather first."

He chuckled, and my chest squeezed at the sound. "Catch ya later, Whitt."

He turned back down the path and I called out to stop him. "Do you want me to give you a ride?" I looked up at the sky, still gray with heavy clouds. From here, his house was almost on the other side of the lake.

"Nah. I think I'd like to take a walk in the rain."

7

ZACH

AUGUST

I sat on the edge of the dock, swishing my feet through the water and contemplating everything that had transpired over the last couple of years. I thought about little things like making team captain of my club soccer team, winning homecoming king, and going to State with the Astaire soccer team this year. Even though I'd only played for Astaire this past season, going to State had still been a cool experience.

I thought about the big things, the life-changing moments that had forever sent my life down a different path. My mom's passing, moving to Astaire, choosing to attend UCLA. And in the last couple of months, my friendship with Jason. Odd that a friendship that had only developed in the last six weeks could feel so life-changing.

When I thought about leaving this place, about what I would miss, it was the sound of Drea's laugh and the way she could read me better than anyone. The way she acted like every other fifteen-year-old girl one moment, then came at me with the wisdom of a forty-year-old. It was my Aunt Amy and the way she looked out for us. She hadn't tried to be a replacement for Mom, but she'd been there when we needed her. She'd taken me shopping yesterday for things for my dorm room when she'd found out my dad hadn't done it yet.

And it was my morning runs with Jason. Meeting him on the trail as the sun rose had become the best part of my day. Whether we ran in silence with only the sounds of our feet slapping against the pavement and the rhythm of our breathing or if we chatted about the happenings of the people in our small town, those runs had been comforting, like pulling on a hoodie fresh from the dryer.

It was the people I was going to miss. I hadn't wanted to move to Astaire, hadn't wanted to leave my childhood home and my friends, but this small town had welcomed me, and I'd made good memories here in a way I hadn't been able to in the aftermath of Mom's death.

Unfortunately, the one person who hadn't quite made the list was my girlfriend. Leslie and I had started dating shortly after the Fourth, and while I'd enjoyed hanging out with her, my feelings for her weren't strong enough to withstand a fifteen-hundred-mile long-distance relationship, and I'd gotten the feeling she wanted to give that a try.

I would have to figure out how to break it to her gently. I was dreading it. I cared about her enough to not want to hurt her but not enough to continue with a relationship I wasn't interested in. Hopefully, she'd understand.

I heard the smack of flip-flops approaching from behind me but didn't bother turning to see who it was. I didn't need to look to know it was Drea, who always seemed to know when I was in a contemplative mood. She slipped off her sandals and settled beside me, dipping her lavender-painted toes in the water. She sighed as she rested her head on my shoulder but didn't speak.

The sun's rays streaked low across the lake, cutting through the trees and casting everything in a golden light. I watched as a pair of dragonflies chased each other across the surface of the water before flitting off into the distance.

"I'm going to miss you, big brother."

"Same, sis." I put my arm around her, squeezing her into my side. "Even if you *are* a pain in my ass."

She snorted and pulled out of my grasp. "I think you have that backwards."

"I'm not a pain in the ass. I'm a delight."

"You're full of shit, is what you are."

I shoved her playfully, and she laughed, just as I'd intended.

"It's going to be quiet. Just me and Dad." She looked down, playing with the edges of her cutoff shorts.

"I hate that I'm leaving you here to deal with him by yourself." The edge in my tone was harsher than I'd intended, but it had been weighing on me for months, and I was struggling to contain it.

"He's not always as bad as you make him out to be."

I snorted. "You always defend him."

"Because he's not as bad as you think. He loves you, you know, even if he doesn't do a great job of showing it."

"How do you know that, Drea? Did he tell you?" I laughed without any trace of humor.

"He didn't have to," she said softly.

My eyes suddenly burned with unshed tears. I hated how much I wanted him to love me, even now. No matter how much I told myself it didn't matter, that my path was my own to walk, with or without his support, it always came back to whether or not he *cared*. I could take all those little digs, critiques, and criticisms if I knew that underneath it all, they came from a place of love. Of a misguided attempt to make sure I was taking the best path. But it didn't feel that way and hadn't for a long time.

Hell, I wasn't sure if he even liked me.

"Just promise you'll let me know if he starts in on you. Tell me you'll call or text if he starts mistreating you."

She looked at me, sadness written all over her face. "I will, but I don't think I'll have to." She attempted a smile, though it was a little watery. "Besides, I've got Aunt Amy and Mandy. What are you going to do about it all the way from California?"

"I'll call Jason and have him come over and kick Dad's ass."

"Jason. You're going to have Jason kick Dad's ass." It was said as a statement, her tone dry with complete disbelief. "He may look like he'd win in a fight, but I'm willing to bet he's never laid a hand on anyone in his life."

"You might be right, but he could at least *look* intimidating."

She shook her head, but her face turned serious once again. "What's going on with you and him?"

"What are you talking about?"

"You talk about him all the time. Spend more time with him than anyone else, even more than with Leslie."

I shrugged, unsure what she was getting at. "He's my friend. Besides, the Leslie thing is about to fizzle out."

"Shocking," she said, her tone dry once again. "No one could see that coming when you started dating her a month before you leave for school."

"Shut up. It just sort of happened. I wasn't looking for it."

"Nope. But she was."

"What are you saying?"

"Nothing. I like Leslie."

I gave her a hard side-eye.

"Stop it! I do. I just think she's a little unrealistic in her expectations for this whole thing. And I think you're oblivious to it."

"Maybe. Or maybe I'm just a selfish asshole who enjoyed having someone around who actually paid attention to me."

"You're not an asshole. At least not most of the time. You're just…"

"What? Please tell me," I said sarcastically. "What am I?"

"I think you're lonely."

I pulled my feet out of the water, ready to bolt up the dock and out of this conversation, but she put her hand on my knee, stopping me. She'd hit a little too close to home, and I didn't like the lump that had formed in my throat as a result.

"It's okay. I'm lonely too."

Even as words of denial bubbled up, I knew it was true. I'd seen that faraway, haunted look she sometimes got, even in a crowd of people. I recognized it because I felt it too. And though I thought I did a pretty good job hiding it, I'd never been able to hide anything from my sister.

"I'm scared, sis. I'm scared to leave, and I'm scared to stay."

"It's not like you're leaving forever. You can always come back here. You'll always have a home."

I looked across the lake, where the sun edged toward the horizon. It felt symbolic, that sunset. The close of a day, of one chapter of my life, in order to rise again the next. "I think my home is wherever you are, sis. You're right. I am lonely. But I'll always have you. We'll always have each other."

She laid her head on my shoulder again, and we watched as the sun slipped lower and the fireflies began winking across the lake.

8

JASON

ANOTHER WEEKEND, another bonfire. Except this one felt different. Though we'd graduated in May, this felt like the true end of high school. Starting next week, my friends were scattering. I wasn't the only one from my graduating class signed up for classes at the community college in Brinkley, but the friends I was closest to had chosen universities much farther away. Will was heading to Purdue and Zach to UCLA, and most of my other friends were heading to college in Omaha or Lincoln.

Not for the first time this summer, a sense of loneliness washed over me. Will and Zach had both come to mean a lot to me in a short amount of time. Were the threads of those friendships strong enough to withstand the distance?

Rafi approached, handing me a red cup I accepted gratefully. Rafi was a year younger than the rest of us, and it was nice to know he'd still be around. Though he'd be busy living it up for his senior year. That scene might feel weird now that I was no longer in high school. I sipped the amber liquid, trying to shake off the melancholy that had washed over me. No sense in letting something I couldn't change ruin the night.

"Yo, did you see the blue Lexus in the parking lot? That thing is badass." Rafi's dad owned a car repair shop in Brinkley, and Rafi had always been obsessed with cars, but a blue Lexus in a town the size of Astaire could only belong to one person. My eyes immediately began a scan of the crowd, searching for Zach's dark hair among all the other partiers. "Who are you looking for?"

My eyes snapped back to Rafi. "Oh. Um, Zach. The Lexus is his."

"*Zach* drives that car? How come I never saw it in the lot at school?"

I shrugged, not really sure of the answer. I hadn't thought about it before, but he was right that a blue Lexus would have stood out among the trucks, SUVs, and hand-me-down beaters most of us drove. "Maybe he drove something else and the Lexus was a graduation gift."

Zach was private, so I didn't want to share details about his family's financial status, but it wouldn't have surprised me if his father had done something like that. From what Zach had told me, his father seemed to like showing off his status and wanted his kids to reflect that as well.

"Hey, guys," Zach said, suddenly appearing beside me.

I felt my cheeks heat, hoping he hadn't overheard us. His girlfriend, Leslie, was with him, her slender hand wrapped in his. My stomach twisted at her bright, friendly smile, and I didn't know why.

I'd known Leslie most of my life, at least on a surface level. She was a cheerleader, and everyone knew her dad was in the state legislature. I'd even hung out with her and Zach a couple of times since they'd started dating last month. There wasn't any reason for her presence here to make me feel any sort of way. I didn't know what to make of it, so I did my best to ignore it.

"Hey, Les. You ready for senior year? It's gonna be epic!" Rafi said, voice rising with excitement.

Rafi was the sort of person who felt everything *big*. The guy always had a smile on his face, always looked for the best in everyone, and was always the life of the party. It was impossible not to like him.

As Leslie and Rafi had an animated conversation about which classes they were taking and which teachers they were hoping to have, my eyes found themselves drawn to Zach. Something was off with him tonight. He had a smile on his face and was nodding in all the right places, but something in his eyes told me everything wasn't as it seemed. I was tempted to pull him aside and ask him if he was okay, but another couple joined us, and my attention was diverted.

I offered Will and his boyfriend, Sammy, a wide smile as they approached. They'd rekindled their friendship after the bonfire in June, the one where Will had gotten drunk and Sammy took him home. They eventually realized there was something more between them. Sammy was known for being a prickly asshole. I'd had my reservations about them dating, but he'd softened since he'd been with Will. I wasn't sure what would happen when Will left in a couple of days, but I hoped they figured out a way to work through it.

We fist-bumped and I made introductions, everyone chatting and talking about their end-of-summer plans. Sammy's friend, Joey, and his girlfriend joined our group, and drinks flowed as conversations continued. I took advantage of Sammy's distraction, lowering my voice just for Will's ears.

"Things okay with you two?"

Sammy's face lit up with laughter at something Joey'd said, causing Will to beam. "Yeah, man. Things are good." We both took a sip of our beer. "Leaving next week is going to kill me."

"You guys talk about it? You going to try to keep this thing going?"

"I haven't brought it up. I think we've both been avoiding discussing it." A wrinkle formed on his brow, and he looked down into his beer. "I love him, J."

"Yeah, I figured." I put my hand on his shoulder and squeezed, offering the little support I could. "It's gonna suck not having you around. Crazy that you only just came back a couple of months ago."

"I know. Feels like longer."

"Course most of these fools are leaving. Astaire's going to be a weird place. I've known some of these people my whole life." I didn't mention that he and Zach had come to mean more to me than any of those people.

That familiar sense of loneliness I'd worked so hard to bury earlier came bubbling back up to the surface. But before I could decide what to do with it, raised voices caught our attention, and we both turned to see what was happening.

Zach and Leslie had moved a little bit away from the group, so I couldn't hear what they were saying. But given the way they were glaring at each other and gesturing, it was obvious something was happening between them. I watched as Leslie threw her empty cup into the sand at Zach's feet, then stomped off, leaving him staring after her, his mouth open. Without thinking, I slipped past Will, striding through the sand to where Zach was standing.

"Hey, man. Everything okay?"

He bent and picked up the cup, shaking off the sand stuck to it. "Yeah. Leslie and I just broke up."

"Oh. That sucks."

The words sounded lame to my own ears. It wasn't that I didn't mean them. It was just that while I did feel bad for him, I also had this underlying sense of relief. It was weird.

He let out a dry laugh. "It's alright. I knew it was coming. I just wasn't planning on doing it in front of an audience."

I cringed, but he smiled in return, placing his hand on my shoulder. "Don't worry about it. I'm leaving on Monday. People will move on." He shrugged, like it was no big deal, though I knew he probably cared what others thought more than he let on. "I feel bad for her. She's a nice girl. I didn't want to hurt her."

"You guys dated for what? A month? She couldn't have gotten *that* attached."

"I don't know. I guess I just have that effect on people." He flashed me a shit-eating grin.

"Pfft. If you mean you attract people to you like a fungus, then yes, you do have that effect on people."

He shook his head, laughing, lighter than I'd seen him most of the summer. That weird knot in my stomach loosened.

"Zach! Jason! What's up?" Brody, one of the guys we'd graduated with who had also played on the soccer team with Zach, approached with a couple of other guys from our class.

We stood in a circle, reminiscing about our childhoods, telling stories about each other, and laughing at the stupid shit we'd done over the years. Zach hadn't been around for most of it, but he stood by my side, listening and laughing, occasionally asking a question about something he didn't know.

The bonfire had burned down to nothing more than a red glow when my phone buzzed in my pocket. I pulled it out, surprised to see Will's name on the screen. He and Sammy had left hours ago, and I'd figured I wouldn't hear from him again tonight.

I swiped open the screen, my stomach dropping at the message waiting for me.

> WILL
>
> He dumped me
>
> I don't know what to do

> Where are you?

Several moments passed before his response came through.

> The elementary

> Stay there. I'm on my way.

I looked up from my phone to find Zach's eyes trained on me. "Everything okay?"

I titled my head, indicating he should step away from the crowd. I didn't think Will would want me spreading his shit around, so I kept it vague. "Something's going on with Will. I'm gonna bail."

He looked at me, eyes searching mine. "Are you okay to drive?"

"Yeah. I stopped drinking hours ago." I'd been caught up in the conversation and hadn't wanted to step away to refill my cup after I'd finished my last beer.

"You want me to come with you?"

"No. That's okay. You stay here. You leave Monday, right?"

"Yeah, but my flight doesn't leave until after lunch. You wanna hit the trail one more time?"

Despite my concern for Will, I smiled. "Fuck yeah. See you Monday."

9

———————

ZACH

I stood at the start of the running path with one foot pulled up behind me in a quad stretch while I waited for Jason to arrive. I was early, having gotten up well before my alarm after a restless night of sleep. I was antsy, my body buzzing with so many emotions that I wasn't sure I could identify them all. Some of them were good, some of them not so much. It was like they bounced around my body, bumping against each other, sending aftershocks through my system.

Part of me wanted to run away to California, to start a new life there and never look back. Part of me never wanted to leave Nebraska. I didn't know how to reconcile those two halves, but I supposed I'd just have to put one foot in front of the other and handle it.

Yesterday, on a whim, I'd driven into Omaha for a bit of a goodbye tour. I'd stopped by the soccer club training center, driven past my old high school, and spent an hour sitting in front of Mom's grave, wishing there was some way I could speak to her one more time. To tell her all the things I was nervous about and hoped for. To hug her again. Going to college felt like this heavy, momentous thing, and it didn't feel right that she wasn't here to witness it.

I'd returned to Astaire as the sun was making its descent into the horizon, the sky above the lake burning red and orange. I'd sat on the dock and watched it fade until darkness fell and fireflies winked above the water.

When I'd come inside, Drea and Dad had been watching a movie on the couch. It was such a rare sight that it stopped me in my tracks. Dad was dressed casually in joggers and a T-shirt, and Drea was curled against his side with her head on his shoulder.

I'd had a flash of memory of the four of us curled up on the couch for family movie night. We'd make popcorn and Drea and I would fight over which movie we'd watch, though it never really mattered because we'd both fall asleep before it was over. We'd been happy then. Life had been simpler. Less intense.

My chest had ached as the two images of past and present superimposed themselves in my mind, and wordlessly, I'd slipped out of the room.

A truck turned into the lot, pulling me out of the memory, and I gave myself a mental shake, plastering on a smile as Jason parked and got out of the truck.

"What's wrong?" he asked as he approached.

"What? Nothing. Nothing's wrong."

His brows rose in concern. "Are you sure?"

"Yes. Why would you think that?"

"You gave me your fake smile."

Perceptive asshole. I sighed. "It's nothing. Just...leaving here is weird. I didn't expect to feel so...sentimental about it, I guess."

We turned onto the path and started off at a light jog.

"Sentimental?"

I didn't want to talk about my dad. Or my mom. I'd talked about them enough and didn't want to go there today. But it wasn't only family I was feeling sentimental about. "Yeah. I mean, I've only been here a year, but I'm gonna miss it."

"I can't imagine leaving Astaire. It's...home."

"Have you ever been anywhere else?"

"Like to travel?"

"Yeah. I know you've lived here your whole life, but have you ever been anywhere else, like on a trip?"

He ducked below a low-hanging branch that needed to be trimmed back before responding. "Yeah. I mean, I've obviously been to Omaha, and we used to go up to Okoboji quite a bit."

"I've played in soccer tournaments up there."

"My grandparents used to own a lake house up there and we went as a family every summer."

"Your grandparents have a farm and a lake house?"

"My other grandparents. On my mom's side. It's my dad's parents who have the farm."

"Gotcha. Have you been anywhere outside of the Midwest?"

"A few places. We went to Disney World when I was nine and Mandy was six. Washington, DC in eighth grade. Colorado. Oregon." We moved to a single file on the path to allow another runner to pass. "What about you?"

"I've been all over the place for soccer. And college visits. Florida and Arizona to visit my grandparents, though Arizona was just once. I don't know. We've sort of traveled a lot."

"Do you have a favorite?"

I gave it some thought as we continued along the path. Sweat trickled down my back, making my shirt stick to my skin, and I wiped at my brow to keep it from dripping into my eyes.

"There have been a lot of really great places, and some stand out more than others, but mostly, my favorites haven't really been about the location. They were the places where we spent time as a family."

It felt corny to say it, but I figured if anyone would understand, it would be Jason. I knew how important family was to him.

"Yeah, I get that. Some of my favorite memories are sitting in the hotel playing cards as a family. Or splashing around in the swimming pool. And we almost always try to find someplace to play putt-putt. My family is weirdly competitive about putt-putt, even though we're all terrible at it. I don't know why it takes traveling hundreds of miles to get us to do those things. I guess life here has too many distractions."

Distractions. Soccer for me. Dance for Drea. Work for my dad. My mom had had...us, I supposed. What kind of selfish asshole was I that I didn't even know what stuff my mom had been into outside of her role as a wife and mom? I knew she and Aunt Amy had worked at a bank together once upon a time, but once she had me, she decided to stay home. Had she ever wanted to go back?

We got to the halfway point in our route and automatically turned back in the direction we'd come from. Wanting to change the subject, I asked, "When do you start EMT classes?"

"The week before Labor Day."

"Are you nervous?"

"No. I kind of wish they were starting sooner, if I'm being honest."

"Yeah?"

He huffed out a breath, though he didn't break stride. "Most of my friends are leaving this week, and with the local schools starting back the week after, the pool will only be open on the weekends through Labor Day. I don't know what I'm going to do with myself."

"Is it...?" I trailed off, realizing my question was likely poking at something that was already bothering him.

"Is it what?"

I sighed. "Is it hard? Watching everyone else leave?"

He slowed his pace, coming to a stop. He turned away from me, resting his hands on top of his head while he breathed.

"I know I'm supposed to say it's fine. It's not a big deal. I'm happy for my friends, but..." He dropped his arms and turned toward me. "It fucking sucks. I've known for a long time that staying here in Astaire is what's right for me, but I didn't really think about what it would feel like to watch so many of my friends leave."

He brushed his hands over his short crop of hair and started walking toward the parking lot. "Will's a mess. I don't know if you heard, but Sammy broke up with him. That's why I left the bonfire the other night. He just fell apart."

"I hadn't heard. I was down in Omaha yesterday. They seemed fine earlier in the night."

"It's a long story, and Sammy's playing the martyr, I think." He waved a hand dismissively. "It doesn't matter. The point is, Will's a mess and I'm worried about him, and he's leaving. He's my best friend and..."

That stung. It shouldn't have. I'd known they were close, even though they'd only become friends a few weeks before Jason and I had started hanging out. And Will was a cool guy. It wasn't really personal. It's just that while Jason had me *and* Will, I only had him. Or at least the only one I shared the deep stuff with.

"And I feel like a dick because I know he's hurting, but all I can think about is that he's leaving and I'll be alone."

"I'm sorry, man. That sucks."

Jason turned and started jogging toward the parking lot, though his pace was slower than it had been. I followed, letting him take the lead. We finished the rest of our run in silence, each lost in our thoughts. I regretted asking him how he felt about everyone leaving. He was clearly bummed about it, and I'd only poked at the bruise.

At the end of the path, we stopped, automatically turning to stretch our aching muscles. "I'm going to miss you, Zach. I don't know if that's weird to say..." He trailed off, shrugging and not quite meeting my eye. "I mean, I know I just said Will was my best friend, but I kind of feel like you've become one too."

"Same. I, uh..." I swallowed past the annoying lump in my throat and tried again. "I know we really didn't start hanging out until this summer, but it feels longer."

"Same here." He chuckled a little awkwardly, and I chanced a look at him. He was smiling with the sun shining behind him like a halo and I had to squint to see him properly.

"I'll text, okay? We'll keep in touch. And it's not like I'm never coming home."

"Yeah, that's good." His arm twitched at his side. "Can I, uh, hug you? Is that weird?"

Something fluttered low in my gut, but I ignored it. "Yeah, man. Though I'm sweaty as hell."

He chuckled. "Same." Then he leaned in, wrapped his big arms around me, and pulled me close.

It wasn't a long hug, just a few seconds with a couple of

bro-style back slaps, but when I pulled away, I was surprised to find myself blinking back tears.

"Yeah, so...good luck," he said, an awkward smile tugging at his lips.

I chuckled. We were awkward and ridiculous. "Thanks. I'll text."

"Cool."

And with one more awkward smile, he turned and headed toward the lot. Watching him go left me feeling bereft like I'd just watched a piece of me walk away. But that was weird. He was just a friend. A guy I'd only gotten close to in the last couple of months.

Shaking my head at my thoughts, I turned and headed home.

10

———

ZACH

My roommate is clipping his toenails

Just sitting on the couch clipping away

JASON

Gross

We have a private bathroom. He could
totally do it there

I stared at him really hard, and when he
finally made eye contact, I glared pointedly
at his feet. He went right back to clipping
them

Maybe he didn't understand your glare.
Some people need actual words for
communication

I don't think that's it. I just don't think he
cares

What are you going to do about it?

Text you, obvi

Seems productive

Eh. It beats writing my English paper

JASON

First home football game of the season tonight

Weird to be sitting in the stands

ZACH

I'm sure

picture of Mandy and Drea cheesing for the camera in their dance team uniforms

They look great!

They spent an hour practicing their hair last night at my house. They locked me out of the bathroom

It's just a ponytail, right?

Apparently it had to be curled a certain way and there's some sort of braid thing that goes into it

Looks like a regular ponytail to me

Shh! They'll hear you.

And then I'll never hear the end of it

Lol. Girls are weird

Yup

ZACH

First game is tomorrow

JASON

Nervous?

No

Yes

lol

It's been a long time since I've been nervous
for a game. But I'm the only freshman who's
starting. I don't want to make an ass of
myself

You'll do great!

How do you know? You've never seen
me play

I might have found a video of the game from
State last spring

You studying up on me, Whitt?

I was curious

Do you know anything about soccer?

Kick the ball in the net. Don't use your
hands

lol

It's a little more complicated than that

I figured

Wait until you learn about the offside rule

I don't think anyone understands that rule

11

———

JASON

SEPTEMBER

As August gave way to September, I settled into a new routine. Temperatures slid into a more reasonable range, making my runs more bearable. Though, these days, I'd found a couple of new running routes that didn't take me around the lake. Running the lake path didn't feel right without Zach by my side.

A lot of things didn't feel right with him gone, but there wasn't anything to be done about it, so I tried not to think about it much.

We texted nearly every day. I'd never been much of a phone person—my mom had often complained about my tendency to forget it when I left the house—but I'd found myself attached to it more than ever these days. And when I felt that little vibration in my pocket, I couldn't help but smile.

Sometimes, they were innocuous little messages, and other times, I could tell he was in a more pensive mood.

Whatever the topic, I'd fumble the phone out of my pocket and happily type out a reply.

Mixed in with the texts from Zach were the occasional messages from Will. He was struggling. I could feel it in his texts and social media posts. I'd made an Instagram after everyone left so I could keep in touch, and since he'd left for Purdue, Will's feed had been full of selfies with various men, often with one or both of them holding drinks. I could see in his eyes that he was unhappy, and he looked like he'd lost some weight.

I tried to text him and offer support, but each time, he brushed me off, insisting he was fine. I didn't believe him for a second, but I was helpless to do anything from so far away.

"Hey, can you give me a ride to dance?" Mandy stood in my doorway, dressed in a sports bra and leggings, with a sparkly backpack slung over one shoulder.

"Sure. What time do you need to be there?"

"Ten minutes."

"Cutting it close, don't you think?" I stood, searching for the tennis shoes I'd kicked off as soon as I'd gotten home from class.

"Don't start. Mom was supposed to take me, but she just texted that she got stuck at the train crossing and is going to be late."

I tugged my shoes on, grabbed my keys, wallet, and ball cap, and walked toward her. "That damn train is off schedule at least once a week."

We climbed into my truck, and I started the engine while she buckled her seat belt. Once we were on our way, I asked her how school was going.

"It's alright. We're reading *Of Mice and Men* in English, which is okay, I guess, but we have to take notes in a specific format, which is really dumb because it's not that hard of a book. Biology is easy so far. Mr. Davidson doesn't give a ton of homework, and when he does, I mostly get it done in class, so that's okay. I don't know. It's all the usual school stuff. Probably not that different than it was for you."

"You're probably right. When's homecoming? You have a date?"

"It's like a month away. I'll probably go with Drea and some other girls from the dance team."

"How's Drea doing with Zach being gone?"

"She acts like everything's fine, but I think she's sad."

I glanced at her quickly before returning my eyes to the road. "What makes you think that?"

"I don't know. I mean, sometimes she gets really quiet for no reason, or she just, like, doesn't text me back for a whole evening. But then I see her at school the next day and she's fine."

"How do you know it's because of Zach?"

"I don't, I guess. I just figured that's what it was because I'd probably feel the same if it was you."

We pulled up to a stop sign, and noting there wasn't a car behind me, I turned to look at her. "Seriously?"

She rolled her eyes. "I mean, yeah. You're my brother."

"That's really…"

"God. Don't make a whole thing about it. Just drive. We're going to be late."

I checked the road before proceeding through the intersection. "I love you too, sis."

"Ugh. Don't be all weird."

I laughed. "I'm not being weird."

"Whatever. How's your EMT thing going?"

"It's fine." I shrugged. I liked the coursework and found most of it interesting, but I wasn't sure she wanted to hear all the details.

"That's it? 'It's fine?'"

"Yeah. What else do you want me to say?"

"What types of things do you learn about?"

"We learned a bunch of medical terminology, and now we're learning about trauma response."

"Ew. Like blood and stuff?"

I laughed again. "Yeah, some. Treating patients with shock. Stabilizing accident victims until they can get to a hospital. Stuff like that."

I pulled into a parking space in front of the dance studio and turned to look at her, surprised when she didn't hop out right away. A glance at the clock on the dash told me she was already nearly five minutes late.

"That's really cool," she said, eyes wide, like she was just seeing me for the first time. "I mean, I think it's really cool that you want to do something like that."

"Thanks." I ducked my head, both pleased and embarrassed by the compliment. "You should probably get going." I nodded toward the studio. "You're already late."

"Yeah." She looked at me a moment longer, then grabbed her bag and hopped out of the truck. "Thanks for the ride," she called out just before she closed the door and jogged into the studio.

12

ZACH

How's school?

DREA

Fine. All As and 1 B. And I have a science
quiz tomorrow

You ready for it?

Yeah. It's cell structure for bio. Easy

You always were smarter than me

Not true. I just actually study

That's fair

How's Dad?

When was the last time you talked to him?

After my game last week, when he called to
tell me I should have been more aggressive
on the attack against Rutgers

...

What do you want me to say? I scored my
first collegiate goal on a PK and all he could
talk about was what I should have done
better

> I think he just doesn't know how to talk
> to you

Bullshit

He literally could have just said congrats on
the goal

Why do you always defend him?

> Because the two of you are all I have left
> and I love you both

I love you too, sis

I have to go

> Don't leave it like that

> Zach?

> Fuck you, Zach

> JASON

> Nice game yesterday!

> Was that your second collegiate goal?

ZACH

Thanks! And yes!

> Very cool

Drea came over and watched with me and
Mandy

All 3 of you watched?

We streamed it

Wow. That's cool. Thanks

I've been able to catch most of your games.

Thanks, man. That means a lot

How was Drea? She seem ok?

I wasn't going to say anything but she was
maybe a little quieter than usual

Are there other things you aren't telling me
about my sister? You said you'd keep an
eye on her!

Dude. Calm down

This is the first time there's been anything to
report

Sorry

We got into a fight

Who? You and Drea?

Yeah. My dad was a dick after my last
game. Not the one yesterday. The one
before that. She defended him

That sucks

I'm sure it's hard for her to feel stuck in the
middle

Yeah. I know it is

It just hurts, you know?

I get that

You should talk to her

Probably

ZACH

I'm sorry

DREA

I know

Me too

It just hurts when he pulls that shit with me

I know that too

13

ZACH

OCTOBER

"Happy Birthday," I said the moment Drea's bright, happy face filled my phone screen. And if possible, she smiled even wider.

"Thanks! It's so good to see you!"

"You too!" We'd texted almost every day since we'd argued a couple of weeks ago, but the texts were short and full of safe topics. Neither of us had mentioned my father since. "I'm sorry I can't be there for your Sweet Sixteen."

"That's okay. Just score a goal for me, okay?"

"I'll do my best!" I had to load the bus in about an hour to head to a game across town at UC Irvine. "Do you have anything fun planned to celebrate?"

"Nothing major. I'm going out for pizza with Mandy and some other girls from the dance team, and then we're gonna come home and have a sleepover."

I internally cringed at the thought of a basement full of giggling teenage girls, but I smiled, glad she had friends to celebrate with. "Nice. Did you get your license?"

"They aren't open on Saturdays, but Dad promised to take me on Monday."

She winced when she realized what she'd said. It was the first time either of us had mentioned Dad since the argument.

"It's okay for you to talk about him. I don't want you to feel like you can't."

Her brow creased in worry, reminding me so much of Mom that my stomach clenched. "I just don't want to upset you."

"I know, but he's your dad too. And just because I don't have a good relationship with him doesn't mean I wish the same for you. I don't want you to feel caught in the middle."

She was quiet for a moment, as if picking over her words carefully, but when I expected her to say something else about Dad, she said, "I miss Mom."

"Me too," I said, my voice barely audible. I watched helplessly as her eyes filled and then spilled over, wishing I could be there to wipe her tears away. "She'd be proud of you." I forced the words past the lump that had formed in my throat. "*I'm* proud of you."

"Thanks, Zach. I miss you."

"I miss you too."

She looked off to the side, then back at me, forcing a smile I knew wasn't completely real. "I better go. Aunt Amy's taking me out for a pedicure. She should be here any minute."

"Okay. Have fun. Tell her I said thank you for the cookies she sent last week."

She smiled again, this time a real one. "Will do. Have a good game!"

"Bye."

I clicked off the call but remained in place as a wave of

homesickness washed over me. As if it had a mind of its own, my thumb swiped into my contacts and dialed Jason. It rang several times, but just as I was about to give up, Jason's deep rumble filled the line. Warmth spread through my chest at the comforting sound. All our conversations had been over text since I left. I hadn't realized how much I'd missed the sound of his voice.

"Zach? Everything okay?" He was breathless, as if he'd scrambled to get to the phone.

"Yeah, I, uh..." I felt sheepish. I wasn't even sure why I'd called. "I was just talking to Drea and thought I'd call and see how you're doing."

"Don't you have a game today?" His voice was laced with confusion, but all I could focus on was the thrill that he still kept up with my soccer schedule.

"Yeah, I have to leave in a half-hour."

"Oh. So..."

Shit. This was weird. I shouldn't have called him. We were friends. Buddies. Dudes didn't call each other, did they? Not just to talk.

"I'm sorry. I shouldn't have—"

"So, how's the game looking today?"

We both spoke at the same time.

"I'm sorry, what?"

He chuckled, and the soft sound washed over me, intensifying my longing for home. "I said, how's the game looking today?"

"Oh. Um. We haven't lost to them in the last ten years, so we should have a strong showing."

"Good. How's your ankle?"

Reflexively, I rolled my foot around, testing it. I'd forgotten that I'd mentioned rolling it during practice this week. It was feeling pretty good at the moment, but the trainer would likely tape it just to be safe.

"Feels pretty good. I stayed off it for a couple of days but was back in practice yesterday without any issues."

"Good. That's good."

"What are you up to today?" I asked, trying to think of something to keep him on the line longer, if only to listen to the sound of his voice. The sound of home.

"I was out back helping my dad with yard work when you called. It's still in the eighties here, but Dad insists we need to start getting the flower beds ready for fall."

"Oh. I'm sorry I interrupted."

"Don't be. I needed to take a break anyway. It's hot as balls today."

My roommate, the toenail clipper who was also my teammate, burst in the door, stripping out of his clothes as he made his way over to his bed. I was pretty sure it was the same outfit he'd been wearing last night when he'd headed out to a frat party.

"Bruh, you should have come to the party last night. It was electric. Cops got called, and I had to climb out a window. Went home with some girl named Jessie. Or Jamie. Or maybe it was Jenny. Have you seen my joggers?"

Jason's laugh filled my ears, indicating he'd heard everything Clayton had said while digging through the pile of clothes next to his bed.

"I'm kind of on the phone. I don't know where your joggers are."

Clayton turned and looked at me. "Oh. Right. You know we need to leave soon, right?"

"Yeah, man. I've got it."

"Cool."

He turned around and resumed digging through his clothes, making an even bigger mess than the one he'd started with. It was as if the pile of clothes was reproducing somehow.

"I better go," I said into the phone, "or this guy's going to show up pantless to load buses."

There was that chuckle again. Why had I never noticed the sound of it before? "Alright, man. Have a good game."

"Yeah, I will."

"Hey, Zach?"

"Yeah?"

"It was good to hear from you." Inexplicably, my cheeks heated.

"Yeah. Same."

I disconnected the call and looked up as Clayton pulled his shirt over his head. He flailed for a moment before getting his arms through the sleeves, then ran his fingers through his hair and looked at me as if he'd been waiting for me to be ready for ages.

"You ready to go?"

I chuckled as I rose to stand. "Yeah. Let's go kick some ass."

"Hell yeah!"

14

ZACH

How's the job at the orchard?

JASON

It's alright. Yesterday, I drove the tractor with a wagon full of kids around the pumpkin patch

They were pretty cute

Dude. They let you drive?

lol. Yeah

Badass

You don't have any games this weekend, right? What are you going to do?

I've got homework and laundry to catch up on. Might hit the beach later with some of the guys

It got down into the lower 50s last night. Definitely not beach weather here

Sunny SoCal doesn't suck

I miss the weather back home sometimes
though

You miss rain and wind and gloomy clouds?

I miss sweater weather

The color of the leaves changing

Coming home from school and turning on
the fireplace

The sound of rain hitting the window and
the way fog looks when it rolls across
the lake

Yeah, those things are pretty cool

I don't miss raking the leaves though

Don't rub it in

ZACH

Favorite scary movie?

JASON

I don't know. I'm not much of a scary
movie guy

What? We can't be friends

lol

Scream? I guess?

The 90s movie?

Yeah, my mom likes that one

It's barely even scary

I just never saw the point in scaring myself on purpose

I have so much to teach you

ZACH

Thanks for sending the homecoming pics

JASON

You're welcome

Did they have fun?

I think so. They came back here after and your sister spent the night

She's actually still here, I think. They're still asleep

It's so weird to not be there

It's weird to still be here and not going

Did you like going to those things?

They were alright. I never went with a date or anything. Usually, it was just some guys from the football team and some of their girlfriends

Really? You never took a date?

I've never really dated

Like you've never had a girlfriend?

Nope. Not a boyfriend either

How did I not know this about you?

It never came up, I guess

Does it bother you?

You don't have to answer that. That
was rude

lol it's fine. I'm pretty sure I'm ace

Ace? Like asexual?

I guess? I've never really been attracted to
anyone

Wow. Every dude I knew in high school was
a horny motherfucker

Or so I thought

It bothered me when I was younger, like
middle school and early high school.
Thought I was broken or something. But
then I just figured it wasn't something I
could change, so why worry about it

Plus, everyone else was having relationship
drama, and I figured I was lucky I didn't
have to worry about it

True. Plus, breakups are the worst

selfie with a rumpled but smiling Drea

Look who just woke up

Sis!

She says hi!

I'm gonna let you go

Tell her to call me later

Will do!

15

JASON

"Zach says to call him later." I set my phone aside and turned to face Drea. Her long brown hair still held some of the curls from the previous night, and I could see a smudge of makeup under her left eye. She turned, opened the refrigerator, and pulled out a pop, holding it up to me in offering. When I declined, she shut the door and sat at the island next to me. She cracked open the can, then took a sip before turning back to look at me with an assessing eye.

"Mandy still sleeping?" I asked, feeling a little discomfited by her gaze.

She rolled her eyes. "You know your sister loves her sleep. I'm guessing she won't be up before noon."

I was pretty sure I remembered Zach mentioning Drea wasn't a morning person either, but I wisely kept that tidbit to myself.

I glanced at the clock on the stove, noting the time was just after ten. Our parents were at church, but they'd long ago stopped making us go, so I'd gotten a late run in this morning, then come back and showered. I'd just grabbed an apple when I'd gotten distracted by Zach's text.

"What time did you guys go to bed? It was after midnight when you got home."

"I think it was a little after one. We were going to watch *Mean Girls*, but we both fell asleep." She took another sip of her pop, and I bit into my nearly forgotten apple. "You talk to Zach a lot?"

"Most every day," I said once I swallowed my bite.

"That's good. I'm glad he has you. He's never hurt for friends, but after Mom died—I'm assuming he told you about that?" I nodded in response. "Well, after she died, it was weird for us. It happened during the summer, and when we went back to school in the fall, everything was different. No one really knows what to say when you lose a parent. It's almost like everyone's afraid of saying the wrong thing, so they just stop saying anything at all. People we'd been friends with for years just stopped coming around. I mean, everyone was friendly enough at school, I guess, but no one ever texted to hang out. I was still in middle school, but Zach was a junior. He used to go out with his friends all the time. They'd go to movies or out for pizza or whatever. The invites just stopped. Zach's a people person. I also am, to a point, but I don't mind alone time either. Zach needs to be around people. He'd already lost our mom, but when he lost his friends too, he sort of withdrew."

I could see it, could picture what she was talking about. I hadn't known Zach well during the school year, but from what I remembered, he'd always been surrounded by a group of people. Even at the bonfires this summer, people had sought him out. He was like a magnet for people and fed off their energy.

"I think it was a big part of the reason Dad moved us out here. Zach thinks our dad is an asshole, and I suppose he has a point, but Dad also sees more than Zach realizes. He knew we needed a fresh start."

She hadn't mentioned her own struggles with depression following their mom's passing, but I didn't bring that up, honoring Zach's request to keep his confidence.

"How are things between you and your dad? I know Zach has a rocky relationship with him, but how is it with you?" I was on shaky ground here, but I was genuinely curious. I wanted to understand their family dynamic a little better.

"Dad's...he's a hard person to know. He's hard on me and Zach because he wants what's best for us, but I think there's more to it. From some things Mom told me before she died, Dad had to work really hard to get where he is now, and he made some mistakes when he was younger. I think he pushes us because he doesn't want us to make the same mistakes he did."

"Do you think they'll ever figure out how to get along?"

"I hope so. But they're both so damn stubborn, I'm not sure it'll happen anytime soon."

She chewed on her bottom lip, looking so sad, and I wished I could do something to take that look away.

"He misses you, you know. He asks about you all the time."

"Yeah?" She laid her head on my shoulder. "I miss him too."

16

ZACH

Jason sent me a video of your "Thriller" performance from last night. You killed it!

DREA

OMG! TYSM!

How long did it take you guys to learn that?

We've been working on it for a couple of weeks

Some of the girls were bummed we had a game on Halloween and wouldn't be able to go to any parties, but this was way more fun, I think

Did you do anything for Halloween?

Me and some of the guys from the team dressed up as the Seven Dwarfs

Fun!

Which one were you?

I don't want to say

OMG! You were Dopey, weren't you?

Please tell me you were Dopey

I hate you

Best. Halloween. Ever.

———

ZACH

I hate how hard it is to see the stars here

JASON

Why are you up at 2:30 in the morning?

It's 12:30 here and I could ask you the same
question

lol. Your text woke me up

Don't you have your phone on Do Not
Disturb at night?

What if there's an emergency?

There are settings that will override DND for
certain people in your contacts

oh

lol. Just go back to bed. Sorry I woke you

no. I'm up now. What's going on?

I suppose I'm feeling a little homesick

I think that's to be expected. Is it bad?

Not bad. I don't know. It's weird

I miss random things

Like what?

Sherry's Soft-Serv

It's closed for winter anyway

Oh yeah

Sunsets on the lake

I can go take a pic tomorrow?

Not the same

probs not

I don't know. I only lived in Astaire for a year.
Seems weird I should miss it so much

I don't think it's weird. I love it here

I miss my sister

And you

Is that weird to say? I know we're friends
and shit, but I don't know… I miss our runs.
And hanging at the lookout. And bonfires

I miss those things too. And you

I should let you go. I have an early class

ok

You know I'm always here, right?

Yeah. Thanks

Goodnight

Goodnight

JASON

When will you be home for Thanksgiving?

ZACH

I'm actually not coming home. We only have
the Thursday and Friday off

Dad and Drea are coming out to visit. And
since we made the D1 tournament,
hopefully, we'll be in it long enough to play
games the weekend before and the
weekend after the holiday

Congrats! That's great news!

It is but I'm nervous

About the tournament?

About spending several days with my dad

But you also get to see Drea

Definitely excited about that part

17

JASON

NOVEMBER

IT WAS the Friday after Thanksgiving, and I was officially in a funk. I'd been denying my shitty mood all week. When I snapped at Mandy over a bowl of Cheerios, sending her fleeing to her bedroom in tears, it became evident I wasn't acting like myself. I'd gone after her and apologized, then retreated to the basement to brood in solitude.

I spent most of the afternoon watching football, and after watching the Huskers beat Iowa, I went to my room and spent some time studying. Despite having the house to myself while the rest of the family headed into the city for some Black Friday shopping, I struggled to focus on the material, so after about an hour, I gave up.

I decided to shower and maybe read a little before bed, so I crossed into the hall bathroom and turned on the water. As steam filled the bathroom, I stripped down, going through the mundane task of preparing to shower. Stepping under the spray, I let the hot water rain down on me, running in rivulets down my body. I began to lather up when I realized I hadn't heard from Zach that day. We rarely went a day without texting, though with it being a holiday week and him having another game tomorrow, I supposed he was likely just busy.

I wondered how things were going between him and his dad. Zach hadn't really mentioned him in any of his texts this week, though he spoke plenty about Drea, and I knew he was happy to see her. I hoped things were going well for all of their sakes.

I smiled as I recalled the photo he'd sent of him and Drea on the beach. They'd spent most of the week in California before heading out today to South Carolina. Zach had flown out with the team, while Drea and their father flew commercially and would meet the team there.

Wednesday, Zach sent a series of photos. Selfies of himself and Drea on the Santa Monica Pier. Shots of their feet in the water. And several in a row of a wave that had taken Drea by surprise. She'd rolled her jeans to her calves and had been standing with her back to the ocean when a wave had crested around her waist, soaking most of her torso and her hair. The look of surprise on her face, followed by laughter, had made me smile, but it was the last picture, another selfie of the two of them laughing, that I was thinking of now.

The smile on Zach's face was the most joyful and relaxed I'd ever seen him. His eyes had been alight with merriment, his smile wide and bright. It had sent a wave of warmth through me, and I'd found myself pulling up the picture several times over the last couple of days just to study that look on his face.

As I ran my soapy hands down my body, I realized with a shock that my dick was partially hard. Other than morning wood, I hadn't had an unassisted erection since middle school, when the lightest brush of my boxers would have me springing up and ready to salute in a fraction of a second. These days, I had to coax an erection into existence with my hand, and most days, I didn't bother. I liked an orgasm as much as the next guy, but honestly, most of the time, I didn't think about it. That urge, that *need* to get off, just simply wasn't there.

But now, standing in the shower with hot water running down my body, I took my cock in hand and gave it a stroke. A groan escaped, echoing around the shower walls, and at that moment, I was glad I was the only one home. I continued to stroke, my dick lengthening to a full erection as little jolts of pleasure coursed through me.

I paused, reaching for the bar of soap and slicking up my hands. Turning, I leaned against the wall for support and continued working myself over. I tilted my head back to rest against the wall while lowering my free hand to cup my balls. As I tugged and rolled them in one hand, I stroked my dick faster with the other.

My pulse spiked and my breaths came in pants until I felt the telltale tingle at the base of my spine, indicating an orgasm was imminent. With a few more vigorous strokes, I erupted, coming hot and thick all over my hand. I breathed through it, grunting with each pulse, until eventually, the waves subsided and my cock began to soften once again.

Holy hell. Where had that come from?

I finished my shower, drying off and wrapping a towel around my waist before heading across the hall to my bedroom. Not bothering with clothes, I climbed into bed, pulling the covers over me and thinking about what had just happened in the shower.

Tonight, I'd gotten hard, or at least partially so, out of nowhere. No. Not nowhere. I'd been thinking about Zach and that picture he'd sent me. The way his face had lit up with his smile. His absolute joy. Despite coming just twenty minutes prior, my cock gave a little twitch at the thought.

Oh shit.

Was this what attraction felt like?

Was I attracted to Zach?

18

ZACH

We lost in the quarterfinals. Clemson scored a goal to go up one-nil in the eighty-ninth minute, and with only four minutes of stoppage time, it wasn't enough time to make a comeback. It sucked to have come so close and then walk away with nothing. Especially considering it was Clemson, where my father had pushed me to go to school.

The mood on the plane was somber. Most guys had headphones on or were sleeping. No one wanted to talk. I tried to sleep but couldn't, replaying the game in my mind, contemplating every pass, every shot on goal, every missed opportunity to score.

Over the last several months, I'd gotten to know the guys on and off the field. My roommate Clayton was one of the most random guys I'd ever met, but his focus was unmatched on the field. It was almost as if he used up all his concentration on soccer and didn't have any left in all the other areas of his life.

Shelton and Anderson were the jokesters of the team, always cracking us up with their antics in the locker room, but on the field, they were all heart. Sidney, Bell, and McAllister were the studious types, always studying film, analyzing player statistics, and advising everyone on the weaknesses of each team. All of us, every last one, had put everything we had out there, and it just hadn't been enough.

I fucking hated losing.

Giving up on sleep, I pulled up my phone and scrolled through the pictures I'd taken this week. The first couple were pics of the stadium I'd taken before the game started. When I'd gotten good enough at soccer that I'd started traveling for games, Mom had encouraged me to take pictures in every stadium and the habit had stuck.

With a lump in my throat, I scrolled past those to the ones I'd taken with Drea on the Santa Monica Pier the day before Thanksgiving. I'd had a couple of classes in the morning, but that afternoon had been one of the best I could remember having since before Mom died. Dad had been relaxed, almost like he had been when we were kids. Drea and I had ridden the Ferris wheel, stuffed our faces with churros and ice cream, and played arcade games, all while Dad watched with an indulgent smile. We'd strolled the beach at sunset, getting soaked by a rogue wave we hadn't seen coming. It had chilled us to the bone, but we'd laughed until our bellies ached and tears streamed down our faces.

Despite campus being only fifteen minutes from the pier, Dad had insisted I stay with them at their rental a few blocks away. I'd been nervous about what it would be like to stay with them again after getting used to living independently, but with Dad on his best behavior, it had actually been a nice break from campus, almost like a mini vacation. I'd caught Drea glaring at him in warning a couple of times and wondered if she'd given him a pep talk before they'd flown out. If so, I was grateful for it.

I continued scrolling, coming across a picture Jason had sent me on Monday. After our late-night text exchange earlier in the month, when I'd confessed to being a bit homesick, he'd taken to sending me random pictures from around town.

Monday, he'd gone down to the lake and snapped a photo of the sun setting on the water. The trees in the distance had been mostly barren of leaves, reminding me it was likely pretty chilly in my home state. The lake had reflected the reds, oranges, and purples of the setting sun, casting the water in an almost magical hue. I'd saved the picture before texting my thanks for sending it. He'd returned my text with a selfie of a grin and a thumbs-up, making me smile in return. It was so unlike him to send a selfie, but it was almost as if he knew the first pic would choke me up, and I'd need something silly to lighten my mood. I'd saved that picture too.

"Is that the guy you're always texting? He's hot."

I thought Clayton had been sleeping, but I looked up to see him quite awake and peering over at my phone. And then it registered what he'd said.

"What?"

"This is the guy you're always texting, right?"

"Yeah. My friend Jason from back home. I didn't know you paid attention to my texting habits."

He shrugged. "You've always got your eyes glued to your phone and your thumbs working overtime. I figured there was a guy."

"Why a guy?"

Another shrug. "I dunno. Just a vibe, I guess."

"You said he was hot," I persisted.

"He is. Do you not think so?"

I looked at the picture, my brow creasing as I thought

about it. "I guess? I never really thought about him like that."

"He's not your boyfriend?"

"Dude. I literally had a girl sitting in my lap at the party we went to last week." Never mind that I hadn't really been interested in her and it hadn't gone any further.

"I just figured you were bi or something. I mean, I sleep with girls like"—he scrunched up his face, giving the matter serious consideration—"maybe eighty percent of the time. But the other twenty percent? I'm all about the D."

I stared at him blankly. "Seriously?"

"Sometimes I just need a good dicking down. Like, pussy is great. Really, *really* great. And tits too." His eyes became unfocused like he was picturing the body parts in question. "But sometimes I'm in the mood for a dude. Muscles and a hard body just hit different, you know?"

"No...I don't know. I've only ever been with girls."

His face fell, and if I wasn't so mind-blown by this conversation, I might have laughed.

"Oh. My bad, dude." His eyebrows shot up beneath the shaggy dirty-blond hair hanging over his forehead, and his eyes widened. "Shit. You're cool with it, right? I'm not rooming with a homophobe, am I?"

I did chuckle at that. "Nah, man. It's cool. I just didn't see it coming."

"Oh, well, that's okay. Most people only see what they want to see. For instance, I got a thirty-five on my ACT, but most people think I'm an idiot."

Me. I was most people.

That wasn't actually true though. I'd seen how focused he was on the field and figured there must be more to him than appeared on the surface. I just hadn't given it a whole lot of thought beyond that.

"So this Jason guy. He's just a friend?"

"Yeah. I've actually only known him for about a year, but I really only got to know him better this summer. I guess we got pretty close right before I left."

"Hm," was all he said.

"What?"

"Nothing, man. If you say he's your friend, then that's it."

I stared at him with my brow raised. He clearly had more to say.

"You just, like, you get this look on your face when you're texting him. Like you're sharing some secret joke or something."

"How do you know it's him and not someone else? He's not the only person I text."

"Like I said, you get a look." And with that, he leaned back in his seat, crossed his arms, and closed his eyes, oblivious that he'd dropped a grenade in my lap.

I wasn't into Jason, was I? Definitely not like *that*. He was a friend. Like a brother. And he was ace anyway. No. That wasn't the point. The point was that *I* wasn't into guys. Or him. At all.

Right?

19

ZACH

My Western Civ professor has a handlebar
mustache

JASON

I don't think I've ever seen one of those in
person

Me neither

Also I think he might be drunk

Isn't it like 9:30 there?

Yup

ZACH

Update: He's definitely drunk. He's listing to
one side and has repeated the same
sentence three times

JASON

Are you sure he's not having a stroke?

Could be, but I'm sitting in the front row and
he smells like he took a bath in bourbon

Yikes

ZACH

Update #2: He's started sweating profusely.
Keeps mopping his brow with a
handkerchief that looks like it began its
existence in the seventies

Ope. He rubbed his face too vigorously and
now his mustache is askew

Not a sentence I thought I'd ever type

JASON

lol

Btw. I'll be home Saturday

Looking forward to it

20

____

ZACH

DECEMBER

I STOOD ON THE CURB, shivering in the wind as I watched the cars moving through the airport pickup lane, looking for my father's black BMW. I had forgotten how bitter the December wind could be in Nebraska, and my UCLA quarter zip and jeans weren't cutting it. It had been sixty-four degrees when I'd left, and as I looked down at my smartwatch, I noted it was thirty-seven here with a chance of snow moving in later that evening.

I was about to walk back inside and call my father when a beat-up silver Ford pickup caught my eye. The person in the passenger seat was waving madly, and as the truck slowed to a stop just a few feet away, I realized it was Drea. Before I knew what was happening, my feet carried me forward as a huge smile spread across my face.

Drea hopped out of the pickup and threw her arms around me, and I lifted her off her feet in a bear hug. "I missed you so much!" she said, her voice muffled against my shoulder.

"Back at ya, sis!" I said as I released her and turned toward Jason, who was already putting my suitcase in the back of the cab.

"Hey, man. I wasn't expecting you to pick me up." I stuck my hand out for a handshake, but he pulled me into a hug instead. It was a brief embrace, the kind bros do with a couple of hearty backslaps for good measure, but warmth flooded me at the contact, nonetheless. I couldn't remember a time when someone bigger than me had last hugged me, at least not since I was a child. It was oddly comforting to be engulfed in someone's arms like that. It was another little thought I filed away for contemplation at a future date.

I'd been filing those thoughts away for a little over two weeks now, ever since Clayton suggested Jason was my boyfriend. In my entire life, I'd had no reason to doubt my sexuality, but ever since Clayton had planted the seed, I'd analyzed every text, every interaction, every thought I'd had about Jason since we'd met.

The results were inconclusive.

"Dad had a last-minute meeting, and Jason offered to drive into the city to pick you up. I begged him to let me come along."

A gust of wind swept through, and we all eagerly climbed into the truck, ready to get out of the cold.

The drive was pleasant, mostly filled with Drea's chatter about school, dance, and her upcoming finals, with Jason occasionally interjecting things he'd heard from Mandy. A pleasant thrum hummed in my veins as the voices of my favorite people in the world washed over me.

And that was it, wasn't it? Despite our three-year age gap, Drea and I had always been close, but Jason had become someone important to me in just a matter of months. What did that mean? Because he was definitely one of my favorite people. Surely, those were bonds of friendship, though, and nothing more. I was straight. He was ace. I'd know if there was something more to it.

Confident in that conclusion and surrounded by the warmth of the heater, I relaxed in my seat and let my eyes drift closed.

I HAD A CRAVING FOR RUNZA, so Jason took us through the drive-thru in Astaire where we loaded up on Runzas and fries, with ranch dressing, of course. We headed back to my house where Drea took her food upstairs so she could finish working on a project for biology. She still had another three days of school before she was out for winter break.

Jason and I headed down to the basement, where we spread the food out and sat at the bar to eat. "You're done with classes on Tuesday, right?" I asked between fries.

"Yeah. I've got one more round of clinicals on Monday, and then we have exams on Tuesday."

"But that's not the big test, right? You said there's a national one in January?"

"Yeah, the certification exam is January 5."

"Less than a month away. How do you feel about it?"

He chewed his food and swallowed, wiping his mouth with his napkin before responding. "How do I feel about the test? Or the program itself?"

"Both, I guess. Does the EMT thing still feel like a good fit for you?"

"Yeah, it does. I've enjoyed the clinicals, but I think the ride-alongs have been my favorite. I'm contemplating training to become a firefighter down the line."

"Wow, I can totally picture you doing that." I remembered how he'd always watched out for others at the bonfires. The way he kept a level head. It would be a good fit for him.

"I mean, we'll see. I still want to go through with the EMT thing first and then maybe I'll consider becoming a firefighter in the future."

"That's cool, man. I'm happy for you." I dipped the last of my fries in ranch and then shoved them in my mouth, trying not to be jealous of the fact that he seemed to have it all figured out. I truly was happy for him. I just wanted that for me too.

"How about you? I know we texted, but how was your first semester? How was it living in LA?"

I took a bite of my Runza, contemplating my answer. "It was alright, I guess. Classes weren't too bad. LA is a trip. Obviously, Astaire is tiny, and so is Omaha compared to a city that size. Traffic is insane. It was probably for the best that Dad made me leave my car at home. I didn't have a need to leave campus a whole lot anyway."

"I can't imagine living in a place like that. I like small-town life."

"Would you ever consider moving to a smaller city, like Omaha?"

He took a sip of his pop, washing down the last bite of his Runza. "Maybe? I've always pictured myself living here. But I suppose if the circumstances were right, I might consider it. I don't know if I could do a bigger city though."

I didn't miss the way his cheeks heated when he said the word *circumstances* and wondered just what circumstances he was thinking of.

With both of us finished with our food, I stood and began gathering up our trash. "Movie or video games?" I asked, falling back on our summertime ritual.

"I'm pretty beat. Not sure I'd last through either. Maybe we can watch a couple episodes of *Rick and Morty.* Then I should probably head home. I've got class tomorrow."

After throwing the trash away, we moved over to the couch and I picked up the remote, scrolling through until I found it. I hit play, and we settled in to watch.

He'd been right. He really didn't make it very long before his eyes started getting droopy and he leaned over to the side, resting his head on the arm of the couch. I knew I should wake him and send him home, but I couldn't resist taking a couple of moments to study him.

I pulled out those thoughts I'd filed away for later and tried to consider them objectively. Jason and I had quickly become close in a way I wasn't with much of anyone. And while that didn't necessarily indicate anything romantic, it did represent a bond I'd never had with anyone, including previous girlfriends. In fact, the girls I'd dated had been pretty and fun, but rarely had my relationships with them gone much deeper than that.

I wasn't a virgin. I'd enjoyed sex with women, just as I'd enjoyed the companionship. But it had always been the girls pushing for something deeper, something I'd been unwilling to give. No one had ever been able to unlock those deeper parts of me the way Jason had. Did that mean something? Or was it merely the power of Clayton's suggestion that had me trying to make our friendship into something more?

Then there was the physical. I had never in my life felt any sort of attraction to a guy. And it wasn't like I hadn't had opportunities. I'd seen plenty of fit, attractive men in locker rooms over the years, and never once had I sported an unfortunate boner. Had never imagined what it would feel like to kiss a guy. What it would feel like to have a hard body pressed against mine rather than soft feminine curves.

I thought about the way it had felt when Jason hugged me earlier. There'd been no stirring in my dick, but definitely a thrum in my blood. I'd liked how it felt to be enveloped by such a large guy. I'd felt...safe. But wouldn't anyone?

I looked at him now, my eyes mapping his features. The way his lashes rested on his cheeks. The carved edge of his jaw. The column of his throat. The way his chest rose and fell with each breath. What would it feel like to curl up beside him? To rest my head on his strong shoulders and close my eyes? Better yet, to have his arms around me and my head on his chest? To be wrapped in his warmth? Surrounded by his scent?

My mouth went dry, and it was suddenly hard to swallow. And, *shit*, there was definitely a stirring in my dick now. It twitched as if it wanted to make extra sure I couldn't deny what was happening in my body.

I scrubbed a hand over my face, trying not to panic. Clearly, some sort of attraction was happening here, but that didn't have to *mean* anything. Jason was my best friend. My *ace* best friend. The end. Having those sorts of feelings didn't mean I had to act on them. Nothing had to change. I just had to get through winter break, and then I'd be back in LA, and I'd get over...whatever this was.

Fucking perfect.

21

JASON

THE WEEK FOLLOWING Zach's return was so busy that we only managed to hang out one other time after I fell asleep on his couch, and even that had only been for a chilly run cut short by the bitter wind. We'd texted nearly every day, though, as had become our habit while he was away at school. Still, even through text, things between us felt...different. I couldn't pinpoint how exactly, but it was as if something had shifted. Like there was the tiniest bit of distance between us despite him being just a few miles away rather than a few thousand. I didn't know what to make of it. Was I at fault? I'd felt guilty ever since I'd gotten off to thoughts of Zach. I hadn't jacked off since, which wasn't uncommon for me, but usually, it was because I wasn't interested, not because I was actively avoiding the act.

I'd hoped it was all in my head, that seeing him again would set my mind at ease and we'd go back to normal. But after I'd fallen asleep on his couch, he'd seemed more reserved, and I couldn't quite pinpoint why.

The Saturday before Christmas, Mandy came bounding into the kitchen, dressed in jeans and a sweater, with her hair and makeup done at nine a.m. I actually checked the clock, surprised to see her before noon, since she'd come home yesterday completely exhausted after finishing her finals. I could relate, as I'd finished my exams on Tuesday and had felt the same way, though I was still studying for the certification in January.

"Hey, big bro!" she said with a bright smile, and I immediately went on alert. She was after something. I'd seen that look too many times.

"What do you want?" I asked.

"Can't I just say good morning to my big brother?"

"No. You literally never do that. What do you want?"

She sighed, then pulled out the stool next to where I was peeling an orange at the kitchen island.

"Can you take me and Drea into the city to do some Christmas shopping? Even though Drea has her license, her dad won't let her drive that far yet, and Mom and Dad are busy today. Pleeeeease!" She widened her eyes, giving me her best impression of a puppy begging for a morsel of food.

I eyed her, delaying my response out of pure brotherly torture. The truth was, I actually had some of my own shopping to finish and had thought about going into the city anyway. "What's in it for me?"

"Ugh. Can't you do it out of the kindness of your heart?"

"Nah. Where's the fun in that?" I gave her my widest, shit-eating grin, then popped a piece of orange into my mouth.

"Ugh. Brothers are the worst," she said on a huff, crossing her arms and pouting.

I chuckled at her theatrics. "I'll do it if Zach comes. I'm not dragging your giggly asses around the city without backup."

She had her phone out of her pocket before I'd even

finished speaking, her thumbs working furiously over the screen.

Moments later, my phone buzzed on the counter. I wiped my sticky fingers and picked it up.

ZACH

What did you get me into?

Does that mean you're coming with us?

Yeah

Though I'll probably regret it

lol! Pick you guys up in an hour?

Works for me

I set my phone back down and looked at Mandy. "Looks like you've got a ride into the city."

22

ZACH

THE GIRLS KEPT up a lively stream of chatter from the back seat of Jason's truck as we made our way into the city. They mapped out which stores they wanted to hit and made a plan for the day while I tried unsuccessfully to bury the odd tension I now felt around him. He didn't say much, mostly leaving me to my own thoughts, but I'd felt him glancing my way a few times when he thought I wasn't looking.

Upon arriving in Omaha, we started the day with lunch in the Old Market. Jason and Mandy led the way to Spaghetti Works, unaware it was a landmine of old memories relating to our mom. When they discovered the last time we'd eaten there had been just hours before Mom died, they insisted on eating somewhere else, but Drea put her foot down. She said it was time we stopped letting things like that keep us from moving forward.

Over pasta and garlic bread, we shared stories about our mom, and I had to give credit to Drea—it had been cathartic. And though we'd eventually moved on to lighter topics, the mood remained somber through lunch. But as we stepped out onto the sidewalk, with the sun shining and holiday shoppers bustling across the street, I breathed deeply. Talking about Mom that way had been heavy but cleansing, and I thought maybe Drea was right. It was time to stop repressing those memories. Stop hiding from them to avoid the hurt. Mom deserved to be talked about. Other people—our closest friends—should know just how amazing she was.

Resolved to not let the heaviness of our lunch weigh down the rest of our day, I pasted on a smile and asked, "Where to?"

Jason stared at me with an assessing eye while Drea responded, "Let's head over to the record store. I still need one more thing for Dad."

The girls led the way while we followed a short distance behind. I could feel Jason watching me, shooting little glances my way he thought I wouldn't notice, just like he had on our way into the city. His hand bumped against mine, and I wondered what it would be like to grab it. To thread his fingers through mine and walk down the street like a couple.

I'd been having more and more thoughts like that since he'd fallen asleep on my couch last week. Little *what-if* thoughts like whispers in my ear that I did my best to ignore but couldn't quite push away. No matter how much I tried to fight it, it was becoming evident that my feelings for my best friend had extended beyond platonic into something...more. But even if I wanted to put myself out there and share my feelings, it didn't seem fair to put that on him when I knew he couldn't reciprocate. And knowing Jason the way I did, knowing the kind of person he was, he'd feel guilty, and that was the last thing I wanted. It wasn't something he could help, but I knew he'd feel bad all the same. So I shut down thoughts of holding hands, swatting them away like an annoying gnat buzzing in my ear, and did my best to put it out of my mind.

"I'm okay, you know. You can stop shooting me glances every couple of feet to see if I'm going to fall apart."

"Sorry. I don't mean to. I just…"

I watched as the girls entered the record shop about halfway up the block before stepping out of the way of the other shoppers and turning to Jason.

"So here's the thing. When we went back to school after the accident, everybody treated us differently. No one knew what to say, so they didn't say anything. They stopped texting. Stopped hanging out. Teachers gave us sad looks. In the process of losing my mom, I also lost my friends. And so did Drea."

"Yeah, I remember you saying something about that this summer."

"Right. And I also told you that was why I didn't say much about it when we moved to Astaire. I didn't want to be the sad kid who lost his mom anymore. I just wanted a regular senior year."

"I get that."

"Good. Then stop shooting me the side-eye."

"I didn't mean—"

I put my hand up to stop him. "I know. You're a good guy, Jason. I know it's because you care. But I promise, I'm okay. Please don't treat me any differently. I don't want to lose you too."

His eyes softened, and for the second time since I'd arrived back in Nebraska, he pulled me into his arms. "You aren't going to lose me."

I let my arms come up to return the embrace, allowing myself to explore the sensation of being held by him. A warmth emanated from him that felt so damn good. I wanted to revel in it.

Too soon, he pulled away, leaving me feeling empty. "Come on. Let's go find the girls."

WE SPENT a pleasant afternoon shopping with the girls in the Old Market, eventually making a trip to the outlet mall for a few other things before returning to Astaire exhausted but happy. The girls had dragged us from shop to shop, arms laden with shopping bags, laughing and giggling along the way. Shopping was generally not my favorite pastime, especially the weekend before Christmas when crowds were large and lines were excessively long, but I'd found myself unbothered by it amid the pleasure of spending time with those who mattered most.

The truth was, I'd missed this. The semester had been busy enough that I hadn't had time for any serious bouts of homesickness, but there'd been small moments when I'd been caught unaware and felt a pang of longing for the people who knew me best. This afternoon, there'd been moments when I'd felt that same pang, only this time in gratitude. The way the sunlight caught on Drea's hair. The sound of her laugh. Her eyes twinkling in merriment. Jason's quiet steadiness. The way the corners of his eyes crinkled when he smiled. The sarcastic comments he threw at Mandy, who returned them right back, both of them smiling with obvious affection. Those were the sorts of things I'd missed in LA.

I was tucking my shopping bags in the back of my closet when Drea bounded into the room and plopped on my bed. "You didn't get enough of me today?"

She rolled her eyes but smiled. "Gotta make up for lost time."

I closed the closet door and went to sit next to her on the bed. "Did you have a good day today?"

"Best day I've had in a long time. Thanks for coming with us."

"I'm glad I came," I said quietly. "I missed you this semester."

Her eyes snapped to mine. "Really?"

I chuckled. "Well, yeah."

She searched my face as if trying to determine the truth in my words. "I missed you too," she said with a sigh as she laid her head on my shoulder. We sat like that for a moment, enjoying the quiet after a long, busy day.

After a while, she straightened, turning toward me and tucking one foot under her. "So, what's going on with you and Jason?"

I froze, surprised at the question and unsure how to respond. "Why do you ask?" I stalled.

She laughed. "You have a shit poker face."

"Fuck off." I threw a pillow at her. "You caught me off guard."

She caught the pillow, but rather than throw it back at me, she wrapped her arms around it while she looked at me with a shrewd eye. "You're different with him."

"Different, how?"

"I don't know. You're more...you."

A snort escaped me. "What the hell does that even mean?"

"You've always had this...front you put on with other people. If there's a crowd, you're in the thick of it. Quick with a joke. Flirting with the girls. Ribbing the bros. You're big and loud. The life of the party."

I could feel my shoulders rising, tension creeping in at being called out like that. She made me sound like some sort of attention-seeking douche. Agitated, I moved to get off the bed, but she reached out and stopped me.

"It's not bad, Zach. You're not a dick about it. People genuinely like you. It's why you got homecoming king even though we'd only lived here a few months."

"Okay..." I still didn't know what she was getting at.

"It's just...that guy, while fun and all, was never you. Not the real you. When you're with Jason, you're relaxed. Quiet. Happy to let someone else take the lead."

I thought about it. Tried to see it from the outside looking in. She was right, I realized. About all of it. "He's my friend. He makes it...easy, I guess, to be me."

"Why do you think that is? Why is it easier with him than it is with anyone else?"

I thought about that too, and the honest answer was I didn't know. Going back to that first bonfire of the summer, I'd never understood why Jason had the ability to pry me open when no one else could. I'd stopped trying to figure it out months ago and had just accepted it for the gift it was.

"What are you getting at, Drea?"

Her eyes softened, her head tilting to one side. "I've seen the way you look at him." Her voice was soft. Careful. Patient. "You've never looked at anyone the way you look at him."

"How do I look at him?"

I was giving too much away with the question, but this was Drea, and maybe a part of me wanted her to know. To have someone to talk to. To help me make sense of the craziness I'd been feeling for a while now.

"Like he's a tall glass of water in the middle of a desert."

I could feel my cheeks heating. I looked down for a

moment, fiddling with the hem of my jeans, debating how to respond.

"I think I like him."

My words were tentative, spoken softly, but there was no taking them back. They hung heavy between us, the weight of my admission impossible to measure as one beat of my heart stretched to two, then three, and by the fourth, I looked up, unable to wait any longer for her response.

"Have you told him?"

I scoffed. "Hell no. I wasn't even sure what I was feeling until I got home last week."

"Last *week*? Jesus, Zach. You're such an idiot."

"Thanks, sis." My tone dripped with sarcasm and I ran my hands roughly through my hair before flinging myself back on the bed to stare at the ceiling.

"How long do you think you've had a thing for him? Because, by my estimation, it's been at least since the Fourth of July."

I turned my head to stare at her. "I started dating Leslie on the Fourth of July."

"Right. As I said. Idiot."

I huffed out a breath, returning my gaze to the ceiling as Drea lay next to me. I thought about the time I'd spent with him this summer. The bonfires. The overlook. Playing video games. Hanging with our friends at Sherry's Soft-Serv. Morning runs. And yeah, the Fourth of July. But even looking back with eyes open to the possibility, I didn't think there was one moment I could point to as the source of my... crush, I guessed you could call it.

It was the culmination of a thousand little moments. A gentle smile. A kind word. An ear to listen. How many miles had our feet traveled on our morning runs while I unloaded my shit? My grief and anger, sadness and stress, and fear? Things I'd never shared with anyone.

Then there were the texts. So many texts. He always responded, any time of day. No matter the topic. Sometimes, he made me laugh. Sometimes, he made me think. Always, he made me smile.

I turned and looked at Drea, unsure how to distill those thoughts into words.

"I...I don't think I can pinpoint when it started. I just know he has this way of making me feel...known. He's always been easy to talk to. He has this quiet intensity, you know? Like when I'm talking to him, he actually listens. He doesn't look at his phone. He doesn't interrupt to tell you some story about himself. He just...listens. Like he genuinely wants to hear what I have to say. Like it's the most interesting thing in the world."

She nodded, then tucked her hand under her cheek. "He's an old soul."

"Exactly."

"Okay, but Mandy and I have that kind of relationship, and I'm not crushing on my best friend. So what's the difference?"

It was all so tangled in my mind. I didn't understand it myself. "I don't know if I can explain it. I hadn't even thought about it this way until a couple of weeks ago when my roommate made the assumption that the guy I was texting back home was my boyfriend. He saw a picture of Jason and said he was hot."

"He *is* hot."

"Ew. Ew, no." I sat up and glared at her. "No, thank you. Never say that to me again."

It wasn't that I thought either of them was actually into the other, but just the suggestion left me feeling...icked out.

She laughed and sat up to face me. "You don't think he's hot?"

"Of course I think he's hot. But you...you're not allowed to think he's hot."

"Oh, for fuck's sake, Zach. How many times do I need to call you an idiot in the same conversation?"

"How about zero times? Maybe, like, don't call me an idiot at all?"

"Then don't give me a reason to."

I wanted to argue the point, but I wasn't one hundred percent sure I had a leg to stand on.

"I just..." Deflating, I blew out a breath. "Once Clayton put that out there, that he thought Jason was my boyfriend, I couldn't get it out of my mind. And I started to wonder if maybe there was something there."

"And is there something there?"

This time, I didn't hesitate. "Yeah. I think there is."

A smile spread slowly across her face, her eyes alighting from within.

"What?" I asked. "Why are you looking at me like that?"

"I'm happy for you. Jason's such a sweet guy. You deserve someone like him."

I let out a laugh, completely devoid of humor. "Slow your roll, sis. Pretty sure this is a one-sided thing."

"You don't see the way he looks at you." I raised a skeptical brow but didn't say anything more. I was pretty sure she didn't know he was ace, and it wasn't my news to share. "He looks at you just like you look at him. You're both besotted."

I snorted. "Besotted? Who says words like besotted? You've been watching *Bridgerton* again, haven't you?"

"Don't be a dick. And stop deflecting." She shoved my

shoulder playfully. "I'm telling you, I don't think it's one-sided. You should talk to him."

"Don't get your hopes up."

"Ugh." She stood in a huff. "Why are boys so stupid?"

I was pretty sure I wasn't supposed to answer that.

She started to stomp away, but I reached out and grabbed her hand, stopping her. I tugged a couple of times until she reluctantly turned to look at me. "Thanks for making me talk about Mom today. It was good to talk about her. To share her with Mandy and Jason." Her gaze softened, the irritation from moments before fading. I tugged a piece of her hair. "You remind me of her."

Her eyes filled, and I pulled her in for a hug. We stood there in my bedroom, arms wrapped around each other, giving and receiving comfort. With a sniff, she pulled away and swiped her fingers under her eyes. "I'm going to head to bed."

"Okay. Goodnight," I called out to her.

"Night."

23

JASON

I AWOKE in the throes of an orgasm. Sweaty and panting, hips jerking, I was helpless to do anything but bite my lip and ride it out. With my head thrown back and the sheets gripped tight in my fists, I grunted through it as my cock pulsed in my boxer briefs. Wave after wave rolled through me in what felt like quite possibly the longest orgasm of my life until it finally subsided, leaving me shaky and gasping for air.

I lay motionless on the bed, eyes still closed, as my heartbeat slowed and I finally regained control of my breathing. I released the sheets and half sat up to grab my phone off the charger, groaning at the feel of the sticky mess inside my briefs. I'd need to get up and shower before my cum-soaked underwear started sticking to me.

Tapping the screen on my phone, I sighed as the time read five-oh-three. That explained why it was still dark outside. I set the phone down by my side and scrubbed my hands over my face. As a child, I'd lain in bed at this time on Christmas morning, watching the minutes tick away until the readout finally said seven and Mandy and I could go wake up our parents to see what Santa had brought. Those days were gone now that we'd gotten older and learned what a beautiful thing it was to sleep in. In the last several years, we'd started the day around nine on Christmas, still four hours from now.

No way would I be able to go back to sleep with my underwear full of jizz—might as well get up and shower.

Thankful everyone would still be asleep at this hour, I quickly crossed the hall into the bathroom and started the shower. As the room filled with steam, I contemplated my current predicament. This was the third time in three days that I'd woken up mid-climax, the first being the morning after our shopping trip into the city. Each time had left me feeling guilty, though I knew it was out of my control. I was clearly lusting after my straight best friend like some sort of creep.

At the same time, I felt an odd sense of relief. Feeling attracted to someone was new and scary, but it was also... good. Exciting. The afternoon of the shopping trip, there had been moments when I'd felt my heart race and my hands go clammy just from sharing a look. And when I'd hugged Zach after lunch, even though it had come with the weight of his worry over losing our friendship, warmth had flooded my chest. I hadn't wanted to let him go.

I'd long ago accepted I was ace, and while I knew logically there wasn't anything wrong with that, there had still been a part of me that yearned for that feeling of attraction, that spark that meant you'd found someone who connected with you on a different level. It figured that when I'd finally experienced that jolt of attraction, it would be with my straight best friend, who was currently attending college fifteen hundred miles away.

I peeled off my boxer briefs and stepped into the spray,

trying to recall what I'd been dreaming about that had triggered the wet dream. Much of it had already faded from my conscious memory, but there were glimmers of moments, fragments that I tried to latch onto. In the dream, I thought we might have been shopping, but this time, it'd been just the two of us shopping at a location that didn't exist in real life, a place my brain had conjured up.

Every dream over the last three nights had started the same way, but in this one, we'd been walking along hand-in-hand. A graphic tee with some silly saying had been displayed in a shop window, but when I'd called it to his attention, thinking he'd find it amusing, he'd been looking the other way, seemingly distracted. I couldn't remember what had happened next, but I'd found my back pressed against the wall of a forgotten hallway and Zach closing in with a salacious twinkle in his eye.

He'd leaned into me, pressed his body into mine, and kissed me. In reality, I'd never kissed anyone, but in the dream, my subconscious had filled in the blanks of my inexperience. He'd gripped my face in his hands, holding me still while he plundered my mouth, tongue sweeping in to tangle with mine. He'd pulled back and nipped at my lip, my jaw, my earlobe before trailing kisses down the column of my throat. I didn't remember any more of the dream, and honestly wasn't sure it had taken much more before I came in my shorts.

As I lathered my body, I wondered what it would feel like to kiss him for real. What it would feel like to have his lips pressed to mine. Would they be soft and smooth? Rough? And how did it work with the tongue? I'd obviously liked it in the dream, but I was pretty sure it was entirely different in real life. I'd never spent so much time thinking about these things as I had over the last few days. Previously, thoughts of kissing had seemed...abstract. People did it all the time and obviously liked it, but I'd never understood the appeal.

My dick clearly liked the idea though. Despite coming just fifteen minutes ago, it was making a valiant attempt at a comeback, standing partially erect as the water sluiced down my body. The temptation to stroke myself, to see if I could come again so soon, was strong. But it was one thing to come while dreaming of my best friend when my subconscious was in charge. It was an entirely different thing to do so on purpose. It was not something I was comfortable with.

Doing my best to avoid thoughts that would make the temptation even more challenging, I quickly finished my shower and got out. After drying off and quietly crossing back into my room, I changed into a fresh set of boxer briefs and climbed back into bed. I grabbed my phone, noted it was still not yet six o'clock, and, with a sigh, swiped open the lock screen.

I tapped into Instagram, scrolling through my feed and catching up on my friends' posts. Rafi was smiling with his girlfriend in front of the altar at the Catholic church. They must have gone to Christmas Eve mass. Sonny and Hannah were posed in front of a lit-up Christmas tree with her hand on her slightly rounded belly, just starting to show. Turns out, they'd been absent from the end-of-summer bonfire because she'd just found out she was pregnant, derailing all of their college plans. They'd decided to defer the first semester while they sorted out this abrupt change in their life. Last I'd heard, they were both working in Brinkley and had delayed college indefinitely. They were due in April.

I continued to scroll, smiling at the posts of friends and their families in front of Christmas trees, when a message came through, causing my phone to vibrate, startling me into almost dropping it on my face. I swiped into the Messages app to find a new text from Zach.

ZACH

Merry Christmas!

There was a picture attached of him from the shoulders up with a lazy smile and his hair mussed from sleep. He appeared to be lying in bed with no shirt on. Something fluttered in my chest, and I found myself grinning in response. Jesus, I was going to have to get this shit under control before I embarrassed myself.

Merry Christmas to you!

Wanna go for a run?

I flipped into the weather app and then back into my messages.

It's 14 outside

So?

I'm not running in 14 degree weather

Wuss

If not wanting to run in 14 degree temps makes me a wuss, then so be it

lol

I have a gift for you. Can we meet up?

I looked at the time. It was six-fifteen.

Now?

> I'll be at Aunt Amy's most of the day. I
> figured we could do it now before the day
> gets crazy

I started to respond when the three dots flashed, showing he was typing another message, so I waited for that to come through.

> But it's cool if not. We can meet up later in
> the week.

> I can meet now. Where?

> My house

> See you in 15

My pulse ratcheted up at the thought of seeing him again. Never in my life had I felt this kind of excitement over seeing someone. It was terrifying and exhilarating at the same time.

I grabbed a pair of sweats and started to put them on, then ditched those for a pair of jeans, suddenly finding myself wanting to dress a little nicer for him. As if any of that mattered to my straight best friend. Still, I pulled on one of the few sweaters I owned—the one Mandy said made my blue eyes pop—and ran a hand through my short hair. I pulled on my Timberlands, grabbed my keys, wallet, and the little gift I'd bought him, and headed out to the garage, pulling on my coat before climbing into my truck.

By the time I got to Zach's, I was a jumble of nerves, another new feeling I wasn't used to having. I generally wasn't a nervous person. Not when playing football or baseball. Not with public speaking at school. Not during any of my EMT training. And definitely not because I had a crush on someone.

I parked on the street and turned off the ignition but took a moment to pull myself together before getting out. I was being ridiculous. He was my best friend, and we were exchanging gifts. Just because this was something I'd never done before or I'd developed some sort of attraction to him was no reason to act a fool.

I took a deep breath and got out of the truck.

24

———

ZACH

I WATCHED Jason pull up in front of the house and sit in his truck for a moment. My stomach flipped at his hesitation, wondering what could be the cause. It had been ridiculous to ask him over here this morning, but I'd been up since five and had worked myself into a tizzy as I contemplated the best time to give him his gift. Or if I should even give him his gift at all. I'd bought gifts for girlfriends before, but never for a friend. Would he read too much into it? Did I want him to? Drea had said he looked at me the same way I looked at him, whatever that meant, and I thought there might be part of me that wanted to find out if she was right. Another part hoped it was a secret I'd take to my grave, if only so I didn't scare him away. God, I felt like I was back in middle school with my first crush. My palms were sweaty, my pulse was racing, and I was overthinking the shit out of everything.

Eventually, Jason got out of his truck and made his way up the drive. I opened the door, shivering as I was met with a blast of cold air. He'd been right that it was too cold for a run this morning.

"Hey," I said, my voice quiet in the sleeping house.

He stepped in through the door, his broad chest brushing mine, sending prickles of electricity skittering across my skin. As I shut the door behind him, he kicked off his boots and began stripping out of his coat. He wore a navy-blue sweater that stretched perfectly across his broad frame, hugging the muscles of his shoulders and back. My eyes continued their perusal down to where his jeans hugged his ass, and as he turned around, I admired the way his quads filled out the front. Realizing he'd stopped moving, my eyes snapped up to his, hoping he hadn't caught me staring, but the small smile and flush creeping up his neck into his cheeks suggested I'd been busted.

I cleared my throat. "Let's, um, head to my room."

I led the way down the hall to my room. He followed me in and closed the door.

"I take it everyone is still sleeping?" he asked.

"Yeah. We aren't heading over to Aunt Amy's until noon, but I think Drea wants us to have breakfast as a family and do presents here first, so I'm guessing she'll get up around eight or nine." Since Mom had passed, Drea had tried to keep some of the traditions alive, like monkey bread with sides of bacon for breakfast.

Jason walked over to the wall of glass looking out over the lake and stood for a moment without saying anything. I fidgeted, unsure if I should sit on the bed or go stand next to him. God, I was awkward as fuck.

"It's pretty in winter." He turned and looked back at me.

I stepped over to stand beside him, looking out at the thin layer of ice blanketing the water below. Winter wasn't my favorite season on the lake, but there was something eerily beautiful in the absence of color during the winter months. A clean slate. Mother Nature in her slumber, saving her energy for that time of rebirth in the spring, when the ice melts and the trees awaken again.

"Do you like winter? What's your favorite season?"

"I don't know. I guess there are aspects I like about all of them."

I snorted. "Do you always go for the neutral answer?"

He shrugged, but I thought I saw a flicker of hurt flash in his eyes. "There's nothing wrong with—"

"I'm sorry," I was quick to say, not wanting him to be upset. "I was just flipping you shit. It's actually one of the things I like about you. You're always thinking about things from multiple perspectives, inclusive of everyone's thoughts and feelings."

"You make it sound like I was picking an answer because I didn't want to offend you when I really do like aspects of all of them. I just don't always think there's a clear answer for everything. Most things aren't black and white. I tend to see the shades of gray in between." He blinked, his eyes widening as if he'd just realized something, but he turned away before I could get a good read on him.

I lifted my hand, thinking to place it on his arm, but I pulled up short. I wasn't sure how to act around him. How to hold myself back from those little touches. How to hide the want that burned inside me.

I let my hand fall to my side and stepped back, putting some distance between us. Clearing my throat, I gestured to the chair at my desk, the only other place to sit besides the bed. "Do you wanna sit down?"

He looked between me and the chair. "Uh. Sure." He took a seat, the chair looking ridiculously small under his massive frame, while I sat on the edge of the bed. "So you said you had a gift for me? Oh, wait...shit!" His eyebrows climbed up his forehead. "Hang on. I'll be right back."

Before I could make sense of what was happening, he tore out of my room and down the hall. Moments later, he returned with a small, wrapped box in his hand. "Sorry. I forgot I stuck your gift in my coat pocket."

He held out his hand, and I took the present from him, sucking in a breath as I examined it. The box was wrapped in gold paper, with a smooshed bow, and it looked like he'd used half a roll of tape on it. I let out my breath, relieved to know I wasn't the only one who couldn't wrap a gift for shit.

Turning, I leaned over, grabbed his gift from my bedside table, and handed it to him. It was smaller than the one he'd given me, a flat box wrapped in blue paper with snowflakes and adorned with a simple silver ribbon.

He took it from me but neither of us made a move to open our gift, locked in a stalemate of Midwestern politeness. "Go ahead and open it," I said, but he shook his head. "No, that's okay. You go first."

I rolled my eyes. "How 'bout we go at the same time?"

He smiled and nodded, and we both tore into our paper. He got his open first, his gasp pulling my attention from my own gift that I was still trying to find a way to get into through all the tape. He'd pulled the paper away and lifted the lid and was now holding the box closer, inspecting the contents inside. His eyes flashed to mine, then back, and I bit my lip, waiting for him to say something.

"This is so cool," he finally said, pulling the keychain out of the box. It had a Star of Life emblem painted in blue enamel on a metal disk, attached to a strip of black mesh with a key ring on one end and a small carabiner on the other. I hadn't gone looking for it, but when I'd seen it at the kiosk, I'd known I had to get it for him. "I haven't even passed my certification yet."

I shrugged, rubbing the back of my neck, trying to

ignore the flush burning up my neck and into my face. "But you passed your final with high marks. The cert test is just a formality."

"You give me too much credit, but thank you. This is really...this is cool." His blue eyes watched me with so much intensity that I had to look away for fear he'd see all my secrets. "Open yours."

I dug into the paper, finally finding a corner that wasn't taped down, and tore it open. My mouth dropped open as I got a glimpse of the contents. I pulled the paper all the way off and couldn't help but stare. "Seriously?" I asked. "How did you...?"

"You can design them on their website. It wouldn't let me choose the color of the jersey, but I was able to get your number."

He'd given me a personalized Funko Pop that looked just like me. He was right. The jersey was black instead of blue, but the number was mine, and I was holding a soccer ball in one hand and a gold trophy in the other. I couldn't believe the thought he'd put into this.

"This is amazing. I can't believe you did this." Unable to stop myself, I launched forward and pulled him into a hug. "This is the most thoughtful thing anyone's ever given me."

He wrapped his arms around me, pulling me even closer. I basked in his warmth, in his clean scent, in the feel of his strong arms around me. I squeezed my eyes shut, allowing myself to savor this feeling for just a moment so I could take it with me when I went back to LA. I breathed deeply and thought I felt him stiffen, jerking me back into reality. I pulled away, breaking the connection, reminding myself he was off-limits, at least in that way.

I cleared my throat. "Thanks, man. This is really cool."

He held up the keychain. "Yeah, um, me too. Thank you."

His phone vibrated and he pulled it out of his pocket, smiling when he read the display. He quickly typed out a response, then stood with a rueful smile. "That was Mandy. Her exact words were, 'Where the fuck are you?' I guess I should get going."

"I'll walk you out."

We made our way down the hall, where he pulled on his boots and coat and then turned to look at me. His eyes grew serious, though a soft smile played on his lips. "Merry Christmas, Zach."

"Merry Christmas."

And then he was gone.

25

JASON

In the days following Christmas, I thought a lot about the gift exchange between Zach and me. The whole interaction had felt awkward and clunky in a way we hadn't ever been before and I didn't know what to make of it, nor what to do about it. I wanted the easy friendship back. The ribbing. The random texts. The long conversations about anything and everything.

But I couldn't help but think the awkwardness wasn't all one-sided. More than once, I thought he'd intentionally put some distance between us. Had he figured out I was into him and was uncomfortable with it? Or was there something else going on? I hadn't missed how he'd inhaled when I'd hugged him close, like he was breathing me in. That wasn't something you did if you were uncomfortable. Though, what the hell did I know about any of it?

There had been that moment when I'd talked about not everything being black and white and seeing the shades of gray between that had triggered something in my memory. I'd read about graysexuality and the asexual spectrum when

I'd been trying to figure out why I didn't experience attraction like everyone else. The day after Christmas, I went looking for the post I'd read, and while I hadn't found the specific article, I'd come across a plethora of more up-to-date information and stumbled across the demisexual label.

My heart leapt into my throat as I read the term, realizing that was likely what I was experiencing now. It would explain why I hadn't initially felt any sort of attraction to Zach. We'd needed to establish an emotional connection first. Or at least I'd needed that on my part. As far as I knew, he was straight. His behavior Christmas morning might have given me reason to suspect otherwise, but it was also entirely possible it was wishful thinking on my part.

I pulled the keychain out of my pocket and rubbed my thumb over the little Star of Life medallion in the center for the thousandth time. It wasn't a fancy or expensive gift, but it was so damn thoughtful. Every time I looked at it, I felt a flutter in my chest at the knowledge that Zach had seen it and thought of me.

"Is that what you're wearing tonight?" Mandy's voice interrupted my thoughts, and I looked up at her, trying to focus on her question.

"What?"

She rolled her eyes and came into my room, stopping in front of me with her arms crossed and a very disapproving look on her face. "I asked if that's what you're wearing tonight. You look like you're going to a barn dance."

I looked down at my dark-wash jeans and navy-blue sweater. "What's wrong with this?"

"I swear you're helpless. Zach's dad is a *lawyer*. Drea said this party is being catered. There will be fancy people there. You look like you're going to a fish fry at the VFW."

I was sure she was exaggerating, but she did have me starting to second-guess myself. Still, I couldn't help but razz her.

"Wait. Do I look like I'm going to a barn dance or to a fish fry at the VFW? Cause you said both of those things, and I just want to make sure I understand you correctly."

She didn't even bother to respond. "You wore that to Zach's Christmas morning, right? You can't wear that again."

"Like *ever* again?"

I was rewarded with another eye roll. "Don't be a dick."

She crossed over to my closet and started rifling through my clothes. It was then I noticed she was wearing a jumpsuit, I thought it was called, with some sort of long sweater over it and wedge booties. Her long blonde hair was hanging in loose waves rather than her usual braid, and I thought I spotted lip gloss, though it was hard to tell since she was muttering to herself while partially turned away from me as she slid hangers aggressively from one side of the rod to the other. "Jesus, don't you have any slacks?"

I groaned. "They're in the back. I don't know if they fit though."

She reached in, disappearing momentarily, then came out, her hand held up triumphantly, black slacks in hand. "Try these on while I look for something to go with them." She tossed them at me, hitting me in the face without even looking in my direction.

With a sigh, I headed into the bathroom to change. No way was I doing so in front of my sister. By the time I returned, she had three shirts and two sweaters laid out on my bed. I started to speak, but she held up her hand, stopping me as she assessed me with a critical eye. "I think those will do," she finally said.

"You don't think they're too tight?" I asked. I felt like I

was going to hulk out with the way they were stretched across my ass and thighs.

"Turn around," she said, and I did as she asked.

"They're a little snug, but Zach's going to love your ass in them." My eyes bugged out and I choked on my spit. "Here, try this shirt," she said, completely oblivious to my distress.

Mandy tossed an eggplant-colored button-down at me, and I began putting it on, numbly processing what she'd just said. Unable to stop myself, I asked, "Did you just say Zach's going to love my ass?"

"Yeah. You want that, don't you?"

I paused in the middle of buttoning, spluttering as my brain short-circuited. "What? How? I don't…"

"Oh, for fuck's sake, J. It's super obvious you two like each other. Y'all need to get over yourselves and get on with it."

"Neither of us has ever dated a man or given any indication we were interested in men. What makes you so sure we're into each other?"

"I have eyes in my head, don't I?"

I finished buttoning the shirt, still at a complete loss for what to say. I held out my hands, indicating she should judge the outfit.

"Tuck it in."

I did as instructed and then waited. Mandy narrowed her eyes, signaling for me to turn around. Nodding, she turned back to the closet, muttering something about a belt and shoes, while I stood there, shell-shocked by her assessment of my feelings toward Zach. Which also included his feelings toward me—or at least her perception of his feelings. If she'd figured out I was into him, was it possible she was right about him being into me?

Good God, having a crush on someone was quite

possibly the dumbest emotion I'd ever experienced. How did people do this all the time?

"Mandy, just stop and come here."

She continued muttering to herself, her head buried in my closet. She either hadn't heard me or was ignoring me.

"Mandy!" I said more forcefully. When her head popped out, eyes raised in question, I said more quietly, "Come here."

"But I—"

"Just stop and come talk to me."

Something in my tone must have registered because she finally came out of the closet and sat on the bed. "What?"

"Just...how are you so nonchalant about all this stuff with Zach?"

"What? Because he's a guy?"

"Well...yeah. I don't know. I didn't even figure it out myself until recently."

"Does it matter that he's a guy?"

I thought about it a moment and realized that in all of my confusion over the last couple of weeks, none of it had anything to do with his gender and was more so related to the fact that I'd never been attracted to *anyone*, closely followed by worry that he was my best friend. The gender thing hadn't really played into it. "No, I don't care that he's a guy."

"Then why would you think I'd care?"

"Fair enough. But this is *Zach*. He's my best friend. And he's straight."

"Doubt it."

"Mandy—" I couldn't believe I was having this conversation with my sixteen-year-old sister.

"Look. You can't tell me you haven't caught a vibe off him."

"What, like a vibe that he's into dudes?"

"No, dumbass. A vibe that he's into *you.*"

I thought back, and while I was pretty positive there hadn't been anything there over the summer, I thought maybe I'd noticed something since he'd been back. He'd been oddly distant after I'd fallen asleep on his couch. There'd been a couple of times our hands had brushed against each other when we'd been out shopping, and he'd quickly pulled away. The Christmas gift. He'd invited me over super early to give it to me. The way he'd inhaled when I'd hugged him after. I'd thought those little things were in my head, but maybe they painted a bigger picture, one I'd been overlooking while I tried to figure out my own shit.

"Do you really think he's into me?"

"*Jesus.* You are one of the smartest dumbasses I know."

"Come on, Mandy. I'm serious."

She sighed, pushing her hair off her face and scooting farther onto the bed. "Yes. I think he's into you."

"But how do you know? Did Drea say something?"

"No. But she didn't have to. It's obvious to everyone except the two of you, apparently."

"What do I do? What if you're wrong?"

"Just...I don't know. At the party tonight, look for signs. Like, really look. Pay attention to the way he looks at you when he talks. The way he only has eyes for you. The flush in his cheeks when you look at him. Flirt a little and see if he flirts back."

"Now who's the dumbass? Do you really think I have the first clue about how to...to flirt?"

She rolled her eyes. "Don't flirt then. Just...just hang out with him. Talk. Joke. Maybe put your hand on his arm and see what he does."

I scrubbed my hands over my face. "Oh my God, I feel like I'm trapped in a nineties rom-com."

"Well, you're kind of acting like you're in one."

"So helpful."

"You're going to be fine. As you said, he's your best friend. What better person to fall for than the guy who knows you better than anyone else?"

26

ZACH

Dad's New Year's Eve party was in full swing when Jason and Mandy arrived. I'd spoken to more lawyers and business people than I could count, my father insisting I work the room and make small talk like a good host. No matter that this was *his* party and not mine. But it was easier to go along with it, so Drea and I had moved about the house, floating from person to person as efficiently as the caterers passing plates laden with hors d'oeuvres.

Drea and I stood off to the side, taking a moment to ourselves, comparing notes on some of the guests while we gulped down water. Between the warmth of a full house and all the talking, we were thirsty. The water didn't make a bit of difference, though, when I caught sight of Mandy and Jason coming down the stairs. My mouth went dry at the sight of him dressed in fitted black slacks and a plum-colored button-down, the sleeves rolled up, revealing his muscular forearms. If I had any doubts I could be attracted to a guy, he obliterated them simply by walking into the room.

My eyes trailed him as Jason and Mandy approached,

weaving their way through the crowd. Drea leaned in and said something, but I couldn't hear her over the thundering in my ears.

"Hey," he said when he finally stopped in front of me, but when I tried to respond, nothing but a squeak came out.

I hastily took a sip of my water and tried again. "Hey."

Distantly, I heard giggles next to me, but I couldn't take my eyes off him. "Come on. Let's leave these two idiots alone," Drea said, tugging Mandy away.

And then it was just the two of us. We were in the middle of a crowded room, but my focus had shrunk to him alone, as if no one else existed.

"You look…" I cleared my throat. "Good. You look good."

God, that was maybe the lamest thing I'd ever said, second only to "Hey," but I didn't miss the flush creeping up his cheeks.

"Thanks. Mandy picked it out. I was going to wear jeans, but she insisted I had to dress nicer and then went digging through my closet until she found this. I haven't worn these pants in two years, since my Uncle Frank's wedding, and I'm pretty sure they're too tight, but Mandy said they made my a—" He stopped abruptly, the flush exploding to an all-out blush as he rubbed the back of his neck. He was flustered, I realized. Babbling and flustered and…and…adorable.

I smiled. Full and bright, the expression completely taking over my face like an absolute imbecile. Drea had been right. I *was* an idiot. A total fool for this guy. And I didn't know how I hadn't seen it before, but I was pretty sure that against all odds, he was a fool for me too.

I set my water down on the nearest table and took his hand in mine. "Come on. I need to talk to you."

I tugged him down the hall, away from the noise of the crowd, toward one of the empty spare bedrooms, flipping on the light and closing the door behind us. At the snick of the lock, his eyes darted to mine, but I shook my head, pulling him over to the bed where I sat down. He paused, his Adam's apple bobbing as he swallowed, staring at the bed I was currently sitting on.

I really had brought him in here to talk, but the idea that he thought I might be up to a more nefarious purpose made my dick throb. I'd just barely begun to accept the possibility I was bi and hadn't really thought about what that meant in any sort of tangible way, but just the suggestion that we might do anything requiring a bed had me aching to explore that line of thought.

But not yet. First, I needed to know we were on the same page. I needed to know this wasn't one-sided, that it wasn't somehow all in my head.

"Are you gonna sit?" I asked.

His eyes flashed to mine. "On the bed?"

I chuckled. "Where else?"

His eyes darted around the room, looking desperately for an alternative. *Jesus.* He'd gone from adorably flustered to skittish and ready to bolt. I stood back up but gave him some space, not wanting to freak him out.

"Hey," I said softly. "Why do you think I brought you in here?"

"You said you wanted to talk."

"Right. And I meant it." I wanted to tease him, to make a lewd joke and ask him why else he thought I might have brought him in here, but he was clearly freaking out, and that was the last thing I wanted. "Do you want to go back out there?"

"No." He dropped his shoulders, visibly forcing himself to relax. "No, we can stay."

"Can we sit?"

He nodded, and I gently pulled him down to the bed but purposefully scooted to one end to give him some space.

"Okay?" I asked.

He nodded, but when I opened my mouth to speak, I suddenly realized I didn't know what to say or how to start the conversation. I wracked my brain, trying to figure out where to begin, and as moments passed, the air in the room became heavier, weighted with nerves, tension, and fear. Finally, disgusted with myself, I took a deep breath and on the exhale said, "I think I'm into you."

He blinked, and for a terrifying moment, I thought I'd made a massive mistake. But on the third blink, his expression changed, a smile slowly lighting up his face. It was like watching the sunrise as it moved up from the curve of his mouth to the brightness of his eyes, and I wondered how it had taken me so long to see just how beautiful he was.

"Seriously?" he asked, his voice full of wonder. I nodded, biting my lip, hoping this meant he felt the same but still needing to hear the words. "I, uh, I think I'm into you too."

"Yeah?" A smile stretched slowly across my face.

He nodded, his expression shy and utterly adorable. He caught his lip between his teeth, and suddenly, he wasn't so adorable anymore. He was sexy as fuck.

"Can I kiss you?" The question burst out of me, and he released his lip, his eyes widening in surprise. "I know you said you're ace, so I don't know how this works for you, and it's totally fine if you say no. I mean, I want you to be comfortable, but..." I trailed off when he scooted closer on the bed. *Look who's babbling now.*

"Zach?"

"Yeah?"

"Kiss me."

My breath caught, but I leaned forward and my eyes

locked with his, only fluttering closed at the last moment as my mouth brushed against his. I savored the feel of his lips pressed against mine, warm and surprisingly smooth. My hand came up to rest on his cheek, my thumb tracing the stubble on his jawline. Used to the delicate features of a woman, the feel of him in my palm, with his angular jaw and five o'clock shadow, was foreign but decidedly hot. And when his hand came up to cup the back of my head at the nape of my neck, the strength in his hold had my cock straining inside my pants.

His lips parted under mine ever so slightly, and I took advantage, dipping my tongue inside, testing the waters. When I felt the tip of his tongue slide tentatively against mine, I groaned, just that tiny contact sending a flurry of butterflies swarming in my gut. The hand on my neck applied more pressure, holding me against him, as he swiped his tongue over mine again, this time more boldly. I parted my lips wider, giving him the freedom to explore, to take the lead, and it occurred to me that while this might be my first kiss with a man, this might be his first kiss ever.

The thought of being his first anything had nerves and a possessive sense of pride flooding my chest. I wasn't sure what had changed for him. What it was about me that he'd felt attracted to when he hadn't ever felt that for anyone else, but I knew it was a gift to be treasured.

The kiss went on and on as tentative brushes gave way to tangled tongues and clashing teeth. Mouths slanted first one way and then the other. Bitten lips. Nips. Nibbles. Tugs. Whimpers.

I'd kissed plenty of girls in the past, but never had I been so consumed by someone's mouth on mine. Even as my dick strained uncomfortably against my fly, I never wanted the kiss to end. I'd never felt anything like it.

The raucous sound of laughter from somewhere beyond the door penetrated my haze. It must have done the same for Jason because he slowly pulled away. My eyes opened as if waking from a dream, but I made no move to remove my hand from his face. Staring into his deep blue eyes—*had I never noticed how deep they were?*—I looked for some sign of panic or regret as I traced my thumb over his red, swollen lips. The look in his eyes was intense. He seemed to be searching my face for something.

"Was that okay?" I asked when I finally couldn't take the silence between us anymore.

"That was…" His lips curved, his face taking on a look of wonder. "That was amazing."

Thank God.

I felt my own smile lighting my face. "Me too."

We stared at each other for a moment, grinning like idiots. I dropped my hand from his face, taking his hand in mine instead. "How did this happen? I thought you were ace?"

"Christmas morning? When I said something about not everything being black and white?"

"Yeah?"

My eyebrows drew up in confusion. I remembered he'd gotten a weird look on his face when he said he saw the shades of gray between, but I wasn't sure what that had to do with my question.

"It triggered a memory about an article I read about graysexuality, and I did some Googling and…well, I think I'm demi."

"I don't…know what that means."

"It means I have to feel a strong connection with someone before I feel attraction."

"Oh," I said, processing what that meant in relation to

us. I definitely felt a strong connection with him. It had been that way almost from the beginning of summer.

"What about you? I thought you were straight?"

"Me too." I chuckled. "I guess maybe I'm bi? I've never been attracted to another guy before."

"But you're attracted to me?"

I wanted to laugh, to make a joke—*isn't it obvious after the make-out sesh we just had?*—but I paused at the raw vulnerability in his eyes.

I brushed a hand against his cheek. "Yeah, J. I'm *very* attracted to you."

He leaned into my hand, turning to press a kiss into the center of my palm. It was somehow more intimate than any of the kissing we'd shared moments ago. "Me too. To you, I mean."

A lump formed in my throat. This moment...it felt huge. Simple words. A small declaration. An admission of sorts. And nothing would ever be the same.

I swallowed, nerves and emotions swimming in my system. I'd spent most of my early teen years wondering why I was different. Why I wasn't horny all the time like the other guys in the locker room. Why none of that held any interest for me. I'd later figured out I was ace and had assumed it just meant my life would look different. I thought I had plenty of love to give, but I figured it would be more like the friendship kind of love. Like the way I felt about Will. I hadn't given up on the idea of having a family necessarily, but I had figured it would be a much harder road for me, if at all.

Zach and I had shared a kiss. It would be ludicrous to jump to any sort of conclusions about a serious future for us. But now there was...*possibility*. I was capable of lust and attraction. I now understood what it felt like to *want*. A door had been opened, and I'd taken a step through. But what did that mean when the guy I was finally feeling these things for was leaving in just a few days?

"So what now? What does this mean...for us?"

"Honestly? I don't know. I'm leaving on the third."

The euphoria from only moments before faded as the

mantle of reality settled heavily on our shoulders. I looked down at our hands, still clasped together between us. I studied the way his smaller hand fit in mine, the contrast of his olive-colored tone with my ruddier complexion. I liked the look of it, but even more importantly, I loved the way it felt. Like the final twist of a Rubik's cube when all the colors are lined up perfectly. I'd never held hands like this before, and I wasn't ready to let go.

"Maybe we just take it day by day? This is new for both of us." I squeezed his hand. "You're important to me. I don't want to rush...whatever this is just because you're leaving. We can talk and text just like we did before. Nothing has to change, really."

"Can I still kiss you? At least while I'm still in town."

I smiled. "Definitely."

This time, when our mouths met, it was with intention. Purpose. Passion and lust and...something deeper I didn't know how to name. I gripped his face with both hands, holding him in place as I plundered his mouth. As inexperienced as I was, I was moving entirely on instinct, trusting Zach would let me know if I veered off course.

He didn't though. His tongue met mine, thrust for thrust, tangling and teasing as we devoured each other. My cock wept in my briefs, my too-tight pants like a straitjacket for my dick, but I paid it no mind. At that moment, nothing mattered but the sensation of Zach's mouth on mine. Every nerve ending in my body was focused on the exact spot where our lips connected and our tongues glided. I didn't know if anything would ever feel as good as this kiss with this man.

It was everything.

There was a knock on the door, followed by Drea's voice. "Zach? Dad's looking for you."

We pulled apart, chests heaving as we struggled for air. His lips were shiny and red, his eyes gleaming with unbridled lust, and his hair was mussed where I'd run my hands through it. He looked like he'd been ravaged.

"Zach? Did you hear me?"

"Yeah! I'll be out in a sec!" he called, his eyes never leaving mine. "We should probably head back out there," he said more softly.

I nodded, not wanting this moment to end. We both stood, and I ran my fingers through his hair, smoothing it back down as best I could. I tucked in my shirt where it had pulled out in the back, willing my dick to calm down as I did so. There was no way I was going to be able to hide any sort of erection in these pants. Zach adjusted himself, mirroring my thoughts, which did not help my situation in the least, but I smiled and shrugged, acknowledging I was in the same boat.

He leaned in and kissed me, this time with much more restraint, then smiled. "You ready to go out there?"

"I'd rather stay in here."

He pressed his forehead against mine, a little awkward with the three-inch height difference but endearing nonetheless. "Same."

He backed away, grabbing my hand and pulling me behind him. He tugged the door open and there were Drea and Mandy, standing with arms crossed and wearing smug expressions.

"Did you two finally figure your shit out?" Drea asked with an arched brow.

"God, you're a pain in my ass," Zach responded, flicking her in the nose playfully.

Mandy's face had *I told you so* written all over it, but she didn't offer further comments.

"Dad really was looking for you. So"—she looked point-edly at our joined hands—"how do you want to handle this?"

Zach looked at me as if wanting confirmation that I was in agreement with what he was about to say. "I think we would like to keep it quiet for now. We don't want to rush anything."

When I nodded my assent, he gave my hand a squeeze, then let it go. I missed the contact immediately.

"Totally your call," Mandy said, and Drea nodded.

"There you are." Mr. Jacobs stood at the end of the hall, looking annoyed. "What are you doing back here? I've been looking for you."

We all turned to face him, but it was Zach who responded. "We were just taking a breather."

Mr. Jacobs sighed impatiently. "Well come on out here. There's someone I want you to meet."

<hr>

WHILE ZACH MADE the rounds with his dad, the girls and I made our way over to one of the side tables laden with a mixture of finger foods and desserts. We piled food onto our plates and found a spot to eat and gossip about the people in attendance. A few folks stopped and said hello, making small talk and asking after my parents. It was impossible in a town such as this not to run into at least a few people who'd known you since you were in diapers. Thankfully, I was only left to my own devices for about an hour before Zach returned, grabbing my hand and pulling me away from the girls.

He led me through the throngs of people and upstairs into the kitchen, where he stopped to grab sodas from the fridge before leading the way down the hall to his room. "I thought we could play Xbox while we wait to ring in the new year," he said, flipping on the light and setting the sodas on the table beside the bed.

"Your dad won't come looking for you?"

"Nah. I'm officially off-duty."

I noticed he and his dad seemed to be getting along better since he'd been home. Perhaps the semester away had been good for their relationship. I hoped so.

Zach fired up the gaming system, shuffling through a selection of games. We settled on the latest NBA game, sprawling out on the floor, side-by-side, knees touching. It wasn't long before we got lost in the game, trash-talking and flipping each other shit. It was like old times. Like it had been before he left for LA. And it was a relief that even after our kiss earlier and the evolving feelings between us, we could still have that easy friendship we'd so effortlessly developed over the summer. I didn't want to lose that and hadn't realized how much I'd needed to know it was still there until now.

Just before midnight, he paused the game, setting the controller down and hopping up to stand. "Be right back," he said with a smile before exiting the room.

I stood, stretching my back and legs, as I'd spent nearly an hour on the floor while we played, and crossed over to look out the window at the lake.

Moments later, he returned with two glasses of champagne.

"I wanted to ring in the new year right." He came over to where I was standing, handing me a glass. "Are you going to kiss me at midnight?"

Looking at the time on my smartwatch, I took his face in

my hand, brushing a thumb across his cheekbone. "Looks like you're just in time."

I leaned in, pressing my lips to his, marveling at the way my stomach swooped each time we came together like this. It reminded me of that feeling you get when driving country roads and you crest the hill just right. For a split second, your heart is in your throat while your stomach drops, and you're weightless.

That's how I felt kissing Zach.

Weightless.

He pulled away, smiling in wonder, and I was sure I had a similar look on my face. He held out his glass in a toast. "Happy New Year, Jason."

"Happy New Year."

28

———————

ZACH

JANUARY

EARLY RAYS of sunlight filtered through the windows, casting my bedroom in soft light as I lay on my back with my head turned away from the sleeping man next to me. Jason was lying on his stomach, fast asleep, with one arm thrown across my midsection and his bent leg resting on my thigh. I needed to pee, and I was starting to sweat from the furnace of a human wrapped around me, but I didn't dare move for fear of bursting the cozy bubble I'd awoken in.

Tiny snowflakes swirled against the window before being carried away again on the breeze as I contemplated how I'd arrived at this moment. One off-hand comment from Clayton had opened a door I hadn't even realized was there, yet, as I looked back, I wondered if there were signs I'd missed. Had there been moments of attraction to guys I'd missed over the years because I hadn't been open to the idea? Or was I demi like Jason? Did the connection need to be established before attraction could take place?

Neither theory seemed to fit, no matter how far back I looked within myself. One thing I knew for sure was that the attraction I'd felt for girls had been real. That hadn't been faked or forced, making me think I must be bi. I remembered hearing about some sort of scale for sexuality and figured I just landed more on one side than the other rather than directly in the middle or on either end.

Not that any of that really mattered. The *how* or *why* didn't really make a difference to me, only that I was here in this moment, feeling more alive, more *me* than I had since before Mom passed.

God, she would have loved him. His gentle spirit. His kindness. His warmth. His sneaky humor. She wouldn't have cared that he was a guy, only that I was happy.

My dad, on the other hand...well, I honestly wasn't sure what he would think. Despite our tendency to butt heads, he'd never given me a reason to think he'd be homophobic. Not that I was planning to come out just yet. Jason and I had talked more last night, lying in the dark with my head on his chest while he stroked a finger up and down my arm. We'd discussed where we wanted this to go and who we wanted to tell. We'd agreed we wanted more time to explore this thing between us on our own terms and timeline before we shared it with others.

As he'd placed gentle kisses in my hair, we'd agreed our friendship was the core of this relationship and must be preserved above all else. And while we didn't want to label this thing between us just yet, we also agreed we wouldn't see anyone else while we figured it out.

Talking had given way to kissing, and while hands had roamed and mouths had explored, neither of us had ventured below the waist. Even as I'd ached for release, ached to touch him, *ached* for things I hadn't even begun to imagine, there'd been relief in the restraint. We weren't ready. *I* wasn't ready. And so we'd made out until the need for sleep eventually took over. I'd rolled onto my side and he'd pulled me into him, the little spoon to his big one, and with a sigh, we'd let sleep take us.

Now, in the light of day, I examined my feelings more closely, determining that nothing had changed. In fact, if anything, I felt...*more*. I didn't know how to put a name to it exactly. Love seemed too strong a word, though if I were really honest with myself, I thought perhaps we were headed there. Yet, my feelings, whatever they might be, felt stronger than yesterday. This was more than friendship, more than simple attraction, just...*more*.

"I can *feel* you thinking," Jason's deep voice grumbled into my shoulder, causing me to turn my head back toward him with a smile.

"Hey, sleepyhead."

"What time is it?" he mumbled.

"I don't know. I can't see a clock while someone has me pinned to the bed."

The arm resting across my midsection squeezed harder as if he were afraid my words had been a threat to get up. It made me smile, even as I winced at the additional pressure on my bladder. It seemed a good sign that he was still on board with us continuing to explore this thing we had going.

"It feels good waking up wrapped in your arms. Thanks for staying last night."

We'd had a bit of a disagreement when I realized he had originally planned to go home shortly after midnight. Neither he nor Mandy had packed a bag, but Drea and I had insisted they stay, and after Mandy texted their parents, they'd agreed to spend the night.

"Mmm. I'm glad you talked me into it." He lifted his head, blinking sleepily at me. "This is nice."

I pressed a kiss to his forehead, letting my lips linger for a moment before pulling away. "Do you have plans for the day?"

He winced. "I do, actually. We always go out to my grandparents' farm and spend New Year's Day with them. We usually watch football and play card games with my cousins, then have ham for dinner with potato casserole." He rolled onto his side, propping himself on his elbow and resting his face in his hand. "You should come."

"I don't know. It sounds like a family thing. I don't want to intrude."

"My family won't care. They love you. Besides, I want to spend as much time with you as possible before you go back."

The air felt heavy with the weight of the reality of our situation. It seemed unfair that I was leaving so soon after finally figuring out there was something between us.

"You're right. I want that time with you too." I tilted my head up for a kiss, and he obliged with a sweet brush across my lips. "But before I do anything, I really need to pee."

Jason chuckled but rolled onto his back, allowing me to get up.

THE DAY SPENT at Jason's grandparents was one of the best I could remember. It seemed every day I spent with him was better than the last. He had a way of making me feel good. Happy. He made me really fucking happy.

Happiness that had been hard to contain, as it turned out. Now that I'd let all these feelings out into the world, it was nearly impossible to put them back. I found myself struggling not to touch him or drop a kiss on his cheek while surrounded by a room full of people. At least I'd been able to hold his hand under the table at dinner while he'd pressed his knee into mine. It had been a relief to touch him, though it had left me wanting more. I was beginning to think I'd never get enough. It was going to be hard to leave in two days.

"Pretty sure my mom is on to us," he said as we looked out over the fields below.

After dinner, Jason had driven us up to the overlook where he'd surprised me by turning the truck around so the bed faced the view. He'd dropped the tailgate and pulled out sleeping bags and blankets from the back of the cab, making a cozy little nest for us to settle into. For a guy with zero experience with dating, it was romantic as fuck.

I turned and looked at him, his face illuminated by the moonlight. It was chilly out here, but not unbearably cold, especially under all the blankets and with his arm wrapped around me, pulling me into his body heat. "What makes you think that?"

"I caught her staring at us a couple of times with one of those knowing mom-looks, like she knows we're up to something."

"My mom used to get those looks when we were kids. I never got away with anything." He gave me a gentle squeeze, pulling me in closer, and I smiled through the ache. It always hurt to think of her, but I was trying to speak of her more often. She deserved to be known. "Would it bother you? If she'd figured it out?"

"I don't think so. She might think she knows something, but I don't think she'll say anything unless I bring it up.

She's always been good about letting us come to her with things in our own time. I never told her I was ace, but not once did she ever pressure me to date. Not even for school dances like some moms do."

"I like your mom. She's fun."

I'd met her several other times, but today was the first time I'd spent any time actually getting to know her. She'd been friendly with a good sense of humor and absolutely cutthroat when we played cards. She may love her people deeply, but she played to win.

"She's the best." He was quiet for a moment, then asked, "Does it bother you that she might know?"

"No. If you're not worried about it, then it's cool. I'm not embarrassed to be with you or because I'm bi. It's not really a coming-out sort of thing. I just…" Jason waited patiently as I struggled to put my thoughts into words. "This thing with you feels…different. It feels…significant. Like every relation-ship I've ever been in before has been nothing more than scratching the surface of what I think I could feel for you. Of what I already feel."

I blew out a breath, not having meant to go that deep, but also unable to pull the words back. They were true.

"As soon as we let other people in, there's judgment and opinions and interference, even if it's well-intentioned. There's a subconscious need to take other people's feelings into account, and I don't want that. I don't want this to be about anyone other than *us*. The only person's feelings I care about are *yours*. I don't want to be concerned with all that other noise."

I chanced a look at him, unsure what I would see. His eyes glistened in the moonlight and he reached out his gloved hand, pulling my chin just a little closer to his.

"You're amazing, do you know that?" he whispered against my lips, his breath coming out in little puffs. "Amazing."

He pressed his lips to mine, eyes fluttering closed as we savored the taste of each other. And it was just him and me, kissing by the light of the moon, with only the stars to keep our secrets.

29

JASON

I miss you already

ZACH

Miss you too

JASON

Hey. Do you have a sec? Can I call?

ZACH

Sorry, I'm in class. Unless you need me to
step out?

No, that's ok. I wanted to hear your voice
when I told you, but I can't wait. I PASSED
MY CERT!

YESSSSSSSS! So proud of you!!!

Thanks! I also got a call back from AFD.
They want me to come in and fill out
paperwork tomorrow. I got the job!

That's amazing!

Big day for you!

I wish I could be there to help you celebrate!

Me too. But I'll see you in a little over a
month, right?

Yeah

I better go. My professor is glaring at me

Ok. Talk tonight?

Yeah. 10 your time

Can't wait

ZACH

Good luck today!

JASON

Thanks!

I feel like I should be nervous but I'm not.
I'm just excited

I think that just means you found your
calling

Hope so!

How did your test go?

Eh. We'll see. Pretty sure I did alright on the
multiple choice. Not so sure about the essay

I'm sure you did great!

I love how much you believe in me

Always

30

JASON

I TUCKED my phone into my pants pocket, smiling at the picture Zach had just sent me. It was late afternoon in LA and he had just gotten back to his dorm after he and Clayton had hit the gym for a workout. He'd snapped a selfie of himself smiling, fresh out of the shower, with a caption that read *Thinking of you.*

The sight of him with his hair mussed, skin still damp, and with a bright smile made my heart ache and my cock twitch. I adjusted myself, something I hadn't had to worry about nearly so often until I'd started dating him. I took a deep breath, trying to center myself and tamp down the ever-present longing I felt whenever I thought about Zach.

I'd been worried when he left that with time and distance, he'd realize his feelings toward me had been limited to proximity. Maybe he'd decide he wasn't bisexual after all. Or maybe he'd simply decide the effort of figuring this out long distance wasn't worth it. But in the two weeks since he'd been gone, he'd done nothing but show me how invested he truly was. He texted me off and on throughout the day and we spoke over the phone or by video call nearly every night. He sent me random pictures from his day and told me he missed me often. I'd never had a single person make me feel so...valued.

An alarm sounded in the firehouse, followed by Andrew, my field training officer, popping his head into the breakroom where I'd come in for a snack. "Let's go, probie. You're riding along on this one."

A combination of nerves and excitement coursed through me as I followed him out to the apparatus bay, throwing on my jacket as I climbed into the ambulance. After a week of onboarding and in-house training, I'd finally been cleared to start going on ride-alongs as part of my required field training, but we hadn't had any calls until now.

I listened as information came in from dispatch about the nature of the emergency and where it was located. Apparently, there'd been an accident not too far away involving a single, overturned vehicle. The accident had been called in by a witness who reported that the car had swerved to miss a deer.

With lights flashing and sirens blaring, we took off in the direction of the accident, arriving just a few minutes later. We were just outside of town on the county highway that ran between Brinkley and Astaire. I couldn't see much until I stepped out of the truck, turning to follow in the direction of my FTO and his partner, Jenny.

Time stopped.

Sound ceased.

I forgot to breathe.

Glass. So much glass.

A deer on the double yellow stripe. Lying in its own blood.

An electric-blue Lexus with its wheels in the air.

Zach. That's Zach's car. No, he's in LA. Drea. Drea's been driving Zach's car since he didn't take it with him to California. Mandy. Mandy's always with Drea. They didn't have school today, but they still had dance class. No. No, no, no, no-no-no-no-no!

I didn't remember shoving Andrew out of the way. Didn't remember trying to yank the door open or cutting my hands on the glass. Someone was yelling, pleading for help, and I wasn't even aware it was me until someone grabbed my arms and yanked me back. In the end, it took three fire-fighters to restrain me, to pull me out of sight of the mangled vehicle, and even then, I still pushed against them, fighting to get back to Mandy and Drea, sure I was the only one who could help them.

"You have to stop fighting us!" Chief said. "We can't help them if we're fighting with you."

"It's my sister and her friend. I have to help them. You have to let me—"

"Jason!" His tone was razor-sharp. With both hands on my shoulders, he shook me. "You *have* to stop fighting me. We're going to do everything we can to help your sister, but if you don't stop fighting, I'm going to have Deputy Charlie put you in handcuffs and lock you in the back of his patrol car." He nodded to the deputy standing a short distance away near his car, stopping traffic from entering the area.

All of the fight left my body as I realized he was right. I couldn't help them while I was in this state, and I was only making it harder for them to do their job. He felt the shift in me, his grip on my shoulders loosening from one of restraint to one of comfort. "I'm sorry, son. But I promise, we're going to do our best to get them out of here safely. You just sit tight."

31

ZACH

I STEPPED off the plane with just my backpack and carry-on in hand. I was wearing shorts and flip-flops, which was ridiculous for January in Nebraska, but I hadn't taken the time to change. At least I'd been wearing a UCLA hoodie when I got the call.

After frantically packing, one of the guys from the team who had a car on campus took me to the airport while Clayton searched for flights with remaining seats that could get me to Omaha. Now, at nearly one a.m., I stepped outside into the cold, my breath coming out in little puffs in the frigid night air. Jason's truck pulled up to the curb moments later, and before I could move, he'd thrown it into Park and hopped out, leaving the door wide open as he came around the front of the truck and scooped me into his arms.

Tears pricked my eyes, and for the first time since I'd gotten the news that my sister had been in a bad accident and was life-flighted to a hospital in Omaha, I felt myself starting to break. Before I could stop it, a sob escaped me. Jason's arms were like a vice around me, and I clung to him just as hard, but when I felt a tremor wrack his body, I realized he was crying too.

I pulled back, putting my hands on either side of his face to get a good look at him. His eyes were red and puffy and tears ran unchecked down his rosy cheeks. He'd been there at the scene, I remembered. He wasn't just dealing with the knowledge that his sister had been injured. He'd actually seen it firsthand. I couldn't imagine what that had done to him—was *still* doing to him.

"Come on, baby. Let's get in the truck. Do you want me to drive?"

"No," he said, his voice shaky. He took another breath, swiping at his eyes as he tried to steady himself. "No," he said again, with more authority. "I can drive."

We loaded up my suitcase and backpack and drove toward the exit. He pointed his truck in the opposite direction from Astaire or Brinkley, and I was grateful, knowing that meant we were heading toward the hospital here in Omaha, where they'd been taken to a trauma unit.

"How are they? Has there been any change?"

"No change."

I didn't miss the clench of his jaw or the way he gripped the steering wheel. I rested my hand on his thigh and didn't move it for the next twenty minutes until we pulled into the hospital parking lot.

We parked, and I followed Jason inside and onto the elevator. He punched the button for the third floor, and I didn't question it when he laced his fingers through mine, as if he were drawing strength from the connection.

He released my hand as we arrived on the third level, leaving me feeling empty, but I took a deep breath and followed him down the short hallway to the ICU waiting room. As much as I wanted to cling to him, to draw strength from him just as he'd drawn from me, now was not the time for a coming-out conversation with our families. Our sisters were our focus. They were the priority.

There were three people in the waiting room when we walked in. Jason's parents were sitting in two chairs, side-by-side, gripping each other's hands, much like Jason and I had just done on the elevator. Jason made a beeline in their direction, asking for an update in soft murmurs. I saw Mrs. Whitt shake her head, then dab at her eyes with a mangled tissue as Mr. Whitt whispered into her hair.

My eyes flicked to the other occupant in the room. My father, still dressed in business attire, stood a short distance away, staring out the window into the parking lot below. It wasn't much of a view, but I wasn't convinced he was actually seeing any of it. He hadn't so much as moved when Jason and I entered. Either he hadn't heard us, or he'd chosen not to acknowledge the interruption.

I hesitated a moment, my heart thumping in my chest. For whatever reason, Dad and I had come to something of a truce in the last several months, but that didn't mean I had gotten any better at reading him. I took in his appearance. He was wearing a suit, not unusual for him, even if most of the corporate world no longer dressed that way. There were little wrinkles across the back of the jacket from where it had creased when he sat, the only sign of imperfection in his otherwise impeccable appearance. Except that wasn't true. As I took a few steps closer, I noticed cracks in his armor. He was still wearing a tie, but it had been loosened, the collar open at his neck. And his hair, dark like mine and usually styled to perfection, was mussed as if he'd run his hands through it. He did so now, fingers gliding through the strands, and then he turned, catching sight of me.

The raw vulnerability in his eyes had me stopping in my

tracks. He looked...older, somehow, as if life had worn on him like a boulder eroded by the elements. Ice and rain and snow and hot summer sun battering its surface. He tried to pull himself together, to pull on the mask he'd worn almost my entire life, the one he'd donned like armor in the wake of my mother's death, but he failed, his face crumpling in anguish. I did the only thing I could think of. I crossed to him and pulled him into my arms.

***

JASON and I dozed in fits and starts, curling up in awkward positions in the ICU waiting room. Mandy had suffered a broken leg and had some internal injuries that had required surgery and was also being treated for a concussion. A surgeon had come out an hour ago to let us know Mandy was out of surgery and resting comfortably, but because of the internal bleeding, she would need to remain in the ICU for a few more days for monitoring. Mrs. Whitt had gone back to sit with her, but Jason had stayed in the waiting room with me. I thought maybe he wasn't ready to see her just yet.

In addition to a broken wrist, Drea had a couple of broken ribs, which led to a collapsed lung. They'd inserted a chest tube to reinflate the lung, but because of multiple contusions and a lot of swelling, they'd placed her on a ventilator for the time being. This required her to be sedated, and it would likely be several days before the swelling would come down enough that they could take her off the medication and remove the ventilator.

Dad had gone back to sit with her shortly after I arrived, when the doctor came out to let us know they had her stabilized. And since Mr. Whitt had left a short time ago to go home and pack a bag, I'd stayed with Jason in the waiting room, not wanting to leave him alone. I sat up in my chair, tilting my head from side to side, trying to work out the kinks in my neck. Jason followed suit, standing and reaching his arms to the ceiling in a full-body stretch. He was still wearing his uniform, the black tactical pants and button-down fitting his body perfectly. Under different circum-stances, the sight would have me shifting positions to allow room for my growing erection, but at the moment, I couldn't do more than admire him with a sort of appreciative detach-ment, much as one admires a work of art in a gallery.

"You wanna go see if we can find some coffee?" He held his hand out, and I took it, rising to stand in front of him.

We made our way out of the ICU, quietly walking hand-in-hand, as we navigated the hallways in search of the cafe-teria. I should have been more concerned about someone seeing us holding hands, but I couldn't bring myself to care. It was amazing how much comfort could be drawn from two hands clasped together. I wasn't willing to break that connection.

It was a little after four in the morning when we entered the cafeteria. At this time of day, there was only a limited selection of food items pre-packaged in a refrigerated case, but I could hear the bustle of folks working in the back, starting on the prep work for breakfast.

We grabbed cups and poured our coffees, paying a sleepy-eyed gentleman in cash before taking a table near the windows. It was pitch black outside, still several hours from sunrise.

We sipped our coffee, and I grimaced at the bitter taste, wondering how long it had been sitting there and debating if I could persuade someone to make a fresh pot. Jason let out a heavy sigh, pulling my attention away from my coffee.

He rubbed his hand through his short crop of hair, then down over his face, scratching at the stubble along his jawline. He seemed to be working himself up to saying something, so I waited while he sorted through his words. "I wonder...I wonder if maybe I'm not cut out to be an EMT."

"What?" I took his hand in mine, squeezing gently. "What makes you say that?"

"I lost it tonight. When we pulled up to the scene..." His Adam's apple bobbed as he swallowed heavily and blinked several times. "When I saw your car...and I realized it was the girls...I just...I lost it. I took off running and...and it's all kind of a blur after that. They had to pull me away from the car after I cut my hands on the window glass."

He held up his bandaged hand, the one I wasn't currently holding. "It took three guys holding me down and Chief threatening to have me handcuffed before I calmed down enough to see that I was only making everything worse." He bit back a choked sob. "I'm no good to anybody like that. I can't be panicking in an emergency situation. I need to be able to keep a clear head."

His tone was becoming more agitated, so I got up and stood behind him, wrapping my arms around him from behind. "It'll be different when it's not your sister. You just had the horrible luck of having your first call involve someone you know. With training and experience, you'll learn to put those feelings aside and do the job."

He was sobbing now, his big body shaking with the emotion of it all. I held on, murmuring nonsense in his ear, trying to calm the storm and soothe the panic brewing inside him. I wasn't sure how long I stood there, holding him together while he let it all go, but eventually, the tears subsided, leaving him sniffling.

I kissed the top of his head, then released him, moving

back to the other side of the table, ignoring the coffee that had now run cold.

"Thanks," he said, wiping his nose with a napkin.

"No thanks necessary."

"I hate that this happened, and I hate that you had to drop everything in LA, but I'm glad you're here." He took my hand in his once more. "I don't know if I could do this without you."

"I'm glad we have each other."

32

ZACH

With a numb sense of detachment, I made my way down the short hallway to Drea's room. I'd lived a thousand lives since I'd gotten the call nearly twelve hours before, yet I'd only cried once in that time. From the moment I crossed the threshold into the hospital, I'd felt...worry and fear and frustration, of course, but it had all been muted, as if those thoughts and feelings were outside of my body, a great distance away. I supposed it was what people meant when they said they were having an out-of-body experience.

A part of me felt guilty for not being more upset. For not losing it like my father or Jason had. Yet I also felt a sense of gratitude for being able to be there for them when they needed to fall apart.

I stepped into Drea's room, taking in the sight of my only sister, younger than me, yet often wiser, and it was as if everything, all of those distant feelings, slammed into me all at once. It was a direct hit to the center of my chest, and it *hurt*. Hurt in a way nothing had since Mom died. And even that had been different, though no less acute. That had been sudden, a complete and total shock, followed by utter devastation.

Drea's accident had been a shock, to be sure, but I'd had twelve hours to prepare myself for seeing her. I *hadn't* prepared though. I hadn't allowed myself to think about what she would look like in this moment, lying in bed, her dark hair spread around her on the pillow, with tubes and wires connecting her to God knew what. Her chest rose up and down, but it was rhythmic in a mechanical way as the ventilator did the breathing for her.

Her skin was pale and bruised, in stark contrast to the bright-pink cast on her wrist. It was wrong, all wrong. She'd never have chosen that color. She'd have gone with something more muted if it was available, lavender perhaps.

There was a lump in my throat and a knot in my chest, but the tears wouldn't fall. I tried to pull in a breath, but the air wouldn't come. My body was betraying me. I tried again to draw air into my lungs but only managed a shallow breath. I was having a panic attack.

I turned back, sliding open the door, intending to find a doctor or nurse or someone who could help me, but I ran into a solid wall of muscle. Jason grabbed me by the shoulders, steadying me.

"I...I..." I gasped, trying to get the words out.

"Breathe, honey."

I shook my head, still unable to take in air. The pressure in my chest was squeezing, squeezing, squeezing, and I thought I might pass out.

"Look at me."

My eyes snapped open, locking on his. I hadn't even realized I'd closed them. He placed my hand in the center of his chest, then one of his hands on mine. I could feel the steady beat of his heart underneath my palm. I tried to focus on it, but my mind was racing as I struggled to release the vice squeezing my chest.

"Breathe with me."

I shook my head, squeezing my eyes shut. I'd already tried that. Didn't he know I was *trying* to breathe?

"Come on, honey. Just try. Even if it's a small one. Eyes on me. Breathe with me."

He began taking shallow breaths, matching the pace of my own, coaxing me into breathing just a little deeper each time. He started a counting pattern, tapping his index finger against my chest with each count. In for four, out for seven, repeating the pattern over and over in his smooth bass until, eventually, the vice on my chest released and I could breathe on my own. His eyes never left mine the entire time.

It was then that the tears finally came, a flood of them, running down my cheeks in rivers. Jason pulled me into his chest, wrapping his big arms around me, one hand at my nape, running his fingers through my hair while making shushing noises in my ear. Just like the breathing, I eventually got myself under control and pulled myself out of Jason's arms, surprised to see the tear tracks on his face. I hadn't realized he had been crying too.

I reached up and thumbed away the moisture. "You okay?"

He chuckled. "Are you?"

I took a shaky breath, relieved that I could still take in air despite my bout of tears. "Yeah. I just...seeing her like that... with wires coming out of her and all the bruises and bandages...it just...freaked me out, I guess."

"I think that's normal. It's scary to see someone you care about looking like that."

I nodded, knowing he was likely thinking about his reaction to seeing the girls at the accident scene. "Thank you for..." I waved my hand vaguely in front of me, hoping he got the gist. "Why did you come down here? I thought you were going to go see Mandy?"

He took my hand in his. "You have nothing to thank me for. And Dad got back and wanted to see Mandy, so I came looking for you. I wanted to be close by in case you needed me."

A warm sense of gratitude flooded me. I wasn't sure how I'd found someone this kind. He always put others first, me included. I didn't think I would ever be enough to deserve him. He was truly one of the best people I'd ever met.

I let out a breath. "I think I want to go back in there. Will you come with me?" His eyes flicked to the door behind me, worry creasing his brow. God, I was a selfish asshole. I forgot that he was still dealing with the trauma of finding them on-scene. "It's okay if you're not ready," I rushed out. "I think I can handle it now."

He took a deep breath, releasing it slowly. "No, I think I need to see her. And it'll be easier with you." He squeezed my hand, giving me a small smile.

"Are you sure?" I asked, searching his eyes. He leaned forward and pressed a soft kiss to my forehead.

"I'm good. Promise."

I turned, pulling him behind me as I opened the door to Drea's room and stepped inside. This time, I was prepared for the whir of the ventilator and beeping of the machines, but I kept a close eye on Jason, unsure how he'd react. I knew he'd done some clinical rotations at the hospital in Brinkley, but I thought it was probably different with someone you knew.

He gave me a small nod, and we proceeded farther into

the room, going around to the other side of the bed and taking a seat. I pulled the chair closer, sitting down and taking her small hand in mine. I wasn't in the habit of holding hands with my sister and had most recently adjusted to the feel of Jason's much larger hand in mine, so by contrast, hers felt frail and small. Still, it was a comfort to have that contact, as if I could feel her life force flowing through her fingers.

I heard a sniffle and turned to see Jason swiping at his eyes. I offered my free hand to him, and he took it, lacing his fingers through mine. "I didn't realize until now just how much I care about her. She and Mandy are thicker than thieves. It kinda feels like Drea's my sister too."

My heart hitched. I couldn't say I felt quite the same way with Mandy. I cared about her, of course, but I'd been gone for months at college while Jason had been home. And during that time, I knew both girls had grown even closer than last year. Jason had witnessed their sleepovers and movie nights while I'd been absent. It would make sense that he'd feel a closeness with Drea that I simply hadn't had a chance to develop with Mandy. And Drea just had a way of drawing people in and making them feel special. No doubt, she'd done so with Jason.

I squeezed his hand. "I'm sure she feels the same way about you. You'll have to tell her when she wakes up."

He nodded solemnly, and I turned back to look at her sleeping face.

We sat like that for hours, just watching her sleep, her chest rising and falling with the pump of the ventilator. Nurses came and went, checking her vitals and making notes on their charts. And still, we sat. There was so much I wanted to say to her, so many things I was feeling, but it was locked up tight, like a knot in my chest that I didn't know how to untangle.

So I didn't say anything as I held her hand and watched her sleep.

33

———

JASON

IT WAS around lunchtime when Zach's father returned. At some point, Zach had leaned forward, resting his head on the edge of the bed near where their hands were clasped. I had moved my hand to his back, rubbing soothing circles until the rhythmic rise and fall under my hand indicated he was asleep. My hand was still resting there when Mr. Jacobs' face appeared in the window. His eyes darted to where my hand rested, then back to my face with a raised brow, a question in his eyes that wasn't mine to answer. He didn't look angry though. More...surprised, and maybe a bit curious.

I rose, reluctant to leave Zach, but Mr. Jacobs had more right to be in the room than I did, so I crossed over and stepped out into the hallway, leaving Zach sleeping peacefully.

"Any change?" he asked, and my shoulders dropped with relief that he hadn't asked me a question I wasn't prepared to answer.

"No. The nurses checked on her about twenty minutes ago, but they didn't say much."

"How long has he been asleep?" He nodded toward Zach.

I shrugged. "An hour maybe?"

He blew out a breath. "They've always been close. Even before their mom…" His voice trailed off, and I didn't miss the shake in his tone. He took a breath, drawing on a strength I couldn't see, and surprised me with his next words. "Thanks for sitting with him. You're a good… friend."

I swallowed past the lump in my throat as I processed everything he wasn't saying. He hadn't said the word friend in such a way as to deny what we meant to each other but rather as a way of saying he understood we weren't ready to name it as something more. It felt like acceptance, and I was grateful.

I didn't think I could respond without expressing my depth of feeling for Zach, so I nodded.

"How's Mandy?" he asked, genuine concern in his eyes, surprising me once again. This man had always seemed so cold and distant. And, of course, I knew of the issues he and Zach had had in recent years. But at that moment, he was nothing but warm and kind, asking about my sister while his own daughter lay in a hospital bed just on the other side of the door.

"Mom texted a bit ago saying she'd woken briefly once or twice but wasn't very lucid and had mostly been sleeping. Now's probably a good time for me to go check in."

He put his hand on my shoulder. "I understand you were with the crew on-scene?"

"Yeah, though I wasn't any help." I looked down, color flooding my cheeks. "I kind of lost it when I realized it was Drea's car."

"Hey." He squeezed my shoulder, prompting me to look

at him. "I'm glad to know you were there. I'm glad there was someone at the scene who cared about them."

I nodded, and after one more squeeze of my shoulder, he turned, wordlessly entering Drea's room, leaving me stunned in the hallway. The entire interaction with him had been unexpected, and I wasn't sure what to make of it. Shaking it off, I turned toward Mandy's room just a few doors down.

My steps were slow, while my heart beat faster the closer I got to her door. If I thought seeing Drea was tough, seeing my own sister would be monumentally harder. At least, that was how I'd built it up in my mind. And now I found myself frozen, standing in front of her door, afraid to enter. Afraid of what I'd see. Rationally, I knew she had a fighting chance at recovery. The doctors had said she was in serious condition, but she was young and healthy and had already shown some signs of improvement since she'd come out of surgery this morning.

But I wasn't rational. Really hadn't been since I lost my shit on-scene. Other than some tears shed, I'd managed to put on an appearance that I was holding it together. Underneath the surface, though, there was a tremor in my blood, a feeling that I was coming apart at the seams. It wasn't like me. I'd always been the calm one when everyone else panicked. It had made me a good lifeguard. A good teammate. I'd thought it would make me a good EMT. Now, I wasn't sure if that path was open to me anymore.

I scrubbed my hands over my face and through my dirty hair, and when I let them drop back down to my side, I caught my mom's eye through the glass of the door. No help for it—I couldn't turn back now—I opened the door and walked in.

Dad rose from his spot next to Mom, placed a kiss on her

temple, then pulled me into a hug. I couldn't remember the last time I'd hugged my father. Not because we weren't close, but I supposed I'd outgrown hugs at some point. Perhaps we should do so more often. "I'll give you some time with her," he said in my ear. "Be good to stretch my legs."

He patted me on the shoulder as he released me and headed for the door while I took his spot next to my mom. Wordlessly, she reached her hand out to me, and I took it, noting how soft and smooth it felt compared to Zach's. Odd that I'd gotten used to the feel of a man's hand in mine in such a short amount of time.

Steeling myself, I forced myself to look toward the bed. Mandy's blonde hair had been braided, though I wasn't sure if she'd worn it that way the day of the accident or if someone had taken the time and care to do it that way since. She had some bruising across her temple and cheekbone, and her leg was wrapped in a cast from just below the knee down to her foot, though there was a thick fuzzy sock covering her toes. Unlike Drea's, Mandy's cast was white. All in all, she looked like she'd faired better than Drea. Though I knew she had some bruising under her gown where the seatbelt had done its job, and the doctors had mentioned some internal bleeding we obviously wouldn't be able to see.

I let out a shaky breath, relief flooding through me so fast I almost felt dizzy.

"She was awake for just a few minutes a little while ago," Mom said. "Seemed pretty groggy, which the doc said was normal, but it was still a relief to see her open her eyes for a few minutes."

"That's good." I squeezed her hand. "Zach's with Drea. She's on a ventilator, and they're still keeping her sedated for now."

"Poor girl. She's a sweet one, that Drea. And I'm sure it's hard on all of 'em after losing Zach's mom the way they did."

"Yeah, he sort of panicked when he saw her." I didn't want to go into details out of respect for Zach's privacy, but this was my mom, and I needed to talk about it.

She made a little humming sound of affirmation. "How are you holding up?"

I shrugged, not knowing how to tell her about the guilt I felt, the shame of panicking on-scene like I had. And the fear I wouldn't be able to do my job again. Not to mention the way all of this was tied up with Zach's family and mixed with the complicated feelings I had for him.

"I was terrified for them." I looked down at the bandage on my hand from where I'd cut it on the glass, trying to get into the car. I forged on, suddenly wanting to get it out there with the one person I knew would love me anyway. "I lost my head. Screamin' and hollerin', trying to get to them inside the car. They had to pull me away. Chief threatened to put me in handcuffs."

"Your love may not be loud, but you love big. Always have."

"Maybe. But it's my job to keep a cool head. To survey the situation so I can make life-saving decisions. Or at least that's supposed to be my job. On this run, I was only supposed to be observing. Instead, I made a scene and got in the way."

"You're human. You reacted as anyone would in a situation like that."

I shrugged, dismissing her assessment. She was my mom. She was supposed to say comforting shit like that. But it didn't change the fact that I'd embarrassed myself and, more importantly, gotten in the way of the other folks doing their job. I wasn't sure if I'd ever forgive myself.

"Oh, baby. Come here," she said, wrapping her arm around me and pulling me close.

I went willingly, needing the type of comfort only my mom could offer, resting my head on her shoulder and blinking back the tears that threatened to fall once again. I was tired of crying. Tired of the guilt and self-pity. I should be focused on my sister and Drea. And Mom should be focused on Mandy, not my issues.

My stomach grumbled, reminding me I hadn't really eaten breakfast unless you counted that sludge resembling coffee from the cafeteria, but that wasn't really food. Mom chuckled, and I sat up. "Why don't you boys go on and grab a bite. Maybe head home for a shower and a nap. You've got to be exhausted."

"You'll call if..."

"One of us will get ahold of you if there's any change."

"Yeah, okay." I stood up, yawning as I stretched. I looked at Mandy once more, wishing she was awake so I could tell her...well, I wasn't sure what I'd say, but it would be a relief to see her eyes. To hear her voice. With a sigh, I turned to Mom. "You want me to bring you back anything?"

"No. Your dad picked up everything I need."

"Alright. Then I suppose I'll go see if Zach wants to go." I turned and headed for the door but paused and turned back. "I love you, Mom."

"I love you too."

34

———————

ZACH

I DIDN'T QUESTION it when Jason drove us through Taco Bell once we got into Astaire. Nor did I question it when he drove us back to his house and led me inside, carrying the bag of tacos in one hand and my travel bag in the other. I was still wearing shorts and flip-flops, but I barely noticed the cold as we made our way inside. The exhaustion, both mental and physical, over the last twenty-four hours had left me in a state of numbness. I felt like a zombie.

We pounded the tacos sitting at the kitchen island, too tired to make conversation or do anything more than chew one bite after the other. When I nearly fell face-first into the pile of lettuce and taco sauce on my empty wrapper, Jason scooped up our trash, tossed it in the can in the pantry, then took my hand and led me upstairs.

Absently, I noticed the pictures lining the stairway wall. The hodgepodge of mismatched frames held photos of smiling Whitts at various ages and stages. We'd spent more time at my place than his over the summer since I had a more state-of-the-art entertainment system in my basement, but the few times I had been here, I'd been struck by how cozy it was. Warm and lived in rather than cold and sterile. It was evident that this was a family who loved each other.

It wasn't that there wasn't love within my family. It was just that without Mom, we'd forgotten how to express it. Or at least my dad and I had. My mind immediately went to the worst-case scenario, envisioning a life without Drea and what that would mean for my relationship with my father. As I crested the top of the stairs, I shook my head, ruthlessly shoving that thought aside. I had to believe the universe wouldn't take Drea from me too.

We made our way into Jason's room, which had the same cozy quality as the rest of the house, though it was a little more sparsely decorated. Jason was a simple guy and not the type to have posters and pictures everywhere. Though he did have a few team pictures on his shelf next to trophies and other athletic awards.

He crossed to the window and drew the curtains, blocking most of the afternoon sun. He began undressing, pulling off his boots, then undoing his belt and lowering his pants. Under any other circumstances, my dick would have surely taken interest, but as exhausted as I was, the only thing I could think about was sleep. He finished undressing, then pulled back the covers and slid into bed in nothing but his boxer briefs, reaching out a hand to me.

I blinked a couple of times, realizing I had been standing in the doorway the entire time he undressed. Quickly, I toed off my flip-flops, dropped my shorts, and pulled off my hoodie and T-shirt, leaving everything in a messy pile on the floor. I climbed into the bed next to him, rolling onto my side so my back was against his front.

Jason threw the covers over us, then draped his big arm over me and pulled me into his warmth. I sighed at the feel of his hairy chest against my smooth back, burrowing myself into him, enjoying the little cocoon of warmth he'd created for us.

"This okay?" he asked, ever the gentleman.

"Mmm," was all I managed before sleep took me.

***

I WOKE WITH A START, groggy and confused. A weight was draped over me, and I blinked, trying to clear my vision in the dim light of the darkened room. I was in Jason's room, I recalled. A whimper behind me had me rolling to face him, dislodging the arm he'd had across my waist. As my eyes adjusted to the light, I could see his eyes were scrunched tight and his forehead was creased. The whimpering intensified, along with mumbling I couldn't make sense of, and he began to shake his head back and forth.

"No," he said, a little louder this time. "No. No. No. I have to..." He thrashed, his body jerking back and forth, lost in the throes of a nightmare. One likely based on the trauma he'd witnessed yesterday.

"Jason," I said, shaking his shoulder. "Wake up, baby."

He shook me off. "No!" he shouted. "I have to help them."

I sat up, knowing I would have to get more physical with him if I was going to pull him out of the dream. "Jason," I said, raising my voice in a commanding tone while I pushed him onto his back. He continued to thrash, turning his head this way and that, so I climbed on top of him, straddled his hips, and shook him with both hands. "You have to wake up. Come on, baby. You're dreaming."

He woke with a gasp, eyes bulging and mouth open as he fought for air. Immediately, I leaned over, getting my hands underneath him and laying my torso across his in a fierce hug. "Shh," I crooned into his ear. "You're okay. The girls are okay. It was just a dream."

I continued to whisper words of reassurance in his ear until I felt his pulse steady and his breathing resume a normal pattern. Eventually, his arms came around me, returning the embrace and holding me tight.

Wanting only to offer comfort, I kissed him gently, where his jaw met his ear. I continued trailing kisses across his jawline, his stubble scraping along my lips. When I arrived at his mouth, I kissed one corner, then the other, before placing a gentle kiss in the center, then pulled back to look him in the eyes. "Better?"

He nodded, though his eyes still held a little wildness, telling me fragments of the dream likely still had a hold on him. I pushed forward so I could reach his forehead, placing another kiss in the center, letting my lips linger over the salty taste of his skin. I moved back down, kissing the tip of his nose and then his mouth again.

I brushed a thumb across his lips, then brushed my knuckles lightly across his cheekbone, trying to soothe the fear and worry as best I could. I knew he held guilt for how he'd reacted at the scene and there was nothing I could say to take that away for him. I knew he was scared and worried for his sister like I was for mine. But I thought maybe I could take some of that away, ease it for just a little while.

I bent forward, pressing my lips to his with intention, brushing my tongue against the seam, encouraging him to open for me. He obliged, the tip of his tongue gliding against mine tentatively. Heat shot straight to my dick, just from that tiny bit of contact, and I groaned, slipping my tongue in farther. He opened for me, meeting my tongue with his, this time with more confidence.

I continued my assault on his mouth, pleased when he

moved his hands up to my back, rubbing them up and down my skin, sending sparks skittering through my veins. My cock was hard and aching, pressed against his belly, and I could feel his own hardness nestled against the cleft of my ass. Unable to help myself, I rocked back against him, smiling against his lips when he moaned, the deep rumble of it reverberating against my chest. His hands moved lower, one on each ass cheek, kneading the flesh through my boxer briefs. Then he moved those hands back up to my hips and pushed me down the length of his body, causing my erection to rub against his. I thought I might die from the pleasure of it.

There were so many new sensations flooding my body that I wasn't sure how to process them all, but I knew I wanted more. Desperately. I pulled back, moving my lips down to his chest, kissing and licking my way down the center through the patch of hair on his chest and the length of his happy trail. The feel of that hair against my tongue was foreign...and erotic as fuck. What was it Clayton had said? *Muscles and a hard body just hit different...* He'd failed to mention body hair.

When I arrived at Jason's waistband, I paused. This was new territory. All of this was, really, but crossing this barrier...well, there was no turning back. I'd be lying if I said I hadn't been thinking about this, wanting this, ever since I'd gone back to LA, but Jason was demi, and his relationship with sex might be different from mine. And with the long distance, we hadn't had a chance to discuss it.

My eyes flicked up to his, and the look on his face took my breath away. I saw nothing but *need*, like he wanted to consume me. He'd never looked at me like that before, not even when we'd made out around New Year's Eve. I wasn't sure anyone had ever looked at me like that, like I was a meal they wanted to devour. Still, I had to know for sure. "Are you okay with this?"

"I don't know what exactly you have in mind, but I know I want you. And I trust you."

I smiled ruefully. "I don't have the specifics worked out yet. Kind of running on instinct. Though I may have watched some gay porn. For research purposes." I waggled my eyebrows.

His cock jumped behind his waistband, drawing my focus. I could see a wet spot where he was leaking against the fabric. I wanted to lick it. "Research, huh?" His question pulled my attention back to his face.

"I figured one of us might need to know what we're doing." I quirked a brow.

"How do you know I didn't do the same type of research?"

"Did you?" I shot back, calling his bluff.

His cheeks flushed adorably. "Thought about it. But porn kind of icks me out. I s'pose it's the demi thing?"

"Could be. But I like the idea that you saved this just for me."

He huffed out a breath. "You gonna talk about porn, or are you gonna get on with it?"

I pretended to think about it, but he put an end to that when he started pushing his briefs down on his own. I batted his hands away, wanting the pleasure of unwrapping him myself.

I lowered his waistband slowly. The head of his cock, shiny, flushed, and leaking at the tip, emerged from beneath the fabric, and my heart hammered at the sight. I'd never been this close to another man's dick, had never even thought about another man's cock prior to a month ago, and here I was contemplating whether I wanted to lick it or ride it.

Since it was right there in front of my face, I went with the former, licking from the bottom of the head upward toward the tip, swirling around his slit and lapping up the bead of precum shining for me like a beacon. I savored the salty taste of him, but it was his reaction I enjoyed the most. This guy, usually so stoic and calm, came alive under my touch. He fisted the sheets at his side, and his face was red, his eyes squeezed shut and his jaw clenched as if he were trying to keep himself from losing control.

Challenge accepted.

I pulled the band of his boxer briefs lower, revealing his erection inch by glorious inch until it was entirely free from the fabric, standing proudly in front of me, begging to be licked. I yanked on his underwear, indicating I wanted them all the way off, and he obliged, lifting his hips so I could pull them free. I tossed them on the floor and then returned my attention to the task at hand.

I never knew a dick could be so beautiful. He was long and thick, with a vein running up the front at a slight angle. I leaned forward and licked that vein from root to tip, marveling at the velvety feel of him under my tongue. He moaned then, a sound I thought I'd never get tired of hearing, and I licked him for a second time just to see if he'd moan again. This time the groan turned into a growl, and holy shit, I thought I might come just from the sound of it. My balls were drawn up tight and I was on a hair trigger without even touching myself.

Deciding I better move this along before I embarrassed myself, I took the head into my mouth, swirling my tongue around it before moving lower, taking more of his length into my mouth. When I took as much of him as I could, I pulled back, hollowing my cheeks and applying suction as I did so. I may not have given head before, but I knew what I liked and figured replicating that was the best course of action.

He let go of the sheets in favor of gripping my hair as I took him back into my mouth once again. I continued the action, bobbing up and down on his cock while he whimpered and whined and begged. He was completely incoherent, and I fucking loved it. Loved taking him apart, one stroke at a time.

I picked up the pace, adding my hand to the mix, and with just a few more strokes, he was coming down my throat. I did my best to swallow it down, managing to catch most of it, until I finally felt his body relax into the mattress.

I shoved up to my knees, hastily tugged my own briefs down my thighs, wrapped my hand around my cock, and began to stroke. I didn't even bother with lubrication, knowing this wouldn't take long. With a long grunt, I shot thick ropes of cum all over Jason's belly and spent cock. My vision blurred at the edges, my orgasm relentless, as tremors rocked through my body.

Finally, when I thought my legs might give out, I collapsed, landing half on top of him and half on the bed, the mess I'd made trapped between us.

35

JASON

"Holy shit," Zach mumbled, his face buried in the pillow next to me. Absently, I trailed my fingers up and down his back and over the curve of his ass as we both struggled to catch our breath. I'd had orgasms before—maybe not as many as most guys I knew—but I'd certainly jacked myself off. This, though...this was an entirely new experience. It was like watching a million-dollar fireworks display after only having experienced the thrill of sparklers in your backyard.

"That was...wow," I finished lamely.

Zach chuckled. "Yeah. Wow."

"Is it always that mind-blowing?" I could start to see why guys in the locker room were always chasing tail if *this* was what they were chasing.

Zach rolled off me, turning onto his side and laying his head on my chest, tucking it under my chin. I wrapped my arm around him, pulling him in close.

"I don't know how it is for anyone else, but for me, no. I've always enjoyed sex, but that was on a whole other level."

"Did you like it? Doing...that? To me?"

He lifted his head so he could look at me. "Babe, I don't think I've ever come so hard."

I could feel my cheeks heat, but I pressed on, unable to suppress my curiosity. "Do you think I could...maybe do that to you sometime?"

"You want to give me a blowjob?"

I bit my lip and nodded, feeling shy.

"We can try whatever you want. My body is yours to explore however you'd like."

I liked the sound of that but still felt hesitant. It must have shown on my face because he said, "How about this? I promise if we do anything that makes me uncomfortable, I'll tell you. And you do the same. Okay?"

"Yeah. I can do that."

He leaned forward and kissed me. "I loved it. I loved every moment of what we just did. Did you?"

"It was amazing." I kissed him again. "You sure you've never done that before? You seemed confident."

He raised an eyebrow. "It helped that I knew you had no one to compare me to."

I shook my head as he tucked himself back into my side with his head on my chest. I shivered when he ran his fingers through my chest hair. His touch felt better than it had any right to.

As we lay there, fingers trailing up and down each other's bodies, reality started to creep back into the bubble we'd created, and along with it came guilt. Our sisters were lying in hospital beds with severe injuries while we were in bed chasing orgasms.

"Are we terrible people?" I whispered.

"Why?"

"I don't know. I guess because our sisters are in the hospital and we're here fooling around."

"I think," he started, his words measured, "that some-times when everything's gone to shit, it's okay to take some time for yourself. To find joy in the moments between all the hard stuff." He drew another breath. "And I think the girls would be high-fiving us if they knew what we just did. Well, maybe not every detail of what we just did…"

I chuckled. "You're probably right."

"We probably should get cleaned up and head back." He tipped his head up to look at the clock on my night-stand. "Maybe pick up some dinner for everyone on our way."

I wrapped both arms around him and kissed the top of his head. "Sounds like a plan."

WE SHOWERED TOGETHER, Zach surprising me when he took the soap from me and lathered my body. I thought he'd want to work me over again, maybe we'd get each other off with mutual hand jobs, but he seemed to understand that as much as I'd enjoyed our time together earlier, I needed some space to process.

Instead, he washed me from head to toe, working the soap into my skin with gentle fingers, then rinsed me off, trailing kisses along my clean skin. He repeated the treat-ment with my hair, lathering me up and massaging my scalp as best he could with the height difference. I tried to return the treatment, but he batted my hands away, saying we needed to finish up quickly so we could get back.

My heart squeezed at the tenderness he showed me, his desire to take care of me without expecting me to return the favor. As good as it had felt earlier—my cock in his mouth, coming down his throat—it was tender moments like this that meant the most to me. He made me feel special. Cared for. Worthy.

For someone who'd just figured out his demisexuality a few weeks ago, I was in awfully deep.

After toweling off and dressing, we hopped in the truck and headed back to the city. Zach texted his dad, seeking updates on the girls and checking to see if they wanted us to bring them food.

We arrived at the hospital around eight o'clock, arms loaded with bags of burgers and fries from the drive-thru down the street. Mandy had been awake for about twenty minutes mid-afternoon but otherwise had slept. The doctors said that was normal, that her body needed the rest to heal. With Drea, there was no change. I tried to be grateful that she hadn't gotten worse, but I knew Zach was worried. Having your sister sedated like that was scary.

We stopped outside Drea's room first. There was a moment before Mr. Jacobs realized we were there when we observed him completely unguarded. He wore black joggers and a Creighton hoodie. I'd never seen him dressed so casually, though that wasn't as startling as the look on his face. He was leaning forward, with his elbows on his knees, hands clasped in front of his mouth, and his body angled toward Drea's bed. There were circles under his eyes and his usually perfectly styled hair was a mess, but the shattered look in his eyes had us standing frozen in the hallway. I'd never seen a man look so...lost.

Zach stepped up to the door, knocking gently against the glass. His dad looked up, the corners of his mouth tipping up ever so slightly, but that tragic look remained as if the mask he'd worn all these years had been irreparably shattered. He rose, coming toward us, and we backed up so he could join us in the hallway.

Feeling like an outsider, I tapped Zach on the shoulder, then nodded toward Mandy's door, indicating that I'd head down there. He nodded in acknowledgment, and I walked away.

My parents came out of the room as soon as they saw me, and after confirming with one of the nurses that they'd let us know if Mandy woke up, the three of us headed to the waiting room to eat our food. I couldn't help but look into Drea's room as we passed, noting that Zach and his father appeared to be talking, heads bowed slightly, bodies angled toward each other.

We found a table in a corner of the space and spread our food out. By that point, our burgers were lukewarm, but I didn't think we were tasting much of anything anyway. We ate quietly, lost in thought and worry, and I was grateful I wasn't required to make conversation.

My phone vibrated in my pocket indicating an incoming call, so I set my burger down and wiped my hands with a napkin before retrieving it, surprised to see the call was coming from the station. I stepped away from my family as I swiped to answer. "Hello?"

"Hey, Jason. This is Andrew. We just wanted to see how your sister and her friend are doing."

"Oh, um, Mandy's hanging in there. They had to put rods in her leg, and she had some internal bleeding they had to manage, but she was awake for a little bit today, which the doctors said was a good sign. Drea—my boyfr—um, my sister's friend who was driving the car, is still under sedation."

I'd almost referred to Zach as my boyfriend. I wasn't sure where he stood on that label, but I realized that's how I thought of him, had been thinking of him for a while now. I just hadn't said it aloud. When he'd left in January, we'd agreed we wouldn't see anyone while we explored this... thing between us, but we'd also agreed not to label it either. Now, though, the label felt right for what he meant to me. It was something we probably should discuss.

"I'm sorry to hear that, man. That's tough."

"Yeah," I said awkwardly.

"And how are *you* holding up?"

I felt the flush start to burn up the back of my neck. "Oh, um, I'm fine. Thanks for asking." I wondered if there'd ever come a time when I'd stop feeling embarrassed and guilty about how I'd reacted on-scene. "I'm sorry...for the way I acted yesterday."

"None of that, now. There's no need to apologize. Any of us might have had a similar reaction had it been someone we cared about."

"You're not...mad?"

"Nah, man. None of us are. We just want *you* to take care of yourself. You let us know when you're ready to come back. And Chief's got some numbers for a therapist he recommends everyone see when they go through something like this."

"Seriously? You guys want me back?"

"Yeah. We do. Don't be so hard on yourself, okay?"

I snorted. "I'll work on it."

"Cool. I'll touch base later in the week to check in."

"Okay. Um, thanks for calling."

"Talk soon."

"Bye."

I disconnected the call, a lump forming in my throat at the kindness he'd shown me, that all of them had shown me if he were to be believed. I blew out a breath, running my fingers through my hair a couple of times, the tiniest bit of weight lifting from my shoulders. Mandy and Drea weren't out of the woods, and I was still worried about my ability to handle the job after all this, but at least I knew I still had a place waiting when I was ready.

I returned to my family, my mom looking up with a question in her eyes. "Everything okay?"

"Yeah. That was just the station. They were, uh, checking on the girls. And I guess me too."

"Well, that's sweet of them."

"Yeah. They're good folks. Said I could take the time I needed and come back when I was ready."

Her eyes softened. I was sure she was recalling our conversation from this morning. God, that seemed like three days ago. "That's good, honey."

I nodded, and we finished our meal.

36

ZACH

Jason and I remained at the hospital until around midnight, when his mom shooed Jason home to get some rest. He tried arguing with her, suggesting she needed the rest more than he did, but she wasn't having it, so he'd finally relented.

We fell into bed just after one a.m., Jason pulling me in close like he had earlier in the afternoon. He was asleep almost instantly, the rhythmic sound of his breathing comforting, though my mind wouldn't quiet as easily.

I couldn't stop thinking about the devastated look in my father's eye when we'd arrived at the hospital that evening. Never had I seen him like that, not even when Mom died. I knew he'd been sad. I'd seen his tears at the funeral. But back then, there'd been a stoicism about him, as if he refused to allow any cracks in his facade. I wasn't sure whether that had been for our benefit or because he'd simply been too stubborn to break, but whatever the reason, it had further widened the rift between us. He'd become hard. Difficult. Cold. And at least where I was concerned, impossible to please.

Tonight, though, he'd seemed...unmoored. A man lost

at sea with no hope for salvation. We'd exchanged a few words, mostly an update on Drea's condition, but otherwise, we'd sat in silence, lost in thought. He barely touched the food I'd brought him. When Jason had come by to tell me his mom was sending him home, I'd been torn. On the one hand, I wanted to escape, to flee the room so heavy with worry. The weight of my father's fear was suffocating.

But on the other hand, I was hesitant to leave him alone. It was an odd feeling to want to be there for him, though it shouldn't have been. He was my father, and I loved him. But just a few months ago, I'd wanted nothing more than to escape his presence and run away to UCLA to put as much distance between us as possible. And now, I didn't want to leave him. I didn't want him to suffer in silence. And I didn't want to leave Drea either. What if she took a turn for the worse and I slept through it? If Dad had to be the one to tell me, what would that do to him?

In the end, Dad urged me to go, insisting he was fine and I should get some more rest. I'd relented, if only because I didn't want to add to his stress with an argument.

So there I lay in Jason's arms, wide awake and staring at the ceiling. He'd told me about the call from the fire station today and I was glad to hear of it. I hoped that, with time, he'd see that his reaction in that moment wasn't indicative of his ability to perform his job. It was the action of a man with a huge heart who cared deeply about those who were important to him.

I thought I'd become one of those important people. He was definitely important to me. So much so that it was overwhelming at times. We'd started this thing just a couple of weeks ago, and at the time, it had felt big. Important. But it had been fun and exciting too. Those fun and flirty feelings had deepened, stretched their roots down and down and down, so deep it'd take a hurricane to rip them out.

It was terrifying to feel something that big, that deep, that strong.

I yawned long and hard, my jaw cracking and eyes watering from the force of it. Jason mumbled something in his sleep, his hold tightening around me for a moment before relaxing again. I tried to focus on his breathing, matching my own breaths with his, until eventually, I slipped under too.

I AWOKE with Jason's hand wrapped around my cock, his grip loose as he lazily stroked me. He'd pulled the band of my briefs down below my balls, but I wiggled around, yanking them over my ass and down my thighs, giving him more freedom of movement. He chuckled in my ear but, thankfully, continued to stroke. "I take it this is okay?"

"Mmm. I told you yesterday my body is yours to explore." I shoved my ass back into his erection just to emphasize the point and was rewarded with a low groan. My cock jumped in his hand at the sound.

Abruptly, I pulled out of his grasp and rolled over to face him. "I have a better idea," I said, tugging at the waistband of his boxer briefs. He obliged by pulling them off and tossing them on the floor.

"What did you have in mind?" I gave him a smacking kiss on the lips before yanking my underwear the rest of the way off and tossing them aside. I loved how open he was becoming. How unreserved and willing to explore he was.

"Do you have lube?"

His face colored adorably. "No. I don't, um, have...that."

I brushed a kiss across his lips. "We need to get you some." I waggled my eyebrows ridiculously, hoping to win one of his smiles. I was rewarded with a small one and an even deeper blush. "What about lotion?"

He leaned back, opened the bedside table drawer behind him, and pulled out a small bottle of generic unscented body lotion. He held it out to me with an eyebrow raised, silently asking if this was what I was looking for.

"Perfect," I said, taking it from him and flipping the cap. I poured a dollop in my hand, snapped the cap shut, and tossed it aside, out of the way. "Lie on your back."

Once he was in position, I swung my leg over his hips and lowered myself until our dicks were aligned, both of us groaning at the contact. I watched his face as I took both of us in hand and smeared the lotion around us. His eyes were glued to the sight of our cocks together, a little crease of concentration forming on his brow while his mouth hung open. I wanted to look down, to see what he saw, but I couldn't take my eyes off his face. His eyes flashed up to mine, and I caught a glimpse of those blue depths before they fluttered shut and he tilted his head back on a moan.

At last, I looked down, watching as I glided my fist up and down our shafts in slow, deliberate motions. We were both cut and long, though he was thicker, and the sight of our dicks together, tunneling through my fist, was quite possibly the hottest thing I'd ever seen.

I began moving faster, rolling my hips with the motion, my balls brushing against his with the movement. Little zaps of sensation surged through me with each stroke, the combined friction of my hand and his dick, along with those brushes of our balls, an exquisite kind of torture.

I continued to ramp up the pace, my strokes becoming

more and more frantic as I chased my orgasm. With the way Jason was whimpering and pumping his hips along with me, I suspected he was close as well. "Come on, baby. Let go. Come for me."

His thighs tensed beneath me, his entire body going rigid as hot ropes of cum spurted from his cock, landing on his chest and abdomen. I continued stroking, moments later mixing my cum with his as my dick erupted all over him. I gritted my teeth, doing my best to keep myself upright as my thighs shook from the effort.

Jason leaned up, wrapped his arms around me, and pulled me down for a sloppy kiss. I could feel the mess we'd made smushed between our bellies as our tongues tangled and teased. I pulled away, resting my forehead against his, smiling as we tried to catch our breaths.

"Did you get that idea from porn?"

"Yes, actually. I've wanted to try it with you since the first time I saw it."

He chuckled. "Yeah? What other ideas have you been wanting to try?"

I waggled my eyebrows. "Mmm. You'll have to wait and see."

He tilted his lips up, brushing them against mine. "Can't wait."

37

JASON

WE SPENT most of Wednesday at the hospital, Zach working on the homework his professors had sent while he was missing classes while I fiddled around on my phone, trying not to go crazy. I ran out and got food for us, checked on my mom and dad, and sat in on doctor visits when they updated us on Mandy's progress.

Zach's Aunt Amy came by, insisting Mr. Jacobs take a break and head home for a shower and some rest. He protested, but she had this odd combination of a sunny disposition mixed with fuck around and find out that somehow had everyone bending to her will. It was kind of impressive.

Mandy was a little more alert, awake for longer periods, though she also seemed to be in more pain. It was hard to watch her suffer, but she was a trooper, pushing through it as best she could. She still wasn't strong enough to get out of bed, but they did have her do some exercises to help with circulation. She slept for quite a while after that.

It was evening when she woke again, and it was just me in the room with her this time. Mom and Dad had run home for a shower and a change of clothes with promises to bring back dinner. Zach was spending some time with his Aunt Amy, watching over Drea, who was still under sedation. There had been talk of beginning to wean Drea off the sedatives, but I wasn't sure if they'd started that process or not.

"Hey, big brother."

I looked up with a smile, delighted to hear her voice. Until now, I hadn't really had a chance to speak with her when she was awake. "Hey, sis. How're you feeling?"

"Like shit."

I chuckled. "Probably going to be that way for a bit. Want me to page the nurse?"

"Maybe in a little bit. I'm okay for now."

I leaned forward and took her hand. "I've missed you."

"Yeah?" Her face registered a mix of surprise and delight.

"Of course. Who else do I have to torture?"

"Dumbass," she said, but her eyes were alight with humor. It was such a goddamn relief to see.

Her smile slid off her face. "How's Drea? Mom wouldn't tell me much other than the basics."

I swallowed hard. "You know she's sedated?"

She nodded.

"There's not much to tell. I think they're going to try to start bringing her out of it soon, but it could take a couple of days before she actually wakes up."

Her face fell, and her eyes became glassy with unshed tears. "It's my fault, J."

"What?"

"I was fucking around with the Bluetooth, giving her shit about her terrible taste in music. I had to have the last laugh."

"There was a deer. She tried to swerve to miss it. That's not your fault."

"She might have seen it sooner if she hadn't been distracted. She would have had more time to react." Tears ran down her face.

"Or she might have hit it head-on. There are a million 'could've been' scenarios. You can't carry this on your shoulders. It could have happened to anyone."

I grabbed a tissue and handed it to her. She wiped at her eyes but didn't say anything else.

"Hey." I waited for her to look up at me. "It's not your fault, sis. Not anymore than it's the deer's for being in the road or Drea's for rolling the car. There's a reason they call it an accident. Sometimes accidents happen, and it's not anyone's fault."

"I'm just so scared." The tears were flowing again. "She's my best friend, J. Like, the absolute best. I don't know how I survived Astaire before she moved to town. And I don't want to do the rest of high school without her."

I sat on the edge of her bed, careful not to jostle her leg or bump any of the other wires she was still hooked up to. I brushed her hair off her face and tipped her chin so she'd look at me. "She's strong, Mandy. A survivor. She will push through this, and you girls will be back to annoying me with your late-night sleepovers."

"I just want her to be okay."

"I know. Me too."

MANDY'S BOUT of tears wore her out, and she fell asleep not long after. Zach and I ate with our families, then returned to Astaire once again. The worry over his sister and his dad was starting to take a toll on him. I could see it in the circles under his eyes and how he carried himself, as if he were carrying the weight of their well-being on his shoulders. I knew the stress of missing classes was eating at him too. He was doing as much of the work as he could remotely, but it was difficult to make up lectures and group projects when you were fifteen hundred miles away.

Wanting nothing more than to take care of him, I sent him into the bathroom to shower, hoping the hot water might wash away some of the stress of the day. In the meantime, I put fresh sheets on my bed, then rounded up several candles, spreading them around my bedroom. My mom had a thing for scented candles. Hopefully, the different fragrances wouldn't become cloying, but I could only work with what I had.

Zach entered the room looking sexy as fuck, his hair glistening with moisture and wearing nothing but a towel wrapped around his waist. It was amazing how I'd never found anyone sexy before, but the closer Zach and I got—the stronger our bond—the more attractive I found him. In that moment, I didn't think I'd ever seen anyone look as beautiful as he did with his brown eyes glowing in the candlelight and water droplets trailing down his toned chest. I was pretty sure I was more than a little in love with him. Probably had been for a while, but my dumbass was apparently slow on the uptake when it came to lust and love and everything *Zach*.

"What is this?" he asked, brows raised in surprise as he took in the candles spread out around the room.

I reached out and took his hand, pulling him toward me. I gave him a light kiss, then gestured to the bed. "Lose the towel and lie on your stomach."

"You gonna ravish me, Whitt?" The corner of his mouth drew up in a sexy smirk.

I leaned in close, my mouth just inches from his. "I'm gonna take care of you." I pressed my lips to his forehead, then pulled back, hooking a finger behind the edge of his towel and tugging it free. "No more questions," I said, nodding toward the bed.

He smiled but did as I asked, settling himself on his stomach with his hands at his sides. I stripped down to my briefs, knowing I needed to keep the barrier between us, or I'd be too tempted to skip the massage altogether and ravish him as he'd suggested.

I kneeled on the bed, swinging one leg over his hips to straddle his waist. Bending forward, I trailed soft kisses along one shoulder, moving across his back to the other side. Then I moved to his neck, starting at his hairline, and began a new path downward, kissing each nob of his spine until I reached his tailbone. He sighed, and I could already feel some of the tension melting away from his body.

Bending forward again, I kissed his cheek, then ran my fingers through his hair. I repeated the gesture over and over, each time choosing a new path through the dark strands, gratified to see him sinking into the pillow a little more.

I paused to grab the lotion we'd left on the bedside table this morning. I poured a nickel-sized dollop, then rubbed my hands together, warming the liquid before I placed my hands on Zach's shoulders and began working the lotion into his skin. I didn't really know what I was doing. I'd certainly never given or received a massage before, so I was moving completely on instinct. But given the way he groaned when I pressed my thumb into a knot I found near the base of his neck, I figured I was on the right track.

I continued working him over, using my thumbs to knead his muscles, letting his moans and groans guide me as I moved from his shoulders farther down his obliques, then to his lower back. My cock was straining in my briefs, my tip peeking out of my waistband, turned on by the feel of his body beneath mine, but I ignored it. While Zach had shown me orgasms were a good distraction, that wasn't what this was about. Or at least not at this moment. Maybe this massage would lead there, maybe not. I just wanted to show him how much he was cared for. He'd awakened a sexual side in me I hadn't known I had, but that wasn't all he was to me, and I wanted to show him that.

His moans turned to sighs, then eventually faded to the soft sound of regular exhalations as he finally relaxed into sleep. I slid off him, rubbing the rest of the lotion into my own hands, then made my way around the room to blow out each of the candles, plunging the room into darkness. Zach was lying on top of the comforter, so I grabbed a throw off the foot of the bed, lay next to him, and pulled it over us. He let out a contented "mmm" and burrowed his face into my shoulder. I pressed a kiss to the top of his hair and whispered, "Sleep, honey. I've got you."

My last thought before I drifted off was just how lucky I was to have found him.

38

ZACH

THURSDAY FELT like a carbon copy of Wednesday. In fact, all the days since I'd arrived in Omaha felt like a monotonous blur of endless worry layered between periods of staring at my computer screen in a vain attempt to stay caught up on homework, runs to local fast food establishments, and watching over Drea, willing her to wake up. The doctors had begun weaning her off the sedatives but said it could still be a few more days before she was fully out of it.

The only thing that kept me sane was Jason. He spent time visiting with Mandy and his parents, of course, but the rest of his time was spent by my side. He didn't say much and didn't ask me to either. He was simply...there. It meant everything.

The nights were anything but monotonous. Each evening, we'd escaped to his house in Astaire, sometimes exploring each other's bodies and other times simply cuddled up like bears in hibernation. The intimacy I had with him was unlike anything I'd ever experienced. The relationships I'd had with girls in high school—the feelings I'd had for them—seemed childish and insignificant compared to how I felt about Jason. With him…the intensity of my emotions, the width and breadth of them…were bigger than the both of us.

We sipped coffees as we rode the elevator to the ICU on Friday morning. We'd showered together that morning, jacking each other off until we'd painted our bellies with cum before washing it all down the drain. We'd traded lazy kisses until the water had started to run cold, then toweled off and dressed before returning to Omaha.

We stepped out of the elevator with hands clasped, pulling up short at the sight of Mrs. Whitt waiting to head down. Her eyes darted to our joined hands then back up again. A slow smile spread across her face as she said, "Good morning, boys. I was just heading out to grab some breakfast. Do you want anything?"

"No. We're good. Grabbed a bagel with our coffees." He held out his coffee with his free hand in confirmation.

She nodded. "Great. Back in a bit."

We watched as the doors closed and then turned toward each other.

"Did you just come out to your mom?"

"Maybe? She definitely clocked us holding hands, right?"

"Pretty sure, yeah."

He looked a little shell-shocked.

"You good?" I asked.

"Yeah. I don't know what I expected, but that wasn't it." He chuckled, then rubbed a hand through his short crop of hair. "I should probably talk to her later. Just to be sure."

"I don't know. She seemed pretty happy about it."

"Probably just confirmed what she already suspected New Year's Day." He squeezed my hand. "Come on. Let's go see how the girls are doing."

We walked down the hall but paused just outside the girls' rooms. Yesterday, they'd started allowing Mandy out of bed for short periods using crutches. They were optimistic she might be released tomorrow, barring any major setbacks, and I knew the Whitts were looking forward to having her home. I'd overheard Mr. Whitt mention he was going to spend some time later today getting the guest room on the main floor ready so she wouldn't have to go up and down the stairs to her second-floor bedroom.

Jason shot a quick glance into Drea's room, where we could see my father sitting with his head back and eyes closed. Jason gave me a quick peck on the lips, then squeezed my hand. "Text me if you need anything."

I squeezed his hand back. "Say hey to Mandy for me."

"Maybe you can come say hi a little later."

"Yeah, maybe." I offered a sad smile, then released him and opened the door to Drea's room.

Dad's eyes opened immediately, letting me know he likely hadn't actually been sleeping. He gave me a small smile, but it didn't reach his eyes. "Did you eat anything?" I asked.

"I grabbed a breakfast sandwich from the cafeteria this morning. The coffee down there is heinous."

"Truly awful." I felt bad sipping my coffee right in front of him. "I'm sorry. I should have brought you some."

"Not a big deal."

I fiddled with the hem on my hoodie—well, Jason's hoodie. Turned out I really had done a shitty job packing and hadn't brought appropriate clothes for winter in the Midwest. Jason had loaned me an Astaire High football hoodie that was way too big on me. I didn't mind. It smelled like him.

"Any updates on Drea?"

"The doctors did whatever it is that they do and said her brain function looks good, but it's really up to her to wake up on her own. She's showing some good signs of responsiveness to light and sound but hasn't opened her eyes yet."

He blew out a breath. "I know all the signs look promising, and the doctors seem confident she'll come out of this, but I can't help but worry she'll take a turn or something will go wrong." He scrubbed his hands over his face. "I can't lose her. I can't lose another person I love." His voice cracked on the last word, nearly breaking my heart in two.

It was hard to see him like this. Dad had always been stoic, rarely showing emotion, even after Mom died. To see him consumed by so much fear and worry was heartbreaking. Yet there was a small part of me that wondered if he'd be nearly as distraught if it were me lying in that bed.

"I think she's going to be okay. I have to believe that. She's the fiercest, strongest person I've ever met."

"Just like your mother," he said softly, causing me to turn my head sharply.

"You never talk about her. About Mom."

He blew out a breath. "It's...hard. She was...everything to me."

"What about us?" I blurted. "If she was your everything, where does that leave room for me and Drea?"

He closed his eyes, pain etching itself into his features, the lines and grooves around his eyes and mouth deepening, making him look older than his forty-five years. "I know. And I'm sorry. I just...when I lost her, I sort of shut down. I've never been good at expressing my emotions. I've never been good at letting them out. So I just locked everything up tight. It was the only way I knew how to keep going."

"I get that, Dad. But you said 'when *I* lost her' when it

should have been *we*. *We* lost her. You left me and Drea to process the grief of losing our *mother* on our own."

I ran my hands through my hair in frustration. I could feel the old anger and resentment bubbling to the surface, though I tried to tamp it down. I hated that we were having this conversation now. In this place with Drea in this condition. But now that the door had been opened, I wasn't willing to close it. "Sometimes it felt like I lost both of you."

It was his turn for those eyes to flash to mine. He opened his mouth and closed it, clearly at a loss as to what to say.

Feeling brave and maybe a little bolder than I had any right, I laid it all out there. It felt like it was now or never. "You've been hard on me my whole life, but these last couple of years, it's felt nearly impossible to please you. I lost my biggest cheerleader, my most vocal supporter. Win or lose, Mom was always there, encouraging me, high-fiving me, putting me back in my place when I needed it. I lost all of that in a flash, and then, to add insult to injury, you doubled down on your criticisms. Nothing I did was good enough. If I scored one goal in a game, it should have been two."

I paced in front of him, agitated and too worked up to remain seated. To his credit, he didn't interrupt. "UCLA was a terrible pick for college. You don't like my hair. My shirt isn't right. I don't say the right things. I don't hang out with the right people. I'm sure you'd love to know I'm dating Jason." I stopped in my tracks, turning to face him. "Yep, I'm dating a guy. I'm bi. How does that fit into your mold of the perfect son?"

Jesus. How had we gotten here? One moment, we'd been talking about Drea being a fighter like Mom, and the next, I was unloading nineteen years of anger and hurt and resentment all over him. Then, like a cherry on top of a really twisted dessert, I came out. Just blurted out my sexuality in the middle of my sister's ICU room. What had I possibly been hoping to achieve?

I couldn't look at him, but I couldn't quite look away either. I took three deep breaths, trying to cool my heated temper, and when he still hadn't responded, I said, "You know what? I think I need a breather. I'm going for a walk."

I moved toward the door, my strides long and quick with my desire to escape.

"Zach." The softness in Dad's tone had me pulling up short, hesitating with my hand resting on the door handle.

"If you want to take a breather, that's fine. I think we could both use it. But I don't want you to walk out of here thinking I have a problem with you and Jason. He's a good kid. And I'll always be grateful he was on-scene with Drea. I don't care that you're with him."

I nodded once, swallowing past the lump in my throat, then walked out.

THE THING about calling my dad out on his treatment of me was that it didn't make me feel any better. He'd been hurting all week. I'd worried over him almost as much as I'd worried over Drea. And I'd still taken the time to shove all my resentment in his face when he was at his lowest. Not only that, but I hadn't given him a chance to respond before walking out and leaving him alone.

I'd been tempted to go to Jason as soon as I walked out of Drea's room, but I decided I needed some time alone. I'd spent almost every moment with Jason this week, which had been amazing, but using him as an emotional crutch wasn't fair.

In the time it took to ride the elevator to the main floor, I deflated like a balloon. Gone was the self-righteous indignation I'd burned with moments before, and in its place was a burning desire to know *why*. I knew my father loved me. So why had he been so critical? So distant? So cold? I hadn't given him the chance to explain.

I walked to the cafeteria and bought a couple bottles of the sparkling water I knew my father liked, thinking they'd serve as a peace offering upon my return.

As I approached Drea's room, thinking over what I might say to my dad, I noticed the movement of hospital personnel inside the room that had my heart beating faster and my footsteps picking up the pace.

Sliding the door open, I walked in to see a nurse and a doctor standing over Drea. The doctor seemed to be speaking to her, but I couldn't hear what she was saying. I glanced at my dad, hoping he could fill in the blanks, but he was bent forward in his chair, obviously trying to see what was happening.

Cautiously, I walked over to stand next to my father, not wanting to be in the way but needing to know whether I'd just walked into something good or bad.

Absently, I handed him the sparkling water. "What's going on?" I asked, my voice just loud enough for my dad to hear.

"She opened her eyes," he said without looking at me. "It was just for a few seconds, and she didn't seem aware of where she was, but they were open."

His voice held a tinge of hope that had tears pricking the corners of my eyes. When he grabbed my hand, squeezing it tight, a couple of those tears escaped unchecked down my cheeks.

The doctor and the nurse remained for a moment

longer, then turned to debrief us, saying this was normal and would likely happen with more frequency over the coming days. That it was a good sign of progress. We thanked her, and they exited the room, leaving us alone once again.

My father was still holding my hand.

I looked down, then back at him only to find him staring at our hands as well. "I'm sorry," he said, his voice quiet. His eyes flicked up to mine. "I'm sorry," he repeated, "for being so hard on you. For making you feel like you weren't good enough."

I sat in the chair next to him but still didn't release his hand. I didn't want to break the connection.

"Can you help me understand why?"

"I don't want to make excuses."

"I respect that. But I really think it would help to know."

He sighed. "Tell me about Jason. How did that happen?"

"You're changing the subject?"

"I promise, I have a reason for asking."

Finally releasing his hand, I opened my sparkling water and took a sip. "Right after Thanksgiving, when the team was flying back after that loss against Clemson, my roommate mistook Jason for my boyfriend, and I guess it got me thinking about the possibility. Next thing I knew, we were kissing on New Year's Eve."

"Did you know you were bi before this?"

"No. I had no clue."

"Are you in love with him?"

I was surprised he asked, though not because I hadn't thought about it myself. I'd been giving it a lot of thought this week, actually. "I think I might be. It's kind of new. But I know I haven't felt this way about anyone else I've dated."

"Did you know it only took me a week to fall in love with your mom?"

"I knew you only dated for about a year before you got married."

He took a sip of his sparkling water. "It was your Aunt Amy who introduced us."

I knew this. Mom had told me. "Aunt Amy was a law clerk in your office, right?"

"Yeah. I was young, just a year out of law school, and there were several of us in our mid- to upper-twenties who worked in that office. We liked to socialize outside of work. Your mom was working at the bank across the street, and Aunt Amy invited her to meet us for happy hour. One drink turned into two, and then drinks turned into dinner. We talked for hours, and I was up so late that I almost overslept the next day.

"I'd never met anyone who could get me talking about anything and completely lose track of time. But with her...it was like everything else in the world melted away. That first night, I hadn't even noticed when everyone else tabbed out. I'd been entirely focused on her.

"We saw a movie the next day. Went to a baseball game the day after that. There was brunch and bowling and another night at happy hour. She had this exuberant personality and a radiant smile. I wanted nothing more than to spend every moment soaking up her energy. By the end of the week, I knew she was it for me. I told myself to wait at least six months to propose, but I only made it two, just for her to accept the proposal and then ask, 'What were you waiting for?'"

I was captivated by the way he spoke of her, as if she had been the single most important thing in his life. And I supposed she had been. That was what he was trying to tell me.

"Marrying her was the best day of my life, or at least until you were born, and then Drea a few years later. If I thought I loved her before, my feelings couldn't compare to the joy of watching her become your mother. While I fumbled with diapers and feedings and bedtime routines, your mom handled all of it like she was born to do it. And I don't mean that in some misogynistic bullshit way, implying it's the woman's job, but in a way that honors her skill as a mother. She always knew what to do. And as you kids got older, what to say. I was very much in my element as a lawyer, but I floundered as a father. Your mom tried to help me, tried to coach me. She inspired me to be better."

He rolled the bottle of sparkling water back and forth in his hands. I didn't think he was even aware he was doing it. "And then she was gone. My best friend, my partner, my *wife*…gone. It felt like someone had reached into my chest and yanked out my heart right there in front of me. I was devastated. And there you and Drea were, shell-shocked by her loss. And you weren't little. I think I might have been able to handle it if you'd been little, but you were teenagers. And as much as I tried to be the kind of dad you deserved, the kind of dad she'd be proud of, parenting a teenager was an absolute mystery to me.

"You talked back. You rolled your eyes. Sometimes, you outright defied me. And that was all while your mom was still here. When I—*we*—lost her, I was so scared you were going to go off the rails, I got even more strict. More insistent that you conform to my way.

"It was all in an effort to control the outcome. I had no control over your mom's death, so I think this was my way of overcompensating. If I controlled your lives, maybe I could save you from her fate."

I thought about what it might be like to lose Jason. To have him ripped from me. It hurt to breathe just thinking about it.

"I think I can understand some of that, Dad, but there are a couple of gaping holes in your premise. You suggest that applying control was an effort to keep me safe, but that's not exactly what you did. The type of control you exerted was pressure. It wasn't a strict curfew or an insistence that I only drove certain places at certain times—those things would make sense after losing Mom the way we did—what you did was demand I dress a certain way, get straight As, score the game-winning goal. None of those were meant to keep me safe. You just wanted the perfect son, and I was never gonna meet that standard."

He glanced over at Drea. "Your sister said the same thing to me right before Thanksgiving. She said she was afraid that if I didn't stop being such a dictator—her word—you wouldn't ever come back. We actually argued over it. She said a lot of things that were really hard to hear, but after she stormed out of the house and went to Mandy's, I had no choice but to think about what she'd said. I even called Aunt Amy, who laughed in my face for being so obtuse—also her word—but then gently pointed out all the ways I'd been too hard on you. She helped me see just how deep it had gotten."

That would explain some of the changes I'd seen in him since I'd left for school, but it still didn't make sense to me. "That still doesn't explain it though. I'm glad someone pointed it out to you. But I still don't understand *why*."

"I don't know how to explain it," he said with a sigh, frustration lacing his tone. "Your mom was so *good* at the mothering thing, and instead of trying to mimic what she did, mostly because I didn't know *how*, I tried to muscle my way through. If I applied pressure and exerted control, I could keep you on track to be the person she wanted you to be. You could chase your dreams and be successful."

I snorted an exasperated laugh. "But, Dad...all Mom ever wanted was for me to be happy. To be *me*. She wanted me to be successful, but she never defined what that success would look like because it wasn't up to her to decide. It was always *my* version of success. She wanted me to chase *my* dreams, not anyone else's. She pushed and nudged here and there, but it was only because I was a kid and she was trying to help me course correct. She never tried to push me onto a path I didn't want in the first place or to be someone I wasn't.

"And I think you missed something critical in the first place. You said the greatest day of your life was when you married Mom, at least until Drea and I were born. But even then, what gave you joy was watching Mom become a mother. It wasn't the joy of becoming a father yourself. It's like you were always happy to be on the sidelines and watch her shine, but you forgot to be invested in being a good dad as well. Supporting her in being a good mother isn't the same as *being* a good father."

He winced, but I continued, needing to make my point. I knew what I was saying was hurting him, but it needed to be said if there would ever be a path forward. "It feels like I grew up with two different dads. The one who was distant and sort of took a backseat to parenting and the one who tried to micromanage everything. Neither of those was the dad I wanted."

I ran my hand through my hair again, then looked him in the eye. "I want a relationship with you, Dad. I want to *know* you, and I want you to know me. I want you to ask how my game went rather than point out all the ways I could have been better. As if I don't already know those things. As if I don't already have coaches for that. I want to come home for breaks and sit on the dock with a cup of coffee and catch up on life. I want to laugh with you. We never laugh, Dad."

He'd turned his face away from me as I was talking, so I couldn't get a read on him. I couldn't tell if he was angry or upset or if he'd really even heard me. It was tempting to jump back in, to fill the silence, but I kept quiet, waiting to see how he'd respond.

After a moment, he scrubbed a hand over his face and rose, turning to face me. "I think it's my turn to take a breather."

I rose to stand so we could speak face-to-face. "Dad, I'm sorry, I just—"

He put a hand out to stop me. "You obviously had a lot you needed to get off your chest. And my first instinct is to shut you down and tell you how wrong you are. But that would be the hurt talking, and I don't want to do that anymore. So I'm going to run home, grab a shower, and check on some things at the house." He nodded toward Drea. "You'll call if anything changes?"

"Yeah, of course."

He squeezed my shoulder, then turned and walked out of the room.

39

JASON

I STOPPED by Drea's room just before lunch with a niggle of worry tapping on my brain like the incessant fly-by of a gnat that simply wouldn't leave you be. I'd texted Zach a couple of times since we'd gone in separate directions at the hospital but hadn't received a response. The messages were innocuous, unimportant things, but the lack of even a tapback reaction was unlike him.

When I entered the room, Zach was leaning back in his chair with his eyes closed, much like the way we'd found his dad earlier this morning. He opened those beautiful brown eyes as I approached, his mouth curling up in a small smile, sending my heart tripping over itself like it always did when he looked at me like that.

"Hey," I said.

"Hey." He raised his arms and kicked out his legs in a full-body stretch. I liked the way my hoodie looked on him. Liked the reminder that he was mine.

"How's she doing?" I asked, nodding toward Drea.

"She opened her eyes very briefly earlier this morning. Doctors came in and told us that would be happening more and more frequently as they pull back the sedatives. She's also had some twitching of her hands and feet, which they said were also good signs and totally normal."

"That's great news!" I was thrilled to hear it. I couldn't wait to tell Mandy.

"It is. Hopefully, she'll wake enough for me to say goodbye before I have to leave." My smile fell as my eyes flashed to his. "I spoke to my advisor a little while ago. I'm heading home first thing Sunday morning. I really can't afford to miss any more classes, and with Drea showing every sign of improvement, I don't really have an excuse for staying."

My stomach sank. It wasn't like I hadn't known this was coming. But we'd been in sort of a bubble this week, a really weird one full of intense highs and lows, and while I was absolutely ready to be rid of the lows, I wanted to hold on to those high moments just a little bit longer. "Makes sense. I'm gonna miss you."

"I know." He rose from his chair, standing close enough that his chest brushed against mine, his hands resting lightly on my hips. "I'm gonna miss you too. After this week, it's hard to imagine being separated. But I'm gonna be home in a couple of weeks like we planned before all this happened. We'll just have to find ways to make it work."

I nodded, relieved to know he was still as invested in this as I was. I leaned forward and kissed him but pulled back before we got carried away.

"Where's your dad? I was going to see if you wanted to go to lunch. Maybe get out of here for a little while."

A shadow passed over his face, making me wonder if something had gone down between them this morning. They'd been getting along so much better. I hoped I'd imagined it. "He ran home to shower and check on the house. I can't believe I haven't even been there since I've been home."

"We can stay there tonight instead of my house if you want?"

He wrapped his hands around my waist, and I did the same. "I kind of like staying at your house. Your room is... cozy. I don't know. It just feels like *us*."

I smiled, loving the sound of that. I liked having him in my space. And in my bed. I wasn't sure how I was going to sleep without him when he went back.

"I'm assuming you want to stay here with Drea until your dad gets back?" At his nod, I continued, "Why don't I grab us some lunch and bring it back?"

"That'd be good, thanks!"

I ran out to Runza, knowing how much he missed it when he was gone, and by the time I got back, Mr. Jacobs had returned. Zach and his dad were sitting side-by-side, talking quietly. I could tell from the way Zach held himself there was some tension between them. In fact, Mr. Jacobs was holding himself the same way. But they weren't arguing, so I hoped it was something they'd be able to resolve.

I held up the to-go bag outside the window, catching Zach's attention, and he came out, surprising me when he kissed me in greeting in front of the open doorway. I pulled away, shocked, but he only chuckled. "Dad knows. I told him this morning." His smile dropped. "Shit. Was that okay? I should have asked you first."

"It's fine. I talked to my mom and dad earlier. Exactly as I suspected, Mom wasn't surprised, which is why she didn't say anything when she caught us holding hands this morning. Dad was more oblivious, but he was cool with it. What did your dad say?"

I hoped my relationship with Zach wouldn't be another source of conflict for the two of them.

"He was cool with it. That was the easiest part of our conversation."

"Yeah?"

We sat at the table in the waiting area, spreading out our food and digging in.

"We talked about a lot of stuff, actually. I don't think we totally cleared the air, but it's a little less hazy, maybe?" He shook his head, chuckling. "That was really corny."

"Yup." I smiled at him before popping a french fry in my mouth.

He filled me in on the rest of the conversation about all the ways he'd felt his dad had been hard on him and how he hadn't been there when he'd needed him. I was really proud of him for laying it all out there, though I was surprised his father hadn't been more angry. As someone who preferred to keep the peace, I didn't know if I would have had the courage to lay it all out there like that. I would have feared hurting his dad's feelings or angering him. Maybe both.

But this was healthier, I thought. The wounds had already festered enough. Better to "clear the air" as Zach had said, while there was still a chance at salvaging the relationship.

"I'm proud of you," I told him as we worked through the last couple of fries.

"I don't know if it's something you should be proud of. Pretty sure I hurt him. And I'm not sure we're out of the woods yet. He barely spoke to me after he got back from the house."

"None of that can be easy to hear. It's also something that's going to take time to work through. This likely won't be the last conversation you guys have."

"Great."

I laughed. "Give him some time. Change and growth don't happen overnight. He's already shown you how much he's trying over the last couple of months."

"I just feel bad. I'm happy things between us have been better and I do think it was good to get all of that out there. I just hate hurting him. He really loved my mom, you know? A love like that... I wonder if he'll ever be over it."

I swallowed, my stomach tying itself in knots around the food I'd just eaten. I thought Zach and I could have that kind of epic love. The kind you saw in movies and heard about in fairytales. I didn't want to contemplate ever having to get over him. "I don't know if you're meant to get over something like that. You just have to figure out how to live with it."

He watched me with an intensity that made me want to squirm in my seat. Like he was trying to figure out the answer to a question that hadn't been asked. My phone buzzed in my pocket, breaking the silence, and I slid it out of my pocket, swiping it open to read the message.

ANDREW

Hey man. Just checking in. How are you doing?

Better thanks.

Mandy is going home tomorrow.

"Oh hey," I said, looking up at Zach, realizing we'd been so busy talking about his conversation with his dad that I hadn't told him the good news. "The doctors confirmed Mandy's going home tomorrow. They just want to keep her one more night to see if they can get her pain a little more under control."

"That's awesome!"

"She's nervous about navigating our house on crutches, and she'll still be out of school for at least another week, but she's excited to get out of here. You should go say hi."

"Yeah, let me just check in with Dad again. Make sure he doesn't need anything."

I nodded, then returned my attention to my phone, which had buzzed again with an incoming message.

That's great news! And how's her friend?

> She's not fully awake yet, but she's showing definite signs of progress

Glad to hear it

We miss you around here

> I miss you guys

> I think I'm ready to come back on Monday

That's great news!

You should give Chief a call to let him know

> Will do

See you Monday!

WE SPENT the rest of the afternoon splitting our time between Mandy's and Drea's rooms. Mandy was still somewhat subdued compared to her normal bubbly self, but she was much more animated than she'd been earlier in the week. She and Zach chatted, catching up on what he'd been up to since he'd been back in LA and her eyes had danced with happiness when we'd told her about coming out to our parents.

The only thing missing had been Drea's presence. Those girls had become so inseparable that it was odd to see one without the other. And they had a symbiotic sort of energy that was incomplete with one of them missing.

We'd spent the last hour before we'd left the hospital in Drea's room. She'd had her eyes open for a longer period this time, though she hadn't appeared to recognize anyone or be aware of her surroundings, which was almost scarier than her lying there asleep. But the doctors had reassured us this was normal and seemed encouraged by her progress.

Zach had been quiet on the car ride, seemingly lost in his thoughts. I didn't blame him. He had a lot to think about. We both did. Watching our sisters fight through their injuries, taking our relationship to the next level while going back to the long-distance thing...not to mention his conversation with his dad and dealing with all the make-up coursework, while I was looking at a return to my EMT training. It was a lot.

We were about twenty minutes outside of Astaire, riding with my hand resting on his knee while little snowflakes danced in the headlights, when Zach piped up, his voice hesitant. "I know what I said earlier about staying at your house, but do you think we could stay at mine tonight?"

I squeezed his thigh. "Yeah, of course. I'll just swing by my house and grab a change of clothes."

"Thanks."

We stopped at my house, Zach waiting in the car while I ran inside and packed an overnight bag, taking a moment to repack his bag with his personal effects that he'd left at my house throughout the week. When I returned to the truck, he was turned away from me, staring out the passenger side window with his forehead resting on the glass. I put my hand on his shoulder. "Hey. You okay?"

At that, he finally turned toward me, offering a small smile that didn't quite reach his eyes. "Yeah. I think the week's just catching up with me."

"I feel that." I squeezed his shoulder, then threw the truck in reverse and pulled out of the drive.

Unsurprisingly, his house was dark when we pulled up. The lights under the eaves were on, likely for security purposes, but the inside of the house was dark, giving it a lonely feel.

As we walked in, flipping switches as we went, the air felt stale, and even though Zach had mentioned the cleaners had come by a couple of days ago and his dad had been here at least a couple of times, it had a vacant air about it. Zach didn't seem to notice as he continued to trudge down the hall toward his room.

"You wanna grab a shower?"

"I just want to go to bed."

"Alright." We got ready for bed, brushing our teeth and undressing without speaking. I tried to tell myself that his silence was just as he'd said—the week catching up to him—but I couldn't help but think this felt deeper. Like he was withdrawing.

Shrugging off that thought, we climbed into his bed, and as usual, I pulled him into me, gratified when he came willingly, seeming to finally relax for the first time all evening.

"Goodnight, honey," I whispered into his hair, kissing him softly just behind his ear.

He wiggled a little, burrowing in closer. "Mmm. Goodnight."

40

ZACH

I woke with a start, sitting up in bed and gasping for air as the images from the dream continued to flash through my mind.

There was a car upside down in a ditch, with all the windows busted out and glass spread across the highway, sparkling in the moonlight like glitter.

"No, no, no, no, no," I muttered to myself like a mantra as I raced to get to the nondescript car.

The harder I tried to run, the farther away the car seemed to be, like I was running on a treadmill rather than pavement faded and cracked from the elements. It was a black sedan, unlike any car we'd ever owned, yet I knew someone I cared about was inside. I blinked, and suddenly, I was right next to the car, my feet wet and muddy as if I'd slid down the embankment trying to get to it, though I had no memory of that happening. I yanked open the door to find my mother in the seat, eyes closed and head bleeding. And though the car had been upside down when I'd been running toward it, it was suddenly right side up.

"Mom," I called out, reaching for her, trying to figure out if she was alive or dead, but as soon as I touched her, I realized the face I was now looking at was Drea's. I gasped, pushing her long hair out of her face, trying to see how bad the head wound was, coming away with blood all over my hand.

I stood up, looking around, straining my ears for the sound of emergency vehicles. "Help!" I called out, though we were in the middle of nowhere, so it wasn't likely anyone would hear me. "Somebody help me! Please! We need help!"

I leaned back down, peering into the car, but the face of the driver had changed again, and this time, it was Jason. "No! Baby, no! Not you!" I reached in, clenching his shirt in my fists, heedless of the blood on my hands as tears ran down my face and I sobbed frantically. "Wake up, J. You have to wake up. Please WAKE UP!"

I blinked my eyes rapidly, trying to adjust to the darkness of the room. *It was a dream*, I reminded myself, still struggling to get my breathing under control. I turned back, looking over my shoulder at the sleeping form of the man I was pretty sure I was in love with, reassured that he was still here and very much alive.

I scrubbed a hand over my face, trying to shake off the grip the dream still had on me. My breathing had slowed to a more reasonable rate, though I could still feel my heart hammering in my chest. Knowing I wouldn't be able to go back to sleep for a while and not wanting to wake Jason, I quietly rose from the bed, crossing into the bathroom to get a drink of water.

Feeling a little more settled, I stepped back into my room, pulling on Jason's hoodie and rubbing my hands up and down my arms to warm up. I wasn't sure if there was a chill in the room or if my chill was due to the remnants of the dream. Either way, I was definitely unsettled, and Jason's lingering scent embedded in the hoodie comforted my rattled nerves.

I stepped over to the window, looking out over the lake, which had always brought me peace. Snow was falling a bit harder now, blanketing the trees and banks of the lake in white, while the water remained a dark black mass in the center. It was eerily beautiful.

I hadn't been lying when I'd told Jason the week had caught up with me. The conversations I'd had with my father this morning had left me feeling heavy with worry and anxious over the hurt I'd caused him. He'd been politely distant the rest of the afternoon, making it difficult to tell if he was still processing or if I'd pushed him away for good. Add in the discussion I'd had with my advisor, and I'd turned into a knot of worry.

My professors understood my situation, but there was still no substitute for being present in class, and my advisor had kindly but firmly let me know that the sooner I returned, the better. I'd booked my return flight after lunch, hating that it meant I might leave Drea before she was truly awake and dreading the moment I'd have to leave Jason.

He'd become my rock this week. I'd come to depend on his quiet, steady presence, turning to him when I found myself upset or worried or just needing some comfort. I wasn't sure how I would survive without his big bear hugs or sleep without being wrapped up in his arms.

My father had asked me if I was in love with Jason, and I couldn't help but think about the answer to that question now. I'd said *I might be*, but as I'd thought about it throughout the afternoon, I'd become more and more convinced the answer was *yes*.

No one had ever made me feel the things Jason did. I'd

never experienced the kind of effortless intimacy I did with him. Not just sexual intimacy, which was amazing, but the intimacy of *knowing* someone. Of being known. The vulnerability in sharing your deepest fears and insecurities and still being cared for despite them. He'd opened a side of myself I hadn't even known existed. I was more...*me* when I was with him than I'd ever been with anyone else. And wasn't that what it meant to be loved? To be known and seen and still be wanted anyway?

Jesus. Did that mean he loved me too? He hadn't said as much, but knowing Jason the way I did now, I suspected that was the case. And why was that so much scarier? It was one thing to risk giving your heart to someone, but to hold theirs in return? To be responsible for the care of it? God, the thought of that had my heart rate firing up all over again. Who was I to bear that kind of weight?

"Zach?"

Jason's voice interrupted my spiral. I heard the rustle of bedcovers behind me and then felt the heat of his body pressed against my back as he wrapped his arms around me, looking over my shoulder at the lake beyond.

"What are you doing over here?" he asked, his breath tickling my ear.

I breathed deep, inhaling his scent, drawing on the strength and warmth his body offered. "I had a bad dream."

His grip tightened ever so slightly. "Do you want to talk about it?" His voice was soft, soothing my momentary panic.

"No. I'm feeling better now."

We stood like that, with his arms wrapped around me from behind, head resting on my shoulder, watching the snowfall. I felt my mind quiet, my body relax, and finally, I felt ready for sleep again.

"Let's go back to bed."

He released me, though he kept one of my hands in his, and pulled me back toward the bed. He climbed in first, holding up the covers, indicating I should climb back in. I did so, and he dropped the blanket over us, the bed still warm from his body heat, making me feel like I was nestled in a cocoon of comfort. He wrapped me tight in his arms, just as he'd done every night this week, and whispered, "Sleep. I've got you."

41

JASON

THE CALL CAME in just after six. Mr. Jacobs called to let us know Drea was awake and aware enough to recognize she was in a hospital. She'd been agitated and scared, but they'd gotten her calm enough on her own that they hadn't needed to sedate her again. She'd fallen asleep shortly after, but I could hear Mr. Jacobs's voice through Zach's phone, and it was by far the most animated I'd ever heard him.

Zach and I had showered and dressed quickly, not wanting to waste a moment getting to the hospital, especially considering Zach's flight was scheduled to leave in about twenty-four hours. It felt like we were on borrowed time.

The drive out of Astaire was slow-going, as roads hadn't yet been plowed, but I drove carefully, and my truck did a pretty good job handling the conditions. Thankfully, the streets were in much better shape as we got closer to the city, and we arrived at the hospital without incident.

I thought Zach would be happier, that the excitement of possibly seeing Drea awake and responsive would have eased some of the tension from his body, but that wasn't the case. He'd been snippy before we'd left the house, and now, as we rode the elevator up to Drea's floor, his jaw was set and his shoulders were stiff with tension. I ran my thumb over the back of his hand to offer comfort.

On the ICU floor, we headed down the hall toward the girls' rooms, the path now familiar as we'd traveled it throughout the week. I waited outside the door to Drea's room, torn between wanting to see Drea and be there for Zach and wanting to check in with my own family. Mandy was possibly going home today, and I wanted to make sure I offered them my support as well.

As if he understood my dilemma, he squeezed my hand and then released it. "Go on. Go check on Mandy. I'll let you know if there's any news to report."

"Alright," I said softly, kissing him on the forehead.

He turned and slid open the door. I gave Mr. Jacobs a wave through the window as he looked up, and he tipped his chin in return. I could see Drea through the window. With her eyes closed, she appeared to be resting peacefully. I wanted Zach to get a chance to talk to her before he flew back, but selfishly, I wanted to see her too. I missed her combination of fiery spirit mixed with old soul. I'd have time to see her later though. Zach was the one who needed to see her now.

I walked down the hall to Mandy's room, where I could see through the window that she was sitting up. Mom caught my eye and gave me a huge smile and a thumbs-up, which I took to indicate she was indeed going home. I smiled back, my eyes stinging with unshed tears of relief, knowing she still had a long road to recovery but was out of the worst of it, at least.

Because both of my parents were in the room and appeared to be talking to one of the doctors, I headed down to the waiting area, not wanting to be in the way. I couldn't help but look into Drea's room as I passed, but I didn't see much change from a few moments ago, other than Zach's presence in the room. He appeared to be talking to his dad.

In the waiting room, I pulled out my phone, realizing it had been a couple of days since I'd checked my email. I deleted some of the junk, then opened a message from Chief.

Jason-

Attached is contact information for a couple of counselors in our area who specialize in working with first responders after a tough call. Unfortunately, our department doesn't currently have the budget to contract with these individuals to provide services free of charge, but they do work with several popular insurance providers, or if you find that you will need to pay out of pocket, they offer a reduced rate for first responders. The use of these services is at your discretion, but because of the nature of the situation with your sister and you being so new, I thought you might find this information helpful.

Currently, we have you on the schedule for the day shift Monday, Tuesday, Thursday, and Friday of next week.
See you Monday.

Chief Anthony "Tony" Capello
Astaire Fire Department

I took a moment to type out a quick response, offering my thanks and letting him know I was looking forward to returning on Monday. The thought had my system flooding with nerves, but I knew myself well enough to know that I had to get back on the horse, so-to-speak, or I would only tie myself up in knots to the point I wouldn't be able to return at all.

I was about to pocket my phone when a message came through from Zach.

ZACH

Change of plans

He'd attached a screenshot from his weather app indicating another, more significant chance of snow coming in overnight.

I'm rebooking my flight for this afternoon to try to get out ahead of the storm

My heart sank right through my stomach and into the floor. I'd been looking forward to one more night with him. One more night of holding him. Kissing him. Sleeping with him. I'd planned to soak up every bit of Zach-time I could get.

Damn

That sucks

Those little bubbles appeared and disappeared a couple of times before another message finally came through.

I know. I'm sorry

The short message made me wonder what he'd been debating on saying. I had an odd sense of foreboding—really, I'd been feeling it since sometime yesterday afternoon—that I couldn't shake. On the surface, he hadn't done or said anything that should have me feeling that way, but I couldn't shake the feeling, nonetheless.

What time does your flight leave?

3:25

Shit. That only left us a few hours, especially considering we'd need to get him there early so he could get checked in and through security. At least we wouldn't need to run back to Astaire to get his bag since he'd brought it with him this morning in case we went back to my house tonight.

How's Drea?

Dad said she was awake again just before
we got here, but she's been asleep ever
since

Hopefully she'll wake up soon and you'll
have a chance to talk to her before we go

Yeah

I waited for more, but when nothing came, I pocketed my phone, unsure why things felt like they were unraveling and even less sure what to do about it.

42

ZACH

I was restless and agitated as I sat in Drea's room, hoping she'd wake up before I had to leave. I couldn't explain this itchy feeling just below the surface of my skin, but it was making me feel a little unhinged.

Maybe it was exhaustion. After Jason and I returned to bed last night, I'd thought I'd be able to sleep, but every time I closed my eyes, those images from my dream—specifically the one of Jason unconscious and bleeding—had appeared, forcing my eyes to pop open once again. It felt like an omen. I'd never been superstitious, but they said bad things happened in threes, right? My mom had died in an accident. Drea had been badly injured. Would Jason be next?

The thought of Jason injured or dying was unbearable to contemplate. Was this what my father had been talking about? Loving someone so much that when you lost them, it fundamentally changed who you were? Changed your ability to move forward? Changed the way you interact with those you cared about?

Would I be able to bear it? I'd already lost my mom. Would I survive the loss of Jason?

It was this thought that had silent tears streaming down my face, soaking into my pillow, until I'd eventually cried myself to sleep. My dad's call had come in just a couple of hours later.

So here I sat, contemplating leaving in just a handful of hours, terrified to go and terrified to stay.

Movement from the bed caught my attention, and I looked up to see Drea's eyes flutter open as if it took all her strength to do so. She finally managed it, her eyes roaming the room and eventually landing on me. She couldn't speak while on the ventilator, but the corners of her mouth turned up in a weak smile as she continued to stare at me. I turned to look at Dad, wanting to make sure he'd noticed she was awake, and caught him watching her with a shaky smile.

I stood, taking a couple of cautious steps to get to her bedside, then turned back to look at Dad. "Can I touch her? Hold her hand?"

He nodded, and I turned back, watching in wonder as I took her hand in mine. Her skin was smooth, a little cool to the touch, and her grip loose, but her fingers curled ever so slightly around mine, making my smile widen.

"Hey," I said, a goofy grin spreading across my face.

Dad came around to the other side of the bed, taking her other hand in his and smiling, though I didn't miss the tears in his eyes as he did so.

"God, I've missed you so much," I said, swiping at my own tears. I had so much I wanted to tell her, but it was bottlenecked in my throat, and I couldn't get it out.

Her eyes continued to move around the room, flitting between Dad, me, and the machines she was connected to.

Confusion and fear were in her eyes, and I gave her hand a careful squeeze, trying to reassure her that she was okay.

A nurse came in and began asking yes or no questions, trying to ascertain how aware she was of her surroundings and the reason for her being there. Shortly after, a doctor joined us, asking similar questions and checking the machine readouts. They assured us all that this was very good progress and they would take her for some scans shortly.

Dad stepped out of the room, saying he was going to call Aunt Amy, but I thought maybe he wanted to give us a moment alone, knowing I was leaving later today. Christ, the changes in him this week were drastic. It was as if the accident had unlocked the softer side of him, and while the idea of being thankful for the crash that had put my sister in the ICU was abhorrent, I could at least be grateful for this result. I felt like I had my father back, maybe more than ever before, and for the first time, there was a path forward to mending our relationship.

Drea looked tired, but when I asked her if she wanted me to let her rest, she gave a slight shake of her head, so I began talking, telling her about how close Jason and I had gotten this week, leaving out some of the more intimate details, and about how Dad and I had begun to talk through some things. I kept it light, giving her the bare bones of what had gone down, knowing that a detailed rundown would likely be too much for her to process. She lasted about ten minutes before her eyes closed again, but I was so grateful for the opportunity to see the light in her eyes before I had to leave.

I remained by her side, watching her sleep until Dad returned. He said Aunt Amy would try to make it into the city later in the afternoon, but he wasn't sure if she'd make it before I had to leave. I watched as Jason and his family made their way down the hall, Mandy being pushed in a wheelchair by a nurse with everyone else trailing behind. Jason smiled at me through the window, making my heart clench. Leaving him this afternoon was going to hurt more than I ever imagined it could.

Around eleven, I got a text from Jason asking if I wanted to grab lunch before heading to the airport. I was torn between wanting some time alone with him and wanting to see if Drea would wake up one more time. In the end, I decided I needed the time with Jason, especially knowing Drea would be taken for scans pretty soon anyway.

Dad walked me out of Drea's room into the hallway and pulled me into a hug. I thought back to the night I'd arrived at the hospital when I'd held him while he'd broken apart. We'd come a long way since then. It was hard to believe it had been less than a week.

"I love you," Dad said into my ear as we embraced, causing a lump in my throat.

"Love you too, Dad."

"I'm...trying, okay? Be patient with me."

I released him, pulling back to look into his eyes. "I know. And it means a lot. I'll work on not bottling stuff up anymore. Not letting it fester."

He chuckled. "That would probably help."

Jason approached, walking toward us from the waiting room. Dad nodded toward him, offering a small smile, before returning his attention to me. "You'll text when you get in?"

"I will."

He turned toward Jason, offering his hand to shake. "I'm glad he has you. You're good for him."

Jason's eyes widened in surprise. "Um, thanks," he said as they shook hands.

We wrapped up our goodbyes, and Jason and I headed for the elevator, walking hand-in-hand.

43

JASON

THE CLOUDS HUNG heavy in the sky as we left the hospital, mirroring my mood. I was happy Mandy was on her way home and Drea continued to show strong signs of progress, but I dreaded the moment I'd have to say goodbye to Zach.

We grabbed a quick lunch at a local diner near the hospital before making our way to the airport, neither of us saying much beyond updating the other on how things were going with our sisters and our families. Even that conversation felt stilted in a way it hadn't ever felt with him.

I pulled into the short-term parking garage and found a spot to park.

"You could have just dropped me off at the curb. You're not going to be able to get past security anyway."

I shrugged. "I want to walk you in."

The truth was, I wanted every last second I could get.

He nodded, and we both stepped out of the truck. He just had the one bag and his backpack, but I picked up the bag, wanting to help. We held hands as we crossed the street into the terminal and didn't release them as we rode the escalator up to the main floor. Omaha's airport was small, so it was only a matter of about seventy-five feet to the start of the security line. I pulled him to the side, wanting to say a proper goodbye out of the way of other folks trying to get in line.

"I can't believe we have to say goodbye." I pulled him into a hug, wrapping my arms around him tightly, not caring that we were in a public space.

"I know," he said, his voice muffled by my shoulder. He pulled back slightly, his eyes burning with intensity. "The way I feel about you, Jason...it's like nothing I've ever felt before. You've been amazing this week. I don't know how—" He choked on a sob, squeezing his eyes closed against the tears threatening to fall.

I placed my hands on either side of his face. "Hey," I said, trying to get him to look at me. "We're going to figure this out, okay? I feel the same way about you. I didn't think I'd ever feel this way about anyone, but you unlocked something inside me, and I'm not done exploring it. I don't think I'll ever be done exploring this thing between us. Okay?"

He nodded, blinking as a tear finally escaped, rolling down his cheek, landing on my thumb.

"We'll figure out the distance thing," I continued. "Plenty of people have done it before. We can do it too. We have texts and FaceTime. And you'll be home in a couple of weeks. And maybe I can come out there. And before we know it, it will be summer, and we'll be jogging around the lake and hanging at bonfires."

I felt one of my own tears escape, and I wasn't sure who I was trying to convince more, him or me. He tilted his head up and kissed me then, pressing his lips to mine as if that connection could cement us together for the rest of time. I thought maybe it might.

I parted my lips, inviting him inside, and he hungrily

accepted, swiping his tongue into my mouth and tangling it with mine. I met his energy eagerly, licking and sucking, completely disregarding the fact that we were standing in the middle of the airport. I was desperate to taste him, to savor him, to memorize his flavor. I wanted to imprint him on my soul.

Dimly, I registered a catcall from somewhere off to my right, but I ignored it, focusing only on *him*. Zach must have heard it as well because he broke the kiss, pulling away to rest his forehead against mine. "I don't know if I'll ever get enough of you."

I chuckled. "Same."

"I should probably go," he said, looking over his shoulder at the security line that had gotten longer while we'd been preoccupied, lost in each other.

Sighing, I released him. "Text me when you get in?"

"Yeah. I think it's going to be late though."

"That's alright. I doubt I'll be able to sleep without you next to me anyway."

He leaned forward and gave me one more kiss, keeping it chaste, before pulling back and looking into my eyes. He looked like he was going to say something but instead leaned forward, brushing his lips against mine before grabbing his bag and walking away.

I watched him go, then turned and made my way down the escalator and out to my truck, tears streaming down my face the entire way.

44

—————

ZACH

Made it to LA

JASON

Miss you

Miss you too

—————

JASON

Missed hearing from you yesterday

Hopefully you got some rest

Good luck getting back into your classes today. You've got this!

—————

JASON

Honey I'm getting worried. I haven't heard from you in a couple of days

———

JASON

I had a nightmare about the accident. First one since I went back to work on Monday

I turned over to reach for you but then I remembered you aren't here

I wish I could at least hear your voice

Where are you?

———

JASON

It's been a week since you texted me last and I don't know what to think. Did I piss you off?

I got desperate enough to call your dad. I had to know you were okay

He told me you were just really busy, but there was a hesitation in his voice and now I don't know what to think

I miss you

———

JASON

WTF Zach? You were supposed to come home this weekend but now I hear from Drea that you're staying in LA?

At least have the decency to call me. Shit, I'd even take a text right now

JASON

FUCK. YOU.

JASON

It's been a month. I fell in love with you and then you fucking ghosted me. I don't understand it. The Zach I know wouldn't do this to me. But maybe I never really knew you at all

You know what? Fuck you for making me doubt everything. For making me doubt US

JASON

I love you. I'm so goddamned angry with you. And hurt. But I can't stop loving you

JASON

Goodbye, Zach. I can't keep doing this to myself. I can't keep holding out hope. If you ever want to explain yourself, I'm here, but this will be my last text. Ball's in your court

PART II

ALWAYS

45

ZACH

I STEPPED out onto the deck and breathed deep, the scents of a Nebraska spring edging toward summer wrapping around me like a warm hug. It wasn't that I hadn't been back to Nebraska in the last nine and a half years, but I hadn't been back to this very spot in at least seven, and I'd forgotten just how much this place meant to me.

I took the stairs to the paved patio, moving past the fire pit and down another short set of stairs to the dock below. I walked the length of it, making note of a couple of planks that needed replacing, but when I came to the end, I stopped and took in the view. I could just make out a couple of joggers running along the path on the other side of the water, despite the warmth of the afternoon. Memories of morning jogs along that very same path wrapped themselves around my heart and gave it a bittersweet squeeze.

On impulse, I sat, stripping off my shoes and socks and sticking my feet into the water. It was cool but not uncomfortable, so I swished my toes this way and that, enjoying the feel of the water against my skin.

The sound of flip-flops slapping against the boards had

me looking up to see Drea strolling toward me, a smile on her face as she approached. It reminded me of another time she'd sought me out in this spot right before I left for college. I'd had no idea the turn my life was about to take, the path I'd already begun to take, without even realizing I'd done so.

Unceremoniously, she plopped down next to me, kicking off her sandals and dunking her feet in the water right next to mine.

"I can't believe you bought our old house," she said, her hand over her eyes to block out the sun as she looked at me.

"I couldn't believe it was on the market. It felt like a good sign."

"A sign of what?"

I shrugged. "A sign that coming back here was the right decision."

She sighed. "You sure about that?"

I raised my eyebrows, trying not to be hurt by the question. "You don't want me here?"

"Of course I want you here. But you're not here for me, and we both know it."

I didn't respond to that. What could I say, really? The truth was that she was part of the reason I'd moved back here, but she wasn't the whole reason. "If you hurt him again, I'll kick your ass. I don't care that you're my brother. You fucked up."

"I know."

There was no use denying it. She'd never know how much I'd hurt myself in the process. She and I—we'd fought about it over the years, had even been somewhat estranged for a time after I ghosted Jason, breaking his heart and mine in the process. Or at least Drea had given me the impression I'd broken his heart. I hadn't actually spoken to him other than the text I'd sent last month that he hadn't responded to. Which I deserved.

"You still going to the reunion tomorrow?"

"Yeah. I have to...I have to see him."

"Zach..." Her voice held a hint of warning, but I jumped in before she could lecture me.

"I promise, if he tells me to fuck off, I'll leave."

"You know he won't though. He's still the nicest guy on the planet. Too nice to tell you to shove it." She nudged my shoulder playfully in demonstration. "Seriously, though, what do you hope to achieve?"

That was an excellent question. One I didn't really have an answer for. I'd come to realize Jason was more than just "the one who got away." I'd given a piece of myself to him all those years ago, and it had left a hole I'd never been able to fill. Not with other friendships, relationships, or even a professional soccer career. It had taken years for me to figure that out. To see that no matter what I tried to use to fill that crater inside me, it was never enough. Would never be enough.

"I just want a chance to make it right."

"Jesus, Zach. You walked away from your soccer career and moved halfway across the country for something you could have done years ago. Why now?"

A million words rushed to my lips, tripping over themselves to get out. Explanations, justifications, rationalizations... All the reasons big and small that I'd left my life behind to come back. To come home.

But in the end, I simply said, "It was time."

46

———

JASON

I HOPPED down from the truck, stripping out of my turnout gear and putting it away in the storage area next to the apparatus bay. I walked into the kitchen and pulled a Gatorade out of the fridge.

"How'd it go?" Hannah Gordon called out from the office where she was currently filing paperwork.

"Eh. Mrs. McClaskey's going to get that new kitchen she was hoping for. But thankfully, the house is still standing."

"Geez." Hannah's head popped out from the doorway, her blonde ponytail swinging with the movement. "She didn't set the fire on purpose, did she?"

I chuckled as I fiddled with the cap on my Gatorade. "Nah. She was pretty rattled. I think it was legit. Thankfully, she was quick enough to grab the fire extinguisher and had it out by the time we got there, but not before singeing the geese on the wallpaper border above the stove."

"Geese?" She arched a brow, stepping fully out of the office and leaning against the doorframe.

"Geese. Straight out of the eighties." I walked toward her, leaning on the wall opposite.

"RIP. Glad she's okay, at least."

"Yeah, she'll be alright. Shaken up, but alright."

"You going to the bonfire tonight?"

The call out to the McClaskeys' had been a great distraction, but at the mention of the bonfire tonight, my stomach instantly retied itself into knots. This had been happening more frequently as we got closer to the event, especially after Zach texted out of the blue last month asking if I was going to our reunion.

It was bullshit that his presence here upset me so much at this point. Whatever it was that had passed between us had been done for a long time. It shouldn't matter that he was here. These folks had been my friends long before he came to Astaire and many of them were still friends to this day. He was nothing but a blip—in and out of my life in less than a year. He didn't matter.

I was so full of shit.

"Yeah, I'm gonna be there. Sammy and Will are coming too. And I think Rafi's crashing, even though he was in the class below ours. What about you guys? You got a sitter?"

"Yeah, the kids are spending the night at Sonny's parents. And God, we need the break. We barely see each other since we work opposite shifts."

Hannah and Sonny got pregnant the summer after graduation and married two years after that. Sonny had worked odd jobs to make ends meet, eventually going through training to become a firefighter. After their third child went to kindergarten this year, Hannah began working at the station as a receptionist and office manager but was taking classes to become an EMT like I had.

"Y'all gonna see who can chug a beer the fastest for old time's sake?"

She snorted. "Highly unlikely. Though I'm pretty sure I could still kick Sonny's ass."

"I have no doubt." I flashed her a grin.

"I should get back to it if I'm going to get out of here in an hour."

"See you tonight."

We each went our separate ways, with Hannah heading back into the office while I headed into the locker room. She only had an hour left in her shift, but I still had four more to go and would be heading straight from the firehouse to the lake.

That was four long hours to contemplate what it would be like to see Zach again. Four hours too many, yet not nearly enough.

***

As it turned out, I was late to the bonfire. I'd fooled around with the other guys, shooting the shit, until we'd caught a call for a car accident out on the highway, just past the turnoff to the overlook on Grandpa's property. Even after all these years on the job, I still had to take a moment when heading out to the scene of an accident. These days, that moment consisted of a couple of deep breaths to center myself en route, but it had taken years of training and therapy to get to that point. I'd always be thankful to Andrew and Jenny, my training officers who had since retired, for their patience and advice, which had gotten me through my probationary period once I'd returned to work after Mandy and Drea's accident. They'd helped me push through on those days when the fear seemed impossible to overcome.

Tonight's accident had been fairly minor, thankfully,

with the paramedics and county sheriff handling most of it. Still, by the time the truck returned to the station and I clocked out of my shift, I was an hour late for the reunion and headed straight to the lake without changing.

I parked on the side of the road a little way down from the parking lot and began walking toward the party, following the sound of voices and laughter carried on the breeze up from the beach. I allowed myself to bring up the image of Zach's face, confronting my memories of him rather than burying them as I would have preferred. I knew what he looked like now, of course. I'd followed his soccer career, even when I'd known it wasn't good for me. I hadn't been able to help myself.

It was a shock when he announced his retirement in the offseason. His last several seasons with San Francisco SC had been successful. The team made it to the conference semifinals this year, which was remarkable for a young team only in its third season. So it was a shock when Zach announced his plans to retire just days before the team was to begin preseason workouts in January. In a press conference, he'd merely cited personal reasons and hadn't given up any more information than that despite prodding from the media.

Of course I couldn't help but wonder what those personal reasons might be. He hadn't been celibate in the last nine years, but unless he kept things very private, he'd only had a few relationships that I knew of: two with women and two with men, though his relationships with the men had been the shortest in duration. They'd also been the ones that had hurt the most to see.

For my part, I hadn't dated anyone. Not terribly surprising for a demisexual who was friendly with everyone but not particularly close to anyone. I certainly hadn't lacked social engagements over the years. I'd been to my fair share of happy hours, barbecues, and Super Bowl parties, but I hadn't felt a strong enough connection with anyone to send lust thrumming through my blood. Not since Zach.

I stepped onto the path from the parking lot down to the beach, doing my best to shrug off the melancholic cloud that thoughts of Zach always brought when I allowed myself to think about him. I studied the crowd of people milling about on the sand, looking to catch sight of any of my friends. Finally, I spotted the gang milling about near the fire and headed in that direction.

I watched as Sammy leaned forward and pressed his forehead against Will's, murmuring something I couldn't hear. The way they looked at each other, the love that shone from their eyes, had my heart aching. I was so damn happy for my friend. Happy they'd figured their shit out and really seemed to have a good shot at a solid future, but I couldn't help but wish for that for myself and wonder what could have been.

I was close enough now that I heard Rafi call out, "Get a room!" to a chorus of laughter, followed by Sammy's middle finger shooting up in the air. More laughter ensued and then Sammy was standing, pulling Will with him through the crowd toward the trees a short distance away. I didn't want to think about what they would likely do out there.

"Way to scare them away," I said as I approached the group.

"Jason! You made it! Did you hear the good news?" Rafi's face lit up with the prospect of sharing a juicy bit of gossip.

I smiled wide. "That Sammy and Will are engaged?"

His face fell. "Damn. How did you know?"

"Don't look so sad, man. I went with Will to pick up the ring in Omaha last week."

I'd also had a text waiting for me when I returned to the station that read *He said YES!!!!!!*, but I didn't want to rub it in.

"Damn, I'm always the last to know everything."

"That's because everyone knows your big mouth can't keep a secret." Sonny joined the mix, handing Hannah a fresh beer.

"Rude. I'll have you know, I can totally keep a secret. Just last week, I..."

Rafi's words faded as I caught sight of Zach walking toward us with a red cup in his hand. He was barefoot, wearing gray shorts that hugged his impressive quads and a pale-blue button-down left open, exposing his tanned skin and the smattering of hair in the center of his chest.

"Hey, Zach!" Hannah called out, her expression open and friendly.

"Hi, guys," he said, returning her smile, though his eyes never left mine.

"Wow, the MLS star is gracing us with his presence," Rafi said. "Must be nice to be able to retire at the ripe old age of twenty-eight."

"It doesn't suck," he returned affably while everyone laughed.

Everyone except me. I was frozen, locked in a moment of fight or flight. My tongue felt thick and the sound around me became muffled, as if someone had shoved cotton in my ears.

"Jason? You alright? You've gone pale." Sonny was peering at me in concern, his EMT training taking over.

"I...uh...I'm..." I tried to tell him I was fine, but the ability to make words had fled, leaving me tongue-tied and incoherent.

Everyone was looking at me now, faces registering

various degrees of concern. And suddenly, as if the winner of the battle between fight and flight had been determined by forces I wasn't in control of, I was in motion.

For the first time ever in my life, I clocked someone.

Not just someone. The goddamned love of my life.

IT WASN'T the first time I'd taken a punch to the jaw, but that didn't make it hurt any less.

I lay in the sand, stunned, gingerly moving my jaw from side to side, testing out the damage. I didn't think anything was broken, which was fortunate because Jason was a strong motherfucker.

I'd gotten a good look at him before he'd noticed me, soaking up the sight of him in his black AFD shirt and pants. He'd always been a big dude, built like a linebacker, but the years had matured that body into a man, and the uniform fit him like a glove. Everything about him was thick. Thick thighs. Thick biceps. Broad shoulders. I'd missed what it felt like to be held by that big body.

I was lucky he hadn't used all of that strength when he punched me.

A hand appeared in front of my face and I grabbed it, allowing myself to be pulled up to stand.

"What the hell, Jason?" Hannah shot him a look before turning back to me. "Are you okay?" She nudged her fingers under my chin, taking a look at the left side of my face.

"I'm fine. A little ice, and I'll be okay."

I attempted a smile, but it hurt like a bitch. For his part, Jason stood with eyes wide like he'd surprised himself, clenching and unclenching his right hand. It wouldn't surprise me if it was the first time he'd ever hit someone. The gravity of what that implied, that I was the first person who'd ever made him angry enough to throw a punch, hurt almost as much as my face, but I had no one to blame but myself. It was just an indication of how long the path to forgiveness might be, if that path was even open to me at all.

"Jason, man, I've never seen you do something like that. Not even on the football field back in the day." Rafi turned his attention toward me. "You must have really pissed him off."

All eyes were on me. Some curious. Some edging toward distrust. One thing was clear. Jason hadn't told any of them what I'd done to him. Maybe hadn't told them about us at all, and I certainly wasn't going to out him. Before I could fumble my way through a response, another voice chimed in.

"J? You alright?"

Will joined the cluster of people with Sammy following behind, holding his hand. *Huh. They must have gotten back together.* Will peered into Jason's eyes. He didn't like whatever he saw there because when he turned back to me, his face had darkened like a thundercloud. And *oh shit*. Maybe Jason *had* confided in someone. "I'm not sure why you thought it was a good idea to do this here, at the reunion, but I think you need to go."

I chanced one more glance at Jason, but he was looking away, hands on his hips with his jaw clenched tight.

"Yeah, okay." I bent down and picked up the cup I'd

dropped when Jason laid me out, and without looking back, I walked away.

I WALKED into my house around eleven with a bruised jaw and an aching heart. I made a beeline for the kitchen, where I poured two fingers of whiskey into a glass, then pulled out a bag of frozen veggies and held them to my face. Grabbing my drink with my free hand, I walked to the windows and looked out at the dark lake beyond. If I angled my body just right, I could see a flicker on the shore where the bonfire was still going strong.

I wondered what Jason would tell his friends. Would he tell them what we'd once meant to each other? Would he tell them what I'd done? I wouldn't blame him. I'd only lived here for a year, while he'd known some of those folks his whole life. It was good that he had a support system.

Drea had been right. And so had Will. What had I been thinking confronting him at the bonfire like that? What had I thought to achieve? I'd ghosted the man for nine years. Was I expecting him to welcome me with open arms?

Jesus. I'd made several life-altering decisions in the last year, had come to some conclusions about the status of my mental health and what I wanted out of my life, and once I'd set a new course for myself, I'd forged ahead with tunnel vision. I didn't have any illusions that any of this would be easy. But I also hadn't stopped and thought about what it would do to him if I just showed up out of the blue in front of all of his friends.

God, I was an absolute dumbass.

I walked into the living room and sat on the new couch delivered earlier that day. I set my drink down on the coffee table and pulled out my phone, swiping into the Messages app.

You were right

DREA

I've been waiting to hear those words all my life, but suddenly I'm filled with dread

He punched me

Seriously? Jason?

I sent her a selfie capturing the swelling on the left side of my face. I was going to have a shiner.

Damn

What do I do?

I have to make this right

This isn't just a little spat you're asking forgiveness for. You ghosted the man for nine years

I know

Do you? Because you're asking the question like maybe if you just give him flowers or buy him a nice dinner, you can smooth things over

God, she wasn't pulling any punches.

That was a terrible choice of words under the circumstances.

I know

Those three dots fluttered on the screen, and I waited to see what she'd say.

The phone rang in my hand, startling me, and I nearly bobbled it as I tried to answer.

"Hey."

"I can't help you with this, big brother. I love you. But I love him too, and you didn't see him after you left. What it did to him."

My heart clenched and it was like I was back there all over again. Lying in my dorm room, tears soaking my pillow, trying to get my panic attacks under control while also trying not to let on to my roommate that I was upset. Wanting so badly to call Jason. To hear his voice. And being completely unable to do so.

Over the years, I'd told Drea some of what I'd gone through during that time, but even she didn't have the full picture. I hadn't wanted her to see just how bad it had gotten. "If you can find a way to get him to forgive you or to reconcile, I'll support it. But that's between the two of you. I'm not getting in the middle of it."

"That's fair."

My voice was quiet. Defeated. I knew coming back here was the right choice. I still believed that. But there were demons I hadn't yet faced, and in the end, I might have to accept that my life here in Astaire wouldn't include him.

"I love you, Zach." She softened her tone, letting me know she really meant it. "I forgave you for abandoning us a long time ago. It's up to Jason if he wants to do the same."

"I love you too, sis. I'm just not ready to give up on him yet."

"Good. He deserves someone who will fight for him." I smiled at that because she was right. He absolutely deserved that and more. "It's late. I'm gonna let you go. You coming to Aunt Amy's for the cookout tomorrow?"

"Yeah. I'll see you there."

We said our goodbyes and disconnected the call. I tossed the soggy bag of veggies on the floor, then slouched back against the couch, resting my phone face-down on my chest. I couldn't get the image of Jason out of my mind, the look on his face after he'd punched me. His eyes had been full of so much *emotion*. Sadness, anger, fear, sorrow, regret... I'd known I'd hurt him, but it was one thing to know it and another to see it written all over his face. I had to fix it. Even if reconciliation was beyond the realm of possibility, I owed him an apology. An explanation, at least.

Picking up my phone, I fired off another text, this time to Jason.

> I shouldn't have shown up at the reunion like that. I owe you a conversation in private. That is if you're willing to talk to me at all

> I'd just like a chance to explain

> Please?

IT WAS STILL PITCH black outside when I woke up, slumped on the couch at a very uncomfortable angle. I sat up, rubbing the back of my neck as I tilted my head left and right, cringing as I felt the tenderness in my jaw. I stood, intending to find a couple of ibuprofen and climb into my bed, but paused when my phone hit the floor with a thunk. I'd forgotten I'd fallen asleep with it on my chest. I picked it up, noting a message had come in while I'd been sleeping.

JASON

I'm off Monday. I can meet you at Fred's
Diner at 9am

My heart pounded, and I was suddenly wide awake. He was giving me a chance. The door might have only been open a sliver, but it was an opening, nonetheless.

Quickly, I fired back.

Thank you

See you then

48

JASON

I WALKED into Fred's Diner out on the county highway about ten minutes before nine. Fred's was one of those old-timey-looking diners with checkerboard tile floors and vinyl stools wrapped around a worn Formica counter, where line cooks prepared greasy breakfast, lunch, and dinner three hundred sixty-five days a year. It was one of the few places I'd known would be open on the Memorial Day holiday.

I nodded and smiled at Holly, the only server on duty, then chose a booth in the corner of the cramped space. It was right next to one of the large windows, where I could watch for Zach. I wanted to see him coming, to have that extra moment to prepare myself before facing him again.

For the hundredth time since I'd seen him on Saturday, I wondered if I'd made a mistake by agreeing to meet him this morning. In my defense, I was drunk when I responded to his request to talk. I rarely drank to excess, but I'd felt fully justified in doing so after the shock of seeing him after all these years.

It hadn't mattered that I'd known he would be there or that I'd been preparing for it for over a month. The reality of seeing him in the flesh had sent me over an edge I hadn't even realized I was close to. It was like he punched in the secret code that unleashed all the anger and hurt I'd managed to mostly bury years ago. As a result, I punched him and then proceeded to get wasted with my friends.

A black Acura SUV pulled into the lot and Zach climbed out, surprising me. I wasn't sure what I'd expected him to be driving—something flashier or sportier, I supposed. He was dressed casually in a fitted T-shirt, athletic shorts, and flip-flops. Perhaps he planned on spending time at the lake today.

He entered the diner, spotting me almost immediately, and headed in my direction. He offered a tentative smile, which slid off his face when I simply gave him an up-nod. I wasn't trying to be a dick, but this man had ripped my heart out. I couldn't summon the energy to be polite.

He slid into the seat across from me and grabbed one of the laminated menus nestled among the condiments at the back of the table. Holly approached with a couple of mugs and a pot of coffee.

"Y'all ready to order, or do you need a couple?" she asked as she poured the coffee.

"I'm just having coffee for now. Thanks." I wasn't interested in a meal with him. I wasn't sure I'd be here long enough.

Zach returned the menu to its spot. "Same for me."

She nodded and moved back behind the counter, chatting with the customers sitting there. I studied him, taking in the differences nine years had made to his appearance. He hadn't changed much. He wore his dark hair about the same length, a little longer on the top with the sides trimmed short. There was some swelling and bruising near his left eye from where I'd hit him. He was tan, like he'd spent a lot of time outdoors, and it occurred to me that I didn't know how he was spending his retirement. I didn't even know what degree he'd settled on. He'd taken away my right to know those things when he'd boarded a flight to LA and never looked back.

He squirmed under my scrutiny, but I simply sipped my coffee, waiting for him to begin.

"So, um, thanks for meeting me."

I nodded.

"Okay, so I guess I just...wanted to tell you how sorry I am...for the way I left things between us."

I raised an eyebrow. "Sorry? You're *sorry*?"

He winced. "Well, yeah. I know it's not enough, but..."

"You're damned right it's not enough. Jesus, Zach. Weeks of texting you without a response. Without an explanation. Visiting your sister in the hospital and trying to keep a brave face because I didn't want to upset her or set back her recovery while simultaneously hoping she'd drop a hint as to why you hadn't called. Mom asking me questions about how you were doing because she *cared* and not knowing how to answer."

I brushed a hand through my short crop of hair, trying to calm myself before I gave the entire diner a show.

"I'm sorry. I'm fucking this up."

"Then try harder," I said through gritted teeth.

"Okay. You're right. Okay." He blew out a breath. "So I got back to LA in the middle of the night and slept most of the next day. I think it was a combination of stress and exhaustion, but also, I think it was a coping mechanism. I just wanted to hide from the world a little longer. I didn't want to think about Drea's accident or leaving you or all the coursework I was behind on. I just wanted to *not*...feel for a little while.

"Clayton finally woke me up for dinner Sunday night and forced me to eat something. I was going to text you then, but I was still so tired and overwhelmed, and I just… didn't. I told myself I'd text you the next day or maybe call you after class. I'd just get through that first day back, and then I'd call. I'd hear the sound of your voice, and it would make me feel better. But by the time I got through classes, my workout, and dinner, it was getting late, and I told myself I didn't want to wake you up…"

"So what? You were having second thoughts about us? I don't understand why you kept putting off calling me…"

"No, I loved you, Jason. You have to believe that. I *wanted* to call you. I just…couldn't."

I reared back as if I'd been struck. "Are you fucking serious? The first time you tell me you love me is nine years after the fact?"

The color drained out of his face as he fought to find his words, but I didn't wait for him to figure it out.

"Well guess what? I loved you too. Was worried sick over you. Worried enough that I called your dad. I nearly bought a plane ticket and flew out there to see for myself that you were okay. I held on to hope that you'd be back at the beginning of February and we could finally talk. Work out whatever it was that had come between us. Only you never came.

"Your sister had only been home from the hospital for a few days when I found out you weren't coming. She cried when she told me, Zach. We cried together. Turns out that you were at least texting her some, but even that was minimal, and neither of us could figure out why you'd abandoned us."

I watched as a tear slipped down his cheek. A part of me was glad for it. I wanted him to hurt.

"I'm sorry," he whispered.

"Yeah, you said that." I stood, pulled a fiver from my wallet, and tossed it on the table. "I don't think I can hear any more of this today. I don't know why you're back here in Astaire, and I'm not conceited enough to think it's just for me, but I'd suggest keeping your distance. I'm not interested in anything else you have to say."

I started to walk away but stopped when Zach's hand shot out and grabbed my wrist. "Wait. Please don't go."

"I don't owe you any more of my time." I shook out of his grasp and walked out.

AFTER LEAVING THE DINER, I spent a good portion of the day catching up on yard work. Physical labor seemed like the best way to get out some of the anger that seemed to be constantly simmering under the surface since I'd seen him Saturday night.

I lived in a small two-bedroom, one-story house I purchased about three years ago. I was fortunate that fire-fighting in Astaire was a paid position, but even still, it had taken years of working odd jobs and saving to afford the downpayment. It wasn't a fancy house, but I wasn't a fancy guy, so it worked for me. I kept it neat and tidy on the inside and out and was proud of the life I'd made for myself.

A life I'd once thought might include Zach.

I'd struggled with letting go of that idea for a long time. I hadn't even realized I'd started to think about a life with Zach in any sort of long-term way until that option was taken from me. Somehow, in the time between New Year's Eve and that Saturday when we said goodbye at the airport, I'd started thinking of Zach and me as an *us*. A *we*. A couple with a future.

It was crazy when I thought about it. We'd only been together for a matter of weeks. *Weeks.* How could I have possibly fallen so deep in such a short amount of time? I'd tried to convince myself over the years that I'd exaggerated what I felt for him. I'd taken feelings that were new and exciting and magnified them into this all-encompassing love for the ages. And the fact that I'd never had any closure allowed my imagination to run away with the ending.

In my mind, I'd played out a million different scenarios that might explain why he'd ghosted me. None of them had ever quite fit. I certainly hadn't expected *I wanted to, but I couldn't* would be his defense.

Deciding it was time for a break, I pushed my mower to a stop and cut the engine. I walked into the house, pulling off my shirt and using it to mop up the sweat dripping into my eyes. It wasn't an overly hot day, but the sun was shining, making it feel hotter than the seventy-degree temp. I walked into the kitchen and grabbed a cup from the cabinet, filling it with water from the tap and drinking it in long gulps.

What bothered me the most from this morning's conversation with Zach was that it left me with more questions than answers. There had to be more to the story than what he'd given me. Scratch that, in what I'd allowed him to give me. I'd been too angry to let him finish.

But damn, could you blame me? His reasoning had been weak. My anger was justified. If he'd loved me as he said, wouldn't he have pushed through whatever mental blocks were preventing him from calling? If they were even mental blocks at all. Sounded like an excuse to me.

This line of thinking wasn't getting me anywhere. It certainly wasn't doing anything to cool my temper. Resolved to give the whole thing a rest, I set the glass on the counter and headed back outside.

49

———

ZACH

I settled into a routine, spending time throughout the week in meetings and answering emails regarding the youth soccer club I was helping to get up and running. I went into Omaha for one of those meetings and had lunch with my father.

He'd moved back into the city shortly after Drea went off to college. Our relationship was much better than it had been in my youth, though he was still irritated with me for staying away for so long and struggled to understand why I'd walked away from my soccer career. I supposed we'd likely always have some difficulty understanding each other. But at least we'd found ways to be at peace with those differences instead of constantly butting heads.

I spent an afternoon with Drea, checking out the dance studio she'd recently taken over running. It was the same studio where she and Mandy had taken classes. She was hoping to buy the business outright, but the studio owner wasn't quite ready to let go of it entirely, so for now, she'd taken on a managerial role. She showed me around the space, pointing out some of the updates she wanted to make and her long-term vision for the studio once it—hopefully —became her own.

I'd also taken some time getting the house squared away. Dad had been shocked when I told him I'd bought our old house in Astaire. I'd originally planned on buying a condo in the city and making the commute to the new soccer club when necessary. I'd lived in a great condo in San Francisco, and I loved the hustle and bustle of city life. But when I happened upon the real estate listing for our old house in Astaire, I had to have it. As I'd told Drea, it felt like a sign. Almost like a call to come home. I'd only lived in Astaire for a year, but I'd felt the most *me* there. Especially the summer I became friends with Jason.

I sighed as I released my quad stretch and began to jog along the path. One way or another, my thoughts always seemed to circle back to him. I'd royally fucked up my attempt to smooth things over on Monday, and I'd spent most of the rest of the day sulking on the couch watching episodes of *Schitt's Creek*. But then I'd woken up Tuesday, determined to stay positive and focus on the things I could control while I figured out how I might try again with Jason.

Drea was right. He deserved someone willing to fight for him. I just had to figure out the next step in this battle.

I continued along the path, enjoying the sunshine on my face and the breeze coming off the lake. My body felt pretty good these days, now that the grind of my professional soccer career was over. There were days I missed it, but mostly, I had no regrets over leaving the career I'd once thought was my dream come true. I'd enjoyed the physicality of it and my teammates, but somewhere along the line, the pressure to compete at the highest level had gotten the best of me. In the end, leaving had left me feeling relief rather than regret, and I knew I'd made the right choice.

I rounded a bend and spotted a runner approaching from a short distance away. My heart rate sped up, and I nearly tripped at the sight of Jason coming toward me. He was shirtless, his broad chest glistening with sweat as his feet pounded the pavement. His eyes were focused on the ground, so I was nearly upon him before he saw me.

Jason's eyes widened with surprise, then shuttered before he turned around and started jogging the other way.

I huffed in frustration, then took off after him, determined not to let this chance to speak to him get away. "Jason, wait."

I caught up to him, sliding into place next to him, though he did his best to ignore my presence. We ran like that for several minutes, with only the sounds of our feet hitting the pavement and the rhythmic inhale and exhale of our breaths between us. Suddenly, Jason stopped, turning on the path to face me. "What? What do you want from me?"

"I just want to talk."

"You did so well with that the last time."

"I know I fucked up. I'm fucking it all up. It's just...hard for me."

"Hard for *you*?"

I winced as he spat out the words.

"I'm...sorry. I know I keep saying that, but it's true. And it's hard for me because it's...you. The stakes are higher."

"Stakes? What stakes? Stakes implies there's something to win or lose. Newsflash. You already lost me."

His words were like tiny shards of glass embedding themselves in my skin, cutting me to ribbons. I'd never imagined in a million years that Jason—quite possibly the kindest person I'd ever met—could be so cruel.

He started to walk away but turned back. "What are you

even doing here in Astaire anyway? I heard you moved into your old house—"

"News travels fast," I muttered.

"You can't have come back here just for me. And if you did, you're wasting your time."

I took a breath, pushing past the angry words and the hurt in order to answer his question. "I'm starting a youth soccer club. Or rather, an offshoot of the one I was a part of as a kid in Omaha. It's going to serve Astaire, Brinkley, and the surrounding area. There were a lot of talented kids on our high school team who would have been even better if they'd had the benefit of a club program in the area. I've been thinking about something like it for a long time, so I wrote up a proposal, reached out to a couple of my old coaches, and we worked out a deal."

I watched him carefully as I spoke, trying to gauge his reaction. This project meant a lot to me, and I hadn't been exaggerating when I said I'd been thinking about it for a long time. In truth, it was the most passionate I'd felt about anything since I'd left.

Some of the irritation left his face and he studied me for a moment before saying, "That's...that's actually pretty cool."

"Thanks," I said, my voice soft.

"So you're really back then? Like, for good?"

"I'm here to stay." I took a cautious step closer. "I know you're mad at me. And hurt. And you have every right to be. But I'm not going anywhere. And I want to make things right between us."

"I can't just forget about what happened. I can't snap my fingers and make all the pain go away. You hurt me, Zach. More than I ever thought it was possible to hurt. And there's still so much I don't understand." He swiped at the sweat dripping down the side of his face, wiping his hand on his shorts in an agitated motion. "What if I can't forgive you? What then?"

I swallowed hard. "Then I'll have to figure out how to accept it. I'm not trying to make your life harder by being here. I just...I missed this place. I missed *you*."

He stepped back as if I'd struck him. *Shit*. I was losing what little ground I'd gained. I could see in his eyes that he was pulling away.

"I missed you too. But you're nine years too late."

And with that, he jogged away, leaving me standing on the path.

50

_____

JASON

"Okay, so sounds like you've got all the decorations taken care of, and Mom's taking care of the food. I'm going to pick up the keg at noon, and I'll have coolers with seltzers, pop, and bottled water." Drea and I were just finishing lunch at Arlo's, Astaire's only bar and grill, while finalizing the details for Mandy's baby shower. She was due next month.

Drea snorted out a laugh. "Only in Astaire do you have a keg at a baby shower."

I shrugged but did so with a smile. "Mandy wanted a couples shower. I guarantee some of these dudes are going to want to drink."

"Not just the dudes," she tossed back with a smirk.

"Fair point." I leaned back in the booth, wiping my mouth with a napkin and pushing my plate away. "I'm stuffed. Anything else we need to go over before this thing goes down tomorrow?"

She reached out and grabbed my right hand, making a show of inspecting it. "How about we talk about your thoughts on my brother coming back to town."

"Drea…"

"I heard you gave him a shiner."

I yanked my hand back and glared at her. "News travels fast in this town."

"Duh. It's Astaire. What else are we gonna do? Now, let's see…" She made a show of pretending to think real hard. "I heard Rafi was actually the one who started the fight and you accidentally hit Zach trying to stop it. I heard Zach accidentally spilled beer on you, and you retaliated." She ticked each ridiculous scenario off on her fingers. "But my favorite is that he threw the first punch when he found out you and I were dating."

I choked on the water I'd just taken a sip of. "What? You and me? Is that a thing people think is happening?"

She laughed. "Seriously? How could you not know this? That rumor has been around for *years*."

I supposed I shouldn't be surprised. Drea had come out as bisexual her senior year of high school, but the queer population of Astaire, particularly queer girls, was nearly nonexistent, so most people forgot she liked girls just as much, if not more than, guys. And we did spend a fair amount of time together when our schedules allowed. We'd shared a bond for a long time. In some ways, I was closer to her than I was to Mandy. But there'd never been any sort of spark between us. She was my soul sister.

"I hope you set the record straight on that."

She shrugged. "Eh. I didn't commit one way or the other."

"Drea…" My tone was exasperated.

"What? Like being connected to me would be so bad?"

I reached out and grabbed her hand. "Of course not, but—"

"Look. I didn't think you wanted me to tell people the

truth. So I don't confirm or deny. Let them think whatever they want."

"I don't care if people know the truth. I ended up spilling the whole sad story to a bunch of folks after I punched him, anyway. I'm surprised that's not the version that made it back to you."

"Really? You came out?"

"I mean, I guess? I wasn't really trying to be in the closet. I just never had a reason to tell anyone I was gay or bi or whatever I am since I haven't felt attracted to anyone since Zach."

Her eyes softened into something that looked suspiciously close to pity.

"Don't look at me like that, Drea. You, of all people, should know I don't need your pity."

We were old maids in a town like Astaire, where most people got married in their early twenties. She knew what it was like to watch everyone around you marry and have kids while you were sitting on the sidelines.

"It's not pity. You just have so much love to give. I hate that you haven't found anyone to give it to besides my dumbass brother."

"It's whatever. I can't help who I'm attracted to. Or not attracted to, as it seems to be most of the time. It just is what it is."

She sighed. "I know. I just want you to be happy."

"I'm not *un*happy. I have friends." I squeezed her hand for emphasis. "A job that's fulfilling. I have a good life."

"Do you think...? You know what? Never mind."

"What? What were you going to say?"

"Don't be mad. I just...I was wondering if you thought you and Zach might ever be...?"

I pulled my hand from her grasp and leaned back in the booth. "Did he put you up to—"

"No," she rushed out. "No. In fact, I told him I was staying out of it. Told him I'd kick his ass if he hurt you, actually. I shouldn't have brought it up. Just forget it."

The image of Drea telling Zach she'd kick his ass diffused some of my ire. I had no doubt she'd done exactly that. "You, more than anyone else, know how bad he hurt me. I don't know if there's a path forward after that. He's tried to apologize a couple of times this week, but his 'I'm sorries' have fallen flat. And every time I see him, I get so *angry*. I'm not an angry person. I've never been that guy who fights with his fists, but every time I see him, I find myself wanting to blow."

I could feel it now, the anger simmering just below the surface at the mention of him. It was such a foreign feeling for me. I didn't know what to do with it.

"When's the last time you saw your therapist?'

"I don't know." I thought back. "A couple of weeks, I think. Pretty sure I have an appointment next week."

"Perfect timing."

She was right. I don't know why I hadn't thought about talking to my therapist about all of this.

At that moment, our server stopped by and dropped off the check, swapping it out for some of our finished plates. I set out my credit card as Drea checked her watch. "I probably better get going. I've got someone coming in to interview in an hour."

"Interview?"

"With the baby coming, Mandy's decided to give up her dance classes this year. She said she might come back and teach at some point in the future, but I have a feeling once that baby comes, she's going to be hopelessly devoted, so we're hiring a new instructor."

"Makes sense." I waved her off. "You go ahead and go. I've got this. It's my turn to pay anyway."

"Thanks." She stood, pulling her purse over her shoulder, then leaned forward and kissed my cheek. "You know I love you, right? Regardless of whatever happens with my idiot brother, you're just as important to me. That's not going to change just because he's back."

I hadn't realized I needed to hear that until this very moment. "Thanks, Drea. Love you too."

She smiled, and with a quick, "See you tomorrow," she was off.

THE WEATHER for Mandy's shower was perfect, allowing folks to hang out inside and outside the house. It felt more like a cookout than a baby shower, which was fine by me. I was happy to support my sister, but I wouldn't have known what to do with guessing games and tiny finger foods.

Drea and Mom arrived at my house two hours before the start of the party and promptly kicked me out of my living room so they could rearrange the furniture and transform the house from a bachelor pad to something more appropriate for hosting guests. I'd rolled my eyes but complied with their wishes, not really understanding what they were talking about. I mean, I kept the house neat and tidy. I wasn't sure what more they wanted.

When I came home from picking up the keg and several bags of ice, I realized how wrong I'd been. Not only had they rearranged the furniture to create more room for socializing, but they'd warmed up the space with an area rug, curtains, and framed photographs of my family, friends, and other special moments throughout my life.

Several were specifically of Mandy and her husband, Jeremy. Mandy would take those with her after the party, but the rest were for me to keep. Apparently, Mom and Drea had been dying to get their hands on the space since I'd moved in and this had been their excuse. I was touched, nonetheless.

While they finished decorating the inside, I set up the backyard, filling coolers with beverages and ice, cleaning the grill, and putting out additional chairs and yard games.

I heard the slam of a car door and made my way back through the house to see who had arrived. Mandy and Jeremy walked in the door, and at first sight of the decorations, Mandy promptly burst into tears. Jeremy immediately went into overprotective husband and future dad mode, rubbing her back and offering reassurances. Mandy had chosen a pretty great guy to marry.

Not long after that, other guests arrived and the party was in full swing. I spent most of my time at the grill, serving up hamburgers and hot dogs while guests moved between the inside and outside, visiting and laughing.

"Can I help with anything?" I turned to find Sammy's brother, Jimmy, standing just behind me, holding a seltzer. He and Mandy had a class project together their junior year, and Mandy adopted him as her friend.

"Hey, Jimmy. I think I've got everything under control. Thanks though." I flipped the last couple of burgers and reached for the cheese slices. "How's your summer break?"

"It's good. This last year was rough. Kids were challenging. I don't think I've done much more than sleep and read since school got out."

"Sounds perfect to me."

He grinned. "It doesn't suck."

Rafi and his wife, Elise, approached with their two-month-old sleeping in Rafi's arms. "Hey, Jason. Jimmy. Where's Sammy and Will?"

"Sammy has an art show in Kansas City this weekend, so of course Will went with him." Jimmy rolled his eyes playfully.

"Those two are practically joined at the hip," Rafi said.

"It's good to see. They deserve to be happy," I said, and I meant it. Despite the circumstances of their breakup and everything that had happened in between, I was glad they'd found a way back to each other.

"I wasn't sure you'd be thrilled with that situation," Rafi said.

"What? Why?"

He shrugged. "I don't know. I always wondered if you kinda had a thing for Will."

I snorted a laugh. "Nope. Never. He's always felt more like a brother to me."

"So, just Zach then?"

"Rafi..." Elise elbowed her husband.

"Ow. I was just asking."

"Zach? Isn't that Drea's brother?" Jimmy asked.

"What about my brother?" Drea joined the group with a beer in hand.

"Zach and Jason had a fling the winter after they graduated," Rafi supplied helpfully.

I groaned as I began pulling hot dogs off the grill. The burgers needed another moment for the cheese to melt. "It wasn't a fling. It was..." I grappled with what exactly to call it. Reducing what we had, or at least what I'd thought we had, down to a fling didn't sit well.

"They spent the summer and fall falling for each other

without even realizing what was happening. By the time they figured it out, Zach was already at college. They kissed on New Year's Eve, but when Mandy and I got into that accident sophomore year, things got hot and heavy. Then my asshole brother ghosted him."

I turned, setting the plate of hot dogs aside. "Thanks for that delightful summary, Drea."

"Welcome." Her eyes twinkled as she sipped her beer.

I shook my head, then turned my back on them and began pulling burgers off the grill and onto a platter.

"So, are you, like, gay?"

"Rafi! You don't just ask a person that!" Elise scolded him.

"What? What'd I do?"

"Coming out can be a vulnerable thing for a lot of people. It's up to them if and when they choose to come out," Jimmy offered, not unkindly.

"Oh. Sorry, man. I didn't mean anything by it."

"We're good. I mean, Jimmy's not wrong, but for me, it's not necessarily something I was trying to hide. I just didn't really have a reason to share. And to answer your question, I'm demi."

"Here, let me run those in." Drea set her beer on a nearby table, grabbed the platters of burgers and hot dogs, and headed inside.

"What's demi?" Rafi asked.

"Demisexual. It just means I have to form an emotional connection with someone before I feel sexual attraction. And since the only person I've ever experienced that with is Zach, I don't know for sure whether I'm gay or bi or pan or whatever. The demi label always mattered more to me than the rest."

"Cool. Cool. So then, like, happy Pride! You too, Jimmy!"

Rafi's face lit up, so pleased he'd remembered it was Pride month. Bless him. He had a good heart.

I chuckled, exchanging a glance with Jimmy. "Thanks, man."

Drea rejoined our group, picking up her beer and taking another sip. Ready for a change of subject, I asked, "How'd that interview go yesterday?"

"Oh, it was great! He's still in the process of moving back to Nebraska, so he won't start until August. I'm still debating, but I think he's going to do some of our choreography for the competition team."

"You guys hiring?" Jimmy asked.

"Mandy's not coming back to teach this fall, so we need to hire a new instructor. It was kind of amazing timing, really, because Thomas reached out to me to see if we had any openings. He's moving back to the area to take care of his grandmother."

Jimmy stood up straighter, focus suddenly very intent on Drea. "Did you say Thomas? What was his last name?"

"Sullivan. Why?"

"He's just someone I knew a long time ago." Jimmy sipped his seltzer, but I didn't miss the slight shake of his hand as he tilted the can to his lips.

"Are you okay?"

"Yeah. Totally fine." He drained the last of his seltzer. "I'm just gonna go use the restroom. Anyone want anything from inside?"

We all waved him off and watched as he walked away.

"I wonder what that was about," Drea said as soon as he was out of earshot.

"Me too. There definitely seems to be more to that story." I turned toward Rafi. "Do you know anything about it?"

Rafi's dad had taken Sammy and Jimmy under his wing

when their mom had abandoned them. Julio Salgado had given Sammy a job and rented them an apartment dirt cheap. Jimmy had still been in high school at the time and the Salgados had become something of surrogates for the boys. I knew they were still pretty close.

Julio shrugged. "I don't remember ever hearing that name."

"Do you think it's okay that I hired Thomas? I don't want to upset Jimmy."

"I think that's probably a conversation for you to have with Jimmy privately. You know he doesn't share much about his personal stuff."

"You're right. We should probably talk about something else," Drea said.

The baby in Rafi's arms chose that moment to let out a loud squawk and Rafi and Elise immediately sprang into action, heading into the house to do whatever it is you did with crying babies. "Should we grab some food before it's gone?" I said to Drea.

"Good plan."

51

ZACH

I HATED HOSPITALS.

I'd just finished a meeting with the activities director at Astaire High School in preparation for the camp we were hosting there next week when I'd gotten a call from someone at the county hospital in Brinkley asking if I would be willing to pay a special visit to one of their patients who was a huge fan. I'd accepted the invitation but had spent the entire drive over battling the urge to turn around and back out.

Currently, I was sitting inside my car in the parking lot, willing myself to open the door and head inside. Since Drea's accident, I'd thankfully only had occasion to enter a hospital one other time. And just like now, I'd spent ten minutes in my car doing breathing exercises in an attempt to stave off a panic attack.

In an effort to distract myself, I focused on the reason I was there. The hospital liaison I'd spoken to over the phone had said Sean was a thirteen-year-old boy who'd lost his mother and home in a fire and was inside the hospital all alone. He was supposedly a huge fan of mine, and knowing what it was like to lose a parent, the least I could do was go inside and pay him a visit. I could do this. I could fight through the panic for this kid who'd lost everything. Taking one more breath and blowing it out slowly, I opened the door and started across the parking lot.

With sweaty palms, I entered the building, a blast of cold air ruffling my hair as I stepped across the threshold. A receptionist pointed me in the direction of Sean's room, and I headed that way, wiping my sweaty hands on my shorts as I continued to take deep breaths. As I rounded a corner, I pulled up short when I saw Jason standing in profile, peering into one of the rooms. He was quite possibly the only thing that could distract me from the anxiety of being in a hospital, and for a moment, I forgot all the breathing I'd been so focused on.

It seemed impossible he could look better each time I saw him, yet as I took in the sight of him in a gray fitted polo and navy shorts, I couldn't help but admire all the ways he'd matured into the man before me. He'd allowed the stubble he'd been sporting the last time I saw him to grow into a full beard, and while I'd never given it any thought before, it would appear I was shaping up to be a beard guy.

Our last meeting a couple of weeks ago hadn't gone well, and I wasn't sure how he'd react to seeing me here now, so I proceeded with caution, hoping he'd at least give me a chance to explain my presence. As I approached, he turned toward me, his face registering surprise and then concern.

"What are you doing here? Are you okay? You're pale."

I waved him off, trying to act casual, though I felt anything but. "Over the years, I seem to have developed an aversion to hospitals."

His brows drew up. "Are you sure you're okay? Why are you here?"

"I'm fine. Or at least as fine as I can be. And I'm here because apparently this kid"—I nodded toward the door—"is a fan. I got a call from the hospital to see if I'd do a visit."

"Did you know the hospital would be a problem before you got here?"

I laughed without humor. "Yeah. I had a similar reaction last time I was in one."

"And you still came?" His eyes were wide with surprise or maybe concern. Possibly a mix of both.

"I know what it's like to lose a parent," I said quietly. "But why are you here? Do you know this kid?"

He blew out a shaky breath, dragging his hand through his hair, and it was my turn to show some concern. "I was the one who pulled him out of the house Sunday night. Him and his dog."

"Shit, J." Instinctively, I put my hand on his arm, wanting to offer comfort. "Are *you* okay?"

"I'm uh...I'm..." He swallowed hard, and I didn't miss the way his voice shook when he continued, "I'll be okay. I just needed to see him. To see for myself that he's alright."

The rhythmic click of heels coming down the hall had us both turning toward the sound. A woman with a no-nonsense bob and wearing a smart-looking pantsuit approached, introducing herself as Betsy Sullivan, the liaison who had contacted me earlier. She gave us a brief update on Sean's condition, stating that he was being placed in his aunt's care and she would be coming by to pick him up later, and then led us into the room.

Sean didn't move as we entered, continuing to look out the window. Poor kid. He had to be pretty messed up over what had happened. I remembered those first couple of days after losing my mom. I went through a thousand different emotions. I figured he was probably feeling the same.

"Sean? I wanted to introduce you to my friend, Zach." When he still didn't turn his head, Ms. Sullivan repeated herself, adding in my last name. "Zach Jacobs. Retired soccer player from San Francisco SC."

At that, Sean finally turned, his eyes widening when he saw it really was me. "Hey, man. I heard you're a soccer fan."

He nodded slowly, eyes still wide in disbelief.

"You just a fan? Or do you play too?"

"I play," he said, his voice hoarse.

"That's awesome." I crossed over to sit in the chair next to him. "Does it hurt to talk? You can just nod if you want."

He shrugged. "It's okay."

"Cool. What position do you play?"

"Forward."

"Yeah?" I smiled. "Just like me."

He nodded.

"Are you any good?"

"Decent, I guess."

"I bet you're better than you let on." I thought I caught the slightest of twinkles in his eye, there and gone in a flash, and I found myself very interested in seeing what this kid could do.

"Have you heard about my soccer camp through Aksarben SC?"

The kid instantly deflated. I hadn't thought it was possible for him to look even sadder than he had when we walked in, but I'd somehow made things worse with just the mention of my camp. "I wanted to go, but my...my mom said we didn't have the money."

God, the way his voice hitched when he said *mom* just about did me in. I could remember that feeling, that ache that came with the mere mention of her name after she passed. I still felt it now, but those first weeks after her accident were like pouring lemon juice into a paper cut. The temptation to bring up my own loss was strong, but I also remembered how many adults in my life had tried to share some anecdote to show how much they related, and all it ever did was make me feel awkward. The last thing this kid needed right now was my own grief story.

"I'm going to leave a spot open for you. I'd love to see what you can do."

"I don't know if—"

I put a hand up to stop him. "I'll talk to your aunt and see what we can work out. It's ultimately up to her, of course, but I'm hoping we can talk her into letting you come."

"Okay, I guess." He offered another shrug. I figured he was likely trying not to get his hopes up.

We chatted for a few more minutes, but I could see him struggling to focus on the conversation, his eyes flickering back toward the window. I figured he was probably over-whelmed and could use some space.

"I think it's time to head out. You rest up, and hopefully, I'll see you next week."

He dragged his eyes back toward me and nodded. I followed Jason and Ms. Sullivan out into the hall, where she thanked me for coming and assured me she would put me in contact with Sean's aunt. She hurried away with those same rhythmic strides, leaving Jason and me alone in the hall once again.

Unsure what to do with the awkward silence that had descended, I half-mumbled, "I'm gonna head out," then turned to follow Ms. Sullivan toward the exit.

"It was nice of you to come today. You were really good with him." Jason fell into step beside me.

"Thanks," I said lamely. I hadn't come here for any other reason than to try to brighten a boy's day, but his praise filled me with warmth nonetheless.

We walked the rest of the way to the exit in silence. As soon as I was outside, I lifted my face to the sun and breathed deeply, releasing the anxious tension from my body. I opened my eyes to find Jason watching me with an odd expression. I hadn't even thought about what I was doing. It had been instinctive. But now I felt heat rise up my cheeks at his stare.

For the first time since I'd been back, Jason was looking at me with something other than animosity, and while I was glad to avoid another fight, I didn't like how much his look felt like pity.

A sudden wave of exhaustion washed over me. In the last hour, I'd fought off a panic attack, held the weight of sadness at bay over a kid losing his mother, and navigated another conversation with Jason. I was grateful I'd had a chance to speak to him that hadn't ended in an argument, but it left me feeling wrung out to dry.

"It's been a long day," I said with a sigh. "I'm going to head out. It was good to see you, J."

"Yeah, maybe I'll see you around."

I nodded, and we turned in opposite directions toward our cars. And while the afternoon had been weighty, there was a part of me that couldn't help but feel the tiniest sliver of hope because he'd said maybe.

I woke with a start, gasping for air with my heart racing. The sheets were wet with sweat and tangled between my legs as if I'd been thrashing around. I sat up, pushed my hair off my damp forehead, and reached for the cup of water I typically left on my nightstand. I drained the glass, then sat, staring into the dark, trying to shake off the lingering panic the dream had left in its wake.

I fumbled for my phone, noting the time was just three-thirty. I threw back the covers and walked over to the window, looking out over the lake. When I'd bought the house, I'd debated moving back into my old room but had ultimately decided to move into the primary bedroom since it included an en suite bathroom. And since the house was designed so all the bedrooms looked out over the lake, I still had the same gorgeous view. The water was still tonight, the half-moon shining just enough that I could make out a few gentle ripples in the otherwise calm lake. It was soothing.

It had been years since I'd had that nightmare, the one where I stumbled upon a car accident and the driver's face kept changing. The driver was almost always Mom, then Drea, then Jason, but I'd also had versions with Clayton and my father mixed in as well.

I'd had other nightmares over the years, mostly surrounding disaster soccer scenarios. I'd forget my uniform for an away match. Or worse, I'd take the field naked. Those sucked, but the ones that were focused on my game time performance were the worst. I'd score an own goal. Or miss a potentially game winning PK. I'd even had one where every time I scored a goal, it was called back for offsides.

Unsurprisingly, the soccer nightmares stopped when I decided to retire. But the one I'd had tonight—I probably hadn't had that one for at least three years. And it was usually harder to pinpoint the trigger. Not this time though.

The hospital visit. The memories of my own grief had been stirred up by the circumstances of Sean's situation. Those were bound to stir things up.

I yawned, stretching my hands to the ceiling, then crossed back over to the bed. I had a full day of meetings tomorrow and needed to try for a little more sleep. I slid into the other side of the king-sized bed, away from the sweaty mess I'd made on my usual side, and closed my eyes, hoping my sleep would be more peaceful.

52

ZACH

I PULLED into my garage a little after seven, feeling mentally exhausted but physically restless. After a shitty night of sleep, I'd spent most of my day in meetings—with the board of the soccer club about funding, the project manager from Rogers Construction about the new facility, and the coaches planning the camp next week. Meetings, meetings, meetings.

I was used to spending my time in training or in practice, not sitting in overly air-conditioned rooms listening to people drone on and on about things I supposed were important enough. But I had a low-grade headache building at the base of my skull, nonetheless. Add to it a nearly one-hour commute each way into the city, and I was itching for some exercise.

I walked into my bedroom, changing out of my slacks and dress shirt and into jogging shorts and a dry-fit tank. I laced up my shoes, grabbed my phone and AirPods, and headed into the humid night air. It was a little warmer than I typically liked for a jog, but I'd skipped my morning run in favor of commuting to the city, so this would have to do.

I lightly jogged down the street toward the stairs that would take me to the lakeside path. The same one Jason and I had traveled so many times the summer before I left for college and where we'd crossed paths a couple of weeks back and Jason shouted at me before turning away.

Still, I thought about how I bared my soul to him in the rain on the anniversary of my mom's passing. How I shared my fears about leaving for college and not knowing what I wanted to do with my life. There'd also been mundane conversations about town gossip, weekend plans, and all the other little things one might discuss with a friend. A friend who'd eventually turned into something more.

God, I missed him. It felt like I'd done nothing *but* miss him for nearly a decade. No matter how far I'd tried to leave him in the past, to outrun our history, to escape my own guilt for the way I'd cut him off, the memory of him was never far behind.

It was like he was a part of me. As was this place. How many times had I stood at the beach in LA and longed to be on the bank of the lake instead? Or had something as simple as ice cream and wished for a cone from Sherry's Soft-Serv? How many times had I seen a guy in a bar with a short crop of dark hair, who was tall and broad, only to have him turn around and be someone else? I'd once thought my feelings for Jason had roots so deep it'd take a hurricane to rip them out. Later, I'd convinced myself that idea had been the fantasy of a nineteen-year-old, longing for someone to simply *see* him. Now that I was back, though, I thought maybe I'd had the right of it all those years ago.

Those roots *had* run deep.

The question was, had Jason's? Had his feelings run deep enough to withstand the storm of my abandonment?

The animosity he'd shown me since I'd returned indicated he still had some sort of feelings. And while yesterday had felt like a truce of sorts, that was still a far cry from forgiveness.

Even so, I couldn't blame him for being angry. And I didn't have a better explanation for why I'd cut him off. I'd been overwhelmed when I left. Between catching up on classes, worrying over Drea, and wrestling with the intensity of my feelings toward Jason, I'd felt almost paralyzed. I'd battled nightmares and panic attacks and had been unable to handle more than the next item on my to-do list, which was primarily occupied by coursework and training.

And it wasn't only Jason I'd left hanging. Aunt Amy had taken to sending me daily texts with updates regarding Drea's condition, but they'd gone unanswered, and for nearly a month after I left, I didn't speak with Drea or my father, not even by text. I just...couldn't. It was like there was a bubble around Astaire that I couldn't penetrate. But the bubble was a creation of my own mind.

Messages were left on read. I'd pull my phone out of my pocket and stare at it, completely unable to execute the simple task of swiping it open and pressing the button to call. I loathed myself for it. The guilt was so severe some days that I couldn't eat. But I couldn't push past it either.

Oddly enough, it was a phone call from Drea that finally pushed through. She caught me early one morning while I was still asleep and too groggy to process what was happening. I'd swiped open the call out of habit before I'd even realized I'd done so, and upon giving a bleary "Hello," she'd laid into me, her words angry and laced with tears. I'd sobbed like a baby.

Our relationship had been rocky for quite a while after

that. I'd stayed in LA over spring break that year, citing my grades as the reason, but really, I just hadn't been able to bear the thought of going home. Of facing my family, or even worse, seeing Jason. With each passing day that I didn't reach out to him, the barrier to doing so became taller and more impossible to climb. How could I apologize? How could I explain when I didn't even understand it myself? Even now, I wasn't sure I had the words to articulate what had happened. I snorted. That had been evident the last couple of times I'd tried to talk to him about it.

Bringing my thoughts back to the present, I came around a bend in the path, ducking under some trees that needed to be trimmed, and spotted someone sitting a short distance away. There was a small dog sitting near them, and they looked to be grabbing their ankle. With the sun low in the sky, it was difficult to see them clearly, but I slowed to a walk, wanting to see if there was something I could do to help.

My breath stuttered when I realized it was Mrs. Whitt, Jason's mom. What must she think of me after what I'd done to her son? I shook my head. It didn't matter. She was obviously injured—I could see the pinch of pain on her face—and needed assistance.

"Mrs. Whitt? Are you okay?" I asked, though I could tell she wasn't.

She looked up, her eyes widening as she recognized me. "Zach? I wondered when I'd run into you."

"Yes, ma'am." I crouched and gave the pup next to her a scratch. It was a small thing with wiry black fur and a bit of a crossbite. I suspected it was a mutt of some sort.

"I heard you were back in town. How are you?" Her voice was warm, without a hint of malice. Somehow, that only made my guilt worse.

"I'm doing well, thank you. But, um…" I gestured toward her ankle. "What about you?"

"Oh," she said, returning her attention to her foot. I could see it was already starting to swell. "I rolled my ankle trying to detangle myself from Toto's leash."

"Do you mind if I take a look?"

At her nod, I pushed gently at the flesh, probing the tissue to assess where it was most tender and gently moving it around to judge the range of motion. I'd seen my fair share of sprained ankles on the soccer field over the years, and while I wasn't a doctor, I did know what to look for. Based on her reaction to my prodding and the rate of swelling, I'd judge it to be a moderate sprain, but she'd definitely want to have a doctor look at it to be sure. "I'm guessing it's just a sprain, but you'll probably want to go in to have it looked at."

I looked around, assessing where we were and how close we might be to the parking lot. "Is there someone I can call? I can help you get to the parking lot, but it's probably best you don't try to drive since it's your right foot."

"I texted Jason just before you happened upon me. He's already on his way."

My heart beat a little quicker at the prospect of seeing him again so soon. Our paths were bound to cross in a town this size, but two days in a row seemed serendipitous.

I shifted out of my crouch to sit by her while we waited. Toto immediately climbed into my lap and made himself comfortable. "Alrighty then. Make yourself at home," I joked, scratching the fur between his ears.

Mrs. Whitt chuckled beside me. "He's not the prettiest looking thing, but he more than makes up for it with the love he's willing to give."

"He seems very sweet. How long have you had him?"

"Let's see...he was actually a rescue. Jason saved him from an abandoned barn that caught fire. No one claimed him, so we took him in. It was just after Mandy finished college, so three years ago, I guess."

I continued petting him, not meeting her eyes. There were so many questions I wanted to ask, things I wanted to know about Jason, about the life he'd lived since I'd said goodbye. But I didn't have that right. And I certainly didn't want to put his mom in that position, so I didn't say anything.

"We followed your career, you know. A lot of folks from Astaire did. It was exciting to see one of our own make it to that level. Soccer got a lot more popular around here."

"I'm surprised you guys consider me one of your own. I was only here for a year. And with the way I left..." I trailed off, not sure what Jason had told her. Surely, she'd figured something was amiss when I basically disappeared from her son's life.

"Whatever happened between you and my son is just that...between you and him." I chanced a look at her but saw nothing but kindness. "And even if you were only here for a year, your family was here longer. Drea is practically family."

"Am I interrupting?" I looked up to see Jason approaching with the corner of his mouth tipped up in a partial smile. He wore athletic shorts and a dry-fit tank similar to mine, with a black ball cap worn backward. He was sweaty, like maybe he'd been working out or doing yard work when he'd been called away, and all that tan, sweat-slicked skin had my mouth going dry and my tongue tying itself in knots. Not the most appropriate reaction when his mom was sitting right next to me.

It was that smile, though, that really did things to me. It

was the first time I'd seen it since I'd been back, and it was like watching the sun break through the clouds after a storm. I knew that smile was for his mom's benefit, but I basked in its warmth nonetheless.

"I can't believe my clumsy self. Thanks for coming out here. Your father's on a fishing trip with Uncle Frank."

"It's not a problem. I just got done mowing the lawn." He crouched, examining her ankle much the way I had done. "Looks like a sprain, but you should probably have Dr. Miller look at it. Do you think you can stand?"

"If you boys help me."

Jason looked at me and I nodded, standing and holding out a hand to help her. She reached for it, and between the three of us, we got her upright.

"You ready?" he asked her.

"Ready for what?"

Without warning, he effortlessly scooped her up in his arms. She let out a screech of surprise but laughed as he jostled her a little to get a more secure hold. "Goodness. Being carried by my son was not on the motherhood Bingo card."

"Yeah? Do they hand those out at the hospital, or…?"

She swatted at him. "Such a smartass."

I scooped up Toto, forgoing the leash entirely, and gestured for Jason to lead the way. We weren't too far from the parking lot, so it only took us a few minutes to get to Jason's truck. He got her settled in the front seat with Toto and shut the door, turning toward me.

"Thank you for staying with her until I got here."

"It wasn't a problem. Do you want me to follow behind in her car? Then you can bring me home after and she won't have to worry about picking up her car later."

I watched as he weighed his options. "Yeah, I guess that

would be helpful," he said, almost reluctantly. I tried not to bristle at the response. No matter how much I thought I deserved his anger, it still stung when faced with it. "Let me just grab her keys."

53

JASON

AFTER SETTLING my mom in at home and promising to check back first thing in the morning, Zach and I climbed into my truck and headed back toward the lake.

It had been surreal to have Zach inside my childhood home again. I'd been flooded with memories, particularly of that week we'd spent there while the girls were in the hospital. My bedroom had become our refuge, a place to escape the stress and worry of the hospital where we could wrap ourselves in each other. I wouldn't ever wish to experience that week again, but I couldn't help but long for the feeling of holding him in my arms, if only for a moment.

That week had been absolute hell, but so had the weeks following, when I'd been consumed with fear and worry over why he wasn't returning my calls until, eventually, that had given way to grief over the relationship that had only just begun but had meant everything. As much as I longed for those days when he'd been mine to hold, the reality was that he wasn't mine. No matter his reasoning for removing himself from my life or the apologies he'd made in the last several weeks, he'd chosen to leave. We couldn't go back.

It was quiet in the truck, the silence weighty with all that lay between us. The anger I'd initially felt when he returned had dissipated over the last couple of weeks, leaving a sense of deep weariness in its wake. There was still so much I didn't understand about the way he'd left me, but I was so tired of thinking about it. Of trying to make sense of what he'd told me. His presence here was dredging up hurts I'd long since buried. Things I'd moved on from. I'd built a good life here without him. There was no sense in rehashing the past and reopening old wounds.

And then I'd run into him at the hospital yesterday. He'd been so pale as he'd come down the hall toward me, his eyes just a little wild, like he was trying to keep himself from flying apart. I'd seen that look on his face once before when he'd had a panic attack outside of Drea's hospital room. For a moment, it had been like we were back there, and I'd wanted to pull him into my arms, just as I'd done back then. And then I'd watched as he'd pulled himself together, pushing past the panic so he could attempt to cheer up a kid who'd just had the rug pulled out from under him.

Watching Zach interact with Sean had been a sight to behold. I'd been so captivated by how Zach handled the conversation that I'd barely said anything. He'd been pale and shaky in the hallway, and then right before my eyes, he transformed into a confident professional soccer player. A kid's sports hero. He'd been compassionate and warm with his offer to hold a spot for Sean at camp, seeming to antici-pate the boy's concerns before he'd even expressed them. And while most adults didn't know how to talk to teenage boys, especially ones in the middle of a life-altering event, Zach had seemed completely at ease. Though I supposed he might understand better than most after losing his own mother as a teen.

It wasn't until we were outside, when he took a few deep breaths, that I remembered just how tense he'd been when he first approached me outside of Sean's room. For a moment, I'd forgotten about all the old wounds of our split and had only been impressed by the man who'd battled his own demons to show up for a kid he'd never met.

I'd thought of little else over the last twenty-four hours.

I pulled into the driveway of his house, noting how little it had changed over the years despite being under different owners for some of that time. "I was surprised when I heard you bought your old house."

"I was going to buy a condo in the city, but I happened upon the listing and couldn't pass it up. I have complicated feelings about this house, but it felt like a sign."

"A sign of what?"

"That it was time to come home. Time to stop running."

I turned to look at him. "Is that what you've been doing all this time? Running?"

"Yeah. I think so."

"Running from what? From me?"

"Not from you. From what I did to you." He averted his gaze to look out the window but turned back toward me now. "I'm just so damn sorry. You deserved better."

He'd apologized a couple of times over the last month, but there was an intensity and a sadness I hadn't noticed before through the haze of my anger. I didn't know what to do with it.

"Why now? After all this time, why come back?"

"How much of my soccer career did you follow?"

I snorted. "More than I should have."

One corner of his mouth lifted up in humor. "You know I played three years with San Fran and that I just retired?"

"Yeah. You took everybody by surprise. By all accounts,

you're in good health and a leader on the team. There was talk of you playing in the Olympics. No one saw it coming."

"That's right. And you know I bounced around a couple of teams before that?"

I nodded.

"Any guesses why? You know me pretty well."

"I thought I did once."

"I'm not much different, J," he said softly.

I huffed but didn't respond.

"I looked good enough for scouts that I got picked up in the draft, but I barely saw any action. I struggled to adjust to the faster pace of play in the pros. By the end of the first season, I got traded. My second season was only moderately better, and I couldn't figure out why. I trained hard in the offseason. Worked hard throughout the season, but I just couldn't find my groove. The trade to San Fran was a last-ditch effort to save my career. With it being an expansion team, there was a lot of energy and excitement surrounding that first season. It sparked something in me that had been missing for a while, and I finally felt like I was finding my place. I found joy in playing again. But it didn't last. I started having soccer-related nightmares. I began to dread game days. And despite the next two seasons being some of my best, I realized any love I'd had for playing had long since been replaced by a constant fear that I wouldn't live up to expectations.

"I don't think I'm wired to be a professional athlete. I have the skill and the talent, but the pressure to perform takes all the fun out of it. My body constantly ached, and it seemed like I was always battling some minor injury. The travel felt never-ending. Do you know I've always wanted a dog? As a kid, we never had one because Drea and I were so busy, and as an adult, I was always traveling. But I really think I want a dog."

I thought what he was saying actually made some sense. He'd always seemed to have a love-hate relationship with soccer. I knew the weight of his father's expectations had worn on him, but I had hoped that would change in college. It seemed that while his father had let up on him, the pressure had shifted to a different source. I figured you really had to love a sport to make it worth that kind of stress.

"Okay, so why Astaire? You could live anywhere in the country. Any city you want. Why here?"

Someone like Zach had always been meant for someplace bigger. He'd traveled all over the country and even parts of Europe for his career. Why return to the tiny town of Astaire in the heart of the Midwest?

His eyes met mine. "Because it's home."

I understood the intent behind his words, but I chose to ignore it. I wasn't ready to face the possibility that his answer was *me*. "What about Omaha? You grew up there. Your dad's there."

He took a moment to respond, staring into the distance as he contemplated his answer. "The Zach who grew up in Omaha was an entirely different person. And even that year I was in Astaire, I was still hanging on to that old persona to some degree. But the summer after graduation...that was the most *me* I've ever felt. I didn't feel pressured to act a certain way or be the life of the party. To always put on a smile and act like I had the perfect life. I could be sad sometimes or angry. I could take time for myself, sit out on the dock, and just...exist."

"What happened when you went to college? Which Zach were you in LA? Or San Fran?"

I waited once again while he gave his answer some

thought. "A hybrid, maybe? I was probably a little more myself than I was in high school, but no one has cracked me open the way you did."

There it was again, the implication I was avoiding. I let out a sigh. "Zach...you're putting a lot of weight on one summer. Has it occurred to you that you might be placing more significance on it than you should?"

"Am I? Is it all in my head? What we meant to each other?"

I wanted to deny it, but I didn't have it in me. "No. But what if you've come back here, searching for that feeling, and I can't give it to you? It seems to me this whole idea of getting back to who you really are is intertwined with our relationship. What if I can't give you what you want?"

"Can't or won't?"

"Does it matter? The result is the same."

He blew out a breath. "You're right. And I won't pretend I didn't come back here in the hope I could repair the damage I caused when I left or that we might find our way back to some sort of friendship, at least. But you're not the only reason I came here. Don't forget that my sister and Aunt Amy are here too. And I'm serious about the youth soccer club. It's the most excited I've been about anything...maybe ever. I might not have been wired to be a professional athlete, but that doesn't mean I can't give other kids the opportunity to reach their full potential. Maybe I had to do all that other stuff so I could show future athletes the way."

His eyes lit up as he spoke about the club, and I couldn't deny that it was good to see him so excited about something. I thought what he was trying to achieve here was admirable, and a part of me was proud of him for choosing this path, for walking away from his professional sports career because he knew deep down it wasn't the right path for him. And he was still trying to do some good with his knowledge and experience. But that didn't mean I had to open up a place in my life for him.

"I don't know where to go from here, Zach. I don't know what you want from me."

"I'm not asking anything of you." I snorted, but he pressed on. "I know it may seem that way, but my initial goal in seeing you again was to give you a long overdue apology. The way I left things...I know I've tried to explain, but that doesn't excuse my actions, and I wanted to tell you how sorry I am. Anything beyond that is up to you."

I looked into the distance, letting his words settle inside me, mulling them over while I considered my response. I opted for the truth. "What you did...ghosting me like that after everything we went through that week...it hurt me in ways I still haven't recovered from. And if I'm honest, I still don't completely understand. I want to forgive you. In a town this size, and given my friendship with your sister, it would be so much easier. I just...I don't know if I can let it go. I can be polite, but for anything beyond that, I need some time."

"That's fair."

Silence descended in the truck, leaving me with a feeling of overwhelming sadness. I wanted to move forward, if only so peace could exist between us, but I didn't know how. There was a gulf between us that I didn't know how to cross.

"How are you feeling about the fire the other night? You seemed a little shaken up yesterday. Do you want to talk about it?"

The change in topic surprised me. I'd been a little shaky yesterday but hadn't realized Zach noticed. There was a time I would have poured my heart out to him, but that wasn't something I was prepared to do tonight.

"Nah. I'm fine." I looked at my watch. "I think it's probably best I get home and go to bed. I'm gonna try talking Mom into heading to the doctor first thing in the morning."

We sat staring at each other awkwardly in the dim light of the cab. Once upon a time, I would have leaned in and kissed him. Instead, I said, "Thanks for your help with my mom."

"No need to thank me. I'm glad I was there to help."

He turned and climbed out of the truck, and I watched as he punched in the code to the garage and headed inside.

I made my way home, showering off the dried sweat and grime from the yard work I'd been doing before Mom texted. I brushed my teeth and set my alarm before climbing into bed. But sleep wouldn't come. Thoughts of Zach and everything we'd discussed played on a loop in my brain like some sort of earworm.

I may not be able to forgive him, but it seemed I couldn't stop thinking about him either.

54

JASON

It had been nearly a week since I'd dropped Zach off at his house following Mom's fall. The sprain had been minor, and Mom was well on the mend, thankfully. My thoughts regarding Zach were much more complicated.

It had been so much easier to be angry. To be full of self-righteous fury. To see him as a cold-hearted asshole who'd cut me off without a word. Even when he first tried to explain himself, it had sounded weak, further cementing my own conclusions about his character. It hadn't mattered that painting him as a cold and calculating villain didn't jive with the guy I'd known and loved. His betrayal hadn't jived with that guy either, so it was clear my original assessment of his character wasn't to be trusted.

And then I watched him battle his own demons to support a kid he didn't even know. Offering compassion and hope in a place that was clearly difficult for him. I watched how he helped my mom, showing genuine concern for her well-being. He could have fled the scene the moment I arrived, but instead, he stayed to help, going above and beyond by following behind with her car. And in the conversation afterward, he apologized once again, patiently answering my questions, never denying his responsibility for what had happened between us.

It left me mired in confusion. The image of Zach I'd seen last week was much more consistent with my memories of the guy I'd fallen in love with all those years ago. So, what about the guy who ditched me without a word? Where did that leave the villain in my story?

I wasn't sure of the answer, but in the last five days, I'd realized I very much wanted to find out.

I pulled into the high school parking lot around nine. I told myself I was only there to check in on Sean, but even I didn't believe my own bullshit. I'd woken up this morning with a burning need to see Zach. To try to reconcile my memories of him with the guy he was now. To verify that my image of him as a good person had been real. And if that were true...well, I wasn't sure where I'd go from there, but I had to know. And when I remembered the soccer camp started this morning, I hadn't been able to let go of the idea of stopping by.

As I stepped out of my truck, I turned my ball cap to the front, attempting to block out some of the late June sun already beating down on the asphalt. I hoped they had plenty of water down at the field. It was going to be a hot one.

I made my way down the steps to the soccer field, sliding into the row beneath the box so I could sit in the shade. I surveyed the field, impressed with the amount of activity. Middle school-aged kids had been divided into groups of six or seven and assigned to skill-based stations where coaches took them through drills.

I scanned the field, looking for Sean, but like a homing beacon, my attention was instead drawn to Zach standing on the sideline, talking with another coach. The guy said something, and I watched Zach tip his head back and laugh, the sun glinting off his sunglasses. My confused heart lurched at the sight.

He looked down at his watch, then blew a long whistle, shouting for everyone to come over and grab some water. They had pop-up canopies set up for everyone to grab some shade while they took their break, and I watched as kids clumped in groups, laughing and teasing each other while drinking out of their water bottles.

Finally, I spotted Sean standing with another boy farther down the field. They were talking, though less animatedly than some of the others, but I was relieved to see that he had at least one friend.

"Hey, stranger. Fancy seeing you here."

I turned in surprise to find Drea standing next to me, leash in hand, with a medium-sized dog of an indiscernible breed by her side. The dog's tail wagged a mile a minute. I'd been so distracted that I hadn't even heard them approach. I automatically reached out to give the dog a scratch and it stepped forward, leaning into my hand, tongue hanging out enthusiastically.

"What are you doing here?" I asked, squinting into the sun in confusion as I looked up at her.

"Same thing as you, I'm guessing."

"Checking on Sean?" I raised an eyebrow in challenge, knowing damn good and well that was not who she meant.

She sat next to me on the bench, completely unfazed by my sarcasm. "Sean's the kid you guys rescued last week?"

"Yeah." I nodded in his direction. "He's the taller one toward the end with the dark mop of hair."

"Zach was so nervous he wouldn't show up today. Even though Zach waved his fees, Sean's aunt wasn't sure she'd be able to get him here. I'm guessing the kid Sean's standing with is his cousin. The only way she'd agree to him coming this week was if the cousin could come too so they could ride their bikes up here together. Zach even found clothes and cleats for him to wear since he lost everything in the fire."

I blew out a breath. "The department put the aunt in touch with an organization that could help him with some new clothes, but I hadn't thought about anything soccer-specific."

"It's pretty much all Zach talked about when we had lunch over the weekend. Well, not just Sean, but Daisy and the camp too."

"Who's Daisy?"

"Daisy's the dog you've been petting since I got here. You don't recognize her?"

I looked back at the dog, cocking my head to the side. "Should I?"

"She's Sean's dog. Or she was. You rescued her last week."

My eyes widened as I examined the dog closer. Sean's house had been heavily filled with smoke, making it difficult to see anything clearly. There'd been a dog in the room with him, who'd been barking its head off, alerting us to their position, but I hadn't gotten a good look at it under the circumstances. Everything had been chaotic as we'd worked to get the boy and the dog out safely.

"Seriously? This is Sean's dog? How...?" I trailed off, stunned.

"When Zach spoke to the kid's aunt last week to get him set up to come to camp, she mentioned the dog. Said she couldn't afford to keep her. So Zach went to the shelter and adopted her the next day." I remembered he'd mentioned always wanting a dog, but still, this seemed impulsive.

"How'd you end up with her today?"

She rolled her eyes. "Zach was paranoid about leaving her alone all day for the first time since she's still getting used to her new home. I told him I could take her for the day. He's done at three, and I don't have my first class until four. Oh shit." Her face screwed up in frustration. "I forgot I have an appointment at two-thirty." She started fishing in her bag for her phone. "I'll just have to call and reschedule."

"I can take her." The words came out before I thought them through.

Drea cocked her head. "You want to help out with *Zach's* dog? Are you sure that's a good idea?"

I shrugged. I hadn't really thought any of this through. I'd mostly just thought I'd be helping Drea. "We're grown adults. I can have a two-minute conversation with him while I return his dog. It'll be fine."

She stared at me for a long time, making me squirm. "What?" I finally blurted out.

She opened her mouth, then snapped it shut. "Nope. I said I wasn't getting involved."

I let out a sigh. "Drea...don't make this into a thing."

"I'm not making it into a thing. *You're* making it into a thing."

"How? How am I making it into a thing?"

Apparently tired of all the conversation, Daisy plopped down on the concrete and laid her head on my foot.

"Listen. When I found out Zach was coming back here, I told him I'd kick his ass if he hurt you again. But..."

I followed her gaze to find Zach looking at us. Busted. When our eyes met, his face lit up with a smile and he gave a wave. Then, as if remembering where he was, he turned back toward the field and blew his whistle, signaling for all the kids to drop their water bottles and gather around him so he could give the next instruction.

I turned back toward Drea. "But?" I persisted.

She huffed out a resigned breath. "I don't want you to hurt him either."

"Me?" My voice was incredulous.

"I don't want you to give him false hope. Whatever his intentions are in returning to Astaire, his interest in you is genuine. And you have every right to be pissed at him. I'm *still* pissed at him sometimes. But if you can't forgive him, if you don't have any intention of having any kind of relationship with him, don't give him mixed signals."

"I'm not..." I trailed off because even as I tried to protest, I realized she might have a point. I'd shown up at his camp uninvited, and now I was volunteering to help with his dog. Dammit. "Look. I'm not trying to lead him on. I'm just..."

"Just?" she prompted when I didn't finish my sentence.

I blew out a breath, trying to figure out how to explain myself. "When he first came back, I was so angry. His presence here dredged up so much pain I thought I'd buried. It was easier to convince myself I hated him. To see him as an asshole who broke my heart."

"I mean, I love my brother, but he kind of *was* an asshole who broke your heart."

"But he's not really an asshole, is he? The guy I remember wasn't like that. He could be moody sometimes, sure, but he was also kind. He listened. He comforted. Do you know how worried he was about leaving you behind when he went to school? You had such a hard time after losing your mom, and with the pressure your dad put on him... He was worried he'd put that same pressure on you. I just wanted to be the guy who looked out for him since he was so focused on looking out for everyone else.

"I've been convinced for years that my memories of him are distorted. That I made him out to be something he wasn't and it was only when he ghosted me that he showed his true colors. But then I saw him with Sean last week and then again when he helped my mom the next day, and he was that same compassionate guy I remembered. I can't figure it out. Which one is he? Is he the good-hearted guy I loved or the asshole who ghosted me?"

"Can't both be true? Sometimes good people do really shitty things."

"Of course, but we're not talking about someone snapping at me because they had a bad day or sideswiping my car without leaving a note. He sobbed on my shoulder at the airport because he was so upset about leaving me, and then, with the exception of one text letting me know he arrived in LA, I didn't hear from him again until this past April. It's hard to believe those were the actions of the same person."

"Have you guys actually had a conversation about why? Like, has he explained himself to you?"

I snorted. "Just that he wanted to call but *couldn't*. I don't even know what to do with that, Drea."

She chuckled. "I got a similar explanation when I finally got him to talk to me that spring."

"And you just accepted it?"

It was interesting, now that I was thinking about it, that Drea and I had never talked about this in much detail. I'd known he'd given her the silent treatment for a time and that, eventually, she'd forced him to talk to her. I knew in the vaguest of terms that things had been rocky between them for a while and that they'd slowly rebuilt their relationship. But I'd never pressed for details, and she'd never offered them up. I think we had both understood the topic of Zach was off-limits. Neither of us had wanted to risk our friendship by bringing him into it.

"I didn't accept it at first. I was hurt, just like you are now. But over the years, I realized I wanted a relationship with my brother more than I wanted to hold on to old hurts. I don't know if it helps, but I can tell you he hasn't wavered from his rationale over the years, and I'm pretty sure he holds a lot of guilt for it. In all honesty, my brother probably needs therapy, but I haven't been able to convince him to go."

She said it almost flippantly, but I took a moment to absorb that thought. Could it be possible something deeper was going on that he'd left unresolved all these years? I'd been seeing a therapist regularly since the month after the girls' accident. It was just such a regular part of my life. It was hard for me to remember that not everyone sought out therapy as a matter of course.

I huffed a sigh before admitting another truth I'd been thinking about over the last couple of weeks. "Sometimes I just miss my friend. Part of me wants to let go of it all just for the chance to have that back. Like you said, to let go of the hurt in favor of the relationship." I pulled off my ball cap, running my hand through my hair before putting it back on. "When he left...I didn't just lose my boyfriend. I lost my best friend."

"I know," she said, laying her head on my shoulder. "So what are you going to do about it?"

I watched the kids for a moment, thinking through my response. What *did* I want to do? It was becoming evident that I couldn't keep my distance, no matter how much I tried not to think about him. And there was a part of me that wanted to understand *why* he'd left me hanging. To reconcile the guy I loved with the guy who'd left without a backward glance.

"I think I want to get to know him again. I don't know if I can go back to what we once were, but I think I want to at least try to know who he is now. Maybe...maybe then I can move past what he did."

"Are you sure you can handle that? What if you catch feelings? Or what if he does?"

"I'm not stupid enough to think it's not a possibility, but I'm just gonna have to be careful. And I'll talk to him. Let him know where my head's at. I don't want to give him mixed signals."

"You're a good man, Jason Whitt. Some guys might use this as an opportunity to get revenge."

I let out a snort. "I'm not the vengeful type. Who has time for that bullshit?"

"You'd be surprised."

55

ZACH

It was hard to concentrate, knowing Jason was sitting behind me. I had no idea how long he and Drea had been there, but I couldn't deny it set a thrill of excitement humming in my veins. I only hoped he'd still be there when we dismissed the middle school group so I could talk to him.

I returned my attention to the field where the kids were running a passing drill. I tried not to focus all my attention on Sean, but even if I hadn't known a little about his history, I think my eye would have been drawn all the same. The kid had talent. His ball-handling needed a little work, but he was lightning fast and showed promise with his goal-scoring. We planned to reassign the groups tomorrow so the players could work on their weaknesses and build on their strengths. The kids would all be working the same skills with different areas of focus based on their needs. Unfortunately, I would have to split him up from his cousin. Rusty just didn't have the same level of skill as Sean. I hoped it wouldn't cause any issues, but ultimately, I had to do what was best for both boys.

With about five minutes left in the morning session, I blew the whistle, calling for everyone to grab their water and meet me in the center of the field. I resisted the urge to turn to see if Jason was still there, keeping my eyes focused on the kids.

Once I had everyone sitting on the turf in front of me, I addressed them. "Nice work today. I saw a lot of potential in each of you. We'll spend the rest of the week building on that potential to make you stronger players. Make sure to drink plenty of water for the rest of the day. Tomorrow's going to be another hot one and it's important to hydrate ahead of time. Coaches? Anything to add?" I looked around at the other coaches, who all shook their heads. "Alright then. You're dismissed."

The kids hopped up, grabbing their water bottles and soccer balls, breaking off in twos and threes to make their way up the stairs and out of the stadium. I finally allowed myself to turn, and there Jason was, standing in the shade of the press box, a small smile on his face. With a black fitted T-shirt stretched across his broad chest and his AFD ball cap on, he looked like the twenty-first-century version of a Greek god.

He started making his way toward the steps and I realized Drea must have left at some point. That was probably for the best. I wasn't sure how Sean would react to seeing his dog for the first time since the fire.

I wasn't opposed to giving him the opportunity to see Daisy. In fact, it was part of the reason I'd adopted her, but the soccer field was likely not the best place for this first reunion. I needed to talk to his Aunt Sarah to see what we could work out.

"What are you doing here?" I asked as soon as Jason was in hearing range.

"I came to check on Sean. The kid looks good out there."

"He definitely shows promise. I'm just glad he made it today. His aunt seemed a little unsure about getting him here."

"Yeah, that's what Drea said. She said you agreed to let his cousin participate so the two could ride their bikes up here."

"Yep. His cousin did alright, but I'm not sure he was super into it. We'll see how he fares the rest of the week." I took a sip out of my own water bottle. "Where'd Drea go, anyway? I was surprised to see her up here."

"I think she just wanted to see you in action. But she left a little while ago. She wasn't sure you wanted Sean to see the dog."

"She was right. I'm going to talk to his aunt about bringing Daisy by for a visit, but given the circumstances, the soccer field is probably not the best place for that reunion."

"I agree." He took his hat off, ran his hand through his hair, then replaced it. It was a little habit he'd always had when he was nervous or unsure what to say. I'd always found it endearing. "I wanted to let you know that I'm taking Daisy for a couple of hours this afternoon. Drea had an appointment that she forgot about and I told her Daisy could hang with me. I hope that's okay."

"Oh. Um...yeah, that's totally fine. Thank you." I could feel a different kind of flush rising under my already heated cheeks. His offer was so sweet and honestly such a surprise that it had me off-kilter. I felt like I was in high school all over again.

"What time do you want me to bring her by?"

I waved him off. "I can just swing by your house and pick her up. That way, you don't have to make a trip over."

"It's alright. I don't have anything else going on today. You finish here, and I'll bring her over whenever you want her."

"Okay. Is four good?"

"That works. I'll see you then."

"Sounds good. Thanks."

"You got it. I'll just get out of your way."

I nodded, but as he turned and started heading up the steps, I called his name, stopping him. "It was really good to see you here today. Kind of made my morning."

His lips turned up in a shy smile, but he didn't say anything, opting for a wave before heading up the steps.

The whole interaction left me feeling confused. And hopeful.

Shit. Hope was a dangerous thing.

56

JASON

As I HEADED over to Zach's later that afternoon with Daisy's nose pressed to my truck's passenger window, I contemplated what I wanted to say. I'd told Drea I'd be upfront with Zach and do my best not to lead him on, but how did I start that conversation? *I want to get to know you again, but don't get your hopes up because I still don't know if I can forgive you* didn't seem like the best way to start. Offering to be "just friends" seemed trite. This was real life, not a teenage rom-com.

Then there was the pesky detail of the hint of attraction I'd felt this morning as I watched Zach working with the kids. He'd been so good with them, demonstrating competence and leadership while also establishing a friendly rapport. And after hearing how he'd once again gone above and beyond for Sean, making sure he had clothes for camp and adopting the dog, I'd been unable to deny those faint flutters of attraction stirring in my blood. The feelings were rusty, like a voice that had gone scratchy from disuse, but I still recognized them for what they were.

All the more reason to walk away.

All the more reason I didn't want to.

Daisy was asleep in the passenger seat when I turned into Zach's neighborhood, and I was no closer to determining what I wanted to say. I pulled into the driveway, and with a sigh, I got out of the truck, walking around to the passenger side to get Daisy, who was now awake and doing a happy dance at the prospect of going on an adventure. I thought this dog might just be the happiest ball of sunshine I'd ever seen. Her name suited her.

We walked up to the door, but before I could ring the bell, a text message came through from Zach, telling me to walk around to the back. Daisy and I made our way around the side of the house, using the pavers to get down the hill to the patio where Zach was sitting with a beer in hand, hair still wet from either a shower or a swim.

Damn, he looked good. It was so rare that I paid much attention to someone's appearance, but that had always been different with Zach. As a high school athlete, he'd been fit, but these days, that tight, muscular build came with the maturity of a grown man. He still wore his hair a little longer on the top, but while he'd always been clean-shaven before, these days, he seemed to prefer having permanent scruff, the length just shy of being a full beard. I found myself wanting to kiss him so I could feel the scrape against my smooth skin.

Fuck. Thoughts like that weren't helping.

I bent and released Daisy from her leash, giving myself a moment to calm my erection—it had been a long time since that had been an issue for me—before taking a couple more steps onto the patio.

"How'd the afternoon camp go?"

"Great until the very end. You want a beer?"

He gestured toward the bucket filled with ice and long

necks sitting on the edge of the unlit fire pit. I pulled an Infusion Vanilla Blonde from the bucket and took a seat while Daisy sniffed around the trees separating Zach's property from his neighbors.

"So what happened at the end?" I asked as I twisted off the top and took a sip.

He huffed out a frustrated breath. "You saw that the camp is coed? That I don't separate the kids by gender?"

At my nod, he continued, "Some asshole dad came up at the end of the day demanding I separate the girls and boys for the rest of the week or he would pull his kid from camp. Said he hadn't paid all that money just for his kid to play with girls."

"Who was it?"

"Last name was Jensen, I think? The kid has potential and seemed embarrassed by his father's behavior, which I totally relate to. I'd love for him to continue, but I'm not changing the structure of the camp, so it's ultimately up to his dad whether or not he continues."

I shook my head. "Chad Jensen is an entitled dick. He's the type of guy who'll leave a two-dollar tip on a forty-dollar bill and then brag about it. Colby, his kid, is going to be a senior and seems to be a decent sort. Stays out of trouble. I think he's going to be captain of the high school team next year, actually. You should definitely stick to your guns."

"Oh, I plan to. The other coaches like the format. A couple of them are with the high school program, so they already know quite a few of the kids and believe the players worked harder under this format. The girls had something to prove and the boys didn't want to look bad in front of the girls. And any kid who might be nonbinary or trans didn't have to feel any awkwardness about their identity. I figure it's the same set of skills anyway, so there's no reason they can't work out together. The only place the girls lagged was in some of the running drills, though not by much, and I bet some of them will outpace the boys by the end of the week."

"I wouldn't doubt it." I took another sip of my beer. "You're doing a really good thing here, Zach. I'm...I'm proud of you."

He'd gotten some color on his face while standing out in the sun all day, but that red deepened at my praise. *Shit.* That was just the kind of talk that would send mixed signals.

"Thanks, J. That means a lot. Even with the incident with that Jensen guy, it felt good to be coaching again. I haven't worked with kids since those camps I did the summer after senior year."

The mention of that summer made my stomach clench as thoughts of that time always did. In some ways, it had been the best summer of my life, made all the more tragic when he walked away just a few months later. That reminder brought back all those feelings of confusion I'd been having trying to get to the bottom of who Zach really was and why he'd left me hanging. And I couldn't figure any of that out until I let him in a little bit. But first, we had to talk about expectations.

I set my beer down and leaned forward in my chair, resting my forearms on my knees. "I wanted to talk to you..." I began.

"Shit. Okay. That sounds ominous."

"It's not meant to, but Drea brought something up this morning, and it's been weighing on my mind all day."

"Okay..."

"She suggested my presence at today's practice, combined with volunteering to take Daisy for the afternoon, might send you mixed signals. She thought I'd be getting your hopes up or something along those lines."

He relaxed, his features softening. "I appreciate my sister looking out for me, but you've made yourself pretty clear that you need some time to…process my return and all the baggage that comes with that. I'm under no illusions that you might forgive me or that there might ever be any sort of relationship between us, even a friendship, though you're too nice of a guy not to at least be polite when our paths cross."

I snorted. "Polite? I punched you in the face."

He grinned at me. "Eh. I had it coming."

He leaned forward in his chair, mirroring my posture while his expression turned serious. "Drea wasn't completely wrong though. I can admit to feeling a little hopeful when I saw you this morning."

I winced at that, knowing he was right.

"Don't stress. It's not all on you. I came back to Astaire with my hopes already up. I told myself not to. I told myself there was every chance you'd never want to speak to me again. But it was too late. From the moment I sent that text in the spring, asking if you would be at the reunion, I was already conjuring a thousand different scenarios for what would happen when we saw each other again. I gotta say, none of them had you punching me…"

"Ugh. I'm never going to live that down."

"No, you're really not. But what I was going to say was that for every scenario I created with a negative outcome, I had ten more that were positive. Maybe we could find our way back into a relationship again. Maybe we'd simply be friends. Either way was good because it meant I got to have you in my life again." He stood, moving so he was sitting in front of me on the brick edge of the fire pit. "I've missed you."

I hated how much those words hurt. I'd missed him too. I still missed him. Right now. In this moment, with him physically sitting right in front of me. I missed my friend. I missed the guy I'd only just started to fall in love with. I missed what could have been. The relationship we never really got to have. The joys and celebrations and fights and tears. The physical aspects we'd only begun to explore. I'd been robbed of that, and the person who'd stolen it from me was *him*.

But where thoughts like this would have fueled my anger a couple of weeks ago, tonight, I felt hollow. Bereft. Unbearably sad. And I had a burning desire to understand *why*.

"I missed you too. But the difference is that you could have done something about it. And you didn't. For *nine* years."

"I know," he said quietly, watching me with sad eyes.

"Because you couldn't."

He nodded.

"I still don't understand. And I'm not trying to be a dick. I'm not trying to start a fight. I'm not even angry anymore. Or at least not much. But it hurts, Zach. To hear you say you didn't call me for nine years because you just *couldn't*. It feels like there's something you're not telling me. Something that would explain what was stopping you."

He let out a breath, dropping his head so I couldn't see his eyes, his posture defeated. When he looked back up, it was with tears in his eyes. "I know it sounds lame. It *felt* lame. Like, why couldn't I just make a fucking phone call? There were days I wanted to throw my phone against the wall and smash it into a thousand pieces. It was like there was a door I wanted to open, but I didn't have the key. And the longer I stood at the door, the bigger, thicker, and more impenetrable it got until, eventually, it became evident I wouldn't ever be able to open it."

I watched as he tried to gather himself, seemingly trying to will the tears away. But I liked the tears. Not because I wanted him to hurt, but because, for the first time, I could see how much it had cost him, whatever this imaginary barrier was that had prevented him from calling me.

"Did you ever consider seeing a therapist?"

"For not being able to make a phone call? That just seems...I don't know. I feel like therapy is for people who have bigger issues."

"You don't think being unable to make a phone call to your boyfriend or your sister, people you were close to, is a sign of a bigger issue? Unless there's something else you're not telling me. Some other reason..."

"No," he was quick to say. "There wasn't any other reason. And I guess maybe you have a point. I just kept thinking if I gave it more time, I'd figure out how to push through it on my own."

"But you didn't." I spoke the words softly, not meaning it as an accusation, but unable to let the point go just the same.

He stood, taking a couple of steps away and running his hand through his hair. I could tell he was getting frustrated, but I didn't think his frustration lay with me or my line of questioning. I thought it was some internal struggle he was having.

"I'm trying to understand, Zach. But I can't do that if I don't have all the pieces of the puzzle. I need you to explain it to me."

He turned back and looked at me. "After I left...after it

had been weeks and then months without contact, I started to accept that I wouldn't ever be able to reach out. I spent the summer in Washington with Clayton. Pissed off my father and upset Drea that I didn't come home. Piled on more guilt. But I couldn't risk seeing you. It was the oddest feeling...needing you so bad it hurt to breathe and being equally as terrified that once I did, I'd have to explain something there wasn't a logical explanation for."

He began to pace. "I think I slid into some sort of depression. The self-loathing made it hard to get out of bed. I withdrew, barely speaking to any of Clayton's family, even though they'd generously allowed me to stay with them. The only thing that got me through was Clayton's persistence that I go outside and do things with him. We hiked and fished and did all sorts of outdoorsy shit. For a guy who seems so derpy on the surface, there's a lot more to him than most people realize. He clearly knew something was going on with me, but he never pressured me to talk about it, and by the end of summer, I could almost pretend everything was okay. I convinced myself that with enough time passing, you'd get over it. Drea and my father would get used to not having me around. Plenty of families have adult children who rarely come home to visit. Everyone would adjust until this became the new norm."

"Zach...that sounds...lonely."

"It was. But that was how I wanted it. With what I had done to you and the way I'd distanced myself from my family, I no longer felt like I deserved to have any of you in my life. The harm I'd done felt irreparable."

God, the picture he painted was almost...tragic. For the first time since he'd come back to Astaire, I was able to set aside my own anger and hurt and see just how difficult that time had been for him. I was glad he'd had Clayton, but if what he was saying was true, he'd needed professional help. He likely still did.

He stopped pacing on the far side of the patio and stood with his back to me, looking out at the lake. Daisy, who'd been lying on the corner of the patio, gave a little whine before trotting over to where Zach was standing and licked his hand.

My heart ached for the nineteen-year-old boy who, for reasons I wasn't sure either of us understood, hadn't been able to reach out and then had punished himself for it. I ached with the need to go to him. To wrap my arms around him and be his refuge. To tell him everything was okay.

But it wasn't okay. At least, not yet.

"Do you still think it's irreparable?"

He turned back to face me. "I don't know. I'm still working through things with my family. Drea says she's forgiven me, but I suspect she still holds some resentment. And things with my father are about as good as can be expected. The animosity from my youth is gone, but I don't know if we'll ever be super close. We're just different people. Or maybe we're too much alike. I don't know."

"And with me?"

He walked back over and sat on the edge of the fire pit in front of me again. Daisy followed and lay at his feet, keeping a close eye. "I think that's up to you. I'm being as open and honest as I can be. And you can continue to ask me questions if you need to. I'll answer all of them. I owe you that. But the ultimate answer of whether the damage I did is irreparable is up to you."

"Why now? If it was so difficult for you to reach out nine years ago, how were you able to do it now?"

"As I was debating what I wanted to do after retirement and had the idea of opening a soccer club, I kept coming back to the thought of doing it in Astaire. But that meant I would have to reach out to you or, at the very least, be prepared for us to cross paths. And when I really thought about it, I wasn't scared anymore. Whatever block I'd had before was gone. I was nervous for sure, but I realized I didn't want to live the rest of my life without trying to explain what had happened. If I came back here and you wanted nothing to do with me, I'd figure out how to live with that. But what if I could make things right, and there was a chance I could have you in my life again?"

"What would that look like? Me in your life again? What are you hoping for?"

"I'll take whatever you're willing to give me."

"That's not what I asked. Disregard what you think I might or might not be willing to give. What do *you* want?" My heart beat faster as I waited for his answer.

He blew out a breath. "I want to try again. A relationship. Maybe we're too different now and it would never work, but I want to try."

"That's a big leap."

"You wanted the truth."

"I'm scared," I whispered.

"Me too."

"I thought about this all the way over here. About what I wanted to say to you. What I wanted moving forward."

"And…"

"I think the only way out is through. I don't know if a relationship is something I'm willing to contemplate just yet, but I do think the only way to understand what happened and to move past it is to continue getting to know you again. To keep having these conversations."

"So what are you suggesting?"

"Let's start with this. You still run every day?"

He dropped his arms, his expression lightening. "I do. But with camp this week, I have to go early as fuck."

"How early?"

"Five forty-five."

"You up for a run with me? Thursday?"

"Seriously?"

"Yeah. Just a run. No more, no less."

He nodded. "Understood. Thank you."

I stood, and he did the same. "You don't have to thank me. But I'm going to head out. I'm on shift for the next two days and need to get some things done around the house this evening."

"Alright. Thanks again for watching Daisy this afternoon."

At her name, she perked up, excitedly looking between us. I leaned over and gave her a scratch behind the ears. "It wasn't a problem. She's a sweetheart. I'll see you Thursday."

57

ZACH

No AMOUNT of coffee would be enough today.

My conversation with Jason last night had left me bouncing between cautious optimism and fear that all my efforts would be in vain and I'd never be able to make things right between us. My racing thoughts had made sleep elusive and when I finally managed to find my way into slumber, it had been interrupted by another nightmare just like the one I'd had the night I met Sean. As a result, I'd woken this morning feeling like someone had poured sand directly into my eyeballs, then held them open and blown on them with a high-speed fan. The result was that the inside of my eyelids felt like they were lined with sandpaper and my eyes were so red that I looked like I'd gone on a three-day bender. Thankfully, it was perfectly normal for me to be wearing sunglasses for my job, so I'd at least be saved from a million questions about why I looked so tired.

"Dude. You look tired. Rough night?"

So much for that idea. I turned to look at Lauren Simpson, the girls' soccer coach from Brinkley, who was helping with camp this week.

"Just a bad night of sleep," I said with a weak smile. "Let's have the kids run laps for warm-up, then we'll give them their new group assignments. Did you give any more thought to which group you want to put Asher in?"

We talked about group assignments while other coaches joined the conversation and gave their input before the kids arrived. Promptly at eight o'clock, we started with the kids running laps. A couple of kids showed up a few minutes late, looking frazzled and apologetic but at least showing some hustle as they joined the other runners. But by eight-thirty, we were still missing two kids—Sean and his cousin, Rusty.

I checked my email, not finding any messages regarding their absence. At eight forty-five, I called Sarah, but she didn't answer, so I left a voicemail. Camp continued, but I found myself distracted and irritable with worry. Finally, a little after ten, I received an email from Sarah thanking me for the opportunity but letting me know the boys were not continuing with camp. I was relieved to know the kids were safe and accounted for but frustrated by the lack of further explanation.

I ran home to check on Daisy during the break between the morning and afternoon sessions. I'd opted to leave her home today but wanted to check on her just to be sure. She happily greeted me at the door, and I was pleased to see she hadn't gotten into anything or left any messes for me to clean up. I let her out back while I quickly made a sandwich for lunch.

After a moment of internal debate, I pulled out my phone and texted Jason.

Sarah pulled Sean and Rusty from camp for the rest of the week

JASON

Shit

Did she say why?

> Nope. She didn't even notify me until I called and left a message that I was worried. She finally sent me an email around 10

> Sorry. I hope I'm not interrupting your day

I'm working but it's slow at the firehouse.
You're good

> How well do you know Sarah?

> Do you think I should talk to her?

I don't really know her at all. Astaire's small,
but not that small

> I was trying to figure out a way for Sean to see Daisy anyway. Maybe I'll give her a call

Let me know how it goes. I feel bad for
the kid

> Me too

I pocketed my phone, finished my sandwich, let Daisy back in, and headed back to the high school.

By the end of the day, I was hot, exhausted, and pissy. Colby's dad had let him return to camp but had sat in the stands for every minute of the three-hour session, watching everything I did like a hawk. It had left me feeling jumpy and agitated, in addition to the lack of sleep and worry over

Sean. I made a mental note to include language in next year's brochures indicating camp would be closed for observation in the future. I likely needed to include something about closed practices in the fall paperwork as well.

I ran home and showered, debating my options once again. I had a feeling my phone calls would go unanswered, so I rounded Daisy up and hopped in my car. Sarah's house was on the edge of town in an older, run-down neighborhood. Rusted-out trucks were parked on the street. The houses were dingy and dilapidated, some with overgrown yards. Here and there were tidier homes. Small but clearly maintained, with fresh-cut lawns and flower beds blooming with color. I held out hope that I'd find Sean in one of those homes, but my stomach sank as my map guided me to the address I'd entered before I left.

The house in front of me was a small split level that looked like it had once been painted a dark blue, but the sun and the elements had faded the color, giving it a splotchy, mottled appearance. The yard was more weeds than grass and littered with children's toys. I spotted a small pink bicycle, a play basketball hoop, several bouncy balls, and a jump rope. Two bigger bikes lay on their sides on the other side of the driveway. I'd known Sarah had two kids, and now, with Sean, four people were squeezed into this tiny house. The knot in my chest tightened.

Taking a breath, I stepped out of the car, grabbing Daisy's leash and pulling her out with me. We made our way up to the door and rang the bell. I'd met Sean's Aunt Sarah one other time last week when I'd dropped off some athletic clothes for Sean at Fred's Diner, where she worked. Tonight, she opened the door with a look of exhaustion. Her dirty-blonde hair was pulled into a messy bun and she wore her work uniform. I wasn't sure if I'd caught her after her shift or as she was getting ready to leave, but either way, she did not look happy to have a visitor at her door.

"What are you doing here?" she asked, frowning at me through the dirty storm door.

Sean and Rusty came up behind her, curious eyes trying to see who might be at the door, but when Sean spotted Daisy, he pushed past his aunt and opened the door, falling to his knees and wrapping his arms around the dog. Daisy's entire body wiggled with excitement as she tried to lick his face and any other part of him she could get to. Tears streamed from Sean's eyes as he sobbed into her fur, the first bit of emotion I'd seen from him since I'd met him in the hospital.

Sarah's expression softened as she watched Sean and the pup, her eyes glistening with unshed tears. This wasn't a woman who didn't care. This was a woman doing her best to keep it together, who'd been handed another mouth to feed without warning. And while Sean had lost his mother, Sarah had also lost her sister. I had no idea what her relationship with Sean's mother had been like, but I had to imagine losing your sister and having your nephew placed in your care in one fell swoop would be the type of thing that might push you to your limit. I'd come over here feeling frustrated and angry with the woman who I felt was limiting Sean's potential, and now I felt like an insensitive jackass.

"I'm sorry to just show up like this. Do you have a few moments to talk?"

She looked at me warily but nodded, opening the door wider so I could step inside. I left Daisy with Sean and followed her up a half-flight of stairs to the living room. There were toys strewn about, and the furniture was mismatched and worn, but there were homey touches as well. Pictures in frames next to the TV. Children's drawings hanging proudly on display. A cozy blanket draped over the back of the couch. A little girl with the same shade of dirty-blond hair was sitting on the floor, quietly coloring. She looked to be around seven or eight.

I sat on one end of the couch while Sarah sat in an adjacent chair. "Look, I'm sorry I pulled the boys from camp, but Rusty wasn't really feeling it and I don't want Sean riding his bike up there by himself. And frankly, I need the boys here at home. I was off yesterday, but I had to work today, and the childcare I thought I had arranged for Lauren fell through, so I needed the boys here with her. The rest of the week is more of the same. I know you went to all the trouble for Sean to get all the soccer gear, but I'm sorry. I just don't think I can make it work."

"Would you be open to allowing me to give him rides to camp?"

She tilted her head, studying me. "Why are you so invested in him? Is he really that good?"

"I think he has potential, yes. But it's more than that. I lost my mom when I was sixteen. It changed so many aspects of my life, but I still had my sister, my father, and my home. I can't imagine what it's like to be a boy his age and lose everything. I can't give him any of that back, but I can give him something to look forward to. Something that allows him to just be a kid for a little while and leave all that other stuff behind."

"You lost your mom too?"

Sarah and I turned our heads toward the stairs, where Sean stood about halfway up with Daisy in tow. I turned the rest of my body in his direction. "Yeah. She was killed in a car accident."

He nodded, coming up the last couple of steps. "How come you have Daisy?"

"When your aunt told me you guys couldn't keep her, I adopted her. I was thinking about getting a dog anyway, so it was perfect timing. And I thought maybe you could visit her sometime."

His face brightened at that. "Really?"

"Absolutely. I can even bring her over here if that's easier." I spared a glance for Sarah, who nodded.

"Aunt Sarah, do you think I can finish the camp since Coach says he can drive me? It's just three more days, and I can do extra chores or something to make up for it."

Her eyes flicked to mine. "Are you sure?"

"Of course."

She turned back to Sean. "Honey, you don't need to do any more chores than you're already doing. And yes, I suppose you can go."

"Yes!" He gave a joyful fist pump, then ran back down the stairs, shouting for Rusty, no doubt to tell him the news.

"He's always trying to do extra chores," Sarah said as soon as he was out of earshot. "I think he feels like he's a burden and wants to make up for it somehow. It breaks my heart."

"He seems like a sweet kid."

"He is. His mama and I were close growing up. Rusty and Sean are just a few months apart. I just wish I could do better for him. This isn't the life my sister wanted for her boy." Her voice shook, but she didn't let the tears escape. "Thank you for helping him."

"Thank you for allowing me to."

She nodded. "If you'll excuse me, I've gotta get dinner ready."

"Yes, of course. I'll be on my way."

I headed down the steps and back outside, where Sean

and Rusty were sitting on the porch with Daisy lying between them.

"I have to be at practice early since I'm the coach, so that means I'll pick you up around seven-fifteen. Can you be ready then?"

He nodded. "Um, do you think you can bring Daisy with you?"

"It's going to be awfully hot again tomorrow. I think Daisy would be more comfortable at home. But how about we stop by my house after practice and you can have a quick visit before I bring you home."

"That would be so awesome!"

"I better get her home now so she can have dinner, but I'll see you tomorrow?"

He handed over the leash, giving her one more scratch behind the ears, his eyes watching her longingly. "I'll be ready."

I PULLED into Zach's driveway just a few minutes after five on Thursday morning. We moved the start time earlier to account for the extra time he needed to pick up Sean before camp. Zach was sitting on the front step with his head in his hands, and when he looked up, he offered me a weak smile.

"Morning," I called out, my smile faltering as I wondered if everything was alright.

"Hey. We should get going."

At the sight of the dark circles under his eyes and the weariness of his tone, I put my hand out and stopped him. "What's wrong?"

He waved me off. "I just didn't sleep very well. I'm fine." He turned toward the path but stopped when I didn't follow. "Are you coming?"

"Zach, if you're not up for it, we don't have to do this today."

"What makes you think I'm not up for it?"

"You're barely holding yourself up. Come on, let's go sit on the deck and talk. I'm sure I can't talk you into taking the day off, but let's at least take it easy until you have to get ready to leave."

His posture slumped in defeat, but I thought I saw a hint of relief in his eyes. We made our way around to the back, climbing up the steps to the deck and into the kitchen, where he pulled out a couple of mugs. "I started a pot of coffee so it would be ready by the time I got back. You want?"

"Sure."

He poured us a couple of mugs, then led the way back out to the deck. The lake was peaceful this morning, with just a hint of a breeze sending ripples across the otherwise still surface of the water. After a few moments of sipping our coffee in silence, I asked, "So why the trouble sleeping? Are you still worried about Sean?"

"I am. And his situation isn't helping, but I've actually been having nightmares again."

I paused with my mug halfway to my lips, my eyebrows drawn up. "Again?"

He closed his eyes for a moment, then opened them and blew out a breath like he was steadying himself. "You probably don't remember, but the night before I went back to LA, I had a bad dream. You asked if I wanted to talk about it, but I brushed it off. It became a recurring thing after I went back to LA, but eventually trickled down to a few times a year, usually around the anniversary of either Drea's or Mom's accidents. I have other nightmares sometimes, usually stress-related, but it's been a couple of years since I've had this particular one. I thought maybe they were gone, but they started coming back the night I met Sean, and I've had several since."

My stomach dropped and I set my mug down, giving him my full attention. "Do you want to talk about it?"

He shrugged. "It's always a car accident. Not always the same car and not always the same location, but it's always overturned on its roof. I run to the door and wrench it open to find... Well, that first time, Mom was the driver, and then she morphed into Drea, and then you, but over the years, the faces have varied. It's still typically one or all three of you, but every so often, Clayton and my dad get added into the mix. I shake you, or whoever it is, screaming at you to wake up, and then I usually wake up myself."

"Jesus, Zach." I couldn't imagine experiencing a dream like that once, let alone over and over again for *years*. "And you said they started up again after you met Sean?"

He nodded. "It's not hard to figure out why. Sean wasn't in a car accident, but I've been thinking about Mom more lately because of his situation."

Zach looked so lost. So fragile. More even than he'd looked when I'd run into him at the hospital. My fingers twitched with the urge to pull him onto my lap and hold him close. Even after all this time, I just wanted to soothe his hurts.

"Is there anything that helps?"

He shook his head and shrugged at the same time in an awkward gesture of defeat. "Not really. I'm usually able to go back to sleep after I get up and stretch. But the only thing I've found that keeps them at bay long-term is time. Hopefully they've reached their peak frequency and then will start receding again. I haven't found anything else that works."

I thought about the conversation we'd had about therapy, wondering if all of this was related somehow. These nightmares had started just before he'd hit that mental wall that wouldn't let him call me. It didn't seem too much of a stretch to think those things might be related. The timing certainly checked out.

"I don't want to be pushy about this, but do you think you might reconsider seeing a therapist?"

"For having nightmares?"

Giving into the impulse, I reached for his hand. I couldn't stand allowing him to sit there looking so lost and confused without any physical contact. "What if the nightmares and the mental block about calling me are all related? And seeing Sean now is some sort of trigger?"

"Do you think so?"

I squeezed his hand. "I think it's worth looking into."

He thought about it for a moment, then sat up a little straighter, spine straightening with resolve. "I'll make some calls."

"I can give you the contact info for my therapist or I'm sure Drea'd give you the number for hers."

"You see a therapist?"

"Started seeing someone not long after you left. You weren't the only one having nightmares after the girls' accident."

His eyes shot to mine. "You had one that week, didn't you? I'd forgotten about that." I nodded. "Did the therapy help?"

"It took some time, but yeah, it helped. I still go in about once a month just to talk about whatever might be bothering me."

Zach looked down, and I followed his gaze to where our hands were clasped together on his thigh. I knew I should let go, but I couldn't bring myself to do so. The feel of his hand in mine, skin pressed palm-to-palm, felt too damn good. He looked back at me, eyes holding mine with a glimmer of hope.

This was the type of mixed message Drea had warned me about, but I wasn't sure how mixed it was. With each of our interactions, I gained a little more insight into the events that transpired in the weeks following his return to college, and I was becoming more convinced that his withdrawal from my life had been a symptom of something deeper. Something he still hadn't addressed. And despite everything, or maybe because of it, I wanted to be the one who helped him through it. So, instead of withdrawing my hand, I held on a little tighter and changed the subject.

"How's Sean doing this week? I know a little from your texts, but tell me the rest."

He hesitated, and for a moment, I thought he wouldn't allow the change of subject. But then he told me about how frustrated he'd been on Tuesday with Sean dropping out of camp and how his perception that Sarah didn't care had changed when he went over to their house. He told me about their living situation and his concern that while he was able to get Sean to camp this week, he was worried about Sean's future. And not just Sean, but the whole family. He told me how helpless he felt.

"Could you suggest being a mentor of some sort for him? Like a big brother kind of thing? Or could Sean help out with the elementary camp next week? You could keep an eye on him and give him something he can take pride in."

"I like that idea. I'll have to see if Sarah is okay with it. It's only three half-days. Plus, he could get some more time with Daisy. You should have seen him when he caught sight of her for the first time. He burst into tears."

With my free hand, I picked up my mug and sipped my now lukewarm coffee while Zach continued, "I was actually thinking about inviting his whole family over for the Fourth. I want to host a gathering and thought the kids might enjoy seeing the fireworks over the lake. I don't even know if Sarah will go for it, and maybe she has to work anyway, but I want to ask."

Well, shit. Was there anything more attractive than a guy wanting to help others? He was wearing me down bit by bit without even realizing it.

"Would you, um, be interested in coming over on the Fourth?"

The way my stomach swooped at the question indicated I was very interested, and I was disappointed I had to say no. "I'm scheduled to work on the Fourth. It's usually an all-hands-on-deck situation."

"Oh. Well, that makes sense for a firefighter, I guess. I hadn't thought of that."

"Let me check with Chief and see if there's any way I can get out of it."

"You don't have to do that. It's fine." Abruptly, he released my hand.

"Zach." I pulled his hand back into mine. "I *want* to be there."

"Really?"

"Yeah. I do."

59

JASON

WE'D BEEN able to run together twice in the last week since that first time had been a bust. The other two times, Zach had seemed much more himself, and I hoped that meant he'd been getting more sleep. He had also talked to Sarah about the party on the Fourth, and surprisingly, she'd agreed to come. The diner closed around four that day, so the family would be able to come over after that.

Zach's joy and enthusiasm were contagious, and I found myself slipping a little further toward the point of no return. That place where I'd have to admit I had feelings for him, and then I'd have to decide what I was going to do about it. It was why I'd hesitated asking Chief if I could have the Fourth off. It was a way of pumping the breaks, of making sure I was proceeding with caution.

And yet I'd found myself knocking on Chief's door Tuesday morning, just a couple of days before the holiday, requesting the time off. He'd been hesitant, but when I reminded him that I hadn't taken a single Fourth of July off since I'd joined the AFD, he'd relented. I should have been scared by just how excited I was by the prospect of attending

Zach's party, but I think I'd known I was always heading this way, toward Zach, since the moment I'd punched him at the end of May.

Okay, maybe not at that exact moment, but not long after. I'd always been drawn to him. Why should it be any different nine years later?

I arrived a little after five with a plate of watermelon and a dozen ears of corn ready for the grill. I'd been restless with nerves most of the day, so I'd kept myself busy by doing household chores and prepping the food. I'd driven into Brinkley to see Mandy and my new nephew she delivered yesterday. She and her husband looked exhausted but happy. Mom and Dad had been there visiting, too, but were planning on heading out to Grandma and Grandpa's house later.

I stepped around to the back of the house, where the sounds of a party could be heard floating on the breeze. There was a good crowd of people milling about. Some on the deck, some on the patio around the fire pit, and more still down on the dock. I stopped at the food table, dropping off the watermelon, then headed for the grill where Zach was flipping burgers while laughing with Drea. She said something that made him throw his head back in laughter, and time stood still. I took a moment to absorb the sight of him looking so happy and free.

It was so rare to see him radiate unrestrained joy like that, I realized. Even back in the day, when he'd put on the appearance of being carefree, there'd always been something deeper lurking just behind that smile. Grief over losing his mother. The weight of expectation from his father. The pressure he put on himself to be the person he thought everyone expected him to be. I thought he might have shed some of that weight over the last nine years, but I wondered if it had just been replaced with new worries and challenges, especially after what I'd learned, or at least suspected, about the state of his mental health. At that moment, though, I was grateful for this glimpse of true happiness. He was so goddamned beautiful.

Time moved forward again and our eyes met, his face lighting up impossibly brighter at the sight of me. I was helpless to do anything but smile in return.

"Hey! You made it!"

"I brought corn for the grill."

"Perfect. I'm going to finish these burgers and hot dogs for the kids, and then I've got chicken legs and thighs to go on next. I'll put the corn on with that."

"Sounds good."

I handed over the corn, which he transferred to a small table he'd set up next to the grill to act as a workstation. The three of us chatted while he worked. Drea had also visited Mandy earlier today, so we compared notes on my new nephew. She talked about the dance studio and how summer classes were going.

It sounded like the guy she'd hired, Thomas, would be here toward the end of the month, just in time to start choreography boot camps for the competition team. Drea seemed pretty excited to have him on board. Apparently, he'd been working in New York and had toured with a couple of Broadway shows for several years. It sounded like he had quite the resume.

As food was served and bellies were filled, Zach was free to move away from the grill, and we found ourselves sitting on the dock with our feet in the water. Most of the kids were done swimming for the day and had moved on to playing yard games while they awaited the fireworks. I noticed Drea chatting with a woman near the fire pit. She looked around our age or maybe a couple of years older and had her dirty-blond hair pulled into a messy bun.

"Is that Sarah over there talking to Drea?"

Zach looked over in the direction I indicated. "Yeah, I was surprised when she accepted my invitation." We watched as Drea laughed at something Sarah said, both of them smiling and talking animatedly. "It's good to see her smiling."

"Who? Sarah or Drea?"

"Both. Is Drea happy, do you think? I mean, I know you guys are close...closer than you were back in the day."

"She's like a sister to me. In a lot of ways, I'm closer to her than I am to Mandy. We just always...connected. As for her happiness...that's harder to answer and probably a question you should ask her."

"I'm glad she had you while I was off...avoiding the people I should have been here for."

On instinct, I reached for his hand, threading his fingers through mine. It didn't sit right with me, hearing him beat himself up like that, and I realized I didn't want him punishing himself for that anymore. I didn't want him beating himself up for things I now knew he had no control over. I believed him when he said he wanted to reach out but couldn't. And I didn't want him to suffer over it any longer.

Oh shit.

With that realization came a shift. I was ready to let go of it. Of the hurt and anger and resentment. Zach couldn't change the past. What was done was done. He was trying to make it right, and that counted for something, maybe counted for everything.

"Maybe. But you also had a pro-soccer career. Don't minimize that accomplishment."

"But look at what I almost missed out on." He nodded to our hands that were clasped between us, his voice filled with anguish. "I hurt you. And her."

He nodded toward his sister, his words coming out faster and faster as he became more agitated. "The two most important people in my life. I'm sorry, Jason. I'm so so sorry."

His eyes overflowed with tears, and I could see he was struggling to breathe.

"Hey, hey, hey." I placed my free hand in the center of his chest, pulling his hand up to the center of mine and holding it there. "Look at me. Breathe, okay? Just breathe with me."

His eyes locked on mine, and we inhaled and exhaled together in slow, measured breaths until he was calm again. I'd done this one other time with him at the hospital after our sisters' accident, only that time had been much worse and had taken longer for him to settle.

"Okay?" I asked, and he nodded. "How often does that happen?"

He shrugged his shoulders, averting his gaze. "It happened a lot after I went back to LA. Nowadays, maybe once or twice a year."

I tipped his chin up so he was looking at me. "Did you make that therapy appointment?"

"I meant to, but I've been busy wrapping up the camps. I'm sorry."

"Honey, you don't have to apologize. I don't want you to do this for me. I want you to do it for yourself."

He held my gaze for a long moment, then nodded his head. "You're right. I'll make the call." He stood and offered me his hand. "I should probably check on my guests. Come with me?"

60

ZACH

I HATED that Jason had seen me so upset. I'd thought retiring from soccer would alleviate most of the pressure I'd been under, but it would seem that coming back here had just stirred up a different type of stress. Between the nightmares and worry over Sean, on top of trying to reconnect in whatever way I could with Jason, my nerves were frayed.

I knew Jason was right. I needed to make an appointment with a therapist. I didn't have anything against them. Drea had been seeing one for years and swore it was a huge help to her. I just hadn't particularly thought I needed one. And I *had* been busy with the camps. But those were finished, and I really didn't have an excuse to put it off anymore.

At the moment, though, I wanted to concentrate on other things. Like the feel of Jason's hand in mine as we walked toward the house. He hadn't let go of my hand since I helped him stand at the dock. In the last week, his attitude toward me had seemed to soften, and I'd noticed his gaze lingering on me when he thought I wasn't looking. This was the second time he'd held my hand in the last week and both times had sent butterflies swirling in my stomach.

Dusk was beginning to fall, so we grabbed the glow-in-the-dark necklaces off the kitchen counter before heading back out to distribute them to the guests. I had plenty of extras, and some of the kids took two so they could create longer necklaces or connect them and twist them around their arms.

A few minutes before ten, everyone began settling into their spots to watch the fireworks show. I smiled when I saw Sean and Rusty sitting with some other kids. Daisy was in the middle, basking in the attention.

Jason pulled me over to a lounger near the fire pit, straddling it with his back resting against the back rest. He shocked me when he tugged me down in front of him and wrapped his arms around me until my back was firmly pressed against his chest.

"This okay?" he asked, ever the gentleman.

"No complaints here," I said once I remembered how to breathe.

The first booms sounded across the lake a half-second before the sky lit up in bright bursts of color. Oohs and ahhs rang out around us, but all I could think about was Jason holding me.

Jason was holding me.

His warmth...his strength...his scent enveloped me, ten times more effective than a weighted blanket. It was the most peaceful I'd felt in a long, long time.

We watched the display for several minutes, and then I felt his lips near my ear. "I want to try again. I want to date you."

Surprised by his words, I twisted my head to look at him. "Seriously?"

"You said you didn't want to live the rest of your life without trying to make things right…"

"Yeah."

"Well I don't want to live the rest of mine without giving this another chance. I think that if I don't, I'll always wonder."

A slow smile spread across my face. "You're sure?"

In answer, he leaned forward and kissed me. We were at an awkward angle, but I didn't care. The feel of his lips on mine was like coming home. We broke apart, staring into each other's eyes as the night sky erupted behind us in what sounded like the grand finale.

"I'm positive," he whispered, brushing his nose against mine.

Applause rang out at the conclusion of the fireworks show, followed by the chatter and commotion of everyone trying to gather their belongings in the dark.

"I better say goodbye to my guests. Stay a while?"

"Yeah, I'll stay."

As the last guests left, Jason and I stood on the back deck, assessing the cleanup situation. I blew out a breath. "Sorry. When I asked you to stay, I didn't think about cleanup. This is going to take a while. You wanna grab coffee tomorrow?"

"We can grab coffee tomorrow if you want, but I'm not letting you clean this up by yourself. It'll go faster if we do it together. I'm off tomorrow, so I'm not in a hurry."

"You don't have to do that. You're a guest."

He stepped closer, placing his hand against my face and

rubbing his thumb across my cheekbone. "Is that all I am? Just a guest?"

I shook my head, entranced by the look in his eye, my head spinning with this change in his demeanor toward me.

"Do your guests do this?"

He leaned forward and brushed his lips against mine. His touch was featherlight, but I felt it all the way to my toes.

"Keep doing that, and cleanup's going to take all night."

He grinned, then released me, turning toward the table where we'd arranged all the food. "I'll start working on this if you want to go down and work on the rest of the yard."

We worked efficiently, with Jason putting away leftover food and cleaning up napkins and plates that hadn't been deposited in the trashcan while I cleaned up the yard games, water toys, and life jackets. I threw a load of wet towels into the washer, and together, we wiped down the tables and furniture outside, and the countertops in the kitchen. Forty-five minutes later, I declared it close enough.

"Thanks for your help. I'll do another round outside in the daylight tomorrow morning. I'm sure there's stuff we missed. For now, I'm beat."

He grabbed my hand and tugged me forward, pulling me into him and wrapping his arms around me. "Mmm. You feel good. I've wanted to do this all night."

"Yeah?"

"Are you going to question it every time I say something like that?"

"Probably. It wasn't that long ago that you told me you weren't sure if you could ever forgive me."

"Zach?"

At his change in tone, I pulled away slightly, just enough to tilt my head back so I could look at his face. "Yeah?"

"I forgive you."

"Just like that? You said you didn't understand and—"

"Do you understand why you did what you did?"

I frowned, not sure what he was getting at. "I told you I wanted to call, but I just couldn't."

"Right. But do you understand *why* you couldn't?"

"No, actually. I've never been able to figure out why I couldn't push past it."

"Maybe we can work on figuring that out together. But in the meantime, I realized tonight that even if I don't understand it, I believe you when you say you couldn't. You wanted to call me, but it was a hill you couldn't climb. I believe that, for whatever reason, you didn't have a choice. And if that's the case, then there's honestly nothing to forgive."

He was giving me the words I'd longed so desperately to hear, but I couldn't accept them. This sudden change was too good to be true.

"But I hurt you. Badly. You said I hurt you in ways you haven't recovered from. How can you forgive so easily?"

He released me but grabbed my hands, not allowing me to go too far. "You're a good man, Zach. You've done nothing but show me your goodness since you got back. The way you care about Sean. Not just Sean but his entire family. The excitement you have for the soccer program you're building. A program you created not for yourself or the glory of coaching but because you want to give back to this community. And with us, with me"—he moved my hands to his waist, then rested his on my hips—"you haven't pushed, not once. You've offered apologies but never begged for forgiveness. You've given me your words, but your actions have shown me who you truly are."

"Who am I?" I whispered, mesmerized by his speech. I thought I might be dreaming.

"Someone who cares, deeply, about others. Someone who's been beating himself up for the actions of his nineteen-year-old self for nine years. Someone who, despite all of the fear and guilt, is trying to make it right." He brushed a thumb under my right eye, swiping away the moisture I hadn't even realized had gathered there. "It's time to let it go. We can't move forward if we're still living in the past."

I closed my eyes, blowing out a shaky breath. "I'm scared," I admitted.

"Me too."

I opened my eyes. "What if I fuck it up? What if I hurt you again?"

"You won't."

"How do you know?"

He shrugged. "I don't."

"And you still want to try?"

"I do."

"I'm scared."

He chuckled. "You said that."

"I can't help it. You...this...it's what I've wanted since the moment I decided to come back, probably long before that if I really think about it. I just didn't believe I deserved it. I didn't think I'd ever be able to earn your trust again. And now, all of the sudden, you're all in? It was only a week ago that you offered to go running with me. 'Just a run. Nothing more. Nothing less.' Remember? It feels too good to be true. Like the rug is going to be pulled out from under me. What if everything I ever wanted finally happens, and it gets taken away?"

I choked on a sob. I could feel the panic climbing up my throat, making my thoughts spin faster and faster, but I couldn't grab hold of them.

"Shh. Honey, you're getting worked up again. C'mere."

Jason pulled me into his arms, holding me close so his chest pressed against mine. He took deep, steady breaths, and I instinctively matched his pace. When I calmed down enough to breathe properly again, he pulled back, cradling either side of my face in his hands. He peered into my eyes intently, making sure I was okay.

"That's twice in one night. I'm really starting to worry."

"I'm sorry. I've had a hard time controlling my emotions lately. There's just been so much going on, and I'm still not sleeping well."

"Still having the nightmares?"

"Not every night, but yeah, they're still making regular appearances."

He rubbed his thumb over my cheekbone. "Want me to stay here tonight?"

"You don't have to. This is all still new. I don't want you to feel like we're rushing things. I'll be okay."

"What if I want to stay? What if I want to hold you all night and chase those bad dreams away?"

I closed my eyes, battling between what I thought was the right thing to do and what my heart so desperately wanted. When I opened them again to find his eyes fixed so tenderly on mine, there was really only one answer.

"Then...stay."

61

———

JASON

I woke at first light, far earlier than I wanted to, but I rarely slept in these days. My body was used to waking up for work. This morning was different though. I didn't have anywhere I needed to be. I was free to savor the feel of Zach sleeping in my arms.

He'd crashed hard last night, the emotion of the day catching up with him, and thankfully, he hadn't had any nightmares. I hoped he'd catch up on some of the sleep he'd missed over the last couple of weeks.

I marveled at how we'd gotten here. From a punch to the face to an argument at the diner. Running into him at the hospital and again when he helped Mom the next day. Showing up at camp. Watching his dog. The conversation after that. Going for runs. Each of those times our paths had crossed had been like opening a window into his heart until, eventually, the window was open wide enough that I could climb through. It may have seemed like I'd made a sudden shift last night, but when I looked back, I could see each small step that had led us here. And now that we'd arrived, I didn't want to waste any more time.

Zach squirmed in my arms, stretching his toes toward the foot of the bed. Daisy, who'd climbed up to join us sometime during the night, dismounted with a snort of protest at being kicked.

"Mmm, what time is it?" Zach asked, his voice raspy with sleep.

I lifted my head, not finding a clock anywhere in sight. "I have no idea, but I'm guessing by the light, around six."

"By the light? Are you a pioneer? Do you need to throw another log on the campfire while I go rustle us up some breakfast?"

"You're ridiculous," I said, kissing him on the top of his head. "I think we both know that if anyone was going to do some rustling, it would be me."

His answering chuckle warmed my heart, especially after seeing him so upset last night. "How are you feeling this morning?"

"Better. Though I still worry this is a dream, and I'm going to wake up to an empty bed."

I kissed the top of his head again, squeezing him just a little tighter. "It's not a dream, and I'm not going anywhere."

Daisy whined, her collar jangling as she danced by the door.

"I should probably let her out and feed her. What about you? Can I make you breakfast?" Zach asked.

"I'd love that."

WE ATE outside on the deck, enjoying the view of the lake as it came alive to face the day. Temperatures were down a little from the oppressive heat earlier in the week, making the breeze comfortable as we enjoyed scrambled eggs, bacon, and toast while Daisy sniffed around the yard.

"Do you have anything going on today?" I asked around a mouthful of eggs.

"Nope. After a week and a half of camp, followed by hosting for the Fourth, I planned to spend most of the day lounging around and catching up on laundry." Zach took another bite of bacon, then asked, "Did you have something in mind?"

"Not specifically. I just thought we could spend the day together, if that's alright with you? I'm happy to lounge here while you do laundry and take it easy. A day like that sounds perfect."

His face lit in a smile and I was so glad to be the one who put it there. "Let's do it."

We finished our breakfast, then made a round of the yard, picking up a few stray pieces of trash we'd missed the night before. Zach ran the towels through the wash again since he'd forgotten to move them to the dryer before we'd gone to bed. Then, we settled on the couch to watch a European soccer game Zach had been looking forward to while I pulled up a book in the Kindle app on my phone.

I must have fallen asleep because I woke with my head in Zach's lap and my phone resting on my chest. Zach was playing with my hair while he watched the game. Daisy was curled up in her bed below the TV, and a gentle breeze blew through the open window. The simplicity of the moment hit me square in the chest. This was the life I had always dreamed of. Lazy days with the guy I was pretty sure I'd never stopped loving. Could this become something more permanent for us? After rushing us forward what felt like thirteen steps last night, I didn't dare bring it up, but the seed had been planted in my mind. I wanted to put down roots with Zach. Roots that would spread and sustain us as we built a life together. Was that something he might also want?

Jesus, Whitt. Slow your roll. He's here in Astaire to stay. You have time to figure all of that out.

The game ended and Zach looked down at me. "How was the nap?"

A slow smile spread across my face. "Perfect."

"Good. Want to grab lunch? I thought we could run over to Fred's."

"Can we stop by my house to change first? I'd rather not do the walk of shame."

He chuckled. "Sure. Let me go move the towels to the dryer."

I sat up, allowing him to stand.

"Do you mind if I take a quick shower?" Zach asked.

"Hmm..." I pretended to think about my answer. "Can I join you?"

"Baby, that is a question you *never* have to ask."

62

ZACH

I HURRIED to move the towels to the dryer, my heart racing with the implications of sharing a shower. Everything felt like it was coming so fast, and the last thing I wanted was to take things to a physical place only to have it result in a setback. I was terrified of losing the ground we'd gained. What if we took this step only to take three more back? Alternatively, what if this drew us closer? It had been *his* suggestion to shower together. I had to trust he knew his own mind.

Resolved, I made my way down the hall to my bedroom, where I could already hear the shower running. Smiling, I pushed the door open only to stop in the doorway, stunned by the sight in front of me. Three-quarters of the shower walls were made of glass, allowing me to see every inch of Jason, from head to toe, including his cock, which he was lazily stroking while I gawked at him.

"You gonna get in, or did you want me to put on a show?"

Jesus. For a guy who had always been a little reserved

when it came to sex, he'd sure found his confidence. It was sexy as hell. *He* was sexy as hell.

I began stripping out of my shirt and shorts, never taking my eyes off him as he continued to leisurely rub his soapy hands all over his body. I'd admired the physical changes in him since I'd returned to Astaire, but looking at him now, stark naked with water sluicing over every one of those carved muscles, my mouth ran dry and my cock leaked.

As a teen, Jason had played football and baseball, and he'd had the body to show for it, but now, it was evident that as he'd matured out of his teens and into adulthood, he'd put in the work to build strength and definition into his broad frame. I wanted to trace every curve and valley with my tongue.

I opened the shower door and stepped inside, letting the steam billow around me as I acclimated to the water temperature.

"I've missed seeing you like this." I dragged my fingertips down the center of his chest. "You're beautiful."

He closed his eyes, giving a full-body shudder at my touch. "I missed your hands on my skin. It's been a long time."

Something about the way he said it made me think it wasn't just that *I* hadn't touched him in a long time but that there hadn't been *anyone* who'd touched him in a long time.

"Has there been...anyone else?" I shouldn't have been so hung up on that point, but I had to know.

He opened his eyes, his gaze locking with mine. "I haven't felt attracted to anyone since you, so no, there's been no one."

I tried not to sag under the weight of the pressure. He'd gone nine years without this kind of intimacy. I understood it was different for Jason. He didn't have the same lust response most people did, or even really felt the need for sex most of the time. But to not be touched, to not be held or shown physical affection from a lover... It was hard for me to imagine going without that for so long. And it all added another layer of guilt because it was my actions that had put him in that position, and I hadn't lived the same kind of celibate life.

"I've, uh, been with other people. Not like different people every night, but yeah... Does that bother you?"

"I can't say I love it, but, honey, those people don't have any place here. It's just you and me in this shower. I don't want to talk about anyone else." He placed his hand behind my head and pulled me closer. "I don't want to talk at all."

He took my lips in a possessive kiss, effectively erasing any thoughts I'd had about anyone or anything other than him. His taste. His scent. The feel of his tongue tangling with mine. The scrape of his teeth against my bottom lip. The pinch of his fingers as he held on a little tighter than necessary.

I stepped closer, wanting *more*, and hissed when our cocks brushed against each other. I gave up on thinking, and instead, running on instinct, I reached my hand out and wrapped his dick in my fist. Before I could give a teasing stroke, his hand flew to mine, stopping my movement. I pulled away from the kiss, afraid I'd gone too far and crossed a boundary without his consent.

He rested his forehead against mine, breathing heavily. "I'm about two strokes away from this being all over. Nine years, remember?"

I chuckled, relieved I hadn't made a wrong move. "We have all day, baby. I can get you off now, and we can go again later. Really take our time then."

"No...I mean, yes to later...but also, I'm not ready to be done yet."

"Okay. We'll go slower." I kissed him softly. "I'm going to let go of you, then I want you to turn around and face the wall."

He did as I asked while I grabbed the body wash and poured some into my hand. I took my time as I ran my soapy hands along his skin, starting at his wrists, moving up his arms, then across his shoulders and back, around to his chest and belly, skirting his cock and ass, and continuing down his thighs, calves, and all the way to his feet. The entire time I worked, he uttered little sounds of pleasure that went straight to my cock, which was still leaking and straining, aching for more contact. I ignored it, wanting to focus on him and his pleasure. He'd waited nine damn years, after all.

I put my hands back up on his hips, slowly sliding them down the curve of his ass, working my way toward his crease. "Can I touch you here?"

"God, yes," he choked out, making me smile.

I slid my finger between his cheeks, stopping when I found his hole and giving it a little tap. He jolted, and I paused. "Still okay?"

"Yes. Um, yeah."

"You sure?" I started to withdraw my hand. "You can absolutely say no, and we'll try something else."

"No. I mean yes. Yes, you can continue. I just wasn't expecting..."

"You weren't expecting?" I found his pucker and applied the slightest bit of pressure with my index finger.

"I wasn't expecting to like it."

Oh. Fuck.

I'd had penetrative sex with two other men in the last

nine years. One had preferred topping and the other bottoming, which had led me to discover I was vers. I'd be happy to bottom for Jason if that's what he wanted, but damn, I hoped he'd let me inside him too. This seemed a promising sign, but time would tell.

I continued massaging his hole, letting him adjust to the sensation and the pressure. I wanted desperately to reach around and stroke him with my free hand, knowing that would maximize his pleasure, but I restrained myself, not wanting him to spill just yet.

That didn't mean I couldn't take my own pleasure at the same time. I stepped forward so my dick was pressed against the side of his flank, groaning at the friction his skin provided against my sensitive erection. I pressed kisses against the skin at the nape of his neck as I nudged my finger forward. "You gonna let me in?" He was tight, his muscles clenched against the intrusion.

"I don't know how to..."

"Breathe, baby, and try to relax."

I pressed again, but he was still clenched tight. I started to pull my hand away, thinking maybe this was too much for him today, but he reached around and stopped me, holding my hand in place.

"No. Don't stop."

"We don't have to do this today. Or ever if you don't want to."

"I want to. I do. Please." The neediness in his voice convinced me, but I stepped back, trying a different tactic.

He started to turn, his eyes pleading with me to continue, but when I dropped to my knees, his eyebrows skyrocketed. "Hands on the wall. I've got you."

He whimpered but did as I asked, and damn, he was a sight to behold. This big, strong, gentle giant of a man, offering himself to me, trusting me with his body. It was a privilege and an honor to be the only one who'd ever seen him like this. I was his first, and damned if I didn't want to be his last.

His only.

I took hold of his ass, spreading his cheeks to get a better look at his pucker, pink and perfect and ready for my tongue. I leaned forward and teased his entrance, flattening out my tongue and licking slowly across his hole over and over again as he rocked back against me. I kept it up, picking up the pace, savoring his taste and the little needy sounds he made.

I repositioned myself, pointing my tongue and pressing the tip inside before he could overthink it and tense up again. This time, Jason groaned, his entire body shuddering at the sensation of my mouth pressed against the most intimate part of him. I continued working to soften him, adding the tip of my finger alongside my tongue, driving them both in and out as he writhed against me.

I pulled my mouth away while leaving my finger in place, pressing in farther until I was past the first knuckle. I kissed and bit at the meat of his ass as I searched for that sweet spot I knew would light him up.

When I found it, he jolted. "Fuck. Oh shit, what was that? Oh my God, do that again."

I obliged, laughing as he let loose another stream of curse words. I stood, keeping my finger inside him, debating whether I should add a second. He had to be close to coming, based on how he was squirming on my hand. I wasn't sure a second finger was necessary. I kissed his shoulder, sucking a small hickey into his skin. "Can I touch you now?"

"Yes. God yes. Please."

The whiny tone of his voice was so unlike him that it had me smiling. He was so responsive, so *alive* under my touch. I liked to think I was a considerate lover, but I could honestly say I didn't think I'd ever taken so much satisfaction from pleasuring someone. I wanted to come, desperately, but I wanted him to come *more*.

I reached down, grabbed his dick, and stroked in time with the motion of my finger.

"Oh shit. Oh shit. Oh shit."

The phrase got louder and louder with each stroke until he stiffened, arching his back and sucking in his breath as he painted the shower wall with his cum. I removed my finger, grabbing his hip to keep my balance and continuing to stroke him with my other hand while he coated my fist with his release. He grunted and groaned his way through it, his body shaking with the effort of keeping himself upright, until eventually, he pitched forward, resting his forehead against the tile while he struggled to catch his breath.

Desperate for my own release, I wrapped my cum-soaked hand around my cock and began to stroke vigorously and without mercy until, moments later, I painted his ass and leg with my cum.

He turned, pulling me into his arms as we both struggled to catch our breath. "That was...wow. We are *definitely* doing that again."

I laughed. "Maybe we should get some lunch first?"

63

ZACH

WE FINISHED our shower and stopped by Jason's house so he could change into a fresh set of clothes before heading to the diner. I figured I ought to get a gold star for keeping my hands to myself while he changed. Now that I'd had a literal taste of him, I wanted nothing more than to feast on him like he was an all-you-can-eat buffet. But as my stomach gave a growl while I was standing in his living room, looking at the pictures of him and his family, I figured I probably needed to eat some actual food first.

When he came out of his room in a black fitted shirt, paired with his usual backward ball cap, athletic shorts, and flip-flops, I almost said *fuck it* and attacked him where he stood.

Judging by the smirk on his face, he knew exactly what I was thinking.

The diner was hopping when we walked in, busy with customers who had the day off post-holiday and were looking for lunch or maybe just a late breakfast. After about a twenty-minute wait, we were escorted to a booth in the corner, where Sarah greeted us with a smile and some waters shortly after.

She rushed away, saying she'd be back in a few moments to take our order while we looked at our menus. Jason didn't bother looking at his, but since I'd only been here one other time and hadn't actually eaten anything, I needed a moment to look everything over. The only problem was that the feel of Jason's foot running up and down my calf had me reading the description for the same burger half a dozen times until I eventually gave up, figuring I'd just order the same thing he did and call it a day.

I tossed the menu down in front of me to find Jason watching me with a shit-eating grin.

"Having fun?"

"Absolutely. You?"

I reached under the table, trying to discreetly adjust my erection. "I'm finding my shorts have suddenly become a little snug."

He picked up his water and took a sip, reminding me of the Kermit the Frog tea-sipping meme. "That's what you get for wearing chinos. Had you worn athletic shorts, you wouldn't have that problem."

Despite my attempts at adjustment, my cock felt like it was being strangled. "That's not helping."

He reached over and grabbed my hands. "I'm sorry, honey. Was that insensitive of me?"

The fucker had the gall to wink.

"When did you become such a tease?"

"You must bring it out in me."

Warmth settled in my belly, and I smiled. I liked this playful side of him. He'd always been so serious, so thoughtful, which I loved about him too, but it was good to see him having a little fun, even if it was at my expense.

Sarah reappeared, eyes locking on our clasped hands, then darting between us, giving me a moment of concern. From what I remembered, Astaire was a pretty progressive town despite being located in a red state, but there were always those who would disapprove of a same-sex couple, regardless of where you were in the world. When her face lit with a smile, I relaxed.

"So, is this a thing now? You introduced him as a friend, but you guys looked pretty cozy on the lounger last night."

"It's kind of a long story, but yeah, we're, um, dating."

I glanced at Jason, who was beaming. I felt my face flush with warmth and realized it was from happiness, not embarrassment. I'd always been happiest when I was with Jason, but at our closest, we'd been wrapped in turmoil over our sisters' accident. This was the first time we were free to simply enjoy the beauty of what it meant to be in a relationship. It was a damn good feeling.

"Well, I'm happy for you guys. Y'all're sweet together."

"Thank you."

We placed our orders and then chit-chatted about innocuous things. Gossip we'd picked up on last night at the party. Speculation about the new guy Drea had hired. As we ate our burgers, Jason shared pictures of his new nephew while I bragged about what an amazing job Sean had done with the kids at the elementary soccer camp earlier in the week.

When Sarah dropped off our check, I asked if we could take Daisy over to visit Sean, which she agreed to. It was nice to see her warming up to me, and I hoped we could continue to be friendly. I suspected she needed some friendship in her life.

We ran home, picked up Daisy, and then headed over to visit Sean. The pure joy he radiated when he opened the door to us had me smiling ear to ear. We took Daisy around to the back of the house where Jason and I sat on the deck steps while we watched Sean throw an old tennis ball for Daisy to catch. I leaned my head on Jason's shoulder, content with the direction my life had taken in the last twenty-four hours. Jesus, had it only been last night that Jason declared he wanted to date me? My instinct was to worry, to overthink and panic about how quickly everything had changed, but I'd already done that. It was time to let it go and embrace it.

"Do you know Sarah's story? Does she have any family here?"

"I'm not sure. I know Sean's mom was her sister and they were close growing up, but that's about all I know. Why?"

"I was just wondering. The yard could use some work, and I'm betting she doesn't have time to do much more than mow."

"You're probably right. Hey, Sean!" I called out. "Come here a sec."

Sean came loping over, tripping a little on the uneven grass. Daisy came, hot on his heels, and dropped the ball at our feet, looking at us expectantly. I picked up the ball and chucked it, laughing as Daisy shot across the yard like a rocket.

"Who mows the grass here?"

"Oh, well, I would, but I don't really know how. Maybe you could teach me?"

"It wasn't an accusation, bud." I put a hand on his arm, hoping to reassure him. "We were just wondering."

"Well, Aunt Sarah does it whenever she has time."

Jason and I exchanged a look. "Does your aunt work tomorrow?"

"I think so. Why?"

"How would you like to surprise her with a little yard cleanup?"

"That would be awesome! She's always so tired after work. It'd be nice for her."

Jason tapped my arm. "I have to work tomorrow, so I can't be here to help you."

"That's alright." I turned back to Sean. "Think we can get Rusty to help? And maybe even Lauren?"

He pulled a face. "Isn't she too little?"

"Nah. We'll find something age-appropriate for her to do. It's gonna be a lot of work. Are you sure you're up for it?"

He stood tall, puffing out his chest. "I can totally do it."

I grinned and put my fist out for him to bump. "We'll start early before it gets too hot. I'll be over at nine."

Daisy trotted over and dropped the ball at our feet. "Will you bring Daisy?"

"Absolutely. But we're gonna head out now, alright?"

"Yeah, okay. Thanks for bringing Daisy over. I'm, like, really glad you're the one who adopted her. I can tell she really likes you, and if I couldn't keep her, I'm glad she gets to live with you."

My eyes flooded and a lump formed in my throat as we stood and made our way to the front of the house. Jason took my hand in his, giving it a squeeze in understanding.

We said our goodbyes and got into Jason's truck. I was glad he'd driven because I needed a moment to compose myself. He started the truck but didn't pull away. Instead, he turned to face me.

"You okay?"

I blew out a shaky breath. "It just gets to me sometimes, how sweet that kid is. He didn't deserve to lose everything like that, you know? I wish there was more I could do for him."

"You've done more than a lot of folks would do." He pulled me forward and pressed a kiss to my forehead. "You've got a good heart, Zach Jacobs."

I was pretty sure that heart belonged to him.

64

JASON

WE SPENT the remainder of the afternoon and evening at Zach's house. Zach threw in another load of laundry and then joined me on the dock, where I read some more of my book and he caught up on one of his coaching podcasts. We traded glances and small touches—a hand on a knee, a brush of an elbow—as if we needed to remind ourselves that the other was really here.

As the sun sank lower in the sky, we heated up leftover chicken and pulled the cucumber salad out of the fridge, sitting out on the deck as we watched the sunset. I watched the way his dark chestnut hair caught the fading sunlight, the dark strands appearing almost coppery red. Zach caught me staring and raised a brow. "What?"

"You. Just you. You're beautiful."

He set his fork down, color flooding his cheeks, clearly at a loss for words.

"Looks have never been all that important to me. It's not that I don't notice other people's appearance. It's just that it doesn't really factor into how I perceive them. With you... I..."

A thought, a memory, really, popped into my head, and I chuckled. I couldn't believe I was actually considering sharing it. "Did I ever tell you the first time I had an inkling that I might be into you?"

He leaned back in his seat, giving me his full attention. "It was around Christmas, I think? I don't remember if you ever told me the exact timeline."

"It was Christmas that I figured out I was demi. But before that, around Thanksgiving, actually, was the first inkling I had that there might be an attraction happening. I just didn't understand what was going on or how to name what I was feeling."

"Okay..."

"Shit, I can't believe I'm telling you this." I pulled off my hat, running my fingers through my hair while I tried to find my words.

He leaned forward, resting his elbows on the table in front of him. "Well, you have to tell me now. You can't drop a hint like that and then not spill it."

"I'm getting there." I put my hat back on and decided to rip off the Band-Aid. "It was the day after Thanksgiving, I think, because you'd sent me some pictures of you and Drea at the Santa Monica Pier from earlier in the week. I don't know how many times I looked at those pictures, but I remember thinking it was the happiest I'd ever seen you. The expression on your face—your eyes were dancing and you had the biggest smile. I couldn't stop looking at it. You were beautiful. You still *are* beautiful."

"Jesus, J. You really know how to make a guy feel good."

I laughed. "I mean it. I don't usually notice other people's looks, but with you, I suppose I take notice."

"Thank you."

"Should we clean up and take a swim?"

"That sounds perfect."

By the time we'd loaded our dishes into the dishwasher and Zach had moved his wash to the dryer, the sun had set and stars were making their first appearance in the night sky.

We walked back out to the dock, stripping our shirts and shorts as we went, leaving us in just our underwear. Zach slid his thumbs beneath the waistband of his briefs and began lowering them. "What are you doing?"

"Taking off my underwear."

"This is a public lake," I hissed.

He laughed. "Not this part. Besides, I turned off all the lights except the ones that line the path. It's pitch black out here. No one can see anything."

He continued lowering his briefs, but I stood there, the good little rule-follower in me hesitating.

"Come on, where's the confident guy who invited me to shower sex earlier?"

"That guy thrives indoors. Outdoors, not so much."

Zach stepped toward me, closing the gap between us. The heat of his body so close to mine had my skin breaking out in goosebumps. "Come on, J..." He slid his fingers beneath my waistband, teasing the skin underneath. "Live a little."

Slowly, he lowered my briefs, allowing my erection to spring free. He bent and pressed my dick up with his hand so it was touching my belly, exposing the underside. He licked a stripe from root to tip, eliciting a groan. Then the fucker stood, winked at me, took off running down the dock, and jumped into the water.

I stood there for a solid five seconds, mouth gaping open while he splashed about in the lake. "Are you fucking serious?" I called out in disbelief.

"Watch it. Keep up that racket and the neighbors will come out to see what's going on. Do you really want Peggy Anderson from next door seeing you standing on my dock buck-ass naked?"

"Peggy Anderson? My fourth-grade teacher, Peggy Anderson?" I began walking down the dock toward the sound of his laughter.

"Oh shit. I forgot she's a retired teacher. Better get in here before she sees you."

Standing on the edge of the dock, I could just make out where he was treading water. I jumped, landing just enough off the right side of his body that I didn't hit him but close enough to catch him in the splash my big body made when it hit the water.

It wasn't very deep here, so I pushed off the sandy bottom of the lake, kicking my feet until my face broke the surface. I pushed the water out of my eyes and reached for him, pulling him into me for a kiss.

"You're a little shit, you know that?" I said playfully.

"It got you in the water, didn't it?"

I bent my head forward and nipped playfully at his shoulder before sliding my tongue up the column of his throat to the spot just behind his ear.

"Mmm," was his response. I could feel his breath catch as I nipped and sucked his earlobe. We were both treading water, our arms wrapped around each other while our legs worked to keep us afloat. I hadn't known my lifeguard training would come in so handy a decade later.

I worked my hands down his body as my lips traced a path across the line of his jaw and around to his other ear. The feel of his scruff against my lips was even more delicious than I'd imagined. When my hands reached the tight globes of his ass, I grabbed a handful and pulled him into me, groaning as our dicks brushed against each other.

"Fuck it," I said and began moving us closer to the shore until my feet touched the bottom comfortably. I released him so he could stand on his own, sliding my hand in front of me until it came in contact with his cock. I lined mine up next to his, taking both of us in my hand and stroking slowly.

"Jesus, J. That feels amazing."

"Mmm. It does." I slid my hand back and forth a few more times. "You know, I didn't finish my story up there at the table."

"What story?" He'd tipped his head forward so his words were muffled against my chest.

"There was more to the story about the picture."

"Yeah?"

I lost my train of thought for a moment when he flicked his tongue across my nipple, sending a jolt of electricity straight to my cock.

"You like it when I play with your nipple?" he asked teasingly.

"Apparently." I grunted as he continued his assault.

I began working my hand faster, shuttling back and forth over our cocks at a steady tempo.

"What's the rest of the story?" he panted.

"What? Oh. That day, the day after Thanksgiving, I was taking a shower, and I was thinking about that picture, and I realized I was semi-erect."

I lowered my free hand, cupping his sack and rolling his balls between my fingers as I jerked us faster and faster. His forehead rested on my chest again and his fingers dug into my hips as he held on.

"I jacked off in the shower that day. I still remember it

because it wasn't something I did with a lot of frequency. I still don't, if I'm being honest. But I had an erection, and I jerked off, and when I tried to figure out what was different, why I'd gotten hard seemingly out of nowhere, I realized I'd been thinking of that picture."

"Oh God, J. I'm about to come."

"Me too," I ground out, teeth clenched with the exertion and the need to come.

He let out a sound, partial grunt, partial whine, like the keening of some wild animal, and then he was coming in my hand. I could feel the slick heat of it coating my fingers beneath the surface of the water as I continued to stroke us until, moments later, my own release was added to the mix. I gritted my teeth and grunted my way through it, determined to stay quiet enough that I wouldn't alert the neighbors. I certainly didn't need to be discovered frotting in the lake by my fourth-grade teacher.

"So basically," he said, between panting breaths, "you're telling me you jacked off to me in the shower?"

"Yup."

"But that was the first inkling? Like you still didn't *know* you were into me?"

God, Zach was a sassy fucker when he wanted to be.

"Shut up. You didn't know either."

He tipped his head up and kissed me. "It was actually the same weekend Clayton first suggested you were my boyfriend, which is what got the ball rolling for me."

I wrapped my arms around him, savoring the feel of his slick skin against mine and the sound of water gently lapping at the shore. "Our sisters were right. We really were idiots."

"One hundred percent. But we can't ever admit that, or we'll never hear the end of it."

"Oh, I'm not *that* stupid."

We both laughed, the sound of it whisked away on the breeze.

I tipped his chin up to mine so I could look into his eyes. "I know now…that I'm into you."

He kissed me, soft and sweet and tender. "Thank you. For giving this a chance. I know you said you forgave me, but it all still feels so surreal."

"What if I turn it around and thank *you* for coming back? For trying to make things right. It wasn't a small thing to come back here after all this time."

"You're thanking me for doing the right thing?"

"Not everyone would. I think most would chalk it up to a painful mistake they made at nineteen and would do their best to move past it. In fact, I think coming back here was very brave."

"You do?"

"I do. Now, no more unnecessary thank yous and apologies. From here on out, we're looking forward and not back. Okay?"

"You're amazing, you know that?"

Zach's eyes were filled with wonder as he looked at me, but I didn't really think I'd done or said anything that incredible. I just wasn't interested in rehashing the past over and over again. I'd meant it when I said I forgave him. And I meant it now when I said I wanted only to look forward.

"I'm not amazing. I'm just excited to see where the future takes us. I want a relationship with you. I want to call you my boyfriend and hold hands at the diner and have more lazy days like today. I want to take you to the county fair next weekend and go on dates in the city and come to soccer games to watch you coach. I want a future with you, but in order for that to work, we have to be equals."

I brushed my thumb over his cheekbone, then cupped his face. "I don't want you to feel like you're always having to make up for what happened before or like you owe me something. I forgave you, honey. Maybe it's time you forgive yourself."

He closed his eyes, and I pressed my lips to his forehead, holding him under the stars. "That's easier said than done."

"I know. It's going to take some time." I kissed him again, leisurely sliding my tongue between his lips before pulling away. "Should we head inside? I should probably get going since I have work in the morning."

"Oh. Yeah, okay. That's probably a good idea."

He pulled away from me and sloshed through the water to the shore of the small beach. He shook off the water, then walked around to step onto the dock, where he pulled his briefs back on, then picked mine up and held them out for me. I pulled them on, then followed him up to the house, picking up the rest of our clothes as we went.

We stepped into the basement, the cool air a shock to our damp skin, sending goosebumps rippling all over our bodies. Zach grabbed a couple of extra towels off the shelf and we wrapped ourselves in them, grinning at each other as we shivered in the air conditioning. We pulled on our clothes and Zach walked me through the house to the front door. Daisy hopped down from the chair she'd been snoozing on and trotted over to nudge her head into my hand.

I gave her a scratch behind the ears before turning my attention back to Zach, who seemed more subdued than he had before.

"You know it isn't that I don't *want* to stay, right?" I placed my hands on his waist, wanting to keep us connected. "It's been an intense twenty-four hours, and I think it would be good for us to have some time to process. And if I'm in your bed, *processing* is the last thing I'm going to be doing." I waggled my eyebrows at him, eliciting a laugh, which was my goal. "Text me tomorrow and let me know how the yard cleanup goes over at Sarah's?"

"I can do that."

"And I was serious about the fair next week. We're going to have a firetruck there and I have to work a shift from eight to noon, but then I'm free the rest of the day. Let me win you a giant overpriced stuffed animal and feed you all the fried food you could ever imagine?"

He laughed. "I'm in."

"Good."

I pulled Zach closer, basking in the warmth of his smile, feeling happier than I'd felt in a long, long time. I leaned forward and kissed him, savoring the feel of his lips against mine. We'd traded so many kisses today, and I was still marveling over the fact that I now had the freedom to do so whenever I wished. I didn't think I'd ever get tired of it.

65

ZACH

I ARRIVED at Sean's with Daisy and a half-dozen doughnuts just before nine on Saturday morning. Sean and Rusty answered the door together, with Lauren pushing her way through the two of them to say hello. She giggled when Daisy greeted her with enthusiastic kisses to the face until Sean grabbed Daisy's collar and convinced her to give Lauren some space. The kids eagerly snarfed down the doughnuts while I sipped my coffee, pretending not to notice when they snuck Daisy a few nibbles. Once the doughnuts were gone and we'd washed sticky fingers and faces, I declared it was time to get to work.

Two and a half hours later, we'd wrangled the yard into something much more manageable. We'd cleaned and organized the yard toys, both boys had taken turns with the mower, and we'd removed the weeds that had climbed the back fence like a trellis. For her part, Lauren had covered the driveway, patio, and sidewalks with a colorful display of chalk art, and we finished by arranging the potted flowers I'd bought in front of the garage and on the front steps. I thought they added some cheer to the place.

We stepped back to admire our handiwork and I snapped a couple of pictures and sent them to Jason before we packed up the tools and put everything away. Sean and I took a moment to sit on the front stoop with Daisy while Rusty took Lauren inside to help her clean off the chalk she had all over her and then get started on lunch. The kids had done a great job today, not complaining once, despite the rough work and heat. I only wished I could be here to see Sarah's face when she got home.

"Thanks for showing me how to do all that stuff today. Now I can help out more."

My heart clenched, remembering what Sarah had said the first time I came over about Sean always offering to do extra chores. "It's a nice thing you did for your aunt, and you guys did a great job. It was fun hanging out here today."

He snorted in that way only teenagers could, conveying his skepticism. "Yeah, right. I'm sure you would've rather been hanging out with your boyfriend."

I couldn't help but smile at his use of the word boyfriend, despite the snarky tone. I was still wrapping my head around the fact that Jason and I were actually dating. Being able to call him my boyfriend was a gift.

"Jason had to work today, but even if he hadn't, we still would have been here hanging out with you guys. We just would have had an extra set of hands."

"Why? You could probably be doing a thousand cooler things than yard work with us."

"I happen to like hanging out with kids. I'm a coach, remember?"

I wanted to put my arm around him. I wanted to hug the kid and give him the reassurance he so clearly needed. I knew now that Sarah really did care about him, but I had no idea what kind of affection she showed him. After my mom passed, I'd become touch-starved and hadn't realized it.

As a teenage boy, I'd been past the point of needing hugs, or so I'd thought, until the one person who still regularly hugged me was gone. It wasn't until I found Drea crying one day and had pulled her in for a hug that I'd realized how much I needed one too.

But Sean wasn't mine to hug. He wasn't a sibling or a cousin or any other kind of relation to me. He was a kid I coached, though I supposed I was more invested in him than I typically would be with any other kid. Still, I refrained, opting instead to nudge his knee with mine.

"You got quiet. Everything okay?"

"Do you still miss your mom?" He pulled one of his legs up and rested his chin on his knee.

"Every single day."

He turned his head away from me so I couldn't see his face, but I still heard him when he said, "I just want it to stop hurting. Does it ever stop hurting?"

I swallowed past the lump in my throat, thinking through my response. The responsibility my words carried was heavy. I didn't want to fuck this up.

"Honestly, no. I still miss her and it still hurts." I heard a sniffle and suspected he was crying. Daisy wiggled herself next to him and laid her head on his feet with a sigh. "And this first year without her...I won't lie. It's going to be tough. But you sort of just put one foot in front of the other and figure out how to live with it."

"What if I can't? What if it's too hard?"

"Have you had days like that? When it feels too hard?"

"All the days are hard." God, I ached for him.

"They are," I agreed. "What do you do when it's especially hard?"

He sniffled again, his arm coming up, I was assuming to wipe at his eyes. "I don't know. I just sort of get quiet and don't say much. Keep to myself. Sometimes I get pissy and say shit...sorry, stuff...to my cousins, and then I feel bad later. Sometimes, I go to my room and cry. Except I share with Rusty, so sometimes I go in the bathroom."

"I do all of those things too."

Finally, he turned and looked at me, his face tear-streaked and his eyes red-rimmed. "You cry?"

"I do. I cried just the other day. Sometimes life is overwhelming and the emotions bubble up and spill out. It's part of being human."

"I hate it."

I chuckled. "I don't always like it either, but I often feel better after. And you know what helps the most? I still talk to her. Sometimes out loud, sometimes just in my mind. Sometimes, it's just a few words about my day, and sometimes, I ramble on and on. It makes me feel like she's still with me."

"I don't know. I might feel weird doing that."

"Maybe. And just because it works for me doesn't mean it will work for you. But you could try it. And if you feel weird talking, maybe you could write it down. It could be like you're writing her letters."

"Yeah, maybe."

I was a little out of my depth here, and I realized that perhaps I wasn't the only one who might benefit from therapy. I made a mental note to find a way to bring it up with Sarah later.

"You can talk to your aunt about this stuff, you know. She loves you."

"She's always busy with work and her own kids. I don't want to bug her."

"You know you're not a burden, right? Your aunt is busy, but that doesn't mean she doesn't want you here."

"Yeah, I guess." His voice was so sad, so dejected, and I didn't know how to fix it. I felt helpless when he stood up. "Thanks again for helping today. I'm gonna go see if Rusty needs help with Lauren."

My heart sank. I couldn't help but feel like I'd bungled this whole conversation, but I didn't know how to backtrack and make it right. "Okay. I'll bring Daisy over again soon."

"Thanks," he muttered, then turned around and went inside.

Dammit.

I STEWED about the conversation with Sean all afternoon. Jason wasn't there to provide a distraction and I'd called Drea to see if she wanted to hang out, but she was spending the day with some friends in Omaha. After all the work I'd put in before and during camp, I'd been looking forward to some downtime, and now that I had it, I didn't know what to do with it. I'd been training or competing my entire life. I wasn't built to sit idle.

Which left me with way too much time to think. About the changes in my relationship with Jason. About the things Sean had told me. About my own mental health concerns. All of it. If they ever made overthinking an Olympic sport, I'd be the fucking gold medalist.

I was sitting in the lounger out back, reading the same paragraph in my book for the third time, when my phone rang. Seeing it was Sarah, I swiped to answer, my heart flip-flopping in my chest, suddenly nervous about her reaction to our surprise.

"I'm told you're responsible for helping the boys tackle the yard today?"

"I hope that's okay. The kids and I just wanted to—"

"Zach, this is maybe the nicest thing anyone has done for me in a very long time. I can't believe you did this for us. I just...I don't know how to thank you."

"You work hard, and I just wanted to help. And now the boys know how to mow, so they can help you with it more."

"I've been meaning to show them, but there just never seems to be enough time. I just..."

"I get it. And look, you are clearly a strong woman, but you're also human. Everyone needs help sometimes."

"Asking for help isn't something I've ever been very good at. Sean's mom and I leaned on each other a lot, but with her gone..." There was a quiver in her voice, and I heard her take a couple of deep breaths before she continued, "Anyway, I just wanted to thank you."

"You're very welcome. I enjoyed hanging out with the kids. I'll send you a couple of pictures. Lauren was covered in chalk by the time we were finished."

"Oh, believe me, I heard all about it. She was chattering ninety miles an hour when I walked in the door."

I smiled, picturing Lauren's blue eyes shining brightly and her cheeks flushed with excitement as she told her mom all about making the yard "pretty."

"I'm not surprised," I said with a smile, already thinking about the next time I could bring Daisy over and hang out with them. I'd connected with this family because of Sean, but I was becoming smitten with all of them.

An idea occurred to me, and without thinking it through, I asked, "What are you all doing next weekend?"

"I'm working the day shift on Saturday and the dinner shift on Sunday. I thought I might take the kids to the pool on Sunday before heading to work, but I hadn't decided for sure. Why?"

"Jason and I are heading to the county fair on Saturday. I thought maybe I could take the kids."

"You want to take three kids to the fair?" Her voice was laced with a fair amount of incredulity. "Do you have any idea what you'd be getting yourself into?"

I laughed. "Oh, I have no doubt I'll be in over my head, but Jason will be with me. I bet we can manage between the two of us."

"You're serious?"

"I am."

"Why? Don't get me wrong. I appreciate you taking an interest in my kids. Lord knows they could use a positive male role model. But I've been a single mom for nearly two years. Longer, really, since their father was in and out of our lives for a long time before he died. Then you show up, and suddenly, you're invested. I just want to know why? Why us?"

"Honestly, I don't know. I liked working with kids when I was younger, but I can't say I spent a lot of time around them until I started the camp. And then I got to know Sean, and you guys, and I just...I find myself wanting to make your lives a little better. I'm sorry if I'm overstepping, and if you want me to back off, I will. I'll be bummed because I genuinely like your kids, but I'll respect your wishes."

My heart beat faster as I waited for her response. I was sure that from her perspective, it did seem odd that a guy like me had inserted himself into their lives, and I could only hope she wouldn't cut me off.

"I can't say I understand it, but no, I don't want you to back off. I'm pretty sure they'd revolt if you did, and I'd never hear the end of it. Are you wanting to take them on Saturday or Sunday?"

"Saturday."

"Alright, if you're sure you can handle them, go for it."

"Awesome!"

We disconnected the call, agreeing to touch base later in the week to firm up our plans. It wasn't until after dinner that I realized I hadn't brought up my concerns about Sean's mental health. I decided to research therapists who worked with children and figure out what financial options were available before presenting the information to her when we talked later in the week.

In the meantime, I'd just have to do my best to keep an eye on Sean when I could and hope that was enough.

66

JASON

I DIDN'T SEE Zach again until Monday, and then it was only for a run. He had some appointments in the city that day, including dinner with his dad, so we weren't able to hang out. I worked again on Tuesday and Wednesday, but since I wasn't scheduled to work on Thursday and wouldn't need to be up early, we agreed to see each other for a late dinner after my Wednesday shift.

I was desperate to see him.

For the first time in my life, I found myself in a near-constant state of horniness. Even those weeks between New Year's Eve and when Zach had returned to Nebraska following the accident hadn't been as painful as the last couple of days. I'd jerked off every morning in the shower, and we'd even resorted to phone sex last night, which had been hotter than I'd expected but not nearly as satisfying as being with him in person.

Even more frustrating than the lack of physical sex was the lack of physical touch. I missed being in his proximity. The heat of his thigh resting against mine while we sat on the couch. The brush of his fingertips against my elbow as he slipped past me in the kitchen. The comfort of his body wrapped up in mine as we slept. I'd gotten a taste of all those things over the weekend, and I was greedy for more.

Suggesting we take some time to process had seemed like a good idea in theory, but in practice, it had only made me miserable. It was ridiculous how much I missed him, considering he lived less than three miles away, and it was completely my fault. Zach had let me take the lead every step of the way, and I was sure he was doing so in this as well. So it was up to me to do something about it.

Keeping things simple, I'd showered at the station and then picked up a pizza from Valentino's on my way to his place. I'd even packed a bag that morning and left it in the truck just in case. But when I stepped out of my truck with the pizza in hand, I grabbed the bag too. I was fairly confident there'd be no need for "just in case."

I didn't bother knocking since I'd already texted him I was on the way, so I walked in through the front door, calling out his name as I took off my shoes and dropped my bag on the floor near the door. When he didn't respond to my shout, I walked back through the kitchen, set the pizza on the counter, and looked out the window to see if he was out back.

I scanned the yard and finally caught sight of him standing on the dock with his hands on his hips, looking out over the water. He was dressed in board shorts and nothing else, and the way the setting sunlight highlighted the toned muscles of his back and shoulders had my mouth running dry and my cock swelling.

As if sensing my presence, he turned and gave me a bright smile and a wave. I was moving before I'd even thought to do so, opening the door and making my way across the deck and down the steps to the dock. He met me halfway, and I grabbed him, hauling him into me for a blistering kiss. He let out an "oomph" and sank into me, meeting my frantic energy with the same intensity.

I needed him. I needed him *now*.

We grappled with each other, hands roaming, grasping, tugging, fighting for dominance as we each sought to claim the other.

"Inside," I said as I shoved my hands down the back of his shorts and gripped his ass, pulling him into me and grinding my needy dick against his.

His groan was guttural, coming from deep in the back of his throat, and he began to walk me backward toward the basement sliding door. My foot caught on something, and I nearly went down, but he caught me, keeping me upright.

I turned, grabbing his hand and tugging him the rest of the way. The moment the door was closed behind us, I dropped to my knees, pulling his shorts with me.

"Not that I'm complaining, but what's gotten into you?"

"I missed you," I said simply, then without waiting for anything more, I took him to the back of my throat in one swift motion. I choked a little, my enthusiasm getting the best of me, but I was determined to continue despite my lack of experience, so I pulled off and tried again, this time a little slower.

The feel of him, steel wrapped in velvet sitting heavy on my tongue, was addictive, and while I'd experienced the pleasure of receiving a blowjob, I now finally understood why someone might actually want to give one.

My senses were on full alert. I slid back again, the taste of his salty precum settling on my tongue, then slid forward, inhaling the musky scent of him as my lips met the neat patch of hair at the base of his cock. I looked up then, and when his eyes met mine, pupils dilated and hazy with lust, lips red and swollen from our kisses, I had to squeeze my own dick to keep from coming on the spot.

He grabbed a fistful of my hair, holding me in place. "Damn, baby. You look so good with my cock buried in your mouth. You gonna let me fuck your face?"

Without breaking eye contact, I shook my head.

His eyebrows shot up. "No?"

In response, I reached up and cupped his sac, kneading his balls lightly. At the same time, I hollowed my cheeks and pulled back, applying as much suction as I could manage.

"Fuuuuck."

As his eyes slid closed in ecstasy, I slid forward again, picking up the pace and applying suction each time I withdrew. Feeling more confident, I slid my hand back, away from his balls and across his taint until I found his hole. I liked it when he fingered me the other day, enough that I'd experimented a little on my own, and now I wanted to return the favor.

I tapped his opening and his hips jerked forward, causing me to gag a little. "Shit, sorry. Baby, stop for a moment."

I pulled off immediately and looked up. "What's wrong? Do you not like that?"

"I fucking love everything you're doing." He ran his hands through my hair, trying to reassure me. "But if you're going to play with my ass, you gotta get your finger wet at the very least."

"Oh shit. Sorry."

"You don't have to apologize. Give me your finger."

I held up my hand and he leaned forward, grabbing me by the wrist and pulling my finger into his mouth. He wrapped his lips around the base of my finger, then pulled it out slowly, his eyes never leaving mine. My cock was hard as granite, aching and begging for attention, but I kept my eyes locked on his, absolutely entranced by the lasciviousness of the gesture. It was hot as fuck.

He released me, breaking the trance, and I immediately went back to work, sliding my finger back toward his hole and taking his cock in my mouth once again. This time, though, I added my tongue to the mix as I applied the suction, massaging the underside of his dick as I worked my jaw. I pressed my finger against his entrance, enthralled by the tight heat as I pushed inside. He groaned, his hand in my hair tightening its grip, spurring me on.

I continued the motion of my mouth at a slower pace as I explored his ass, pushing farther inside until I was two knuckles deep.

"Keep going, baby. God, that feels so good."

Encouraged, I pulled out a little before pressing back in until my finger was seated all the way inside him. He shuddered, rocking his hips forward a little, encouraging me to move. So I did, bobbing my head faster as I began to explore his ass in earnest, searching for that same spot he'd hit that I knew would light him up from the inside out.

I knew the moment I found it because his cock jumped in my mouth and he let out what could only be described as a screech. I doubled my efforts, hitting that spot again as I worked him over with my tongue.

"Baby. I'm gonna...shit. I'm gonna..."

I hit it one more time and that was all it took. Zach's body tensed, his quads straining with the effort of keeping him upright as he unloaded down my throat. I swallowed, trying to keep up with the amount of cum he was shooting into my mouth, but he just kept going, and I couldn't quite contain it all. Some of it ended up dribbling down my chin.

Finally finished, he pulled himself out of my mouth and

immediately dropped to his knees in front of me. "Your turn."

He flashed me a grin, then nudged me to lie on my back. He wasted no time yanking my shorts and briefs down my thighs and pouncing on my dick, pulling it into his mouth and giving me the same treatment I'd just given him. The difference was that I was so primed, so fucking worked up over the blowjob I'd just given him, that I was coming down his throat in seconds rather than the minutes it had taken him.

My orgasm hit me like a tsunami, an all-consuming wave of sensation that had my legs shaking and my vision tunneling. I grunted through it, helpless to do anything other than ride the wave until, eventually, the roaring in my ears abated and all the tension left my body at once, leaving me feeling like Jell-O.

Zach climbed up my body, collapsing on top of me like a starfish as we struggled to catch our breaths. My hand stroked his back absentmindedly, my fingertips dancing along his skin. I hadn't even taken my shirt off, I realized. I'd been so blind with lust that I hadn't even thought of it.

"Holy shit," he mumbled into my neck.

"Me too."

He gave a halfhearted laugh. "I think you sucked my brains right out of my dick. I'm surprised I can even form a sentence."

"Not bad for my first blowjob, huh?"

"It was a fucking stellar blowjob. A-plus. Ten out of ten would recommend."

"You're recommending my blowjob skills to other people?"

"Absolutely not. I amend my statement. Ten out of ten, back off, he's mine."

God, he made me laugh. "Alright, get off me. Let's go eat."

"Hang on. I'm still waiting for feeling to come back in my legs."

I pinched his ass, and he yelped, scrambling to get off me. "Fine. Let's eat."

WE ATE lukewarm pizza on the deck under the starlight, washing it down with a couple of beers while Daisy supervised, hoping for scraps. Even though we'd talked on the phone every day since Friday night, we rehashed our lives over the last couple of days while our feet tangled together under the table.

I couldn't stop touching him, couldn't take my eyes off him. To anyone on the outside looking in, we probably looked like a couple of codependent teenagers rushing into our first relationship, but the fact was, our foundation had already been established a long time ago. Perhaps that foundation had acquired some cracks, but I liked to think we'd patched them up and were working toward making sure it was stronger than ever. And now we were making up for lost time. Time I was no longer willing to waste.

"I packed a bag. I hope you don't mind. I was going to leave it in the truck and then run out and grab it if you asked me to stay, but I guess I'm the one doing the asking. So...can I stay?"

The smile that lit his face could have powered the entire fire station. "I'd love for you to stay."

We stood, gathering the pizza box and beer cans before heading inside. "I'm off tomorrow. What do you have going on?"

"I've got a haircut around eleven and planned to spend the afternoon organizing some things for tryouts later this month."

"So nothing in the morning?"

Zach set the empty pizza box on the counter and turned to face me. "No, why?"

I stepped into him, placing my hands around his waist and giving him a wicked smile. "Because it means we don't need to be in a rush to get out of bed."

He tilted his head up for a kiss. "Mmm. I like the sound of that."

"I thought you might."

"I like this side of you. It's like I've unleashed some sort of sex fiend."

"Did you just call me a sex fiend?"

"I mean…if the shoe fits…" He drew his brows up in challenge.

"You little shit. Just for that, I'm not putting out tonight."

"Bullshit."

"Bullshit?"

Zach reached out and ran a finger up my length. I was already half-hard just from this little flirty thing we had going and his touch sent shivers skittering along my spine. "Bullshit. You're already hard for me. Sex. Fiend."

I stepped even closer, nudging my leg between his thighs, deliberately pressing my quad into his crotch. My hands rested on the counter behind him, caging him in. He was just as hard as I was. "Who's calling who a sex fiend?"

"I never said I wasn't one. Only that I'd awoken yours."

I nuzzled my nose against his ear, nipping at his earlobe playfully. "Maybe you have. Think you can keep up?"

"Bring it on."

67

ZACH

I AWOKE WITH A START, sweaty and shaking and blinking in the darkness. I tried to sit up, but there was a weight across my chest and I nearly panicked until I realized it was Jason's arm, warm and sturdy, holding me, not restraining me. Without even knowing it, he was keeping me from flying apart.

The tears started then. It felt like that emotional comedown after an emergency, when you've gone into the zone and done what you needed to do, but after it's all over, you fall apart. I was lying in bed, staring into the darkness, with the man I'd never stopped loving wrapped around me, and I was falling the fuck apart.

I tried to keep the tears quiet, but Jason woke anyway, immediately alert and concerned. "Honey, what's wrong? Did you have another dream?"

I nodded, hoping he could see it in the dark because my words were trapped in my throat.

"I'm going to get you a glass of water."

He started to pull away, but I latched onto his arm.

"No," I choked out. "Stay."

"Shh," he crooned, settling back down next to me. He wiped away my tears, but they just kept coming. I couldn't figure out how to make them stop.

"I have an idea. I'm going to sit up with my back against the headboard. I want you to sit between my legs and rest your back against my chest. Then I will wrap my arms around you, nice and snug, okay?"

I nodded, and we shifted positions as he'd suggested. He wrapped his arms around me, adding his legs over my thighs as well, and pulled the blankets over both of us, anchoring me to him. We hadn't worn clothes to bed, so the skin-to-skin contact, combined with the weight of his limbs wrapped around me and the warmth of the blankets, made me feel like I was wrapped in a cocoon of safety. A place where bad dreams would never, ever become my reality.

As the tears subsided and my thoughts coalesced into something less fragmented, I realized Jason was taking deep, measured breaths, and I'd subconsciously matched them. I took one more breath and let it out, then went completely still, feeling like I'd run a marathon.

"Better?" he asked, sensing the worst had passed.

"Yes. Thank you." I sniffled, wiping my eyes with my hand.

"You want to talk about it?"

"Not really. There's not much to tell anyway. It was the same dream I always have."

"The car accident?"

"Yeah. It always starts with Mom, but this time, the other faces were you and Sean."

I couldn't see him, but I could envision his forehead creasing with worry. "Sean? Is that new?"

"Yep. The kid isn't even old enough to drive, so that's a fun addition."

He placed a kiss near my ear and then rested his chin on top of my head. "He's becoming important to you."

"He is. And I'm worried about him."

"I know. Did you find out any more info about therapy options for him?"

"Yeah, a couple. I just haven't figured out how to bring it up with Sarah. I know it will be another point of stress for her."

"She needs to know though. She'll *want* to know. And we can help out with driving him to appointments and stuff."

God, he was so sweet. I'd shoved my way into this family's life, and he never questioned it. He'd simply supported me and them in whatever way he could. For roughly the millionth time, I marveled at how lucky I was to have him.

"I'll try to bring it up when I talk to her tomorrow. I need to touch base about our plans for the fair on Saturday." I'd felt bad that I'd invited the kids without talking to him first, but like everything else, he'd taken it in stride, saying he thought it sounded like fun.

Jason moved his arms, running his hands up and down my shoulders. "How are you feeling about your appointment on Tuesday?"

I snorted. "I was kind of dreading it, but after that dream, I'm thinking it can't come soon enough. I want some peace."

"I took the day off. I want to be there to support you."

I twisted around so I could look at him. "You didn't have to do that. I can go by myself."

"Do you *want* to go by yourself?"

What I wanted was to feel strong enough to handle it on my own. But the reality was that I wasn't sure I could. I hated how weak it made me feel, but the truth was, I did want him there. I shook my head.

"Then I'll go. I can drive you and sit in the waiting room. Or I can wait in the car if you'd rather. Wherever you want me, that's where I'll be."

I leaned up and kissed him. "Thank you."

"Of course. Do you think you can sleep?"

"Yeah, I usually don't have the dream twice in one night."

We slid under the covers, rolling onto our sides with my back against his front. He pulled me in close, as he always did, and locked safe in his arms, I slid right back into sleep.

68

___

ZACH

THE SKY WAS heavy with clouds the morning of the fair, but a quick check of the weather app indicated that the rain should hold off until later that evening. Jason had left a tumbler of coffee next to the bed before kissing my forehead and telling me he'd see me later. I'd managed one more hour of sleep before getting up and preparing for the day, nervous and excited to hang out with the kids and spend time with my boyfriend.

We arrived at the fairgrounds just in time to catch Jason for the last half-hour of his volunteer shift. The AFD booth was not far from the entrance, and once Lauren caught sight of it, she was tugging my hand in that direction. "Come on, guys. Mr. Jason is waiting!" Sean and Rusty rolled their eyes at her antics, but we all followed along, letting her lead the way.

The booth was popular, with kids waiting to climb into the firetruck while AFD personnel handed out stickers. Jason looked up as we approached, and when his face lit up brighter than the sun, I slid a little further in love with him. There was no use denying it or turning away from it, nor did

I want to. Despite everything that had happened, he'd given us another chance and I was determined to never let him go.

He stepped away from the line, greeting me with a kiss on the cheek before swinging Lauren onto his shoulders.

"Put me down! Put me down! I wanna get in the truck!" she exclaimed, her words laced with giggles.

"Oh, you do, do you?" He lifted her back up, flipping her over his head and suspending her upside down. "What's the magic word?"

She kicked her feet, her little cheeks turning pink as the blood rushed to her head. "Pleeeease!" she begged, and he flipped her right side up, carefully setting her on her feet.

"Let's go check it out." He held out his hand, and she took it, following him over to the apparatus.

Lauren climbed into the truck while Jason showed her all the buttons and let her explore. The boys tried to act unimpressed, but I could tell they thought it was pretty cool too. Lauren took three stickers, immediately putting one on her shirt and one on each of the legs of her shorts, then proceeded to charm everyone else in the vicinity.

At noon, Hannah and Sonny arrived to take the next shift and we all set off in search of lunch. We stuffed ourselves on turkey legs, grilled street corn, and way too many items that weren't ever meant to be battered and fried. Though I had to admit the fried Oreos were pretty fucking good.

The kids wanted to head to the rides, but Jason wisely suggested letting our food settle first, so we made our way to the livestock area. Jason and I strolled hand-in-hand behind the kids, watching as they looked at the various animals.

I was struck suddenly by the mundanity of it all. I didn't think most people would be thrilled to hear a date described as "mundane," but this slice of life was exactly what I'd wanted when I walked away from my soccer career. I'd craved a quieter life where I wasn't constantly training, traveling, and dealing with the pressure of competing. I thought it was probably why the idea of buying my old house had been so appealing. I'd been craving the peace I'd always felt living there. And today, strolling hand-in-hand with my boyfriend and a gaggle of kids at the county fair, I could see a future I really, really wanted.

"Do you want kids?"

We stood by a wooden fence with our feet propped up on one of the slats, watching the boys follow Lauren from animal to animal. I hadn't fully formed the thought before the question had burst out, and now I waited with my heart in my throat for his response.

I chanced a look at him, trying not to flinch at the intense look in his eyes.

"Yes."

"That simple?"

"Does it need to be complicated?"

"No, I don't suppose it does. I've just never really thought about it before." Lauren squealed, and I watched her drag Rusty over to show him one of the sheep. I turned my attention back to Jason. "I take it you've thought about it?"

"Not in a concrete, specific way, but I've always figured I'd have a family. Though I didn't always know what that would look like. I mean, for a long time, I thought I was ace, and then after you left... Well, there wasn't really anyone else I was interested in, but I thought maybe I'd adopt." He paused, the corner of his mouth tipping up in a smirk. "Or there was always the option of marrying your sister. Drea and I joked that if we didn't find anyone by forty, we'd marry each other and be platonic spouses."

The only appropriate response to that statement was a glare. "I hate everything about what you just said."

He laughed big and hearty, his head thrown back with the force of it. It was almost impossible not to return the smile.

"Let's never speak about you and my sister entering into any form of a relationship other than friendship ever again." I gave an exaggerated shudder.

He reached over and grabbed my other hand, turning me so we faced each other, our hands clasped between us. "What if it's an in-law relationship?"

My body registered the implication of what he was saying before my brain did. My smile faded as my palms began sweating, my heart beating like a bass drum while those fried Oreos threatened to make a reappearance. Still, I had to be sure I was understanding him completely.

"Are you saying you want to marry me?"

"I think we still have some things to figure out, but yeah, I do. I told you I want a future with you."

I gaped at him like a fish, completely flummoxed.

"Say something, honey. Did I freak you out?" A crease of worry formed between his brows at my lack of response.

"N..no," I stammered. "I'm just shocked. I thought when you said you wanted a future, you were talking about next week or next month. I didn't really allow myself to think any further than that."

"Which is why we still have some things to figure out. But for me, a future means a *life*. I want to build a life with you." He moved his hand up to cup my face. "Is that okay?"

"Yeah, I mean..." A slow smile spread across my face as the full impact of what he was saying hit me. "Yeah, that's so much more than okay. It's...I love you, J."

"Are you guys gonna kiss?"

We turned to see the three kids standing a couple of feet away. Lauren had her hands clasped in front of her and a big smile on her face while the boys were looking everywhere but at us.

"Sorry, um, to interrupt." Sean broke the awkward standoff. "Lauren says she has to go to the bathroom."

That spurred everyone into motion as the reminder of why they'd come over had the hearts fleeing from Lauren's eyes and she started doing what could only be described as the potty dance.

"I think I saw one back that way," Jason said, pointing over his right shoulder.

I scooped her up over the fence and walked quickly in the direction he'd pointed with the boys hot on our heels. The moment her feet hit the ground outside the door, she was scampering in, her little legs moving faster than I would have thought possible. The boys headed into the side designated for men while Jason and I stood outside, trying to shake off the adrenaline.

As our breathing returned to normal, Jason linked his pinky with mine. "Hey," he said, drawing my attention. "I love you too, you know."

"Yeah?" My face lit with a smile at the wonder of it. That despite everything, he'd not only forgiven me, but he *loved* me. It felt like a fucking miracle.

At his nod, I pulled him into a kiss right there outside of the restroom at the county fairgrounds.

It was mundane and ordinary and *wonderful*.

THE REST of the afternoon flew by in a blur of carnival rides, games, and more junk food. We stopped by Sammy's booth, where he had some of his metalwork on display. Zach ended up buying an eighteen-inch sculpture of a dancer for his sister's birthday, which wasn't for several more months, but he said he always had a hard time finding the perfect gift for her, so he had to have it. Will was there, too, and I caught him giving Zach the side-eye a couple of times when he thought I wasn't looking. I pulled him aside and suggested lunch later in the week. Summer was flying by, and we had some catching up to do, including an explanation of how things with Zach had escalated so quickly.

We were about thirty steps from Zach's car when the sky opened up. We ran the rest of the way, the kids shrieking and laughing as the rain soaked us through. Sean helped Lauren get buckled into her booster seat while I loaded the giant stuffed puppy I'd won into the back. Since we'd driven separately, I jogged a couple of rows over to where I'd parked my truck while Zach headed out to take the kids home and then meet me back at his place.

The fairgrounds were about twenty minutes from home —Zach's house, I mentally corrected—and I spent most of that time reflecting on the day's events. Zach's question about kids and wanting a family had surprised me, but it shouldn't have. The way he'd become involved in Sean's family's life, along with his love of coaching, should have clued me into the fact that he was made for being a dad. I got the impression he hadn't given that much thought in the past, but he had such a natural instinct for it and was so good with them that I was glad to know it was something he was thinking about now.

As for my response, well, I hadn't had to think about it. Family had always been important to me. So much so that I'd remained in Astaire, while many of my friends had left. My parents and my grandparents were here. Mandy and her little family. I wanted that for me too. I wanted it with Zach.

I pulled into the garage at Zach's house. He'd given me a door opener yesterday, saying I might as well use it since I was always over there anyway. Daisy was there to greet me, her nails tippy-tapping on the tile, no doubt hoping I'd feed her. I poured some food into her bowl, which she quickly inhaled, and then let her out back to do her business while I waited for Zach. With the rain coming down, Daisy made quick work of it, so I let her back in and wiped her down with a towel. At the sound of the garage door rising, both of our ears perked up, our attention swinging toward the door from the garage to the house, which Zach walked through just a moment later.

Daisy ran over to greet him, and while he gave her a couple of scratches behind the ears, his eyes were locked on me.

Want rolled through me like a flash of liquid heat. I walked toward him and, with the dog still dancing between us, placed my fingers under his chin, tilting it up for my kiss. As our lips met, I slipped my tongue inside, hungry for a taste. That first touch of our tongues lit a fuse inside me, setting off a detonation of lust that had my dick rock hard in seconds. Desperate for more, I slid my hand behind his head, gripping his hair as I deepened the kiss, fucking into his mouth with my tongue.

Zach grabbed my ass, pulling me into him, squeezing and kneading at my flesh so hard I thought there'd be bruises. I backed him into the closed door, grinding my erection into his hip, desperate to show him just how badly I wanted him. I pulled away, tugging his lower lip between my teeth before releasing it in favor of nipping at his jaw, then his earlobe. He groaned in response, pulling my shirt free so he could get his hands underneath, sliding them up and down the contours of my back.

"Want you," I panted into his ear, my voice gravelly with lust.

"God, yes." His hips jerked up, bringing his erection flush with mine.

"I want you to fuck me. I want to feel you buried inside me until I don't know where you stop and I begin. I want you to own my body like you already own my heart."

He went completely still, his eyes finding mine, and for a moment, I thought I'd gone too far. "Fuck, Jason. The things you say. Every time I think I've got my feet on solid ground, you do or say something that has me turned upside down again. I love you so goddamned much."

He kissed me again, then nudged me back so he could step past me, taking my hand and pulling me down the hall to his bedroom. He stepped over to his nightstand and flipped on the lamp, casting the room in a soft glow.

We hadn't made it this far as young men, fumbling

through sex with another guy for the first time. In fact, I hadn't been sure penetrative sex was something I'd ever want, top or bottom. But what I hadn't realized back then, and had only just discovered about myself in the last couple of weeks, was that it wasn't that I'd become a sex fiend as Zach claimed. It was the intimacy I craved. The complete deconstruction of oneself in order to allow your partner access to the deepest parts of you. And in so doing, he allowed you the same until there was no longer him and me. There was only us.

Orgasms were great. Fantastic, even. But experiencing that kind of intimacy with Zach was quite possibly the greatest gift of my life.

So, as we undressed each other, stripping our still-damp clothes from our bodies, exploring each other's skin with fingers and lips, I didn't feel nervous. There was no hesitation. Only a sense of rightness. A surety that whether we'd been separated by days or months or years, it would have always come down to this.

I was always meant to be his.

I reached down and stroked him, smearing the bead of precum around the crown, swollen and glistening. "Tell me what to do."

His eyes rolled back, and his mouth parted as I gave him a few more leisurely strokes. With some effort, he opened his eyes, refocusing his attention on me. "Lie on your back."

I did as he instructed while he fished some lube out of the drawer and tossed it on the mattress next to us. He climbed onto the bed, kicking his leg over to straddle my waist, and placed his hands on either side of my face while he looked down at me.

"I love you, J. The fact that we're here together feels like a dream come true. I'm going to do everything I can to make this good for you, but promise me that if you're uncomfortable with anything, you'll tell me to stop."

At my nod, he bent forward and kissed me, then began moving lower, his mouth blazing a trail down the center of my body. Each press of his lips felt like a brand, searing his essence into my skin. When he arrived at my cock, he ducked his head lower, licking from the underside of my balls, up my shaft, to the very tip, where he lapped up the bead of precum, moaning in pleasure like he'd just tasted his favorite flavor of ice cream. "I love the way you taste. Can't get enough."

As if to prove it, he swallowed me down, enveloping my dick in the wet heat of his mouth. My hips jerked and danced as he bobbed his head, but he didn't let it go too far, pulling off after only a few strokes and sliding lower to suck one of my balls into his mouth. My eyes rolled back as he rolled it around his tongue and then moved over to give the other one the same treatment.

He sat up and nudged me under my knee. "Pull your legs back, baby. Let me see that hole."

I was not the most flexible guy, but I pulled my legs back as he asked with my hands behind each of my knees. It wasn't the first time he'd seen this intimate part of me, but the position had me feeling exposed and vulnerable. I welcomed it, though, knowing this path would only bring us closer.

His eyes flashed as he slowly traced one finger from my balls down to my hole. "God, the sight of you, open and exposed like that." He picked up the lube, drizzling some on his fingers and down the crack of my ass. "I want my cock to find a new home inside of you." He breached my entrance with just the tip of his finger. "You going to welcome me home, J?"

The only response was my sharp intake of breath. I'd lost all ability for words as soon as his eyes had locked on my ass like he was transfixed by the sight of me open and on display for him.

He pressed his finger farther inside of me, my body welcoming him just as he'd asked. He continued his exploration, never taking his eyes off me while he worked to open me. The steady eye contact felt more intimate than the fingers inside me. When he added a second finger, he took my dick in his other hand, putting a dual focus on both parts of my body.

Pleasure rolled through me, and I broke eye contact, my eyes slamming shut as I began to writhe under his ministrations. By the time Zach added a third finger, I was an absolute mess. Every nerve ending in my body was alive with sensation, ready for the faintest spark to set me ablaze.

My eyes flew open when he withdrew his hand, the absence of his fingers such a profound contrast to the fullness I'd felt just moments before. He grabbed the lube and looked at me meaningfully. "Are you ready?"

"Yes. God, yes." I nodded as if my words needed reinforcement.

"I have condoms in the drawer, but I haven't been with anyone since before my last physical in January. Are you comfortable with me going bare?"

"Please," was all I could manage.

He slicked his cock, groaning as he stroked, then drizzled a little more of the liquid over my hole before tossing the bottle aside. He notched himself at my entrance, locking his eyes on mine once again, and pushed forward. "Bear down, baby. It will help."

I breathed deeply and did my best to follow his instructions, groaning as he sank farther inside. He made a few more shallow strokes before pressing in a little more, moving slowly to allow me to adjust to the intrusion. It burned some, but not unbearably so, and as he continued to work his way inside, my body began to adjust, relaxing to take him more fully.

When he was fully seated, buried to the hilt inside me, he paused, taking in measured breaths like he was trying to regain control of himself. The weight of the moment, the fact that we were joined together so wholly, had tears pricking my eyes, and I reached up, wanting my hands on him. I wanted to pull him closer so that as much of his skin was touching mine as possible.

This was what I had craved. This beautiful moment when two people were joined in the most intimate way. Where there was no room for fear or worry or regrets over what could have been. There was just *us*. Just him and me and the love burning bright between us.

"Move, honey. I want to feel you."

He nodded, a bead of his sweat landing on my chest with the movement. Lowering down to frame my face with his elbows, his face just a few inches from mine, he pulled his hips back slowly before sliding home once again. The drag of his cockhead inside me sent the most delicious sensation rippling through my body. And as he picked up the pace, moving faster and faster, those ripples became waves, washing over me with pleasure.

He continued pumping into me, nipping at my chin and then biting at the skin where my shoulder met my neck. Our skin was slick with sweat, our torsos sliding against each other while we both grunted with the motion. He pushed himself up, propping himself with his left hand and taking my cock in his right. I jolted, letting out a deranged squeal as the change in position had him brushing against my prostate.

"That's it, baby. You're doing so good. Think you can come for me?" He pegged my prostate again while his hand continued to stroke me, his hips pistoning into me with ruthless precision.

"Close," was all I managed, the word ground out through clenched teeth. My balls were drawn up tight to my body and every bit of me felt like a bolt of lightning just looking for a place to strike.

"Look at me." I tore my eyes open, locking with his as he continued the relentless motion of his hips. "I'm gonna come, and I want you to come with me. Please, baby, come with me."

My orgasm blew through me, my entire body going rigid with it as slick heat spread between our bellies. Zach also went still, but I could feel him pulsing deep inside me, filling me with his cum. I dropped my legs and wrapped my arms loosely around him as my limbs turned to jelly and he collapsed on top of me. I winced as his softening cock slipped out of me, feeling the wetness dribbling down my crack. I would be sore, but that was okay. Every bit of what we'd done had been worth it.

His face had landed on my chest when he collapsed, giving me the perfect opportunity to place small kisses on the top of his head.

"Mmm. That's nice," he mumbled into my chest, his words barely decipherable. "I'll move in a minute, 'kay? Once the tingling stops."

I chuckled, tightening my arms around him. "You are welcome to stay just like this for as long as you want."

"Cool. Forever then."

"Fine by me. I can't feel my legs anyway."

He found the strength to lift his head and look at me, forehead creased in concern. "That's a good thing, right? I didn't hurt you?"

"I'm a little sore, but I don't think any more so than would be normal for my first time. And it was one hundred percent worth it."

"It was good, then?" he persisted.

I moved my hands to his face. "It was amazing."

70

JASON

ZACH BARELY SLEPT the night before his therapy appointment. This time, though, it wasn't due to night-mares, mostly because he spent a good portion of the night tossing and turning, never falling asleep long enough to get into a dream state. As a result, we both woke up groggy and irritable, though I knew some of Zach's foul mood was also related to nerves, so I did my best to keep my snark to myself.

Too exhausted for our usual morning run, we took turns in the shower, then dressed and made coffee, hoping that if we drank enough, we might be able to impersonate actual humans.

Forty-five minutes before his appointment, I was sitting on the deck with my third cup of coffee, scrolling through the sports section of the *Omaha World Herald* on my phone, when Zach threw open the door and shot me a glare. "What are you doing out here? We need to go."

I checked the time. "I figured we'd leave in about fifteen minutes."

"Fine," he snapped, then turned on his heel and went

inside. I could see him through the window, aggressively unloading the dishwasher. Knowing this wasn't really about being late, I stood and carried my mug inside.

"Zach."

I set my empty cup in the sink and waited for him to give me his attention. When he grabbed the silverware basket and began tossing forks and spoons into the drawer, I gently took the basket from him and set it on the counter. He glared at me, but I grabbed his hands and pulled him into my arms. He was stiff at first, but after a moment, he melted into me, his arms coming around my waist as he let out a breath.

"It's going to be okay," I said into his hair. "Therapy is hard work, but it's also good work. And I'll be waiting when you're done." I kissed the side of his head. "I'll take you to get ice cream afterward."

He snorted a laugh, exactly as I'd intended. "I have a feeling I'm gonna need something a little stronger."

"I think Arlo's has boozy milkshakes." I kept my tone light. "We could do some day drinking. Maybe see if Drea can pick us up after."

He laughed. "You're ridiculous."

I squeezed him extra tight, then pulled away. "Let me grab my keys, and we'll head out."

I ran back to the bedroom and grabbed my wallet and keys off the dresser, and by the time I returned, he'd finished unloading the dishwasher and seemed calmer.

He pulled the keys out of my hand, examining the keychain. "I can't believe you still have this."

The enamel had worn off a long time ago, but you could still see the outline of the Star of Life emblem stamped into the metal.

"There was a period of time when I debated getting rid

of it, but I couldn't bring myself to do it. It felt like I'd be giving away the only piece of you I had left."

He brushed his finger over it, then returned it to me. "I'm sorry I was a dick this morning."

"It's okay. I can take it."

"But you don't deserve it. And I just...thank you for being patient with me."

"You never have to thank me for supporting you. We'll work through it together, okay?"

He nodded, though I knew he was still feeling guilty. He'd worry over it because he was an overthinker. But all I could do was show him grace and patience and love him through it.

***

ZACH'S THERAPIST shared the same suite of offices as mine and was located just a couple of blocks from the center of town. I dropped him off fifteen minutes early, giving him a quick kiss before he stepped out of the truck, then circled around and found a shady spot to park my truck and wait. I could have sat in the waiting room, but I was actually feeling a little nervous on his behalf and thought sitting in my truck, with the windows open and a cross-breeze flowing, might be a little more comfortable.

When he finally came out a little over an hour later, I held my breath, waiting until he was close enough to the truck for me to see his face clearly. His eyes were red-rimmed, but he was smiling just a bit, clearly happy to see me. The moment he was in the seat next to me, I pulled him into a hug.

"I'm so proud of you!"

"I haven't even told you how it went."

"Doesn't matter. I'm proud of you for taking this step."

He pulled away. "It helped knowing you were here. That you've done this before and I didn't have to do it alone."

"You'll never be alone if I have anything to do with it."

"You're so cheesy," Zach said with a grin.

"It's true. But I'm happy it put a smile on your face." I traced a fingertip across his cheek. "Should we go get that ice cream? Are we heading to Sherry's or Arlo's?"

"Arlo's, but mostly because I'm starving. Can we grab an early lunch?"

"Absolutely."

I kept his hand in mine for the five-minute drive, releasing it when we exited the car and grabbing it again as we walked inside. We chose a booth in the back corner, ordered a couple of burgers and sodas, and then I took Zach's hands in mine once again.

"You gonna ask me how it went?"

"Honey, you are welcome to tell me whatever you're comfortable with, but that's completely up to you."

"Okay, well, I guess the main thing is that she suggested I might want to make an appointment with a psychiatrist to be evaluated for PTSD. She can't give me a diagnosis but said that based on my past trauma and symptoms, it would be fair to think PTSD might be a possibility. She said it's up to me if I choose to go that route, but we could continue our sessions, and she could give me some strategies to manage symptoms either way."

"How do you feel about that?"

"You sound like my therapist."

I laughed. "Maybe. But I genuinely want to know."

"You don't seem surprised."

I shrugged. "I'm not. Though I had thought it might be anxiety. Will has it, and so does Sammy's brother, Jimmy.

Your symptoms, I guess you can call them, aren't exactly the same, but there are some similarities to what I've seen them deal with. PTSD would make more sense based on your history, though, and I bet if we do some research, we'll find that the two aren't a whole lot different in the way they look from the outside."

"Why didn't you say anything?"

"I suspected something deeper was going on back at the end of June, but I only made the anxiety connection in the last week or so, and since you'd already made the therapy appointment, I figured it was best to leave it to the professionals. Plus, I didn't want to stress you out. I'm sorry if that was the wrong thing."

He thought about it a moment, then blew out a breath. "It's okay. You were probably right to leave it for my appointment."

"Do you think you'll make the appointment with the psychiatrist?"

"I'm considering it. I want to do some research first."

I stood and moved to his side of the booth, motioning for him to scoot over. I pulled out my phone, swiping it open and pulling up my browser. "What do you want to know?"

"You want to Google PTSD over lunch?"

"Will it make you feel better?"

"I mean...probably.

"Then let's do it."

71

ZACH

BY THE TIME we went to bed that night, I felt like I had been wrung out to dry. I'd spent most of the afternoon researching signs and symptoms of PTSD, and now my brain felt like it was going to explode with information. For his part, Jason had stuck by my side all afternoon, showing extreme amounts of patience each time I rattled off some new fact I had discovered. By dinner time, he made me put my phone down and take a break. We ate grilled chicken and corn on the cob on the deck, then, after taking a dip in the lake, I was right back on my phone, unable to let go of the quest for more information. I had a visceral need to know what was going on with my mind and the best strategies for dealing with it.

"What I don't understand is how I didn't know this about myself until now." We were lying in bed with the lights out, presumably to sleep, but I couldn't turn my brain off despite my exhaustion. "When I look at all the patterns in my life, it's so obvious. Nightmares. Brain-fog. I really struggled with that in college and just thought it was stress from trying to get caught up, but looking back, it lasted a lot longer than I think something like that typically would. And I've always been a moody bastard, though I suppose I hid that most of the time. Of course, faking it to the world when you actually feel like you're coming unglued on the inside is another sign."

Jason's arm tightened around me, but I barreled on. I was on a roll now.

"It got worse after Mom's accident, but it wasn't until after Drea's that the symptoms really amped up. I had that panic attack at the hospital, remember? I had a few more once I returned to California, but since I was able to get myself back under control, I just attributed it to stress. Then there was the dissociating. I'd be talking to Clayton and just completely check out, or I'd be sitting in class, an hour would go by, and I wouldn't remember a single thing the professor had said."

"Oh my God!" I sat up in bed, dislodging his arm and throwing the covers off me. "Do you think this has something to do with why I ghosted you? It has to, right? What else would explain the fact that even though I wanted to call you, I just couldn't?" I climbed out of bed to pace, too agitated to sit still. "It has to be related, right? And if it is, all of this could have been avoided if I'd just picked up on the signs sooner."

I stopped pacing and turned to face him. He'd turned the light on when I'd gotten out of bed and was now sitting up with the covers pooled around his hips, eyes wide with concern.

"We lost so much time because of what I did. Because of how I hurt you. Jesus, because of how I hurt myself." I scraped my fingers through my hair and climbed up on the bed, kneeling in front of him. "How much time was wasted over something that might have been prevented? We could have been—"

Jason put his fingers over my lips, effectively stopping my spiral. "Stop, honey. You're getting worked up over something you had no control over."

He took my hand, his touch grounding me, and I immediately felt a little steadier. Like I was no longer going to fly apart, all the pieces of me scattered in the wind.

"Maybe things would have been different had we known what to look for, or maybe the accident would have triggered you in a different way. Either way, what happened in the past doesn't change the fact that I love you *now*." He brought my hand up to his lips and brushed them across my knuckles. "We're only looking forward, remember?"

"I want that, J. I want so badly to move on and focus on the future, but the past keeps creeping up on me, and I can't help but wonder if it will happen again. What if I get triggered and ghost you? Or, I don't know, I dissociate and pull away?"

"Do you really think that will happen again?"

"No. But I never would have thought I would have done something like that the first time."

"Okay, but the difference is that now we know what we're battling, so we can educate ourselves and put in the work to get you as healthy as you can be. And we learn to watch for the signs. You work on asking for help and I work on how I can support you better."

"I'm scared, J. My feelings for you back then felt big, but they're nothing compared to the way I feel about you now. It feels like so much more is at stake."

He pulled me closer until I was sitting in his lap, facing him with my legs wrapped around his waist. "I suppose there is more at stake. But that's not necessarily a bad thing.

Because this time, you're not doing it alone. You have me. And as much as I loved you back then, I didn't fight for you."

"J, it's not your—"

"No, honey. I could have flown out to California. I could have made Drea tell me when you were going to be home, and I could have confronted you. Hell, I probably could have figured out how to contact Clayton and pushed my way back into your life. My gut told me something wasn't right, but I let the hurt override everything else because it was easier than doing the work to figure it out.

"But now those high stakes mean I'm invested. And I'm not ever letting uncertainty or doubt come between us ever again. So your battles...those are my battles too. We put in the work together. And if you ever start pulling away, or you ghost me, you can count on the fact that I'm going to do everything in my power to find you. To fight for you. To fight for *us*."

A sob escaped me as I threw my arms around his shoulders, clinging to him as all the emotion I'd been holding on to finally spilled over. Months and *years* of grief and guilt came pouring out of me, along with all the fear and worry I hadn't even realized I'd been holding in. It was as if today's revelations had unlocked something I'd only previously allowed myself to feel in small, contained doses.

Except for the panic attacks I'd had over the years. Those hadn't felt small or contained. I supposed those were my body's way of releasing the pressure when I hadn't allowed it to escape in a healthier manner, like a volcano venting closer to the base rather than a full eruption.

This felt like an eruption. Only instead of spewing lava and ash, it was tears and hiccuping sobs and snot. Jason held me through it all, rubbing my back as he rocked me back and forth. This time, he didn't shush me or try to help me with my breathing. He simply let me ride the wave, recognizing that this wasn't a panic attack but rather a cleansing. Something necessary if we were ever going to move forward.

Eventually, my tears subsided, leaving me feeling even more exhausted than before. I pulled back, climbing out of his lap so I could grab a couple of tissues off the bedside table. "I feel like I'm forever either thanking you or apologizing to you for an outburst."

I wiped at my eyes, then blew my nose. I had to look like an absolute disaster, but I couldn't bring myself to care at this point.

"It might seem that way lately, but I've had my own share of stress and heartache over the years. I still have to practice my breathing when heading to a car accident scene. The night of Sean's fire, I sat in my truck outside the firehouse and cried for ten minutes. It wasn't the first time I lost it over losing someone in a fire, nor will it be the last. There will be moments when I need you to do for me just what I'm doing for you now." He tapped my nose with his finger. "Being in a relationship, loving each other, means it goes both ways."

Jesus, could this man be any more perfect?

"Did you just boop me?"

He chuckled. "I guess I did. You ready to try to sleep?"

As if on cue, I was overcome by a massive yawn. Jason pulled back the covers so I could slip under them. I slid onto my side, tucking my hand under the pillow while he pulled the blankets over us and draped his arm over me. He pulled me into him, the big spoon to my smaller one, my absolute favorite way to sleep.

72

ZACH

THE WEEKS FOLLOWING my first therapy appointment were some of the hardest of my life. Which was saying something, considering I lost my mom at the age of sixteen.

Because of the variety of issues and triggers I was dealing with, my therapist recommended weekly appointments for the foreseeable future. The worst of my problems seemed to center around the nightmares, though those occasional panic attacks were a concern as well, so we focused on trying new strategies to help me cope while tackling the root causes through therapy. To be blunt, it was awful. Rather than eliminating the nightmares, they seemed to pick up in frequency. And the therapy sessions often left me feeling raw and emotional, like someone had peeled back my skin and scraped a dull blade across every one of my nerve endings. My therapist insisted this was normal and all part of the process, but I was so very tired of crying. Still, I continued with my appointments, determined to give it my all, if only so I could be a healthier partner for Jason.

Getting into a psychiatrist for evaluation was proving harder than I thought. Even with my willingness to drive into Omaha, my first appointment wasn't until late August. The more I did the research, the more I was convinced I did indeed have PTSD. Having this official diagnosis wouldn't really change anything—my therapist was already giving me strategies to cope—but there was still a part of me that couldn't help but wonder if there was some sort of medication that might help. While that idea gave me hope, it was also terrifying. I hated the idea of being dependent on medication for the rest of my life, and I knew some of them came with their own set of risks, but if there was a chance it could help...well, there was a part of me that wanted to at least give it a try.

For Jason's part, he made some additional appointments with his own therapist, wanting to make sure he was supporting me but also making sure to take care of himself. He said he felt like he needed it after I'd had the breakdown the night of my first appointment. And to be honest, it was probably the thing that made me feel supported the most. It reinforced everything he'd said about fighting this battle together. His actions showed me I wasn't in this alone.

Those were also some of the best weeks of my life. Jason and I grew closer than I ever thought possible. For all intents and purposes, he'd moved in with me. We hadn't really discussed it, but more and more of his clothes had made their way into my closet and he only went home to check on his house and mow the lawn. I supposed I should have questioned it, but I let it be. The mundane, ordinary life I'd wanted was becoming our reality. We worked. We socialized with friends. We jogged several times a week with Daisy. We made time for swimming in the lake and date nights in the city. And every night, we fell asleep wrapped in each other's arms.

It was everything I wanted.

The last week in July, I held tryouts for the Washington County division of Aksarben SC. Like with camp, Sarah and I had worked out an arrangement for me to take Sean back and forth to tryouts, and I'd gotten the board's permission to waive his fees. He attacked each evening of the tryouts with his usual focus, grinding through the various workouts and skills assessments with single-minded determination. Not only did he demonstrate physical prowess, but he was wicked-smart, showing an advanced understanding of soccer strategy. In scrimmages, he had an uncanny ability to see the entire field of opponents as if they were chess pieces, reacting to their play almost before his opponent had even made their move. The coaches were continually impressed by his abilities and it became evident he would make the team. It was just a matter of making sure we found the right place for him so we set him up for success.

Still, despite his near-dominance on the field, he rode home each night in silence. I would have thought perhaps he was just exhausted from leaving it all out on the field, but the way he fidgeted—picking at the hem of his shorts, untying and retying his cleats, spinning the ball in his lap—made me think there was something else going on.

On the third and final night of tryouts, I pulled into the driveway and put the car in Park, but I stopped him before he could get out. "Everything okay?"

His shoulders slumped and he refused to look at me as he muttered, "Yeah."

"Sean..."

"I'm fine." Before I could say anything further or stop him, he climbed out of the car, slammed the door behind him, and jogged up the steps into the house. I was still sitting there, debating whether to go after him, when Sarah's minivan pulled into the driveway next to me.

We got out of our cars at the same time, rounding the hoods to meet in the middle. She gave me a wan smile as if she were barely standing upright with the weight of the world on her shoulders. Her dirty-blonde hair was piled on top of her head in her usual messy bun, though several strands had escaped and dangled around her face haphazardly. Her diner uniform was rumpled, and she had a smudge of something I couldn't identify on her right cheek.

Instinctively I stepped forward, peering at her in concern. "Rough shift?"

"I worked a double. Come on, let's go inside. I want to sit down."

She led me up the stairs into the house, making a beeline for the kitchen sink, where she washed her hands, then crossed to the fridge and pulled out a can of pop. She held up another can in question, but I declined, so she put it back, and we both sat at the table. She propped her feet up on the chair next to her and sipped her pop while giving me an assessing eye. "You look like you have something on your mind."

"I do. I wanted to talk to you about Sean."

She sat up a little straighter, setting the can down in front of her. "Is he okay? You said tryouts are going well..."

"They are. He's incredibly talented. But that's not what I wanted to talk about."

I took a breath, unsure how to begin. I'd been meaning to talk to her about my concerns over Sean for weeks, but I had struggled with figuring out how to bring it up. I felt like a selfish asshole. I'd been so bogged down with my own mental health issues that I'd failed to help him address his.

That ended now.

"Have you considered making an appointment for Sean to see a therapist or a grief counselor?"

She stood, opened the freezer, pulled out a frozen meal, and took a couple of steps to the other side of the kitchen. Her movements were aggressive and agitated as she unwrapped the packaging and punched the buttons on the microwave. As her food heated, she turned and leaned against the counter with her arms crossed.

"Yes, I've considered it. I have a drawer full of pamphlets social services gave me when Sean came to live here." She gestured toward the drawer in question. "But when exactly was I supposed to find time to take him? And how the hell am I supposed to pay for it?" The microwave chimed, and she turned, taking the food out and stirring the contents before popping it back in and starting it up again.

She faced me once again, her eyes flashing with anger or maybe frustration. "The reason I worked a double today? It wasn't because the diner was short-staffed. It was because I didn't have a choice. School starts in two weeks and supplies for three kids aren't cheap. Then, as if I don't have enough shit on my plate right now, I got a flat tire on my way home. So now I have to take time off work to deal with it—time I can't afford to take—and magically come up with the money to fix it. I'm probably going to have to pick up a second job, not that I have time for that either, but I don't see any other way to keep us afloat."

She turned her back on me, her shoulders slumping as all the fight went out of her.

"I'm sorry, Sarah. Maybe I can help with the car. I think Jason knows the owner of a car shop in Brinkley. You can borrow my car and I'll take yours to get it fixed."

"I can't let you do that. You already do so much for us."

The microwave chimed and she pulled the food out, stirring it again and carrying it back to the table.

"Then let me take the kids shopping for school supplies.

I can take them next week and get them everything they need. The schools put out lists, right? Give me their lists and we'll get everything taken care of."

There had to be something I could do, some way to help them.

"Zach…"

"Please, Sarah. Let me help you."

She sighed. "Why? Why are you so invested in my family?"

She'd asked me a similar question several weeks ago and I didn't have any better answer today than I did then. I just knew in my gut that I couldn't let them suffer. At my hesitation, she narrowed her eyes. "It's not healthy, Zach, this attachment you have to us. You can't just swoop in and save the day every time something goes wrong."

"Why not? I have the time and the means…"

"Because we're not *yours* to save." She leaned forward, pushing her untouched food away. "I know you care, and it's very sweet, but the fact is, these are *my* kids. Sean is *mine*, not yours. And this…bond or attachment or whatever you want to call it is… well, I think maybe we need to redraw some boundaries." She stood, her eyes resolute. "In fact, I think maybe you should go."

My mouth gaped open as I looked up at her, completely flummoxed. I had no idea how we'd veered so far off track, and no idea how to fix it. I'd come in with concerns over Sean's mental health, and now I thought there was a chance she'd cut me off from him completely. She hadn't actually said that, but it felt like that's where her thoughts were heading.

Moving slowly, I rose, my mind frantically searching for the words that might put things back to rights. "Sarah, I'm sorry. I didn't mean to—"

"Please go," she said with a kind of resolute weariness that had my heart sinking. "Thank you for everything you've done, but I need you to respect my wishes."

"Okay," I said softly, not really knowing what else to say. I brushed past her and headed down the half-flight of stairs, pausing at the door to look back one more time. From this angle, I could just see her in profile, sitting at the table with her head in her hands.

With a heart that felt like it was breaking in two, I walked out.

73

JASON

I was sitting on the couch, hair still damp from a shower, finishing a bowl of ice cream, when I heard the garage door open. Daisy's head popped up and she immediately trotted to the door, waiting for her favorite human to walk in. I could relate. After a long shift, including three false alarm calls to the elementary school where they'd just had a new HVAC system installed, I was looking forward to spending some time with Zach and hearing about how the last night of tryouts had gone.

What I wasn't prepared for was the absolutely dejected look on Zach's face when he walked in. Head down and shoulders slumped, he barely acknowledged Daisy as she excitedly danced around in circles and licked his fingertips. I set aside the finished bowl of ice cream, crossed over to him, and pulled him into my arms.

"Honey, what's wrong?"

"Sarah cut us off. She wants to set boundaries or something. I don't know. I'm afraid she won't let us see Sean anymore."

Shit. I pulled him over to the couch and sat him down

next to me, keeping his hand wrapped in mine. "Start at the beginning."

It took a while because his thoughts were so disjointed, and he kept hopping forward and back, telling the story out of order, but eventually, I was able to piece together what had happened. From what he said, he was right to be concerned about the possibility of Sarah cutting ties, which would be very upsetting indeed. We'd become awfully attached to that family—most especially to Sean—but really, all of them had wormed their way into our hearts. It was hard to wrap my head around the possibility of not having them in our lives anymore.

Still, I thought the best thing we could do right now was to take some time to step back and breathe. Sarah was clearly dealing with a lot, and it was entirely possible that with a little bit of space, she might come around.

"Come on. Let's get ready for bed. We can look at the situation with more clarity tomorrow." I stood and reached out a hand to him.

"I don't know if I'll be able to sleep," he said, sounding so utterly lost it nearly broke my heart. But he took my hand and stood, following me down the hall toward our—*his*, I reminded myself—bedroom.

He stopped in his tracks, and I turned, eyebrows raised in confusion, until he pulled his phone out of his pocket and I realized he had an incoming call. "It's Sarah," he said, then swiped to answer.

"Have you seen Sean?" Her voice was frantic and loud enough that I could hear her on the other end of the call.

His eyes shot to mine and he put her on speaker. "I dropped him off at your house, then came straight home. Is he not there?"

"I went to check in with the boys before bed, but Rusty

said Sean came into their room after tryouts, then went right back out. He said he wanted to grab a snack before hopping in the shower. But he never came back upstairs, and I never saw him come into the kitchen. We searched the house, but when we started looking outside, Rusty noticed Sean's bike is gone. I've been driving around the neighborhood, but I can't find him anywhere." Her voice broke. "I don't know what to do."

"Where are you now?" I asked, jumping into the call.

"I came back home in case maybe he came back here, but there's still no sign of him. He doesn't have a phone. I can't even call him."

"You stay there, I'm going to get in my truck and drive around. And I'll call over to APD and see who's on patrol. Let them know to keep an eye out for him."

"I'll come with you." Zach's eyes were pinched with worry.

"I think it's best if you stay here in case he does manage to bike his way all the way across town."

The doorbell rang, sending Daisy into a tizzy of excitement as she raced to the front door, spinning in circles at the prospect of a visitor.

"Hang on, Sarah. Someone's here," I heard Zach say as I slid past him and made for the door.

Every cell in my body sagged in relief at the sight of the thirteen-year-old boy standing with his bike on the front porch. It must have started raining because he was drenched from head to toe, a puddle of water forming at his feet.

"He's here," I called over my shoulder. "Sean's here."

Even from across the room, I could hear Sarah's exclamation of "Thank God," but I turned my focus back to Sean, letting Zach handle the rest of the conversation with her.

"Hey, bud," I said gently. He was shifting back and forth on his feet like he might turn and make a run for it at any moment. He hadn't even acknowledged Daisy, who was excitedly licking any part of him she could get to. "You wanna come in?"

He shrugged and muttered, "Maybe I shouldn't have come here."

"Sarah's on her way," Zach said, coming up behind me and looking between the two of us. "Why don't you come inside out of the rain?"

The porch was covered, so he wasn't technically standing in the rain, but temperatures had dropped, and I could see shivers running through him.

Making a decision, I stepped out onto the porch and gently took the bike out of Sean's hand, propping it against the side of the house. "Inside you go," I said, nodding toward the entryway where Zach stood.

The boy stepped over the threshold, and I followed, closing the door behind us. Zach led him into the living room, plucking a blanket off the back of a chair and wrapping it around him. We nudged him onto the couch, and he went willingly, though he still hadn't said anything since he'd come in the door. Daisy came over and, with a small whine, climbed onto the couch and attempted to curl up in his lap, though she was too big, so only half of her fit. Sean looked down at her, running his hands through her fur in an almost absent way, still as quiet and subdued as ever.

I made eye contact with Zach, not really knowing where we should go from here. Obviously, I wanted to know what had set him off and why he'd decided to come here, but I wasn't sure if we should wait for Sarah.

The decision was made for us when she burst through the door without knocking. She made a beeline for the couch, sat on the coffee table in front of Sean, and pulled him into her arms. "You scared the shit out of me. What were you thinking, running off like that? And on your bike in the dark? In the *rain?*"

"It wasn't raining when I left," he muttered. I hadn't spent a lot of time around teenagers, but it was quite possibly the most gloriously stupid thing I'd ever heard one say.

Sarah reared back, glaring daggers at him. "Seriously? That's all you have to say for yourself? That it *wasn't raining when you left?!*"

He seemed to realize his misstep and sank even farther into the blanket.

"Okay, I think we need to take a moment and calm down. Let's give him some room to breathe."

Sarah's head snapped to Zach, and she rose to her feet. "Are you seriously telling me to calm down? This is *your* fault." She jabbed a finger at him for emphasis. "This is exactly why I told you we needed to set some boundaries."

"How is this my fault?" Zach fired back, sending the tension in the room skyrocketing. "He biked over here on his own. I had no idea he was even missing until you called!"

"Stop it! Stop yelling!" Sean shouted, bringing everyone in the room to a screeching halt. It was the loudest I'd ever heard him be. "It's not Zach's fault. It's not anybody's fault." Sarah sank back down onto the coffee table, giving Sean her full attention. "I don't want to be a burden anymore. You're working yourself to death, Aunt Sarah. I see how tired you are. I hear you cry sometimes."

"Oh, honey." She leaned forward and took his hand between hers. "I'm sorry you heard that, but that's been going on for a long time. Longer than the time you've been with us."

"But that's the point. It was already hard for you guys before, and now you have me too, and I just make it harder on everyone." Tears were running down his face now. I figured the kid had probably been worrying about this from the moment he moved in with them.

"That's not for you to worry about. I love you, kiddo. I'm figuring it out." She tried to brush his hair off his forehead, but he backed away out of her reach.

"By getting *another* job? I overheard you guys talking tonight. You're barely home as it is." He swiped at his eyes. "Zach said he wanted to help us, but you won't let him, so I thought maybe I could just come over here and..." His voice trailed off, and his eyes shifted like he'd thought better of what he was going to say. "It was a really dumb idea, but I was already almost here, and it started raining, so I just kept going."

Zach sank onto the couch next to Sean, angling his body toward him. "What were you going to do when you got here? Before you changed your mind?"

Sean blew out a breath, and he suddenly looked much younger than his thirteen years. "I thought maybe I could live here with you guys. Then Aunt Sarah could focus on her own kids, and I'd be out of the way. But then I didn't even know if you wanted kids, especially a kid my age, and I decided it was a dumb idea, but I was already almost here, like I said, so..."

I watched Zach's face as Sean spoke. Watched as his features flickered from surprise to understanding to yearning. He caught my eye and tried to school his features in a neutral expression, but it was too late. I knew he wanted a family. We both did. We'd talked about it several times since the day of the fair. But it was a future dream, something for us to work toward. Never mind that our relationship had escalated quickly and we were basically living together. We still had things to sort through. Work to do on ourselves and our relationship. I'd hoped we'd work toward marriage and then kids eventually, but we still had time for all of that.

Yet, as I watched all of this play out in real-time, I knew the idea had taken root in Zach's mind. And I couldn't deny there was a little piece of me that thought, *What if?*

Sarah's reaction to the idea was quite the opposite. In the last ten minutes, she'd gone from worried to mad to compassionate concern, but as Sean had confessed his original intent in coming here, I'd seen a flash of hurt in her eyes, and then she'd gone right over the edge into white-hot fury. She tried to rein it in, to get ahold of herself, likely for Sean's sake, but she wasn't entirely successful, so when she told him through clenched teeth to go wait out in the car, he hopped up to comply.

As soon as the front door was closed, she unleashed her anger on us, though it was mostly directed at Zach. "How *dare* you! How fucking dare you put that idea into his head?"

"I didn't give him any ideas, I swear. I had no idea he was thinking anything like that." He put his hands in front of him in a gesture meant to placate, but it had absolutely zero effect.

She stood, and Zach did the same, both squaring off, while I stood by, helplessly trying to figure out how to de-escalate the situation. "*This* is what I was talking about. Blurred boundaries. You've got the kid totally confused."

She got right up in his face. "My sister left him in *my* care, *not* yours. She'd never even met you. You have no rights to him. None. In fact"—she turned and looked at me, making sure I was included in whatever she was about to say—"I want no contact from either one of you. I'll get a restraining order if I have to, but both of you just stay away from him. Stay away from all of us!"

She shoved past him and stormed out the door, leaving us staring after her in stunned silence.

I DON'T THINK anyone could have prepared me for just how much it would hurt to have the kid I hadn't even realized I wanted taken from me in just a matter of hours. Worse still, I was even more worried about his mental health under the circumstances, and there wasn't a damn thing I could do about it.

Jason tried to get me to talk about it, but I couldn't. I knew I should bring it up with my therapist, but I couldn't bring myself to do that either. It was as if everything was locked up inside me, and I didn't have the key to release it.

For days after, I went through the motions. I managed tryouts for the high school age group. I buried myself in the administrative work involved with getting the season rolling in the fall. Walked the job site with the contractors of the new soccer facility due to open in the spring.

Jason and I continued our morning jogs. We had Drea and my father over for dinner. Went to one of Sammy's art shows. Hung out with Rafi and his family. I'd wanted a mundane, ordinary life, and we were living it. But it was empty. Something was missing, and it wasn't hard to identify it.

"School started this week."

We'd taken our coffees down to sit in the Adirondack chairs on the dock. Rain had rolled through the night before, taking the oppressive heat and humidity with it, leaving the air comfortable for the first time in weeks.

Jason turned to look at me. "I know. I've been trying not to think about it all week."

I returned his gaze. "Do you think he's okay? Do you think they got the school supplies they needed?"

He shrugged, but I could see the sadness written on his face. "I think Sarah made it pretty clear that wasn't our problem."

I sighed, trying to release some of the frustration inside of me. It had been bubbling just below the surface for weeks now, making me feel irritable and snappy. Jason and I had bickered more than once recently over really stupid, unimportant shit, and I knew it was because of the toll the situation was taking on both of us.

"Do you think we should reach out? Surely, she's cooled off by now. Maybe she'd be more willing to listen."

"What are you going to say? That you want to adopt him? I know you've been researching it."

"I just want to know our options," I said, feeling defensive. "I figured it didn't hurt to have the information."

He reached out and took my hand, gentling his tone. "There are plenty of other kids out there who need good homes. It doesn't have to be Sean."

"I know. But I can't let go of it. Adopting Sean is a stretch, but I still worry about him. I worry about all of them. A part of me is so mad at Sarah, but I can't help but worry about her too."

"I love your big heart," he said, stroking his thumb across the back of my hand.

"I learned it by watching you."

He leaned over, and I met him halfway for a kiss.

"You have your first practices this week, right? Let's see if Sean shows up before we do anything."

"Yeah, okay. Thanks for being patient with me."

"It's hard on me too. Just remember, we're in this together."

"I know. Some days, I think it's the only thing that gets me through."

75

JASON

WHEN ZACH WALKED in the door Tuesday evening, I knew Sean hadn't been at practice. Everything about him screamed defeat. I tried to coax him into talking about it, but he waved me off, saying he just wanted to shower and head to bed.

When he'd woken in the throes of one of his nightmares, I'd helped him work through it, going through the grounding techniques we'd been taught, until he collapsed in my arms, and we'd both gone back to sleep.

This morning, I'd risen before him, and with a restlessness I couldn't contain, I decided to head over to my house and catch up on some chores I'd neglected since I spent most of my time at Zach's. He'd been so tired that he hadn't even moved when I'd kissed his cheek before leaving.

I was worried that this whole situation with Sean had triggered a depressive episode on top of the PTSD he was still trying to get a handle on. I had no idea if he'd shared any of what was going on with his therapist, and his appointment with the psychiatrist wasn't for another week, which left me feeling helpless.

By lunchtime, I'd scrubbed both bathrooms and vacuumed the entire house, but I was still just as restless and irritable. Needing a break, I headed to my truck and started her up.

Ten minutes later, I was pulling into the lot of the diner. I found a spot and killed the ignition, taking a moment to stare at the front of the restaurant. I had no business coming here like this. Sarah was likely in the middle of the lunch rush, and I honestly didn't even know what I would say to her anyway.

But the radio silence was killing me. I'd been so focused on supporting Zach that I hadn't realized how much I was hurting too. I missed Sean. I missed all of them. It felt like we'd been cut off from half our family.

Resolved, I got out of the truck and walked inside. The diner wasn't as busy as I would have expected during the lunch hour, but I took a seat at the counter, not wanting to take up a table.

"What are you doing here?" Sarah came up behind me, holding a pitcher of water. Her voice held no venom. She simply seemed tired. And maybe a little resigned.

"I just want to talk. Please."

She sighed, surveying the tables in the dining area. "Give me twenty minutes."

I ordered an iced tea and sipped it while I waited, scrolling socials on my phone without really taking any of it in until Sarah sat in the empty chair next to me. "Both of my tables just tabbed out, but if another one comes in, I'll have to cut this short."

I nodded, taking in her appearance now that she was sitting in front of me long enough to get a good look. I assumed she was in her early thirties, but the dark circles under her eyes and the pallor of her skin had her looking several years older. From the moment I'd met her, she'd looked world-weary, but there'd always been a fire inside her. A determination to do what had to be done. Now, she looked like a boxer who'd gone nine rounds and didn't have any fight left. "How are you?"

"I'm fine."

I ducked my head, searching her eyes. "Are you?"

She blew out a breath. "What do you want me to say? I'm the same as always. I work. I take care of the kids. Rinse and repeat."

"Did you end up getting a second job?"

"No." She pushed a stray piece of hair off her face. "Sean was right. There really wasn't a way for me to squeeze it in."

"What about your car?"

"I'm handling it, okay?" She glared at me, a little of that fight coming back into her eyes. "I think we've established that's really none of your business."

"You're right. It's not my business. But I'm not asking just to be nosy. I'm asking because I care. Zach and I have been worried sick about you guys."

She snorted. "Did Zach send you here today?"

"No. He doesn't know I'm here. But he was heartbroken when Sean wasn't at practice last night."

"Even if I could get him to practice, I don't think that's a good idea. Zach and Sean...they're too attached to each other."

"Is it really such a bad thing? The two of them being so close? For Sean to have someone else looking out for him after all he's been through?"

"It confuses him. He wanted to move in with you guys, for fuck's sake."

I was silent a moment, weighing my words. It was very possible I could make this entire situation worse if I wasn't careful. "Look, I won't deny that Zach would adopt Sean in a heartbeat if you allowed it—"

"I knew it! I knew he was trying to take Sean away from me!"

"It's not that he wants to take him away, it's just that…" I ran my hand through my hair, picking through my words. "Okay, so his mom died when he was sixteen. His father was hard on him, and he and his sister were close, but I think he felt that because he was older, he had to be the strong one. He put on a brave face for the world when everything inside him was crumbling. So, while his family circumstances were different from Sean's, I think he sees a lot of himself in the kid. There's a bond there that I don't think you or I could ever understand.

"So, yes, he wants to adopt Sean, but it's not because he wants to take him from you. He's just a man with an over-abundance of love to give, and he wants to give that love to Sean."

"What about you? What do you want? The two of you are pretty serious, right? Are you going to add a thirteen-year-old kid with trauma into the middle of your relation-ship? You guys think you're going to play house?" She snorted, the sound of it full of sarcasm and snark. "Wait until he comes home sullen and barely talks for days. Or gives you an attitude for asking him to do something as simple as picking up his socks. What about when he just stops doing his homework and nothing you say or do can convince him to do it?

"Raising kids is hard. He's past the age of middle-of-the-night feedings and diaper changes. Everyone thinks that's the hard part, but raising a teen—that's when the real work starts. Once they hit middle school, you get just a few more years to keep them on the right track before launching them into the world and hoping they're good, self-sufficient humans."

The door chimed, announcing new customers. "I need to get back to work." Sarah stood from the stool and turned to look at me. "For what it's worth, I think you and Zach have good intentions. But I don't think you have any idea what you'd be getting into. And the bottom line is my sister left Sean in my care. I love that boy, and I'm honoring my sister's wishes to the best of my ability. I need you to leave it be."

She started to push past me, but I put a hand on her arm to stop her. "Will you at least consider letting us see him again? Even if it's just for soccer practice? We miss him. We miss all of you."

She peered up at me, her gaze inscrutable as she considered. "I'll think about it."

76

ZACH

"WHAT DO you think Will's big news is? Did he drop any hints?" Wearing briefs and freshly showered, we were in the process of dressing for dinner in the city with Sammy and Will.

"Nope. I couldn't get a damn thing out of him. He insisted on waiting until tonight at dinner." Jason stepped into a pair of slacks, pulling them over his hips and zipping them up. Pity.

"Okay, so do we think wedding news or moving in together? Or something else?" I pulled on my shirt and began fastening the buttons.

"I don't know. They kind of already live together, don't they? Maybe they set a date for the wedding."

"Possible, though it wouldn't surprise me if they just up and went to the courthouse without telling anyone."

I lost my train of thought as I watched Jason do up the buttons on his shirt, fingers efficiently brushing against the fabric. It wasn't often that he needed to wear anything more formal than athletic clothes or his uniform, but when he did, he made it hard for me to concentrate.

"What do you think about us moving in together?"

The seriousness of his tone pulled my focus back up to his face. He was looking at me with a hesitant expression. It took a moment for his words to register, but when they did, a slow smile overtook my face.

I stepped toward him, closing the distance between us. "Finally. Ugh," I said with a playful roll of my eyes. "I thought you'd never ask!"

He grabbed my hips and pulled me into him. "You're the one who should do the asking. It's your house after all…"

"I didn't want to assume you'd move in here. Maybe you want me to move into your house?"

"Honey, we've never even spent a night together at my house. I think it's safe to say *this* is my home. Here with you."

"Mmmm," I said, my lips brushing against his. "I love the sound of that."

I kissed him, as always, savoring the feel of his lips against mine. This time, I couldn't help but feel a sense of wonder that I'd been so lucky. Not just that he'd given me a second chance, but that he loved me so deeply, despite everything that had happened.

"I guess we'll have our own news to share tonight." I started to lean in for another kiss when the buzzing of my phone interrupted me. I turned to where I'd tossed it on the bed while I was changing and picked it up. My eyes shot to Jason's. "It's Sarah."

I swiped to answer, but was surprised when it wasn't Sarah's voice I heard on the other end of the line. "Zach, you have to come over here. She's on the ground, and I don't know what to do."

"Slow down, Sean. Who's on the ground?" I switched to speakerphone so Jason could hear.

"Aunt Sarah. We just got off the bus and found her on the floor in the kitchen. She's not moving."

Jason jumped in, his EMT training taking over. "Can you tell me if she's breathing?"

"Um, I don't know. I can't tell." I could hear the tears in his voice.

"Sean, I know this is really scary, but I need you to—"

A faint moan sounded on the other end of the line. "Aunt Sarah? Wake up, okay? We need you to wake up." Sean's voice came through a little softer, as if he'd pulled the phone away from his face.

"Sean," Jason said, volume pitched a little louder to be heard. "We're going to head over there, but I need you to hang up and call 911." We'd already put on the nearest shoes we could find and were heading toward the garage. "Sean? Can you hear me?"

"Yeah, I can hear you."

"Okay. We're on our way. I'm disconnecting the call. Call 911, and they'll tell you what to do."

WE TOOK MY CAR, getting across town in record time while Jason texted Will to cancel our dinner plans. The fire station was located on this side of town, so the medic beat us there, and I could tell Jason was warring with whether to barge into the house or stay out of the way. In the end, the kids decided for us, making a beeline straight over to us as soon as we got out of the car.

Jason scooped up a frantic Lauren while I pulled Sean and Rusty forward, wrapping my arms around their shoulders and squeezing them tight. Moments later, Sarah was wheeled out on a stretcher, her eyes open and responsive, though her color was quite pale.

"Mommy!" Lauren called out, trying to launch herself out of Jason's arms so she could get to her mom.

Jason kept hold of her but carried her across the yard toward Sarah and the other medics from his department, while the boys and I followed at a distance. I saw Jason speak to one of the EMTs and then lean over so Lauren could give her mom a hug. One of Sarah's arms came around her, patting her back weakly, and then Jason pulled Lauren away so they could load Sarah into the ambulance. I caught sight of Sarah swiping at her face just before they shut the doors.

"They're not entirely sure what's going on. It doesn't appear to be a cardiac event, but there are a lot of reasons a person can collapse, so they're taking her to the hospital to get her stabilized and run some tests."

"Can we go there?" Lauren asked, her big brown eyes swimming with tears. "I want my mommy."

Jason's eyes met mine, and I finally understood how couples had entire conversations without speaking. He was letting me make the call. "Yeah, honey. We can go."

77

———————

JASON

OVER THE NEXT couple of days, I watched Zach step into the role of caregiver like he'd been born to do it.

In between trips back and forth to the hospital in Brinkley, we made sure the kids were fed, answered their questions as best we could, and spent each night with them at Sarah's house, Zach and I each taking turns on the couch or the floor. I'd watched him console a crying Lauren, talk Sean through a nightmare, and distract Rusty with card games.

Friday evening, we'd loaded the kids into Zach's SUV and followed the rig to the hospital in Brinkley. After a couple of hours in the waiting room, we'd finally been able to go back and see Sarah, who'd looked exhausted but relieved to see the kids. We only got about fifteen minutes with her, but we promised to return the following day and visit.

Saturday had been more of the same, with Zach and I driving the kids out to the hospital and supporting them at home as best we could. On Sunday morning, Sarah called to say she was being discharged and asked if I could pick her up. The kids had wanted to pile in the minivan and go get her, but we'd talked them out of that, instead encouraging them to plan a low-key welcome home celebration. Zach stayed back at the house with the kids, making homemade cards and signs while I headed to Brinkley to pick Sarah up.

She gave me a small smile when I entered her room, and I immediately noticed her color was much better. Her eyes were brighter and the circles under her eyes had faded. They'd determined her episode had been the result of a combination of exhaustion, stress, dehydration, and an untreated urinary tract infection, none of which was surprising considering how hard she pushed herself to make sure her kids were taken care of. A nurse came in and reviewed her discharge paperwork, instructing her to drink plenty of water and finish all the antibiotics she'd been prescribed, and then we headed out to the truck.

Sarah was quiet as we made our way out of Brinkley and onto the highway that would carry us back to Astaire. Her face was turned away from me as she stared out the window, apparently lost in thought. The last thing I wanted to do was add to her stress all over again, but I thought there were some things we should discuss without the kids present. "The kids are excited to have you home. Lauren was chattering a mile a minute before I left."

She didn't look at me, but when I glanced at her profile, I caught a hint of a smile. "I missed them. There are so many days I long for just a bit of quiet, but I spent most of yesterday wishing for the noise. They're my whole world."

"I know they are. They're good kids and you're a good mom."

"Am I?" Her voice cracked. "I work my ass off to provide for them, and it never feels like enough."

"You're doing your best, right? Working so hard that you

landed yourself in the hospital. Not that it matters what the hell anyone else thinks, but no one could look at all you do and argue that you should be doing more."

"I could have let you guys help me. You practically begged me to and I shut you down." Her voice shook, and out of the corner of my eye, I caught the motion of her wiping away tears.

"You were just doing what you thought was right. Even as frustrated as we were, neither of us blamed you for that. Honestly, I think most parents are just out there doing their best. It's not like they give out handbooks about how to do any of it."

"Truth." She was quiet a moment, then said, "You really are just a genuinely nice guy, aren't you?"

"I mean...I try to be." I could feel the heat rising in my cheeks.

"Zach's lucky to have you."

"I'm lucky to have him. He's been amazing with the kids. He didn't even bat an eye when Lauren asked him to put her hair in a ponytail yesterday, and then he let her paint his fingernails last night."

"She was probably in seventh heaven. She's always begging to do our nails."

We crossed into the city limit of Astaire, and I still didn't know what future role we might play in their lives after the way the weekend had unfolded, but I wasn't sure how to bring it up either.

"Thank you for jumping in and taking care of the kids this weekend. And after I shut you guys out. I just...I don't know what would have happened if Sean hadn't called you. I think..." She blew out a breath. "I think maybe it's time I admit that I need some help."

I turned into her neighborhood but pulled over to the

curb in front of a random house down the block. I wanted to finish this conversation, and I knew the kids would make a run for the car the moment I pulled into her driveway. I put the truck in Park and turned to look at her. "Do you have something specific in mind?"

"Well, I had plenty of time to give this some thought yesterday, and I think that before we discuss anything else, I need you to know I'm not willing to give Sean up. I think you guys would make excellent parents, and I do want you in his life, but he's my nephew, and he stays with me. Can you and Zach accept that?"

Disappointment sat heavy in my gut, and I knew Zach would likely be upset, but ultimately, this was her decision, and we had to respect it. "I don't want to speak for him, but my guess is he'll be disappointed, just like I am. But that doesn't mean we can't accept it. We just want what's best for him."

"I get that. And believe me, there are days when I doubt everything I'm doing for him and for my own kids as well. But I can't constantly be wondering if you guys are trying to take him. There has to be trust between all of us."

"I agree. And we wouldn't ever want you to doubt our motives. So assuming Zach is on board with dropping the adoption idea, what did you have in mind?"

"Well, I think the easiest thing to start with is letting Sean play soccer. If Zach is still willing to waive his fees and help with transportation, I'd like to let him participate. I don't want him to miss out on the opportunity because I was too stubborn or prideful to allow it."

"That one's an easy yes. I don't even have to ask Zach. I know he'll be on board."

She smiled. "I figured. The rest...well, I'm not great at asking for help, but would you guys be willing to either watch Lauren or help with transportation maybe a couple of days a week? I think there are some clubs Rusty would like to join at school, but he doesn't even ask to participate because he knows I need someone to be home with Lauren, and I just want him to have a normal kid life. I don't want him to be stuck babysitting his sister all the time and never get to do—"

I put my hand on her knee, stopping the flood of words that had burst forth. "It's a yes. Between Zach and my schedules, I think we can work something out."

"Are you sure? It feels like so much to ask and you guys don't even get anything out of it. I literally have nothing I can pay you back with."

"We get to spend time with some pretty amazing kids and help a *friend*. We don't need anything in return."

Without warning, she launched herself at me, wrapping her arms around me in a tight squeeze. I hadn't seen her show much physical affection, so it took me by surprise, but I put my arms around her and hugged her back.

"Thank you." The words were muffled, her head turned away from me where it rested on my shoulder. "I've had no one to depend on but myself since I was eighteen years old, and you guys just seem too good to be true."

"If it makes you feel better, spending time with your kids can be like practice for when we adopt our own. So, really, you're the one helping us."

She pulled away, shaking her head, but with a smile. "You're ridiculous."

"You ready to go home and see your kids?"

"Yes, please!"

I put the truck in gear and drove down the block to the house. Four faces peered out at us through the storm door, smiling and waving madly as I pulled into the driveway. We got out of the truck, but she paused a moment, turning back to look at me. "You guys are going to make excellent dads someday."

"You really think so?"

She nodded toward the door where Zach stood behind the kids, one hand on Lauren's shoulder and the other on Sean's, looking completely natural. "What do *you* think?"

"I think that as long as I have him, there isn't anything we can't do."

EPILOGUE
ZACH

WE HOSTED another gathering over Labor Day weekend, this one a little smaller than the one Zach had hosted on the Fourth. We limited invites to family, so Jason's parents and Mandy's little family were there, along with Dad and Drea. And since we now considered Sarah and her kids family, they were included in the guest list as well.

It had been a little over a week since Sarah collapsed, and besides taking Sean back and forth to soccer practices, I'd spent Thursday afternoon hanging out with Lauren after school while the boys participated in the Strategic Gaming Club at school. She'd insisted on changing out my nail polish, so I was currently sporting hot pink on one hand and neon green on the other. I loved it.

I'd initially been disappointed when Jason shared the news about Sarah keeping Sean, but I respected her decision and was thankful we could still be so involved in their lives. And on the positive side, the whole thing had led to several really good conversations with Jason about our future plans to adopt. And while I was anxious to get started, I knew I still had work to do on my mental health.

I'd finally had my appointment with my psychiatrist this week. To no one's surprise, she'd confirmed the suspected PTSD diagnosis. She'd started me on a prescription, with plans to continue work with my therapist and then return for a med check in six weeks.

As for Sean's mental health, well, that had been my only request after Jason, Sarah, and I sat down to talk about how this relationship between our two families would work going forward. I convinced her to let me help cover the cost of Sean's therapy and help with transportation as needed. In the end, it hadn't taken much convincing since it had never been a question of her *wanting* to provide that for him. I thought she was learning that leaning on people, especially when they were offering help, could be a really good thing for everyone.

Jason approached, handing me a fresh beer as I stood on the deck, taking a moment to watch my favorite people laughing and talking below. "Coming back here was the best decision I've ever made."

"No regrets leaving soccer behind?"

"I didn't leave it behind. I've just changed my relationship with it." I turned to face him. "But no, I don't have any regrets leaving my pro career behind. Especially because it means I get to have you."

He leaned forward and kissed me briefly before pulling away. "My house is officially on the market as of about an hour ago."

"Yeah?" A smile spread wide across my face. He'd taken a couple of days off work this week, first going through everything with his real estate agent, then cleaning, reorganizing, and staging it to get it ready to list. In the process of cleaning out his house, he'd also started moving some of his belongings into my house permanently. I'd enjoyed seeing little touches of him sprinkled throughout the house, making it feel like a home more than ever. "She came over and took pictures yesterday, then texted a bit ago to tell me the listing is officially up. We're holding an Open House next Sunday, but she thinks that with the way the market's looking, it might sell before that."

"Really? That fast?"

"Yup." He pressed his forehead to mine. "In just a few weeks, you'll be officially stuck with me."

"Mmm. As far as I'm concerned, it's official *now*." I tilted my head to press my lips to his, marveling once again at just how lucky I was to have him in my life after everything we'd gone through to get here.

"God, you guys are disgusting. Is this my life now? The two of you sucking face all over the place without any regard for others? I mean, there are *children* present."

We broke apart, turning to look at Drea, who was standing just a few feet away with a smirk on her face. "Why are sisters so insufferable?"

Mandy approached, her sleeping baby boy tucked into a sling across her torso. "You should be thanking us for helping you pull your heads out of your asses ten years ago. Who knows if you ever would have figured yourselves out otherwise."

Drea held out her beer and Mandy tapped it with her seltzer.

"I don't know," Jason said, eyes trained on me. "I'm pretty sure we were always going to end up here."

"I love you."

"I love you too." He leaned forward and kissed me again, this time making a bit of a production out of it. I matched his energy, licking into his mouth and tangling my tongue with his.

"Oh, good grief," I heard Drea say. "And they said we were the insufferable ones."

As their footsteps faded, I pulled back once again. "Welcome home, baby."

"Mm. I love the sound of that."

THE END

Jimmy and TJ's book will conclude the series! Stay up to date on their story and all future book news from Melody Claire in Melody's Lane on Facebook!

Want a peek into Zach and Jason's future, including Sammy, Will, and the rest of the gang? Click HERE for the *Roots Run Deep* Halloween Bonus Scene!

ALSO BY MELODY CLAIRE

When He Saved Me

Jamie & Finn

When He Saved Me is an emotional new adult MM romance featuring a broody barista and a sunshiney college student navigating love and loss. It's a standalone and comes with a guaranteed HEA.

Wrapped Up In You

Jonathan & Hayden

Wrapped Up In You is a steamy, opposites attract, age gap, stepbrother, MM Romance, featuring a lovable guy with ADHD and an uptight divorcé in need of a shake-up.

Once and Always Series

The Once and Always series features stories about men finding love and their second chances.

Something Good

Sammy & Will

Book 1

Something Good captures those feelings of young love in the summertime. It's small town, and fireworks, and bonfires, and walks in the woods. Getting soft-serve at the local ice cream shop. Cruising the highway, holding hands with your love. It's good boy/bad boy, hurt/comfort, and second chances. It's all of that and so much *more*.

This was the book that almost broke me. And it wasn't for the reasons I would have expected.

I started writing Jason and Zach's story during a very busy spring. Youngest Daughter graduated high school and the spring semester is very busy for band directors. Added into the mix was a change in my husband's job that meant he was away from home even more than usual. All of that meant many days went by when I wasn't able to get a single word in. Then, when I finally sat down to write, I was too exhausted to string together words in any coherent sense. I had hoped to get this book out in July, but as the school year wound down and graduation parties concluded, it became evident a July release wasn't feasible.

I was disappointed but determined to give readers (you!) the very best possible story, so with school out and more time available to write, I dug in and got to work. Only the story didn't go where I expected and the characters didn't cooperate. I realized I'd painted myself into some corners with the little bit of foreshadowing I'd dropped for Jason and Zach in *Something Good,* and now I had to make them do things I didn't want them to do (massive side-eye to the end of Part One).

There's a lot of myself in Zach. Everything else I listed above was frustrating, but it was this aspect that nearly broke me. I don't have PTSD, but I do know what it's like to discover you have undiagnosed mental health issues that you weren't even aware of. Writing him felt personal in ways it never has with any of my other characters and it took me almost three-fourths of the story to figure out that it was because I'd baked so much of myself into his character.

I didn't set out to write a character with PTSD. And I know there are folks who might say Zach's behavior didn't make sense, but that's the thing about mental health. It often doesn't make sense. Thankfully, Zach had Jason, with his gentle, patient spirit, to see and accept him, despite the way Zach had hurt him. And I'm lucky enough to have a husband who's patient with me too!

I don't want to close without a note regarding the demisexuality rep in this book. I always knew Jason would be demi, and so it was important to me to show him develop the relationship with Zach first, before the awakening happens. This made the book considerably longer, but as I said, it was important to me that the reader saw that evolution. Demisexuality is often portrayed in friends-to-lovers books where the friendship is already well-established, which makes a lot of sense in terms of good storytelling, but the way I've portrayed it in this book feels more realistic to me and is more in line with the way I have experienced attraction throughout my life. As we know, sexuality is a spectrum, so your experience might be different than Jason's, but I hope at least some readers might see a bit of themselves represented between these pages.

As always, thank *you*, amazing readers, for picking up my books. It is still a marvel to me that people choose to read my words. Thank you, thank you, thank you!

~Mel

ACKNOWLEDGMENTS

Writing a book takes a village and these folks deserve my utmost gratitude!

To my husband - you are the best human I know. I absolutely could not do this writing thing without your support.

To my daughters - you are my world. I am incredibly proud of who you are becoming. I learn from you every day.

To Gena - This book literally would not be what it is without you. You are forever and always the best ledge talker-offer a girl could ask for. Even more than that, I'm so glad to be able to call you my friend!

To Amanda - I don't know how to tell you how much your friendship, support, and mentorship have meant to me over the last couple of years. I am so thankful for you!

To Breanna - I have to give you the shoutiest of shout outs for your help in making sure the mental health aspects of this book were realistic and accurate. Any mistakes are one hundred percent my own!

To Francesca, Aiden, and Ian - Your feedback was invaluable in shaping this book. I appreciate you allowing me to slide into your DMs at all hours! I adore you all!

To Abbie - I think we've found our groove! Thank you for your support of Zach and Jason and for helping me polish their story to perfection!

To Kate - Thanks for another beautiful cover. I love how it turned out!

To the Authors Fire/Rescue group - what a valuable resource you all were in the writing process! Thank you for your patience in answering all of my questions!

ABOUT THE AUTHOR

Melody Claire writes emotional contemporary MM romance stories with moderate heat and a whole lot of heart. She hails from Kansas City but resides in Omaha and loves setting her stories in the Midwest. She is married with two almost grown kiddos, a dog, and a kitty. By day, she teaches middle school, and by night can be found writing on her laptop or curled up with her Kindle. She's addicted to Pink Drinks and the sound of her husband's laugh, and loves nothing more than to escape into a love story.

Connect With Me!

www.ingramcontent.com/pod-product-compliance
Lightning Source LLC
Chambersburg PA
CBHW031951150726
47990CB00005B/1665